Murder on the OBX

Henrietta F. Ford

Henrietta F. Ford

PublishAmerica
Baltimore

ISBN: 1-4241-3274-6
PUBLISHED BY PUBLISHAMERICA, LLLP
www.publishamerica.com
Baltimore

Printed in the United States of America

DEDICATED TO

My mother, Mildred Forbis Ford,
Whose love and respect for the sea was contagious.

Acknowledgements

I would like to express gratitude to:

My brother, Henry Ford, who shared his law enforcement stories with me.

The employees of the National Park Service who patiently answered many questions about the Outer Banks.

And most importantly to my husband, Jim, without whose help and support I could not have written my Outer Banks mystery.

CHAPTER 1

SATURDAY

He watched her sitting behind the wheel of the new red SUV. She wore a yellow sundress with tiny red birds, and her sun-bleached blonde hair was tied back in a long ponytail with a red checked bandana. She explored the dashboard and stroked the luxurious leather seat. Positioning her hands on the steering wheel in driving position she faced him with a widening grin. Then she reached across the passenger seat and held out her hand. He laughed and took her soft, outstretched hand, and pressed it gently.

Unexpectedly the SUV began to move. He jerked his hand away. At first the car moved slowly as if it were making a left turn, then its speed increased, faster and faster until it was spinning. He heard her terrified scream and saw the look of panic on her face. He stood helpless, horrified as the car spun round and round until it looked like a gigantic, whirling red blur. Suddenly her screams were obliterated by an explosion…a horrific blast. His ears rang, and he felt intense heat. His arms, his face, his back drawing, burning, searing mercilessly. He couldn't breath, and as the flames leapt higher and higher his cries mingled with hers in the thick, humid September air.

He was awakened abruptly by the metallic clatter of an alarm clock that jolted him back into reality. He swung his feet off the bed and stared around at the cluttered room. Clothes were strewn everywhere…on chairs, tables, in dirty piles in the corner. Travis had not shut a drawer nor closed a closet door in two years. He looked at the messy desk, where unpaid bills hid under junk mail. The chaos was a metaphor for his life. He sat shaking on the side of his bed. His breath was labored, and he sweated profusely. The sunburn he got the day before while weeding the garden stung and itched. His head throbbed, and he realized that tears streamed down his cheeks. The dream! He felt so alone. Alone with his nightmare.

Travis had not always lived alone in the small, brick, two bedroom house. Travis married the only woman he ever loved. Actually, Virginia was the only girl Travis ever dated. He'd had a crush on her since second grade. A peanut butter and jelly crush his mom used to say. He could see Virginia now sitting at the lunch room table eating a sandwich...peanut butter stuck between her teeth and purple jelly on the collar of her white blouse.

Virginia and Travis grew up in Seaboard, a small eastern North Carolina town located in Northampton County on the coastal plain. As kids they walked to school together, roller skated down the sidewalks, shared big orange drinks and cinnamon buns, and watched television while stretched out on her living room rug. When they were teenagers, they walked hand in hand down the long halls of Seaboard High School amidst giggles of classmates and indulgent smiles of teachers. On Wednesday and Friday nights they drove to basketball games in Travis' old Buick. Travis played the position of forward, and Virginia jumped and whirled in her blue corduroy cheerleader skirt with as much enthusiasm as a Dallas cheerleader and much prettier. On Saturday nights, they went to the Starlight Drive-In Theater, and when some monster roared out at them from the giant outdoor screen Virginia feigned fright and hid her head in Travis's coat. After the movie, they'd stop by Frankie's Drive-In and ordered ham sandwiches and milk shakes brought to the car by a curb hop. Their senior class voted them most popular and most likely to succeed.

And so it went, that after high school graduation Virginia attended nursing school in nearby Roanoke Rapids. Travis took a two-year law enforcement course at North Carolina State University in Raleigh and trained at the North Carolina Justice Academy in Salemburg, North Carolina before becoming an Alcohol Beverage Control officer. Time away from Virginia was almost unbearable. Finally one hot August evening in the quaint Seaboard Methodist Church by the glow of white candles and the scent of gardenias, Virginia and Travis were married. For them it seemed the natural evolution of their lives. They were perfect together, complete. And when their marriage failed to produce children, they found that just being together filled that void.

Travis loved his job as an ABC officer. He mostly checked applications for liquor licenses, sleuthed out whiskey stills, and took part in drug busts. Occasionally, he'd do crowd control at rock concerts or ball games. Virginia worked long hours at the hospital in Roanoke Rapids as a pediatrics intensive-care nurse.

But Travis's life changed when he received a phone call one stormy August night. It seemed surreal. A strange voice told him that Virginia had been in an accident, and he should come to the hospital immediately. His mind couldn't process what was happening. Maybe it was a wrong number, or a mistaken identity, or a sick joke from some low life he'd busted. After all he didn't recognize the voice. When Travis tried to speak, his words were incomprehensible.

"Mr. White, just try to understand. Your wife was in an automobile accident, and we need to airlift her to Duke University Hospital. Come as soon as possible."

Travis remembered very little about the ride to the hospital. Sam Barnett, a friend and fellow ABC partner, drove him. But he knew when he walked into the emergency room that Virginia wouldn't need to be airlifted. He could tell by the faces of her co-workers that Virginia was dead. He heard a few words...gasoline truck...rain...head injuries...burns...but it didn't come together. It didn't make sense. Over the next few days, Sam patiently explained the accident to Travis over and over. It was raining hard and visibility was poor. So when Virginia pulled onto I-95, she never saw the eighteen-wheel gasoline truck barreling over the overpass. The impact was horrendous, and mercifully Virginia probably never knew what hit her.

Travis shivered and shook his head violently. "I'll never get past it. NEVER."

His eyes fell on the stuffed canvass bags and fishing equipment piled in the corner of the room. He swore, jumped from bed, and rushed into the bathroom. He let a spray of cool water pound his smarting back, face, and arms. His head began to clear, and he jumped out of the shower, grabbed a towel, and twisted it around his waist. As he hopped barefoot towards the bedroom he heard the squeal of brakes in front of his house. Suddenly a horn blasted, and the voice of Elvis Presley belted out Jailhouse Rock. Travis hobbled to the front door clutching the towel around his waist and threw open the screen door.

"Hey shut that down, Sam. You want to wake up all of Seaboard?" Travis shouted.

"Wouldn't hurt none. Somebody ought to wake it up," said Sam.

"Just shut it off," said Travis.

The music went low, and as he turned to go back in, Travis caught a glimpse of his neighbor peering through parted curtains.

"Sorry, Mrs. Bernice," Travis said. The curtain dropped suddenly. Remembering that he wore only a towel, Travis ducked back into his house.

It took Travis only a few minutes to throw on cut-off jeans, a faded tee-shirt with OBX, Outer Banks, North Carolina printed on it, and a pair of badly worn boat shoes. He grabbed his gear and was out the door. He threw his gear into the back of the Cherokee and swung into the front seat. Simultaneously, with Travis's bottom hitting the seat, Sam turned up the volume on his tape player. Elvis had moved on to another memorable hit, and Sam squealed the jeep Cherokee onto the road.

"Sam cut that thing down!"

"Hey, man, the King lives!"

Travis reached over and turned the volume down. "I wish you'd grow up."

"Good Lord man, you look like hell," Sam said concern etched in his voice. Travis didn't reply.

"The dream again, huh?"

Travis shifted nervously. "No, got sunburned yesterday weeding the garden. Kept me awake."

"What? That's what you did on the first day of your vacation—weed a garden? Hey, man, you're supposed to be relaxing this week. That's why they call it a VACATION."

"Well, I can't just let it go," Travis said remembering that Virginia planted the flower garden. She chose lilies, Turks caps, spiderwort, hosta, yarrow and several other perennials, explaining to Travis that now they wouldn't have to plant every year. "They're like us, Travis; they'll be here year after year." But Virginia wasn't here...not now, not ever again.

"Say Trav," said Sam, "I know you don't want to hear this again, but have you thought about getting some kinda counseling. These nightmares are really messing you up. It's been two years now. (pause) Trav, Ginny would want you to move on. Maybe you need a little nudge. Maybe a psychiatrist can give you that nudge."

"Sounds like a bunch of psychobabble to me. That's all I need, Sam, for it to be on my law enforcement record that I went to a shrink. I can hear them now—they're letting a crazy man walk around with a gun."

"It ain't like that any more, Trav," Sam said. "Therapy is treated like any other medical treatment now days. Hell, it's even covered by our HMO."

Travis wasn't really concerned about how counseling would look on his record, he just didn't want to share intimate memories of Ginny with anyone else. Especially a stranger. Memories were all he had left of Ginny. Travis laid his head back and closed his eyes. "Think I'll grab a few," he said.

Now Sam, on the other hand, had a different attitude about women and psychiatrists. Sam sought counseling when Angie, his wife of two years, took off with a fertilizer salesman to Florida leaving behind an empty bank account, her house key, a sink full of dirty dishes, and a quart of spoiled milk in the refrigerator. Sam relished his counseling sessions. He enjoyed the attention. He had a captive audience. He talked at length about the rush he got from his job, about how to build a deer stand, the best bait to use for surf fishing, the hazards of kayaking in the ocean, wind surfing techniques, camping in the mountains, and so on and so on. After only three sessions, the psychiatrist suggested that Sam had already gotten on with his life and didn't really need his help. But he did mention that Sam exhibited what he referred to as a Peter Pan personality. In other words, like Peter Pan, Sam refused to grow up. This diagnosis delighted Sam, and he wore it like a badge of honor.

Sam headed the Cherokee down Seaboard's Main Street pass the Farmer's Bank, post office, Seaboard Grocery, and a John Deere farm implement dealership. He drove pass lovely old Victorian homes that peered out from behind lush, magnolia and pecan trees. He drove pass the Baptist and Methodist churches, that struggled to maintain small town values. Finally, he reached a sign that read, LEAVING SEABOARD—COME AGAIN.

Seaboard, North Carolina was home for Sam Barnett and Travis White for almost half a century. It was a small town of less than 700 people and surrounded by miles of fertile farm land in Northampton County. In 1751, settlers came from nearby Virginia and built the small settlement which they called Concord.

But in 1832, when the Seaboard Railroad (then known simply as the Seaboard Road) was built to run from Portsmouth, VA to Weldon, NC, the name of the town was changed from Concord to Seaboard in anticipation of progress the people hoped the railroad would bring. And when the trains rumbled through the town shaking the earth and coughing black smoke into the air, the people of Seaboard reaped small rewards from the railroad's presence. Young girls waved as sailors rode by in the trains heading to the naval base in Norfolk. Nervous young students with large trunks of new smelling clothes boarded the train on their way to colleges in the large cities.

Salt-water fish arrived from markets on the coast every evening to be sold by a local black man in his fish market behind the drugstore. Often the fish were still flopping about in the trays of shallow ice water used to transport them. The modest Victorian town had been home to farmers, legislators, lawyers, doctors, law enforcement people, as well as a famous writer, Bernice Kelly Harris, and an entrepreneur, Paul Rose, founder of Rose's Stores. But the day came when the train was no longer king, and like other small southern towns Seaboard declined with the railroad.

Sam stopped his Cherokee at the intersection of highway 158. He looked at Travis who slept fitfully on the seat beside him. His fingers twitched and through the thin skin of his eyelids, Sam could see his eyeballs darting from side to side. Sam shook his head, turned left and headed east to the Outer Banks.

They stopped just over the bridge at Elizabeth City for lunch. The diner was built on pilings that extended into the Pasquotank River, and they were seated at a window with a full view of the harbor. They watched a 36 ft. Catalina sailboat motor into the mariner and struggle to maneuver into a narrow slip. A waitress brought them sweet tea that was so thick with sugar that you could stand a spoon up in it. Then they ordered the daily special from a menu written on a chalkboard. They ordered eastern North Carolina barbecue, hush puppies, corn on the cob, and cole slaw. Dessert was fresh peach cobbler with a scoop of ice cream. Sam watched intently as the sailboat squeezed into the slip, and a tall, tan woman with short dark hair and a more than adequate figure bounced about securing the lines. Sam always enjoyed a beautiful view, and he gawked unashamedly.

"Is everything okay?" the waitress asked as she peeled their check from her pad.

"Huh? Oh, yeah," Sam said. Then looking out the window again he winked and added, "Everything is just delicious."

The waitress rolled her eyes and clicked her tongue. Travis laughed and shook his head. Sam felt relieved that Travis was relaxing.

Travis offered to drive, and Sam sat in the passenger seat yammering on and on about anything that popped into his head. The men knew this part of the North Carolina well. A large portion of North Eastern North Carolina plus the Outer Banks from Corolla to Ocracoke Island made up their Alcohol Beverage Control turf. After years of working this area, the side roads, swamps, and small coastal towns were as familiar to them as hometown Seaboard.

The men continued on towards Nags Head. They never tired of being out on the Outer Banks. (OBX as it is affectionately known) In fact, Sam once joked that he'd do this job for nothing if he could work the beach all the time. The vehicle rumbled onto the Wright Memorial Bridge crossing the Currituck Sound. A gull with a head that looked like it had been dipped into a bottle of black ink swooped down and soared just ahead of the Cherokee. Suddenly, the bird looked back, made a loud squawk that sounded like a laugh, tacked swiftly off the wind, and disappeared over the sound.

Sam laughed. "Our reception committee."

Travis nodded and smiled. "What happened to the King?"

"Now you're cooking," laughed Sam, and he popped in a tape. Soon the voice of Elvis shouted at the cars behind them...YOU AIN'T NOTHING BUT A HOUND DOG.

CHAPTER 2

Travis continued pass milepost markers and city limit signs that read Kitty Hawk and Kill Devil Hills. They passed the enormous granite monument in Kill Devil Hills that designated the dunes chosen by Wilbur and Orville Wright for their first flight. The men watched as a hang glider soared from atop Jockey Ridge and disappeared behind the migrating sand dune. Finally Travis turned onto Virginia Dare Trail and drove along the shoreline, until he reached Nags Head.

The Cherokee pulled onto the crushed shell parking lot of the sprawling Sand Trap Motel. Additions to the motel were made haphazardly over the years, and now the Sand Trap was a tangle of rooms and efficiency apartments. The exterior of the buildings was constructed of weathered clapboard, and the complex was horseshoe shaped with the office and swimming pool situated in the center. On the outside, it appeared to be one step above seedy, but inside it was clean, the appliances worked, and the sheets fit the beds. Travis and Sam always stayed at The Sand Trap. In fact, it was the motel of choice for most of the ABC officers on vacation, one reason being it was cheap. But the biggest reason was that it was oceanfront, making the job of lugging fishing equipment to the beach easier.

The two men walked into the office, and a heavy set woman with dyed black hair and too much make-up smiled and said with a true Outer Banks accent, "Well, if it ain't the Seaboard boys? Didn't know as you was coming in today."

"Hey, Reba. How's it going?" said Sam.

"Any fish left out there?" asked Travis extending his credit card.

Reba laughed and reached for the card. "I don't know. You better go on

14

down and check it out. They been abringing 'em in by the buckets full today. How long you gonna be our guest?"

Travis pocketed his credit card and said, "Reba, you get to enjoy our company all week."

Sam and Travis unloaded their gear. "What say we go check it out, Trav?" said Sam.

"Might as well claim our spot," said Travis. "You want to try it this afternoon?"

"Naw, let's just pick a spot and get at it early in the morning. Besides, I intend to drink some serious beer tonight," Sam said with a wink

Travis shook his head and feigned disgust. "I wish you'd never had a head session with that damned shrink. Every since he told you that you have a Peter Pan complex, you been trying to live up to it."

They walked up the steps to the top of the dunes and gazed down at the backs of a multitude of fishermen armed with heavy surf rods, eyes glued to the ocean. Sam and Travis watched the ritual taking place with reverence as if they'd never seen surf fishing. They watched the fishermen bring up their long rods for an overhead sweep, push up with the right hand, pull down with the left, and turn in the direction of the cast. They heard the whirr as pressure on the spool was eased to let the line out, and they watched as the sinker hit the water at just the intended spot.

Sam and Travis walked down to the beach and moved from one fisherman to another talking "fish speak". When they learned that bluefish were running strong, they discussed lures, whether to bait with cut mullet, menhaden or artificial bait.

When they'd gleaned all the information they needed for tomorrow's fishing, they decided to walk down to the pier before dinner. Iridescent gems of twilight tripped across the water, and the ocean became a mesmerizing combination of beauty, mystery, and power.

East of anywhere USA, the Outer Banks of North Carolina is especially pleasant in the fall. Schools are in session. Tourists with their out of state license plates are gone taking their litter, blaring radios, and children with them. Locals slowly emerge from their air-conditioned hibernation. Dogs with impressive pedigrees and dubious parentage romp up and down the beaches accompanied by owners with poop scoops and plastic bags. Restaurants post off-season rates and prices are slashed in the shops along the Beach Highway. All seems right with world.

Travis and Sam chose Guthrie's, a local mom and pop restaurant over on the by-pass. It overlooked the water just below the Washington Baum Bridge that spanned the Roanoke Sound. Sam pulled the Cherokee onto the restaurant's crushed shell parking lot. In the off season, Guthrie's was a gathering place for the locals…a sort of de facto country club. The place was comfortable, the view tranquil, and the food to die for.

"Well, bless my soul. The Seaboard boys. Didn't expect to see you this week. Thought you were on vacation," said an attractive thirty something year old, redhead with green eyes, freckled shoulders, big boobs, and white teeth.

Sam's face immediately took on that "you're the sexiest gal I've ever seen" look. "Hey beautiful. Missed me huh?"

"Yes, Sam, like a cold sore." She picked up two menus and led them to a table by the window.

They looked out over the shallow marshes of the Roanoke Sound. Channels provided boats access to deeper water. Clumps of black needle rushes were so thick in places that it looked like you could walk on them were it not for their sharp dark needles. Travis and Sam watched a pair of mallards and a tern vie for corn and bits of bread a little boy tossed into the water. Suddenly there was a slight movement in the rushes across the channel. The water rippled and a creature with long whiskers, bulging eyes, webbed feet, sleek dark fur, and a furless tail glided effortlessly through the water toward the birds. Soon two companions joined him. The ducks and tern appeared undisturbed by their company and willingly shared handouts with the nutrias.

"I can't stand those damned nutrias," said Sam.

"Why?" asked Travis

"They look like big old rats to me."

"Well, they are rodents. In the muskrat family, you know."

"Yeah, see. MuskRAT. I told you," said Sam

"Some people think their fur is beautiful. Early fur traders trapped nutrias, dyed their fur, and sold the pellets as beaver skin," Travis added.

"Where you get all this stuff, Trav?" asked Sam.

"Well, some of us read, you know."

They ordered chowder, a green salad, soft-shell crab sandwiches, and French fries. Lemon chess pie was today's special dessert so they had an extra large slab, compliments of the cook.

Travis said, "That's got to be the best lemon chess I've tasted since....since..."

"Since when, Trav?" pretty freckled waitress asked. Then she turned, and extended her hand toward the kitchen door. "Tra da," she said in a loud voice.

The two men looked toward the kitchen. A hollow black face with course gray hair clipped short around his receding hairline popped out of the kitchen door. He was thin and his big, yellow eyeballs were mapped with tiny red streaks. When he grinned a large gold tooth shined out at them. There was no mistaking him.

"Doo-Wop!" the two men shouted in unison. The other people in the restaurant laughed and clapped.

Then Sam and Travis stood up and began snapping their fingers rhythmically and chanting, "Doo-Wop, D Doo-Wop, Doo-Wop, D Doo-Wop...." as the Doo-Wop slithered out of the kitchen.

Other diners joined in snapping their fingers and clapping. Crouching low, elbows clenched to his side, fingers snapping to the beat, Doo-Wop moved slowly in cadence to their chanting. His eyes were scrunched shut, and his face took on a look of ecstasy, as he threw his head back and rolled it from side to side. He shuffled slowly across the room finally ending at his friends' table. The men laughed and exchanged high fives.

Doo-Wop was an Outer Banks legend. He was born Jabiz Abraham Early over on Roanoke Island. He lived with his granny who took in ironing and his pop who worked on a shrimp boat. When Jabiz finished high school, he went to work as a shrimper, too. Everything seemed to be going according to God's plan as granny put it. But granny hadn't figured on the one thing. She hadn't figured on the power of music. All day, every day on the boat and at the dock, Jabiz listened to the new sounds, especially the blues and jazz coming out of Memphis and a doo-wop sound called Motown emanating from a warehouse in Detroit. He was especially partial to doo-wop recordings, and he'd add his doo-wops to the back-up groups he heard on the radio. Thus, Jabiz earned his nickname Doo-Wop.

Soon Doo-Wop was no longer content to just Doo-Wop around the shrimp boats. He left the Outer Banks to try his luck in the music industry leaving his granny brokenhearted and his pop shaking his head in disgust. It was years before anyone saw Doo-Wop again. Then one day he just appeared as if he were simply coming home from a vacation. He returned with nothing to show for his adventure but a gold tooth, a claim that he had once been in a back up group on a Motown recording, and a tiny little baby girl he called Short Sugar.

That was seventeen years ago. Now Doo cooked in the restaurant and took care of Pop and Short Sugar. Occasionally, he would disappear for a few days, but then he was back spinning yarns about his former music career and bragging about Short Sugar.

"Say Doo," said Sam, "What's happening?"

"Yeah," said Travis. "Where you been? You were gone a long time this trip."

Doo-Wop bent forward with a laugh and slapped his knee. "Questions. So many questions. And ya ain't ebin axed me 'bout Short Sugar." Doo-Wop spoke in an Eastern North Carolina Black dialect, a combination of African, early English, and Scottish influence that was slowly disappearing.

"Right," said Travis. "How is the little girl?"

Doo-Wop lifted his eyebrows and gave a soft whistle. "Lil girl? Guess ya ain't seen Short Sugar fo' a while. If'n ya had ya'd know Short Sugar ain't no lil girl." He turned toward the kitchen and said in a loud voice. "Short Sugar, git on out cheer."

Sam and Travis looked towards the kitchen as Short Sugar slowly stepped from behind the swinging door. She was tall and slim, a lovely young woman of seventeen with clear, golden brown skin. She had brown almond shaped eyes set above her high cheekbones. Her hair hung in shoulder length braids tied off by multi-colored beads. The sun had bleached the tips of the braids leaving the effect of a halo around her innocent face. She wore no make-up and although she smiled, she diverted her eyes shyly. One other feature was particularly noticeable. Short Sugar's figure verified that she was indeed no longer a little girl.

"Wow, Short Sugar, you sure have grown up," stammered Sam. He wasn't exactly sure how to act around a little friend who had blossomed into womanhood over night. Short Sugar blushed.

"We'll have to find another name for you. One's that more suitable for a young lady," Travis said.

"Naw, Short Sugar's okay fo' my baby," said Doo-Wop putting his arms around her and giving her a squeeze.

"My teachers call me Elizabeth," she said. It was the first time she'd spoken, and her voice was soft and clear, and there was not a trace of the northeastern North Carolina black dialect.

"And you know what else? Nex year she be goin' to college. Dat's right…college. Cin you magine dat?" said Doo-Wop his arms still around Short Sugar's shoulder. "Me…the ole Doo-Wopper wid a baby in college. Umm."

"College? That's great Elizabeth," said Travis. "Where you going?"

"Elizabeth City State University. That way I won't be so far from home."

Doo-Wop grinned, "See. She ain't lack ole Doo. She ain't a-frettin to git way from home lack her daddy." He gave her another squeeze.

Sam and Travis left the restaurant. They talked about how touching it was to watch Doo-Wop with Short Sugar—Doo whom they had never known to dedicate himself to anything but doo-wop music.

"What a difference a pretty little girl can make in a person," said Travis.

"Pretty little girl? Did you see those..."

Travis cut him short, "Knock it off, Sam, she's still a kid."

"You're right. I've got to adjust. By the way, you decided what kind of bait you're going to use in the morning?" Sam asked changing the subject.

"Yeah, thought I'd use cut mullet."

"Me, too. Want to stop up here at the bait shop and get it tonight?" asked Sam.

"Might as well. Then we can get on down to the beach early in the morning," said Travis.

Even though it was eleven o'clock, the shop was full of customers. Some fishermen were buying bait for the morning. Others were examining artificial lures. Others just yammered on and on about anything to do with fishing.

The Outer Banks' reputation among serious fishermen is world class. The waters of the Artic move south creating a cold current called the Labrador Current, while the warm waters of the Gulf Stream flow north. When the two forceful currents collide, abundant sea life is thrust upward, providing bountiful food for all kinds of fish.

So year after year men who have nothing else in common converge on the Outer Banks and bond with one mutual interest...fishing. Sam and Travis saw several familiar faces, as they moved about the shop engaging in "fish talk", examining lures, and waiting their turn at the cash register.

"Hi," a low soft voice said behind Travis. "You're out late tonight."

"What?" Travis said with a start and turned to look into the bluest eyes he ever saw.

"I said, may I help you," the woman said, a rosy blush spreading across her face. She wore jeans, a red halter top with large white flowers, and short brown hair stylishly framed her oval face.

"I didn't mean to startle you," Blue Eyes continued, "Do you need some help?"

19

"Oh, you didn't…I mean I wasn't…Well, yes I could use some help," Travis stammered.

Blue Eyes smiled. "Well, how may I help you?" They both laughed.

"I want…I mean do you have any bait?…Uh…Well, of course you have bait. This is a bait shop. What I mean is do you have any cut mullet?" Travis continued to sputter.

"Pint or quart?" she said moving away from him.

"Better make it a quart," Travis said following behind her. "That way I don't have to keep coming back for more…Not that I don't want to come back for more, it's just that well, you're fishing and…," He stopped and swallowed hard. "Just make that a quart, please."

Blue Eyes left for a few seconds and returned with a quart cardboard container. She told him the price, and Travis fumbled for his wallet and removed the wrong bill three times. He finally settled on one and handed it to her. As he turned to walk away, she said, "Wait."

Travis froze in his tracks. His mouth was dry, and he slowly turned to face Blue Eyes again.

"You forgot something," she said holding out his change.

Travis swallowed again and extended his damp palm. "Thanks," he whispered and forced himself not to run from the shop.

When Travis got outside, Sam, who saw the whole terrible thing, was leaning against the Cherokee doubled over with laughter.

"And what the hell is so funny?" Travis snarled.

Sam could hardly speak he was laughing so hard. "A quart….then I don't have to keep coming back….NOT that I don't want to come back…." Sam laughed so hard that tears ran down his cheeks, and he began to hiccup.

"Get in the damn car," Travis said plopping down in the driver's seat. "It's clear to see that you are in no condition to drive."

Travis roared out of the parking space, tore from the lot in a spray of crushed shells, and barely missed a rusty pickup tooling slowly down Virginia Dare Trail. This resulted in another explosion of laughter from Sam who rolled onto the floorboard and pounded the seat with his fist.

CHAPTER 3

SUNDAY

Travis and Sam didn't need an alarm clock to wake them up the next morning. The sound of gently lapping waves mingled with the hungry cry of gulls was all that was needed to propel them out of bed and down to the beach.

They armed themselves with heavy surf rods, rod belts, sand spikes, braided nylon and monofilament lines, sinkers, net, bait, lures, and any other paraphernalia they might need for a heavy session of serious surf fishing. They climbed to the top of the dune and looked out over a scene so beautiful as to be sacred. A dazzling orange sun ascended from the eastern horizon and a stunning copper brilliance danced on the water like shining pennies cast upon the gentle waves. A light breeze carried the scent of salt and fish and brine. They hurried down to the beach to join the battery of solemn fishermen facing east, rod in hand, as if in divine meditation.

Travis and Sam chose a spot where the waves were flat and the water slightly darker indicating an inshore slough created by a dip through a sandbar. Years of fishing these waters taught them that a slough was a perfect spot to drop their sinkers because breaking waves stir up food and trap it in the slough.

Their ice chests filled with fish even faster than they hoped. They caught mostly bluefish, but they also landed a few spotfin croakers and a couple of channel bass. Then as the sun climbed higher, the fish became inactive and hid from the glare that exposed them. This gave Sam and Travis time for breakfast and rest before the late afternoon session.

Their favorite breakfast place was Don and Ollie's on Virginia Dare Trail. No reservations required. No signs prohibiting bare feet and chests. No elegant breakfast foods with fancy sauces. No espressos or lattes. Just plain Outer Banks breakfasts of home-baked biscuits topped with white gravy, local sausages and bacon, eggs to your liking with grits and lots of real butter. You could almost hear the arteries clogging, but this was fishermen food, designed to eat quick, fill up fast, and let the next fellow take your seat. An old pool table was in the back, and if you were lucky, you could find a cue and sink a few balls while you waited for a table. The parking lot was full and Sam took a spot with several other cars along the road in front of the weathered clapboard building.

Ollie said the wait would be about twenty minutes so they used the time to exchange fish stories with the other sweating, sunburned fishermen they knew from other seasons. Most men reported a good morning. The blues were still running well, and the weather looked like it was going to hold. As Travis reached down to pet a motley colored hound-type dog waiting for a handout, he stared across at the bait shop.

"Need some bait, Trav?" Sam laughed loudly and slapped his knee.

Travis's face turned an even brighter shade of red. "Back off, Sam," he whispered.

Ollie called their names and led them to a small table that was squeezed into the corner by the kitchen.

"Hey this is good, Ollie," Sam said, "Now they can just hand me those hot biscuits right out of the oven."

They ordered the fishermen's feast that consisted of some of everything in the kitchen, along with a pot of strong, hot coffee. When Ollie brought the breakfast out and laid it on the table, Sam bent over his plate and breathed deeply.

"Marry me, Ollie," Sam swooned. "Marry me and fix me biscuits like these every morning."

"Sam, you fool," Ollie laughed. "Don might have something to say about that."

Suddenly Don stuck his head out of the swinging kitchen door. "You hitting on my woman again, Sam?" he said.

"It's not fair, Don," Sam said. "Not fair that you got to her first."

Ollie waved her hand at them and walked off laughing.

The breakfast crowd was thinning out, so Sam and Travis enjoyed a third cup of coffee and planned their evening fishing strategy. Then a thin, tanned man with straw colored hair and wearing a wrinkled Dare County law enforcement uniform sauntered to their table. He pulled up a straight back chair, turned it around, and straddled it.

"Well, if it ain't the Seaboard boys," he said. "Thought this was your vacation week. You on assignment or you just like our company?"

"Hey, Shucks," said Travis. "We missed you, what do you think?"

"Huh," scoffed Shucks. He reached in pocket and took out some salted boiled peanuts. He shelled them, popped them into his mouth, and simply dropped the shucks on the floor thus demonstrating the origin of his name, Shucks.

"Shucks, you dropping those peanut shucks on my floor again?" Ollie called across the room.

Shucks crushed them with his heavy boot and kicked them under his chair. "No kidding. What's going on that you two come out here this week?"

Shucks was an ABC wanta-be. He felt that working as an ABC officer would be more adventurous and prestigious than a Dare County law enforcement officer. So he was constantly pumping Sam and Travis for information about their assignments…drug bust, still stakeouts, arrests etc., as well as tips on any job openings.

"This week, Shucks, we're on vacation," said Travis. "Simple as that. We're fishing."

Shucks looked doubtful. "That's right," said Sam. "We're down at the Sand Trap. Want to go out with us tonight when you get off work?"

"So sure 'nuff, you're just fishing?" Shucks asked dubiously.

"Just fishing."

"No, think I'll pass this time. Say you hear of any jobs with ABC ?" Shucks asked for about the hundredth time.

"Not yet, Shucks," said Travis. "But we'll keep you posted, buddy."

"Thanks," Shucks said, reaching into his pocket for more boiled peanuts. He stood and turned his chair around. "Catch you two later."

"Well, what do you want to do now?" Travis asked Sam. "We've got a few hours to kill before we go back out."

"I don't know, Trav," said Sam. "Could go over and buy some more bait."

"Get off it, Sam," said Travis. He pushed his chair away from the table and headed for the cash register leaving Sam doubled over in laughter.

Sam and Travis drove back to the Sand Trap stretched out on their beds, and watched a game between Atlanta and the Redskins. Travis fell asleep, but

Sam kept looking at his watch, coaxing the hands to move faster. About four thirty, he roused Travis.

"Hey, let's go on down, Trav."

Travis stood up, stretched and gathered his fishing gear. Soon they were climbing the dune. Since they'd been lucky earlier, they set up at the same spot that they'd fished that morning. Their afternoon efforts were disappointing, however. So they just relaxed, breathed the warm sea-scented air, and listened to the song of the waves. They watched the waves gently lap the shore like soft white hands. They watched as a pelican floated onto the inshore slough they were fishing and wished him more luck than they were having. The ambience was so peaceful and serene that it was of little consequence that the fish seldom disturbed them, and their ice chests contained not fish but beer.

"Looks like we're off our game this afternoon, partner," said Travis.

"Yeah, this is about as exciting as watching a car rust," said Sam.

When they heard the first waves of the incoming tide, they gathered their equipment and trekked up the dune to the Sand Trap. They gave the fish to Reba who cleaned and froze them in milk containers filled with water.

The sun and the quiet afternoon left Travis tired and reflective. A hot shower, German food, and a cold draught beer at the Bavarian Place were what he needed. But his thoughts kept going back to the girl at the bait shop. Blue eyes...the bluest eyes he'd ever seen. Suddenly, he'd felt guilty, unfaithful and he struggled to remember exactly what Ginny had looked like.

CHAPTER 4

When Sam and Travis arrived at the Bavarian Place on Roanoke Island, they found the front parking lot full.

"Packing 'em in tonight, Trav," said Sam.

"Try the back lot," said Sam, his eyes searching the crowd.

They took the last space in the back lot and walked into the outdoor beer garden. Traditional German décor featured picnic tables, an old-world clock tower, a children's playground with boats, and a Gingerbread House. Smiling waitresses in short Bavarian style pinafores held large round trays ladened with frosty beer mugs. Sam and Travis worked the crowd, laughing, joking and lamenting with other fishermen their less than successful afternoon of fishing.

They ran into Shucks, who stuck to them like a "tick on a blue hound dog" as Sam characterized him. They almost didn't recognize him in street clothes, and Shucks joined them when they went inside to eat. The atmosphere of the restaurant further energized their festive mood. Delicious smells and robust sounds of German music infused their senses, and servers dressed in Bavarian attire brushed by them balancing trays of scrumptious German fare. The white walls, high ceiling, and exposed beams were hung with Bavarian ornamentation, and the booths and tables were of sturdy dark wood creating an atmosphere of old-world hospitality.

The hostess seated them in a booth and a smiling waitress with blonde hair, blue eyes, and wearing richly-colored garb designed to accentuate her best qualities arrived at their table.

"Hi I'm Brita. I'll be your server tonight," she said.

Sam looked into her eyes, affecting his 'I can't believe I've finally met you' look and said, "Brita? Like the German name, Brita? For real?"

"Yes, that's really my name," she giggled. "I was named for one of the Von Trapp children. You know, in the movie, The Sound of Music. My mother saw the show fourteen times."

"Fourteen times? That's amazing," Sam said, raising his eyebrows feigning surprise. "Isn't that amazing, Trav?"

"Yeah, real amazing. You'll have to excuse my friend, Brita. He thinks it's his mission to engage every woman he meets in conversation whether he makes any sense or not," Travis said. Shucks laughed.

Sam continued undeterred, "Well, Brita, why don't you bring me and my friends a beer. I know ole Trav and I want a couple of Black Radishes, how 'bout you Shucks?"

Shucks ordered a Corolla Gold, and the men set about the serious business of considering the menu. By the time Brita returned with sweating, cold mugs of beer, they'd made their decisions. Sam ordered Sauerbraten, and Travis ordered Wiener Schnitzel. Shucks ordered a hamburger and French fries.

They ate slowly, and Sam and Travis entertained Shucks with accounts of their exploits as ABC officers. Their degree of embellishment was commensurate with the number of beers they consumed. Shucks listened, riveted to every word.

"Okay, here's one for you two. Something I've always wondered. Where did the word *bootlegger* come from anyhow?" said Shucks who fired question after question at Sam and Travis relishing every word that came out of the mouths of the two men he tried to emulate.

Travis took this one. "You see, Shucks, in colonial times it was illegal to sell whiskey to Indians. So whiskey traders hid a bottle of whiskey in their boot. That's where we got the term bootlegger."

"Well, I'll be," said Shucks. " I knew it had to be something like that."

After dinner Sam made sure that Brita knew he'd left the biggest tip. It took the three men another half hour to make their way through the crowd and to their cars in the back lot.

"So, what ya gonna do now?" asked Shucks.

"Well, Shucks, I guess we'll go on back to the Sand Trap," said Travis.

"Going to sleep or are you going to watch TV?" he asked.

"We're gonna hit the sheets, Shucks," said Sam. "We're on the beach early tomorrow."

Sam and Travis followed Shuck's car out of the parking lot and turned towards the Washington Baum Bridge. When Shucks' car reached the Dare

County Justice Center, the car signaled right, drove into the paved lot, and pulled into a space designated For Law Enforcement Officers Only.

"Thought this was Shucks' day off. Doesn't that guy ever give it a rest?" asked Travis.

"Yeah, he needs to get himself a woman," said Sam.

"You've got a one-track mind, Sam."

As they stepped out of their car back at the Sand Trap, a yellow moon hung large and low. A small bank of charcoal gray clouds lined the horizon to the south. The sound of gently lapping waves could be heard beyond the lee of the dunes, and a pungent briny smell filled their nostrils. Breathing deeply, Sam stretched his arms above his head and yawned.

"I won't have any trouble getting to sleep tonight," Travis said.

"And I won't have any trouble getting up in the morning," said Sam. "I'll make the coffee. Like to be the first up before the day cracks down on me."

Once inside, Travis and Sam caught the last part of the local news, listened to the weather forecast, and got ready for bed. Satisfied that a slow-moving storm from the south would not make tomorrow a complete washout, they stripped and stretched out on their beds. The room scarcely clicked into darkness, when they heard the crunch of a car on the shell driveway, a car door slammed, and a fist pounded on the door.

Sam jumped out of bed, reached for his thirty-eight-caliber revolver, and slowly parted the curtains. "Shit, it's Shucks," said Sam.

"Shucks?" echoed Travis

Sam threw the door open. "Shucks, this better be damned important."

"Important? You think hit and run is important? You think a helicopter taking a victim to Albemarle Hospital intensive care is important?" Shucks retorted dramatically.

Travis was up and to the door. "Say what you mean, Shucks."

"Yeah, what's going on?" Sam added.

Shucks pushed himself into the room. "You a friend of that black guy who works over at Guthrie's Restaurant?"

"You mean, Doo-Wop?" Travis asked anxiously.

"Yeah, I believe that's his alias. His real name is," Shucks took out a small tablet and began to flip the pages pretentiously as Sam and Travis watched impatiently.

"Alias?" Sam shouted. "That's no alias, that's his nickname."

"Get on with it, Shucks," Travis said impatiently. "Hell, we know who you're talking about."

Shucks would not have anything to do until he found the page in his pad on which Doo's real name was scribbled. "His real name is Jabiz, Jabiz Abraham Early," Shucks said with some satisfaction.

Sam stepped toward Shucks, fists clenched at his side. "Shucks if you don't want me to cram that damned notebook down you throat, the next words that come out of your mouth better tell us," and he leaned forward menacingly and yelled, "WHAT HAPPENED TO DOO?"

Shucks retreated with a startled look on his face. "Get outa my face, Sam. Did I say anything happened to Doo? Ain't nothing happened to him..." Sam took another step forward, and Shucks quickly added, "It's his girl. The one that helps out down at Guthrie's. The one they call Short Sugar. Except her name is not really Short Sugar it's...."

Sam and Travis were not listening. They threw on their clothes, gathered their wallets, badges, guns, and keys, and headed out the door.

Travis and Sam slapped open the door labeled Intensive Care Unit Waiting Room and walked hastily to the desk.

"You can't come in here," said a red-haired nurse with a smear of orange lipstick on her front teeth.

"We're here about Elizabeth Early. How is she doing?" Sam asked.

"I'm sorry. I can't give that kind of information to anyone but family....You're not family are you?" She grinned at her own tasteless joke.

Travis ignored her insipid remark. "Where's the family waiting room?"

"Down that hall and to the right. But you can't go down there. It's reserved for family members only," she said.

The two men turned to start down the hall. "I'm calling security," she added and reached for the phone.

Travis turned and pulled out his badge, "No need to call security. We can handle this ourselves." They left the nurse sitting there with her mouth opened.

They found Doo-Wop in the family waiting room with other desperate family members hoping, praying that their loved one would survive whatever brought them here in the first place. Doo sat with his elbows on his knees, his face in his hands. He shook his head from side to side. They called his name, and when he looked up his face seemed thinner, his eyes yellower, his hair grayer. Tracks of tears streamed down his cheeks, a necklace of perspiration beads was implanted in the creases of his neck, and wide sweat stains ringed the underarms of his soiled chef's shirt.

"WHY?" he threw his head back and wailed. "Why day do dis to my baby? Why day hurt sweet lil Short Sugar? Why Sam? Why Travis?" He dissolved into tears and shook uncontrollably.

Sam and Travis walked across the room and sat one on each side of Doo.

"I don't know the answer to that one, pal, but we're gonna find out," Sam said.

"Sure are, Doo. Don't you worry about it, we'll find the bastard. But, hey, right now we're gonna take it one step at a time. First, how about Short Sugar. What are her injuries? What does the doctor say?" Travis asked.

Doo-Wop looked up and wiped his eyes with the sleeve of his food-stained, chef's jacket. "Dey says two tings. First off that she be lucky to be alive. When de car hit her, it hit her real hart, but it threw her aside and didn't run ober her. Dat de good part. Second part ain't too good. She was throwed so hard dat her hed just banged on de road and gave her a percussion."

"Could he have said concussion, pal?" Sam asked.

"Believe so. She ain't come to yet," said Doo-Wop. As he talked, Doo-Wop became calmer. "She gots a bruised kitney and all kinds of cuts and scrapes, but the ting that gits me is she jest not coming round."

"Sometimes it takes time, partner," said Travis squeezing his shoulder gently.

Sam and Travis sat with Doo until the first light of dawn seeped through the waiting room window. After what seemed to be a thousand cups of coffee, a young Indian doctor walked into the waiting room. Exhausted family members turned their weary, expectant eyes his way and waited for him to call a name.

"Early," he said in a loud voice. "Mr. Early."

Travis and Sam supported Doo-Wop as he stood shakily. "Here." His voice quivered.

The doctor looked questionably at the trio, then spoke to Doo-Wop. "Mr. Early, we think your daughter is out of danger now." Sam and Travis grabbed Doo as his knees buckled with relief.

The doctor continued, "She is awake. She has some double vision now, but that will go away soon. The bruises and scrapes will heal with time and her kidneys are functioning normally. She is experiencing quite a bit of pain, but we have her sedated. We need to keep her for a few days for observation."

"When cin I see her?" Doo-Wop asked. The doctor told him that he could see her within the hour, but added that only immediate family was allowed to visit.

Travis showed his badge. "Doctor, this young lady was injured as the result of a crime…hit and run. It's important that we talk with her as soon as possible."

The doctor frowned. "Against better medical judgment, I will allow policemen five minutes. That is all you can have." And he walked away.

Sam and Travis waited outside the room while Doo-Wop went in to see his daughter. Although he was in there only a few minutes, it seemed like an eternity. When Doo came out, he was trembling and crying again. He collapsed in a straight-back chair and looked up at the men.

"I jut don't unnerstan it," he said shaking his head. "How come anybody do sumping like dat to my baby? She ain't done nuffin to nobody."

"We know, partner," said Sam.

"I ain't no violent man, Sam. But I tell you one ting, if'n I finds out who done dis, I'll whup some ass," he said resolutely.

"I don't like to hear you talk like that, Doo. You let us take care of this," Travis said. "And you take care of Short Sugar."

As Sam and Travis walked down the hall to Short Sugar's room, Travis whispered, "He's gone from grief to anger now.'

"I for one would rather see him mad than crying. Not much to be gained by crying," said Sam.

"Not much to be gained from anger either," said Travis. "That's when things get crazy."

They walked into the room. Short Sugar was lying motionless on stiff white sheets. The multi-colored beads that tied off her braids were scattered about on the white pillow like flower petals on a white table cloth. She was hooked up to several machines and an IV needle was in her arm. As a result of her head striking the hard pavement, both eyes were black. The doctor told them that her jaw was broken, but they were startled to see wires holding the bone in place. A nurse held a glass, as Short Sugar drank a pink liquid through a straw.

When she saw the two men, the nurse removed the straw. As she left the room, she mouthed the words, "Five minutes."

They approached the bed cautiously as if their movement might shake the bed and disturb the pitiful girl shackled there by tubes and wires.

"Hi, good looking," smiled Sam.

"Hey there Elizabeth," said Travis. "You're going to be alright now.

We've talked to the doctor ourselves, and he says it will take a while, but none of this is permanent. You're going to be okay."

A single tear rolled down her face. "Can you speak, Elizabeth," asked Travis. There was a slight movement…barely discernable…as Short Sugar indicated "no".

"That's alright," Sam said reassuringly. "Now, we're going to ask you a few questions and you just nod your head very gently, yes or no. Okay?"

She nodded, yes. "Good," said Sam. "Now, did you recognize the car that hit you?"

She shook her head, no. "Okay," said Travis, "Did you recognize the driver?"

She shook, no. "Let's talk about the color of the car," said Sam. "Was it a dark color?"

She nodded, yes. "Could you tell exactly what color the dark color was….like dark blue or black or green. Could you tell exactly what dark color?"

Using this system of questioning, they went through type of vehicle, make of car, year, model, etc.

"Now Elizabeth," said Travis, "What about the driver? Did he slow down?"

"Did he look back…in other words did he seem to know he'd hit you?" said Sam.

She nodded, yes. "One person?"

Yes nod. "White?"

Yes nod. "Young?"

Yes. At that point, the nurse returned and firmly announced that their five minutes were up, and she did not budge from her post until Sam and Travis began to move away from the bed.

"You've given us a lot to start with. You take care now," said Travis.

"Yeah, and we'll handle this," said Sam. "And we'll keep an eye on Doo, too."

Another tear rolled down Short Sugar's face and dropped onto the white pillowcase leaving a round, wet gray spot.

They couldn't convince Doo-Wop to leave the hospital, so they went to the shopping mall in Elizabeth City, bought him a change of clothes, and stuck a twenty in the pocket of the new jeans. As they were leaving the hospital, they ran into Shucks in the parking lot.

"Hi, pal," said Sam.

Shucks looked grim. "This ain't your case," he said slowly and emphatically. "I went up to question the Early girl, and the nurse told me that two policemen had already talked to her and five minutes was all the time the cops were allowed this morning. Figured it was you. This ain't your case," he repeated.

"Now, hold on there, pal," said Travis, "we don't want a fight over this."

"I don't want a fight either. I don't mind your help, but I mind the way you did it. This is my case," he repeated.

"Okay, I understand where you're coming from," said Sam. "I'd feel the same way. Why don't we sit down over here, and we'll tell you what we got." Sam was moving toward a bench under a giant oak tree.

The three men sat down and Sam and Travis went over the information they gleaned from Short Sugar. White male, 40-50 years old, driving a muddy dark colored four-wheel drive, make of car unknown…possibly a Jeep Wrangler and added that they needed to follow up on that. Shucks took copious notes in his small tablet.

"Well, thanks," he said. "Didn't mean to fire off at you back there. But the chief gave me the case. So it's my case."

"Tell you what," said Travis, "Why don't we work together on this?" Shucks looked doubtful.

"Yeah, we do that all the time at ABC. Someone's on a case and another agent runs across some evidence, we turn it over to the guy in charge. In return, the agent heading up the investigation keeps everyone else informed of his findings. That way, you know what to look for."

Shucks thought for a few minutes. "That way I can say I've worked with ABC officers."

"Yeah, the more men on board, the quicker we'll catch this creep," said Sam.

Sam and Travis drove back to Nags Head in silence. Although they were operating with no sleep, they were restless and uneasy. When they reached the Sand Trap, they saw a shirtless man wearing rubber flip-flops and balancing a steel rod, socket, and tackle box descend the dune. He was sunburned, and a wide dark band of sweat ringed his NC Hurricanes baseball cap. When he spotted Travis and Sam he flashed them a wide grin of recognition.

"Hey, Smitty," said Sam. "You look like a happy man."

"Sure am," he replied. "They're hungry today, man. Thought you two would be the first ones down this morning."

"Had a little problem to take care of," said Travis.

"Well, you better get on down there," the enthusiastic fisherman said as he opened the door to is his efficiency apartment. "They're gonna get tired of waiting for you."

Sam and Travis discussed whether they should go to the Dare County Justice Center now, or wait and give Shucks a chance to report on *his interview* to Sheriff Caffy. They didn't want to give the appearance of infringing on a county case. After all, hit run wasn't their job.

Travis said, "So what do you think? Go to the Justice Center now or later?"

Sam said, "Later. But I'm so wired I couldn't sleep if I wanted to. I need to unwind."

"Me, too," said Travis. "Want to cast a few?"

The fisherman was right. Yesterday's fishing lull had passed. The blues were biting at anything thrown their way, and Sam and Travis slowly began to relax as their cooler filled with fish and emptied of beer. They fished for several hours and watched as gray clouds began to slowly engulf the sun and the wind took on the acrid smell of a storm rolling in from the south and threatening to crash against the fragile dunes.

Sam and Travis gathered their fishing gear, plodded up the dunes, presented their catch to Reba, and trudged to their room. Then without bothering to undress, they fell onto their beds and let the song of the surf lull them into a dark, silent chasm of sleep.

CHAPTER 5

Travis and Sam woke up at six pm. A gnawing feeling in their stomachs reminded them that they had not eaten since morning. They showered and changed clothes. When they stepped outside they smelled the pungent scent of a storm in the warm southeast wind.

"Want to just go back to Guthrie's?" asked Sam.

"Might as well," said Travis, and he drove the Cherokee on the familiar route to their favorite restaurant.

When they arrived the parking lot was full. "Just pull over there on the grass," said Sam. Ignoring the sign that read DO NOT PARK ON THE GRASS, Travis pulled in beside other cars guilty of the same infraction.

They entered the restaurant and found it full of fishermen who had been driven from the beach by the approaching storm. They motioned to the hostess that they were going into the bar. Spotting two empty stools, they moved in that direction. Suddenly a tall woman with long blonde hair pulled back in a French braid and wearing chartreuse green shorts and a tight light blue tee-shirt pushed in front of them and quickly sat on one of the bar stools. She turned a grinning face towards them. She had big jade eyes, and her teeth appeared startling white against her dark suntanned face.

"Gotta move fast if you want to get ahead around here," she said smiling up at them.

"Hey, good looking," Sam said brightly.

They ordered drinks. Black radish beer for Travis and Sam and a Tom Collins for the sassy stool stealer.

"Didn't recognize you without your uniform," said Sam. With his elbow on the bar and his chin in hand, he stared intently at the beautiful face.

"You recognize people only by the clothes they wear?" she quipped and took a slow sip of her drink.

"You know what you need?" Sam asked softly with a wicked smile, and he moved closer.

"No, but I bet you're gonna tell me," she said

"You need a good looking hunk to take you for a long, midnight drive along the beach, up behind the dunes, look down at the beautiful nightlights, count the stars, and…whatever."

"Sounds great. Let me know if you think of any good looking hunks that fit the bill," she said and took another slow sip.

They laughed and Travis took a hefty swallow of his beer. Nona was the only woman Travis knew who could return Sam's passes without a hint of hesitation. Nona Godette was a local girl. When her mother died of ovarian cancer thirty years ago, Ansel Godette was left alone to raise a feisty, smart, independent, and strikingly beautiful three year old girl. Ansel knew nothing about raising children, much less a girl, so he raised her like a boy. She worked along side him on his offshore charter boat, and like the best fishermen she enjoyed reeling in and releasing billfish and was known to have once put up a damned good fight with a bluefin tuna. Ansel taught Nona to swim, surf, hang glide, scuba dive, and Nona was the most aggressive guard on the Dare County High School Girl's Basketball Team.

So when Nona set her mind to become a law enforcement officer, Ansel hid his apprehensions and encouraged her to go for it. Nona proved to be a competent and fearless Dare County law enforcement officer, but Ansel soon realized that Nona's job was not the only authority his daughter had going for her. She was a breathtakingly beautiful woman whose power over men was unmistakable.

Nona fingered the condensation on her glass. Then she said, "Heard about your friend, Doo-Wop. Real bad what happened to his girl."

"Yeah," Travis said. "She's over in the intensive care unit at Albemarle Hospital."

"I know," she said. "I read Shucks' report. Hit and run. Nasty business."

"I know," said Sam. They did not mention that Shucks' report was compiled using the information from their interrogation of Short Sugar.

"Shucks says you're going to be working with him on the case," said Nona.

"Yeah. Doo-Wop is an old buddy of ours," said Sam.

"Poor old Doo's just about crazy," said Travis.

"I'm sure," said Nona. "That's why I was so shocked he's working tonight. Thought he'd have stayed over there."

Travis and Sam looked at each with surprise. About that time, Nona spotted someone across the room. Her eyes brightened, and she flashed a smile unlike any Sam and Travis had seen before.

"Excuse me," she said sliding off the stool and swinging towards a tall well-built man, with a straight-from-the-beach tan and a shock of black hair tousled casually about his face. He wore a tee shirt two sizes too small and flashed a smile that showed that his teeth were every bit as white as hers.

Sam gawked and Travis sputtered as she strutted slowly towards her prey.

"They really compliment each other don't they," asked the very young bartender.

"Compliment each other?" asked Travis.

"Yes, you know…he's so dark and she's so blond. They compliment each other."

The young bartender cleared the empty Tom Collins glass and moved down the bar to wait on another customer.

Sam said, "*Compliment each other,* my ass…How old you think that bartender is? We oughta pull her out and ask for age verification. She looks too young to be working behind a bar."

Travis laughed and took another swallow of beer. "Say, Sam, what say we go talk to Doo?"

"Right," Sam said as he finished his drink and set the empty on the bar. They motioned to the hostess that they were going back to the kitchen.

They swung open the door labeled IN and entered a room full of the sounds and smells of a kitchen in high gear. They heard the clatter of pots and pans, voices rising above the din, the sizzle of food on the grill, and the hubbub of orders being shouted across the room. The smells of coffee and grease and fish mingled with that of human perspiration.

Harried cooks and waitresses waiting for their orders glanced nervously in the direction of the man beside the grill. Doo-Wop, wore a food-stained white apron and the band around his forehead was soaked with sweat. He swore, banged pots and pans, and threw a handful of shrimp on the grill causing small licks of flame to flare up.

Travis and Sam walked over to Doo-Wop. The kitchen staff and waitresses watched anxiously.

"Hey, Doo," said Sam, "Didn't expect to see you here tonight."

"Yeah, we thought you'd stay the night in Elizabeth City," said Travis.

"If we'd known you were coming back today, we could have given you a ride," Sam said.

Doo-Wop turned abruptly and with a contemptuous look said, "What? Ya dunt tink Doo got no otter friends?"

"Sure Doo," Travis sputtered. "Ease up. We just wanted to help."

Doo-Wop stepped forward and shook a long-handled spatula at the men. "Ya tink I cain't take care my own bidness? Well, I cin. I shaw cin."

Sam said, "Hey Doo, we know you can, but we wanted to help and..." Doo shot a seething look at Sam, and Travis lifted his hand slightly motioning Sam silent.

"Ya tink po ole Doo need hup? Ya don't tink I cin take care of my bidness and my girl widout the hup of de man? Well, I got news fo ya, I don't need de man. I done tolt ya I cin take care of my own bidness, and I cin take care of my girl."

Travis and Sam stepped back. "Sure, partner, didn't mean to but in," said Travis.

Doo turned the shrimp he'd thrown on the grill and found that they were burned. He swore and raked the black shrimp into a large garbage can.

Travis and Sam backed slowly through the swinging door labeled OUT leaving the kitchen staff and waitresses with hopeless looks on their faces.

As they walked back into the dining room, the hostess motioned them that their table was ready. She seated them by a window and handed them menus.

"I've never seen poor Doo like this," she said. "We were surprised to see him this evening, but we let him work hoping that it would take his mind off the accident. It hasn't worked."

"Yeah, he just had a conniption fit," said Sam.

They both ordered the jumbo combo fish platter. They ate silently and watched kayakers race through the channels in the marsh trying to beat the storm. After dinner, they went to the bar, reflected thoughtfully on the scene in the kitchen, and just waited for the day to end.

When they stepped outside it was nearly dark. Stars hung heavy in the darkening sky. A rain ring encircled a full moon, and topaz clouds pushed up from the southern horizon and threatened to extinguish its light. On the ride back to the Sand Trap, they drove through little patches of mist that rose and rolled across the highway still warm from the hot September sun.

They barely beat the storm. As they pulled onto the shell parking lot, rain began to fall with all its fury. Drops the size of marbles pounded the windshield.

They ducked and raced to their room, rain peppering their face and neck. The sound of the raindrops on the window air conditioner sounded like buck shot being tossed onto metal. They didn't have much to say that night. Each man was lost in his private thoughts. Sam thought about their interrupted fishing trip, Doo's resentment of their help, Shucks' obsession to become an ABC agent and what a nightmare it would be to work with him. But most of all, Sam thought about Nona and wondered what she was doing on such a gloomy night.

Travis thought about only one thing…the fury he had seen in Doo's eyes. It was a rage he'd never witnessed in this gentle man.

CHAPTER 6

MONDAY

"Hey Caffy," said Travis. "What's up?"

The huge uniformed man with thinning gray hair was seated behind a large, typical government-issued desk. A plastic name plaque identified him as T. M. Caffy, Sheriff of Dare County. He lifted his ruddy face, looked over wire-rimmed glasses and in a husky voice said, "Hey yourself. Thought this was your vacation week. You're not getting to be like Shucks are you? Loving the job so much you won't even take a vacation?"

"Don't even think it," said Sam. "Vacation plans interrupted by weather and a little incident called hit and run."

"You thinking our hit and run had something to do with alcohol or drugs?" asked the Sheriff skeptically.

"Possibly," said Travis. "But more importantly the victim is the daughter of a friend. Thought we'd see if there's any way we can help if it's okay with you."

"From what I hear," said Caffy, "your friend don't want your help."

"What gives you that idea?" asked Sam.

"Well," he said tossing down his pencil and leaning back in his chair, "news travels fast around here you know. Heard about the little scene down in Guthrie's kitchen last night."

"That wasn't Doo-Wop talking," said Travis. "That was anger and fear for his daughter."

"Any way," said Caffy, "mighty hard to help someone if they don't want your help."

"Way I look at it," said Sam, "this is a crime and regardless of friendship, it's gotta be looked at."

"You're right there," said the sheriff. "So what you doing here? Just hanging out till the weather clears?"

"Like to take a look at what you got so far. If that's okay," said Travis.

"Okay by me," said Caffy. "Not much yet. But you're welcome to see it." He tossed a thin folder across the desk.

Sam and Travis pulled up two straight chairs, opened the folder, and took out the first sheet. Sheriff Caffy grabbed the stub of a wet cigar that rested in an ashtray waiting to be lit. "Like I said," he said, "not much there yet." He struck a match on the underside of his desk, lit the cigar butt, and blew a cloud of noxious smoke upward.

Sam and Travis carefully read the printed report of their Interrogation of Witness. It was prepared by Shucks and appeared to be accurate. They didn't tell Caffy that they interviewed Short Sugar and Shucks wasn't present. At this time, no other witnesses had been found. Some night fishermen who had been casting off the Melvin R. Daniels Bridge discovered Short Sugar. They had not witnessed the accident and reported seeing nothing suspicious prior to finding her.

Sam and Travis recalled that Short Sugar said the vehicle slowed down. Apparently it also pulled off the pavement. The CSI officers got a good tire print and concluded that the vehicle involved was a four-wheel drive...possible a Jeep Wrangler. Broken glass from a small headlight seemed to substantiate that.

"You're right. Not much yet," said Sam.

"Told you so," said the Sheriff, "What do you expect? It just happened last night."

"We were thinking about going over to talk to Short Sugar...Elizabeth again," said Travis. "She was pretty much out of it yesterday. Maybe she can give us more detail."

"Know where Shucks is?" asked Sam. "Since you gave the case over to him, we wouldn't want to ah, ah, get in his way."

"Came in, looked at this folder and left. He may be over at Elizabeth City too," said Caffy.

But Shucks wasn't at the hospital...nor was Doo-Wop. This surprised Travis and Sam. They expected to find the men squaring off, protecting their turf, and generally disturbing the peace of the entire intensive care ward.

Short Sugar, on the other hand, was propped up in bed, holding a glass, and sipping a dark liquid through a plastic straw. Sam and Travis were delighted at the improvement a few hours made in Short Sugar. They smiled and crossed the room.

Sam took her hand and said gently, "Hey there, good-looking. You're looking great."

"You sure do look better," said Travis. "When we left here, we were mighty worried. You suppose to be sitting up like that?"

She smiled with her eyes and nodded her head slowly. Then she spoke slowly, gingerly, barely moving her lips. "I'm sore and stiff, but they say I'm going to be fine."

"Oh, Elizabeth," said Travis, "That's great. Where's Doo?"

"He was by real early," she said. "Said he had to take care of some business." She looked worried.

"Now don't you worry your pretty little head. We'll keep an eye on old Doo. He's our buddy," said Travis.

She smiled.

A nurse popped in the door, halted, frowned, and said sternly, "Elizabeth is doing so well that we're moving her up to a room today. But in the meantime, you two are still going to go by our rules down here. Five minutes."

Then her frown quickly vanished as she looked at Short Sugar and smiled sweetly, "How are we doing with that glass, dear?"

"Fine," she said. The nurse turned abruptly and marched out.

"They take real good care of me here," Short Sugar said.

"Honey," said Travis, "we need to ask you some more questions today. Feel up to it?"

"Yes," she said placing the glass on the table and sitting up attentively.

"Now, going back to the vehicle that struck you. You said it was a dark color. You couldn't be more specific?"

"I've thought and thought," she said. "All I can remember is that it was a dark color....dark green, or blue, or maybe even black."

"Anything else about it that was, say, a little different?" Travis said.

"Yes," she said. "The back wasn't enclosed, and it had these pipe-like things...bars across the top part of rear end. They looked like they were wrapped in something black...like canvass."

"Was this a big vehicle?" asked Sam

"Oh, no...at least not real big," she said. "But it felt like an eighteen wheeler."

They smiled. "Elizabeth, this is real helpful. Now do you remember anything unusual on the vehicle? Like the license plate, bumper sticker, or parking permit sticker. Anything like that?"

She smiled real big. "It was a North Carolina plate, and I'm almost sure it started with EV1. I'm almost sure of that," she repeated.

"Great," said Sam. "Any identifiable decorations? Like beads hanging from the mirror...anything like that?"

"No," said Short Sugar. "I couldn't have seen any beads on the mirror anyway. My being on the ground and all."

"Well, just keep thinking about it. Something might come to you," said Travis.

"There was one thing," she said haltingly. "It was sorta cute and unusual. There was this bumper sticker. It read 'I...and then a heart for love...My' and then there was this picture of a furry dog with the biggest smile on his face. It was one of those white dogs you see up north. Like an Eskimo Spitz or something. Except I never thought of an Eskimo Spitz smiling like that."

"That's a great lead," said Sam. "You know, honey, the more your body recovers from this trauma, the more you are likely to remember."

"That's right," Travis concurred. "That's why we go back and talk to witnesses several times. You know what you might want to do? Why don't you keep a pencil and paper beside your bed, and anytime you think of something...no matter how seemingly insignificant, jot it down. That way you won't forget again."

"Yeah, sometimes the mind suppresses traumatic experiences. So writing it down can help us a lot. Here, take this pen and paper...in fact take the whole tablet," said Sam tearing out his notes and laying the tablet and pen on the metal table.

Suddenly a sad, sheepish look shadowed Short Sugar's face, "Sam, Travis I want to tell you something," she hesitated.

"Go ahead," prompted Travis.

"I wanted to tell you that I wasn't walking on the correct side of the road...you know facing traffic. I was walking with my back to the cars. I shouldn't have done that."

"Look here, cutie," said Sam, "it's not unusual for victims to start blaming themselves and wonder what they could have done to prevent the incident."

"That's right, Elizabeth," said Travis. "You just remember, that regardless of the circumstances, that driver should never have driven away and left you like that. That's hit and run pure and simple."

Short Sugar gave them a smile of relief.

Sergeant Nurse reentered the room, looked at her watch, and barked, "Times up." She then marched across the room dismissively and pulled the curtain surrounding Short Sugar's bed.

On the drive back to Manteo, they discussed their interview with Short Sugar.

"Well, that's another confirmation on Wrangler as the make. I'm sure those bars she described are roll bars," said Sam.

"I agree," said Travis. "And that bumper sticker was a real gift. How many dark colored Wranglers with a smiling white dog bumper sticker is there on the beach?"

"If he's still on the beach," added Sam.

They drove in silence for a while. Then Sam said, "I was really surprised that old Shucks wasn't camped out over there."

"And I was surprised that Doo wasn't there," said Travis.

"What kind of business you think he has to take care of?" asked Sam.

"I don't know," said Travis. "But I hope Elizabeth didn't tell him as much as she told us. You know, Doo can be pretty crafty. He's capable of tracking down a dark colored Wrangler with a smiling dog bumper sticker."

"I don't even want to think about it," said Sam.

CHAPTER 7

The sky cleared, and the September heat and humidity returned with a vengeance and seeped into the black pavement on the highway. Shimmering waves of tepidity wiggled just above the shiny asphalt and potholes filled with dirty water.

Sam and Travis crossed the Washington Baum Bridge and returned to the Dare County Justice Center. As they pulled into the parking lot, a familiar uniformed figure leaned idly against a squad car, amidst a mass of peanut shells.

"Hey, Shucks," said Sam.

"Hey," Shucks answered back. "Where you been?"

Travis said, "We drove over to see Short Sugar. Thought we'd find you there since you weren't in the office." Travis didn't want Shucks to think that they proceeded without intending to include him in the interview.

"Yeah, sure," mused Shucks. He threw a handful of peanuts in his mouth and tossed the shells on the pavement. "Well, I couldn't go anyway. Been too busy checking some stuff out."

"What kind of *stuff*," asked Travis.

"The vehicle used in the commission of the crime," Shucks drawled with a wry smile. He cracked another peanut shell and picked out the nuts. Then he cracked another one, and another one.

"Well, you gonna tell us or not," Travis said impatiently. "How did you check the vehicle out and what did you find?"

Shucks tossed the nuts in his mouth, threw the shells on the ground, and began to chew leisurely. At this point, Sam thought it might be a good idea to help Shucks get to the point by cramming all the boiled peanuts down his throat, and he took a menacing step towards him to do so. Travis extended a restraining hand and said quickly, "Are we together on this or not, Shucks? When you're on a team, you can't go off on your own hot dogging and not let your partners know what the hell you're doing."

"Hot dogging? You call this hot dogging?" said Shucks reaching into the window of the car and pulling out a board with several sheets of paper clipped to it.

"Looks real official, Shucks," said Travis positioning himself between Shucks and Sam whose face was blood red and the blue veins on his neck protruded as if they would burst. "But you still haven't answered the question...."

"Yeah, *what the hell have you got,* " yelled Sam.

Shucks flinched and said quickly. "A list. A list of all the people in the county that bought dark colored Jeep Wranglers in the last three years."

"And you got the list from?" asked Travis

"From the Jeep dealer over at Nags Head," said Shucks simply.

Sam relaxed. "Good thinking, Shucks," said Travis. "That's exactly what we had in mind. You beat us to it, and that's good. That's real good. Now, let's take a look."

The three men examined the printouts the dealer had given Shucks. It was three pages of vehicle description and number, color of vehicle, date of purchase, name and address of buyer at time of purchase, and information on service done to the vehicle by the dealer.

"Bingo," said Travis.

"Good start," said Sam. "Let's keep our fingers crossed that the perp is a Dare County resident. Otherwise it gets back to square one."

Shucks' disappointed look showed that he hadn't thought of that. Travis caught his expression, slapped him on the back and said, "Hey that's the way it is Shucks. We have to start somewhere, and this is as good as any...damned good."

Shucks seemed appeased. Each man took a sheet containing the names and addresses of Wrangler Jeep owners from the clipboard. They decided to go to the address listed, try to get a front end visual of the vehicle, check out the headlights and grill. If the headlight was broken or the front grill damaged, they'd call back to the office for a warrant to search. If the visual failed to look suspicious, they'd simply meet back at the Law Enforcement Center at four and go to the next name on the list.

Shucks knew every inch of Roanoke Island. He was born and raised there. He turned left out of the Center parking lot and headed west towards Manteo. He passed the entrance to The Lost Colony Outdoor Drama theater entrance. Shucks' first experience in law enforcement was as a traffic cop at this intersection. At the height of tourist season, cars were backed up for blocks as tourists waited to purchase tickets for the evening performance. But today, there were no tourists, no traffic jam. Shucks liked it like this...quiet, uncrowded, and slow. He loved Roanoke Island with its history and mystery. Shucks was in fact quite a history buff. This was a little known fact about the peanut eating, shuck tossing officer. And the mystery of the Lost Colony of Roanoke Island fascinated him since childhood.

The mystery involved the first attempt at an English settlement in America in 1585. When the governor of the settlement, Governor White, sailed back to England for supplies, he never dreamed that a war between England and Spain would delay his return for three years. When White did return, he found the settlement deserted and no clue to the settlers' fate save three letters C R O carved on a tree. After four hundred years the significance of the letters and the whereabouts of the colonists remain a mystery. As a child, Shucks speculated about the disappearance of these first English settlers and fantasized that he solved the ancient mystery and discovered the fate of the settlers. His investigative zeal took root with these games.

Shucks turned into a luxurious neighborhood located on the west side of Roanoke Island. The subdivision was laid out so the homes faced a stunning, tranquil view of the Croatan Sound. His patrol car snaked down the curbed streets pass elegant, quality-built homes with immaculate, well-maintained lawns looking like something straight out of Southern Living. These were the kind of homes that were built to withstand the fiercest storms of the Outer Banks yet maintain a fabulous ambience. He felt a surge of intimidation as he looked for the first address on his sheet, 102 Raleigh Ave. He turned right onto a street with that name and found that it was a cul-de-sac containing five homes. The one at the very end was 102.

He pulled into the drive behind a shiny black Jeep Wrangler. Trembling with excitement, Shucks got out of his patrol car and walked over to a sweating, shirtless, black man who was attacking the weeds in a flowerbed.

Shucks summoned an air of confidence and said, "Looking for Mr. or Mrs. Johnson. Know if either of them is at home?"

The sweating man looked at Shucks' badge, wiped his brow with a filthy red handkerchief, and simply pointed in the direction of the side yard.

Shucks could have easily cut across the lawn to reach the spot the worker indicated, but he chose to take a more circuitous route. He walked anxiously up the drive and around the front of the black Jeep Wrangler. He looked down eagerly at the grill and the headlights, but much to his disappointment, both headlight and grill were in perfect condition.

At that moment, the automatic garage-door activated. Shucks jumped as a young man wearing a swimsuit and shouldering a surfboard jumped right back at him.

"Jeez," said the young surfer. "You scared the…"

"Charles," a woman's voice interrupted from around the house. "What's wrong?"

Shucks turned to see a fastidiously-dressed lady wearing designer denim overalls, a neatly pressed red checked shirt, garden gloves, and a sassy straw hat. She stepped onto the driveway and a bright smile spread across her impeccably made up face.

"I just opened the garage door and he scared the…."

"That's enough Charles," Mrs. Johnson said calmly. "Officer, may I help you with something?"

Although Shucks felt intimidated, he regained his composure enough to say, "We're just checking on an accident, mam. A dark colored Jeep. Just wanted to see if your vehicle is okay."

"Well, as you can see, officer," Mrs. Johnson smiled, "We're just fine. Thank you for your concern. Will there be anything else?"

"No mam," muttered Shucks.

The surfer turned impatiently and stomped toward the Jeep muttering something like, "…yeah, I'll bet he wanted to know if *we're* alright."

The young man dropped behind the wheel of the Jeep and said, "Do you mind? I gotta catch some waves."

"Sure, sorry" said Shucks, and he hurried much too quickly towards his car.

Shucks backed down the driveway. Before he could turn his car around, the jeep sped pass him. He looked up the drive at Mrs. Johnson who smiled sweetly and waved. He waved back. The handy man stood up, wiped his brow with his squalid handkerchief, shook his head, and went back to work.

CHAPTER 8

Sam could hardly contain his excitement. He was onto something. He felt it in his gut. The slovenly looking man who responded to his knock wore only dingy boxer shorts and held a can of beer. His eyes were blood shot, and he smelled of stale cigarette smoke and sour beer breath.

"Whatcha want?" he'd slurred.

When Sam showed him his badge, and identified himself as an ABC agent, the drunk said, "So what's it against the law to get drunk in your own home? What a man does in his home is his own business."

"Not interested in your drinking habits," said Sam, "as long as you keep it on the right side of the law. I'm checking on a vehicle that was involved in an accident night before last. Dark colored Jeep Wrangler. Understand you own such a vehicle."

"So what? It ain't been in any accident night before last," he said indignantly.

"Then you wouldn't mind if I take a look at it?" Sam asked.

"Would if I could, but I cain't," he said in a sing-song fashion.

"Why's that?" asked Sam.

"Cause it ain't here," he said taking a swig of beer and wiping away some dribble from his chin with the back of his hand.

It was at this point, that Sam usually depended on cool-headed Travis to keep him in line. But Travis was not there, and Sam was surprised to find that this time he could exercise self-control.

Sam cleared his throat and asked patiently, "And where is your vehicle now?"

"My *vehicle* is being repaired," he said not willing to give one bit more than he had to.

"Where? Where is it being repaired and who's doing it?" Sam asked hoping to get more than one question answered at a time.

"Down in Salvo at David Rogers's place."

Hey it worked. Sam pocketed his badge and said simply, "Carry on."

Sam turned onto highway 12 and headed south along the barrier island. He drove pass a marina located on the sound side of the road just north of Oregon Inlet. Sam looked over at sturdy party boats with broad beams and wide sterns. He admired the large charter fishing vessels equipped with outriggers for trolling and fishing chairs for fighting heavy game fish. He noted how the boats strained against their lines and bobbed restlessly in the slips. Resentment surfaced as Sam remembered that he relinquished a fishing vacation to investigate a crime.

Sam continued south and drove onto the Oregon Inlet Bridge that twisted and curved as it spanned the inlet and marshland. In the scheme of the Outer Banks' life span, the Oregon Inlet is a new waterway dating back as recently as 1846 when a furious gale struck the Outer Banks and water poured over the beach and formed the Oregon Inlet. The new inlet was named for the first ship to pass through it, the Oregon.

Sam finally reached Salvo, a tiny picturesque coastal village just north of Cape Hatteras. The village is predominantly residential, not tourist, and the residents make their living on the water. Crab pots and fish boxes, tools of the trade, leaned against houses and were stacked in yards.

Sam turned onto the sound side road where he asked and received directions to David Rogers's garage. A couple of miles into the drive he saw a hand painted white sign nailed to a tree. Black letters read David Rogers, Body Shop and a red arrow pointed to a path through a dense stand of trees. Sam followed the arrow through a tunnel of windswept yaupon trees. Tiny slits of light cut through the thick leaves making eerie patterns on the windshield, and the air was so thick and still that Sam could hardly breathe. Just before claustrophobia gripped him, Sam emerged into a clearing. An unpainted wooden building that looked like it would not survive the next storm stood surrounded by vehicles of different sizes, makes, and with varying degrees of damage.

A sudden movement caused Sam to turn his attention to a corner of the clearing that was almost obscured. A little boy was jumping about trying to get an exhausted puppy to play with him. The child's eyes met Sam's, and he smiled. He looked to be about five years old with dark skin, cold black hair. He wore dirty red knit shorts and no shirt. He said something that Sam couldn't understand. Then he realized that the boy was speaking Spanish.

Sam got out of the car and said haltingly, "¿Como esta?"

The child laughed and ran back to a dusty, battered old Ford Explorer calling to someone inside. The doors were open and Sam could see beads and a rosary hanging from the rear-view mirror. Brown paper bags, empty pop bottles, junk food wrappers, two packages of disposable diapers, and busted toys littered the van. He stepped closer and saw a young, dark haired woman holding a tiny baby. She was attempting to feed the crying infant from a plastic bottle with a pink nipple. Black flies competed for the baby's meal and the mother shoed them away with a cardboard fan that had a picture of the Holy Mother on it.

Sam said, "I'm looking for Mr. Rogers."

The young woman looked frightened and in a shaky voice said something that Sam thought was 'I don't speak English'.

Sam repeated…this time in a louder voice, "Mr. Rogers. I'm looking for Mr. Rogers."

This served only to frighten the woman more. Sam realized that louder wouldn't help her understand what he was saying, so this time he said more softly, "Mr. Rogers. Is he here?"

Then from behind Sam a voice with a heavy Mexican accent said, "He iz not here."

Sam turned to face a Mexican worker who was shirtless, wore dirty athletic shoes with no shoestrings, no socks, and was covered with grease and grime. He shifted nervously from foot to foot and blinked uncontrollably.

Sam approached the man. He took out his badge and showed it to the him. He knew that the worker could not read English, and he also knew that he couldn't make him understand what his badge meant. A law officer meant only one thing to some Mexican workers. Are you an illegal? Apparently, this man was. But sleuthing out illegals was not Sam's game today, and he wasn't going to be diverted from the task at hand.

Sam tried again, "Mr. Roger?" and waved his hand around the shop.

The worker swallowed hard and said, "No English. Mr. Rogers not here."

Sam said, "Cars. I look at cars." He spoke slowly and used hand signals. Then he walked towards the cars in the lot. He checked each one, although he didn't need to, but he wanted the worker to catch on to what he wanted to do.

And he did. In a few minutes Sam looked his way and saw that the Mexican looked relieved. He nodded his head vigorously and smiled to show that he understood. He said something to his wife, and she seemed to relax. The little boy returned to the exhausted puppy.

Then the Mexican walked over to Sam very cautiously and said something in Spanish at the same time motioning toward the garage. Sam let him lead him inside where several other cars were in various stages of repair. There in the very center of the room was a black Jeep Wrangler. Sam's heart raced as he walked towards the front of the vehicle. But much to his disappointment, he found a perfectly intact headlight and a good-as-new grill.

The Mexican worker was saying something in Spanish and pointing to the side of the jeep. Sam walked quickly to where he pointed. There he saw the driver's side of the jeep was bashed in, and streaks of white paint ran from the door to the bumper.

Sam was flattened. He'd been so sure that this was the lead they'd been looking for. His face must have shown his frustration for the Mexican looked first at Sam and then the jeep door. Then his face took on a look of disappointment, too.

Sam recovered, smiled, and said "Gracias."

The Mexican followed him out of the garage chattering a mile a minute. The woman was out of the van now, and the little boy ran up to him holding out the weary puppy. Sam patted the pup and smiled at the boy. Then Sam knelt down and held out both of his fists to the boy. The boy tapped the right fist. Sam opened it and there was a folded dollar bill. The boy snatched the money, squealed, and jumped up and down jabbering to his mother who smiled and stood rocking the baby back and forth.

Sam pulled off of the sound side road onto highway 12. He drove pass deserted campgrounds, and rental cottages boarded up for the winter. They seemed to reflect his mood, sad and empty.

"I sure hope Trav and Shucks got lucky," he said aloud. "My expedition was a real wash."

CHAPTER 9

"Help me out with this Caffy," said Travis as he studied the list of people who own dark colored Jeep Wranglers. He walked around the sheriff's desk and placed the printout on an empty spot of his cluttered desktop.

The sheriff focused on the name Travis had highlighted. "You know anything about a Maynard Drane?" he asked.

"He on that list?" asked the sheriff. "Wouldn't think he could get credit to buy a vehicle."

"Really?" said Travis. "What you got on him?"

"Got a restraining order on him. Seems his wife doesn't like being stalked and harassed…estranged wife, I might add," Caffy said.

"Really?" Travis repeated his curiosity peaked.

"Yeah, they're going through a real nasty divorce. He's just a pumped up, wide-eyed sot of a redneck. He's older than she is and intimidated the hell out of her. Beat the daylights out of her several times. At first she refused to make charges against him. Like so many abused women, she thought if we got him quieted down, they could work things out. Took several violent incidents before she realized that he wasn't gonna change. Never understood what she saw in him to begin with. She's a real lady…pretty as a picture and smart. I wonder how someone with so much class could get mixed up with such a slug. Far as he's concerned, I think he'd be more attracted to the mud-wrestler type of woman, but somehow he latched on to her like a pit bull on a poodle. Just doesn't want to let her go. Acts like he owns her."

"You know, I think that's one of the biggest mistakes a person can make. People just don't own other people," Travis said.

"You're right there," said Sheriff Caffy. "Can't tell a drunk that though. Especially a foul-mouthed red-neck…"

The sheriff's tirade was interrupted. "Hey got'cha a vehicle, Travis," said a man in mechanic overalls stamped Dare County Sheriff's Department. Don't you go messing it up now," he added with a grin on his face.

"Thanks T-Bone," said Travis, "I'll try to keep it on the road." Then he said to the sheriff, "Thanks for the wheels. With three of us checking out the list, a third car will help it go faster."

Travis checked the address on the printout and drove over the bridge towards Kill Devil Hills. He drove down 158 until he reached Pig Pulling Barbecue restaurant. The rumbling in his stomach reminded him that it was lunchtime, but he decided not to stop. Instead, he just inhaled the smell of hickory smoke and turned towards the Nags Head Woods and the subdivisions adjacent to it.

He found the street he was looking for, but the house almost eluded him. It was a small fifties-style brick ranch tucked behind a thick stand of yaupon trees. He drove onto the pebble driveway and parked in front of the stoop. He noticed that a small area around the house was cleared and overlaid with a thick carpet of well kept grass. Yucca plants were planted on each side of the steps and a cheery pot of dazzling red geraniums set by the door. The doormat featured a picture of a pair of red cardinals perched on a dogwood branch, and the name on the doorknocker was Drane.

Travis took the two steps up the stoop and stood before a red door bordered on each side by narrow glass windows. He was tempted to peep inside but instead reached for the doorknocker and rapped hard several times. He could hear the sound resonate through the house.

The knock was instantly followed by a deafening clamor and a cacophony of deep woofs and yaps and the thump of a body being hurled against the door. Just as Travis thought the door would surely give way, the entity from inside regained its footing and charged at the window. Suddenly a mammoth white head popped into view. The animal had a thick snow-white ruff of fur around the neck that framed a beautiful enormous head. Triangular ears with soft rounded tips were held erect and alert. The animal had dark brown almond shaped eyes and a grand velvet brown nose. A brilliant pink tongue dangled from brown lips that curved into the biggest smile Travis had ever seen on a dog. He immediately thought of the bumper sticker Short Sugar described of a smiling white dog.

Travis heard rapid footsteps on the wooden floors and the door slowly opened. As soon as there was a slight aperture, the big brown nose pushed through and launched the door open. Suddenly giant paws pressed against Travis's chest and a head as big as a moose's was thrust in his face.

"My God, I'm going to die," thought Travis.

Then above the sound of his pounding heart, Travis heard a female voice say, "No Misha. Get down. Bad boy. He may not want to be your friend." And Travis could feel the dog being dragged reluctantly off of him.

"I'm so sorry. Misha thinks that a stranger is just a friend he's hasn't met. That's the way Samoyeds are. They like people better than animals." She was bending over the massive fluffy white beast and saying, "No, no, bad boy" as the dog continued to smile and wag.

Travis regained his footing and waited for his heart to slow. His mouth was dry and he wasn't sure he could speak. Then she turned her face towards Travis, and he looked into the bluest eyes he'd ever seen. Her short brown hair was wet and smelled of gardenias. Her blue plaid shirt and matching skirt were neatly pressed and her tan sandals revealed freshly polished pink toenails. He was as speechless now as he was when he first saw her at the all-night bait shop.

"It's you," she said simply. She smiled while struggling to restrain Misha.

"Yes," Travis said. He couldn't think of a thing to say so he reached into his pocket, pulled out his identification, and held it out to her.

She looked at the badge and then at the car. Her smile immediately vanished. "You're a policeman." It was a statement, not a question.

"I'm a law enforcement officer...yes...I'm with Alcohol Beverage Control...that's the same. Well, not exactly the..." Travis was mortified. He was doing it again. For some reason he couldn't put two sensible words together when she was around him. He knew she thought he was a nitwit.

"You must be looking for Maynard," she said. "He doesn't live here any more. But if you're from the sheriff's office you must know that. I have a restraining order against him." The dog was getting tired of struggling, sat down, and smiled up at Travis.

Travis took a deep breath and commanded himself to finish a sentence. "I'm not here about the restraining order," he said. *What do you know, I finished the sentence.* "There's been an accident and we're checking out dark colored Wrangler Jeeps."

She sighed and said, "Well, if Maynard is involved, I doubt it is an accident. Won't you come in...uh I didn't get your name."

"Travis. Travis White," he said.

"Eve. Eve Drane," She stepped inside pulling the dog after her. "Misha loves to have visitors. Don't you boy?"

Travis followed her into a room in the back of the house that served as kitchen, dining room, and den. The furniture was old and the chair and sofa covers faded, but the room was orderly, spotless, and smelled like pine. There was a large fireplace at the end of the room. Over it hung a shotgun and a twenty-two rifle. In the center of the mantle was an antique kitchen clock flanked on either side with an assortment of framed pictures and snapshots and an oil lamp. She motioned Travis to a straight-back chair resting under the breakfast table. He sat down, and Misha immediately trotted to him, leaned heavily against his leg, and smiled up at him.

"When he leans against you like that, he's giving you a hug," Eve explained. "I have to be at work in an hour, but we still have time for a drink. Ice tea?"

He said yes, and she served him a large glass of sweet tea topped off with a freshly sliced lemon wedge. They sipped the tea silently for a moment, as Misha smiled up at Travis adoringly and stuck to him like Velcro.

Finally Eve said, "So...how can I help you?"

Travis felt more relaxed now and answered the question deliberately. "A couple of nights ago, there was a hit and run close to the Washington Baum Bridge. A young girl was very seriously injured. She's still in the hospital. She wasn't able to give us a lot of information, but we do know the driver was a man. He stopped briefly before driving off. The car was a dark color, although she couldn't specifically identify the color. We think the vehicle was a Jeep Wrangler. We're checking out owners of dark colored Wranglers, and discovered that your husband...uh, ex-husband..."

"Not ex yet. I'm still waiting for the final divorce," she interjected.

"Right. Your husband. Anyway we learned that he owns a dark colored Wrangler. Is that right."

"Yes," she said candidly

"I don't suppose the vehicle is here?" he asked.

"No."

"Do you know where I might find your husband?" Travis asked.

"No, Travis, I don't. For the last year I have tried to know as little about my husband as I possibly have to," She said.

"I see," said Travis. "This morning the dealer didn't have the license plate number on your husband's vehicle, and we haven't heard from DMV yet. We know that the first three letters on plate of the vehicle involved were EV 1. I don't suppose you know your husband's license plate number do you?"

Eve stood up walked to the sink and set the glass on the counter. She stood with her back to Travis, and he watched her shoulders rise and fall as she breathed heavily. Then she turned and said softly, "Won't this ever end? This is the way it has been ever since we married ten years ago. I can't seem to be able to get away from him. He's not here, but his problems are. The license plate number is not EV 1, it is EVI-112. Evi. He calls me Evi."

She poured the tea from her glass into the sink and walked to the table. "Are you finished?" she asked reaching for the glass.

"Yes," he said.

She took his glass to the sink. Then she turned to him and said helplessly, "I'll never be rid of him. Not as long as I live….or as long as he lives."

She splashed the tea and ice into the sink. "I'm sorry. I have to go to work now. I have to call a friend to pick me up. I not only don't have the Wrangle, I don't have any car at all. I've been bumming rides from friends ever since my little Honda broke down.

Travis stood up. "Hey, let me give you a ride. I go right pass the bait shop."

"Oh, no," she protested. "I couldn't do that. My friend doesn't mind. She's been my rock."

Travis brightened when Eve referred to her friend as *she*. "Now listen," he persisted. "I insist. In fact, it would be my pleasure."

Travis cringed realizing how corny he sounded, but she didn't seem to mind.

She smiled and said, "Well, if you're sure it won't be a problem for you…being in an official car and all."

She grabbed her house keys and headed for the door. Misha was hot on her heels hoping to be invited to join them. His smile vanished when she turned to him and said, "Not this time, Misha. You take care of things here." She closed the door.

Travis opened the car door for Eve. She slid in and adjusted the seatbelt. She smiled up at him and said something about how much she appreciated the ride. He felt lighthearted and callow as he backed out of the driveway and headed back toward highway 158. As they drove off, a black Jeep Wrangler with a smashed headlight and damaged grill slowly emerged from the woods and headed toward the house.

CHAPTER 10

"So, no luck, huh?" asked Caffy sipping his two hundredth cup of coffee for the day.

"Nope," said Sam. "I did have a nice drive down to Salvo, though. You know, that's a neat village. It's not a touristy place."

"See David Rogers?" asked Caffy. "Now he's a damned good mechanic, and he doesn't charge you an arm and a leg like some of these jerks do."

"No," said Sam. "Saw a Mexican family. Looked like they may be living out of their car. Cute kids. They're probably illegals."

"Well, that's not high on my list right now," said the Sheriff. "What about you Shucks? Feel confident your guy's clear? Say, Shucks, where are you? Listen up."

Shucks was still obsessing about his awkward interview with a possible suspect. His boss's surly voice roused him, and he said weakly, "Yes sir, okay."

"Say, what's the matter with you anyway?" asked the sheriff.

But Shucks was spared the humiliation of reporting the details of his interview when Travis rushed into the office with a look on his face that said "got 'em".

"Hey," said Sam. "Think Trav's got something. Last time I saw a grin like that was on the face of a prostitute when a submarine made port after six months at sea."

"Got him," said Travis. "At least I know who the owner is." Travis tossed the printout on Caffy's desk. He had drawn a big circle around Maynard's name.

"Well, can't say as I'm surprised. He ain't got sense God gave a Billy goat.

Never has, never will. Come on tell, tell, tell…," the sheriff waggling his fingers in an urging motion.

Travis sat down and rubbed his hands together. "It's like this. You were right. The couple is separated, and she is determined to keep him away from her until the divorce is final. She doesn't know where he is or anything about the hit and run. The vehicle is a black Wrangler, and the license plate is EVI, not EV1. Evi is a nickname for Eve, and the numbers are 112. EVI-112. She lives alone, and the house is secluded in a bunch of yaupon trees. She does have a dog. And guess what? It's a giant white monstrosity named Misha. Looks like the picture Elizabeth described on the bumper sticker. He's not much protection, though, unless he licked the intruder to death."

"Bingo," said Sam.

"Good work, Travis," said Shucks half heartedly.

"Okay, Shucks. Get out an APB on Maynard Dwayne Drane. There's not that many places he can hide around here. We want to catch him before he ditches that jeep," said the sheriff. "Well, what you waiting on man. Get on it."

Shucks skulked out the room.

"Don't know what the heck's got into that boy lately," Sheriff Caffy said shaking his head.

"I think one thing that might be troubling him is that there's two many cooks in the kitchen," said Sam. "He probably thinks we're infringing on his territory."

"Not his to say," said the sheriff.

"Well, you don't need us any more," said Travis. "All we wanted was to lend some manpower till Elizabeth's assailant was identified. You'll pick up your guy before morning. Hey, maybe Shucks can pick him up."

"Hummm…well, maybe," the sheriff said tugging skeptically at his ear. "Thanks fellows for your help. Hope you get some fishing in before you go back to Seaboard."

"So, what do you want to do now?" asked Travis.

"Think we ought to celebrate. You identified the suspect," said Sam.

"Celebration might be premature," said Travis. "But I sure could use a beer."

"You're on," said Sam and he bounced behind the wheel, clicked his seat belt, turn on the ignition, and hit the tape button. They drove pass two men clipping grass and dressed in red coveralls emblazoned with large black letters that read Dare County Jail. Travis and Sam waved, and Elvis taunted them with his bellowing rendition of Jailhouse Rock. They drove over Washington Baum Bridge and straight to Guthrie's.

It was five thirty, and the restaurant was only half full. "Well, lookee here. We're graced with the presence of the Seaboard boys again," said Irene, the hostess, who virtually sparkled...sparkling lipstick, three shades of sparkling eye shadow, sparkling nails, and sparkling jewelry on her fingers, arms, neck, and ears.

"Hey, gorgeous," said Sam, "Look at you. Travis, you see what the attraction is at Guthrie's. Now I ask you, where else in Nags Head can you find such a sparkling hostess?"

The hostess rolled her eyes and shook her dangling earrings. "Same old, same old, Sam," she said reaching for a couple of menus. "Got you a table by the window right now if you want it."

"Honey, just put those menus down and point me in the direction of the bar," said Sam, and he headed that way.

Travis said, "Irene, is he working tonight?"

She shook her head. "No, Doo called in this afternoon and said he had some business to take care of." Then she leaned close and whispered, "The kitchen staff and waitresses were relieved. Travis, I know he's upset and all but he's become a real pain in the ass at work."

Travis nodded understandingly and headed towards the bar. He pulled up a stool beside Sam and whispered, "He's not working tonight."

"Good," said Sam.

"You think we pulled out too soon?" Travis wondered aloud.

"What do you mean?" asked Sam.

"I mean should we stick around until they pick up Drane," said Travis.

"Hell no," said Sam. "Look, Trav. I always say leave while you're at the top of your game. You tracked down the perp's identity, you found out the color of the vehicle, you got the license plate number, and you checked out his prior residence. That's really more than you're expected to do. Back off. Give Shucks his chance."

"You're right," said Travis reluctantly.

"Sure, I'm right," said Sam. "Besides, I got some serious business to take care of tonight."

Sam elbowed Travis and nodded in the direction of the entrance. There in all her glory was Nona Godette, and she wasn't wearing a Dare County law enforcement uniform. Nona was wearing an ankle length sleeveless dress made of a blue flimsy material that lazily caressed every soft curve of her well-endowed body. A spray of tiny bell-shaped flowers was planted in her shining blonde hair that was twisted into a bun at the nap of her neck. She smiled and strutted slowly across the barroom enjoying the looks of approval, and headed straight for Sam and Travis.

Without a word she pulled up a stool and joined them. Sam gave her his "you've finally come into my life" once over. She smiled and crossed her knees bumping his leg gently.

The young female bartender walked up and said, "What'll you have?"

Nona ordered a gin and tonic. Travis and Sam ordered a Black Radish.

Then Sam fixed his eyes straight on Nona, "And how about bringing us a couple dozen oysters from the raw bar?" he added with a wicked grin.

"Big date tonight, Sam?" she asked raising an eyebrow.

"Have anybody in mind?" he asked.

"Oh, yes," she said leaning closer. "I most definitely have someone in mind." Then she reached for her drink, slid off the stool, brushed pass Sam, and swung slowly across the room toward the tall, dark, tanned man entering the bar.

"Damn. Shot down again," said Sam.

The young thing tending bar set platters of raw oysters on the half shell in front of Travis and Sam and smiled in the direction of Nona and her latest conquest. She leaned across the bar and whispered, "They look so good together. Don't you think they…"

"Yeah, yeah, we know," interrupted Sam. "They *compliment* each other."

Sam reached for a wedge of lemon, squeezed juice on each oyster, and then shook on a generous amount of Tabasco. He gave an oyster a stir, lifted the shell to his lips, and slid the oyster into his mouth. He followed the mouthful with a hefty swallow of Black Radish.

Sam was already several oysters and a beer ahead of Travis, and he ate ravenously while sneaking glances at Nona Godette.

"She's a strong woman," said Sam. "And smart, too."

"Who you talking about, Sam?" Travis joshed.

"The Queen of England, Trav," Sam said wearily and drew another long swallow of beer. "Yeah, she's smart. Smart enough to pull my chain and not many women can pull Old Sam Barnett's chain."

"Don't break your arm patting yourself on the back, pal," said Travis. Then he added more sympathetically, "You know, strong women can be good actresses. They know how to hide their vulnerability."

"Well, I wish I could plug into her vulnerability, but like I said she's too damned smart," said Sam.

"You're intimidated. Intelligent women sometimes intimidate men. Especially if the woman has the gift of gab. Then men feel like they need to put them down instead of...."

"You saying I put Nona down?" asked Sam.

"Not intentionally," said Travis

"Hell, I'm just fooling around," said Sam.

"You're always fooling around. Damn it Sam, you ought to hear yourself sometimes. If you really like Nona, you got to be straight with her. No more of this playing around. You're not some high school kid. You're not Peter Pan."

"Now don't start with that psychobabble again..." said Sam.

The sparkling hostess interrupted Travis's upbraiding. "Got a table for you," she said. "Not by the window though."

"That's fine by me," said Sam. "I don't like looking at those rats."

"Nutrias, Sam, nutrias," said Travis following Irene into the dining room. "They're called nutrias."

They sat down and the hostess handed them menus. "Only two tonight, huh? Where's your shadow?"

"Oh, you mean Shucks?" said Travis. "He had to take care of business."

"Let's hit the beach early tomorrow," said Sam as he drove towards the Sand Trap. "Try to salvage some of our vacation anyway."

"I'm with you there," said Travis. "Stop by the all night bait shop. Save us a trip in the morning."

They pulled into the parking lot. The lot was almost empty and only a few customers milled about the shop. Sam bought his bait and walked out onto the porch while Travis wandered about inspecting the fishing gear. After a few minutes of dallying, Travis approached a clerk. "Is Eve still working?" he asked.

The weary clerk rubbed his rummy eyes and focused suspiciously on Travis. Travis guessed that he'd interceded for Eve many times.

"It's okay," he said, "I'm an ABC officer and a friend of Evi's. See." He reached into his pocket and took out his badge.

The clerk examined the badge carefully, and when he was satisfied that Travis was not a threat he said, "She left early. We aren't busy so she took off."

Travis walked onto the porch where Sam was leaning against the post, a smirk on his face.

"What?" demanded Travis.

"Why you sly old dog," Sam said. "No wonder you came back to the office with a smile on your face. Eve? You mean 'blue eyes' is Eve Drane? And Evi. You called her *EVI?* Man, you work fast."

Travis shot him a look to kill, stomped down the steps, and marched around the Jeep just in time to see a blue tick hound hose down the back tire.

"Hey, get outta here, you mangy mutt," he yelled.

The whole scene served only to make Sam laugh harder, and he leaned against the post doubled over with laughter. Travis slumped in the front seat, arms folded, and a scowl on his face.

CHAPTER 11

When Travis and Sam arrived back at the Sand Trap, they watched the tide and weather forecasts. Satisfied with the favorable predictions, they settled on a time to head for the beach, organized their fishing gear, and called it a night.

Travis fell asleep immediately lulled by images of "blue eyes". "Blue eyes" smiling behind the cash register, "blue eyes" smiling over a glass of ice tea, "blue eyes" smiling beside him in the patrol car, and "blue eyes" just smiling.

Sleep did not come so easily for Sam, however. He lay awake and listened to the pounding of the surf just beyond the dune. He counted the cars that whirred pass the motel on Virginia Dare Trail and listened to the slam of car doors in the parking lot. He heard the click of the digital clock each time it rolled up another hour, and he thought of Nona Godette. Mostly he thought of Nona.

Just as he was forced into sleep by exhaustion, he heard a car door close just outside their room. He rose up on his elbow and glanced at the clock. Two-thirty. The serious fishermen who stayed at the Sand Trap would certainly be aware of the ideal weather forecast, and Sam wondered why they would stay out this late. Then Sam detected an urgency in the crunch of footsteps approaching their door. Reacting instinctively, he pulled open the chest drawer beside the bed, grabbed his thirty-eight, rolled out of bed, and headed for the window.

"Hey, Trav," said Sam. "Wake up."

"Wh…what?" said Travis, more asleep that awake, but when he spotted Sam moving toward the window with his gun in hand, he was immediately roused into wakefulness and bolted out of bed.

Sam parted the curtains furtively and squinted out the window. Suddenly he dropped the curtain and said, "Whoa. Now we're cooking."

Sam flung opened the door and beamed as he watched Nona Godette walk straight towards their door. This time she was in full uniform.

"Well, what have we here? Miss 'Got It'. I knew you wanted me," Sam said.

"In your dreams," she shot back. "Got something down at the beach you might like to see."

"You've got something right here I'd like to see," Sam cracked.

"Put your pants on, Skinny Legs, and let's go," she barked and turned back towards the squad car.

Sam, who had forgotten he was undressed, looked down at his boxer shorts and said, "Oh, Jeez."

Travis was already dressed, and he opened his canvass bag and took out his firearm. He turned to Sam and said, "Well, don't just stand there with your face hanging out. Put on your pants."

They drove without speaking, only the occasional chatter of the car radio broke the silence. Nona would not tell them the reason for their night-time excursion. Travis sat in the back seat. All he could think about was Doo. Sam sat up front beside Nona Godette. Being so close to her fired his imagination. She turned a stunning profile, and her scent was a mixture of citrus and female sweat that aroused a stirring in him.

She drove until she reached a fork in the road and chose the road to the left. After only a few hundred feet, she pulled onto the shoulder, cut the ignition, and said, "Well, here we are."

They took the small dune in a few steps and looked down upon what might have been a serene setting. A blanket of stars hung from the dark night sky and the white surf washed gently upon the silver sand and then retreated into the blackness of the ocean. And there amidst the splendor of this nocturnal beauty was a scene all too familiar to them. Flood lights and headlights from police vehicles illuminated an area enclosed with yellow crime tape. Uniformed officers and people in civilian clothes milled about outside the cordoned off perimeter.

Travis and Sam hurried down the sand dune. "Hey, what you got here, Caffy?" asked Travis.

"No ID yet. Boys from the crime lab don't know him. We're waiting for them to finish before we go in," said Caffy.

Caffy pointed his flashlight beam on broken glass lying beside the body. When Sam and Travis took a close look, they recognized it was fragments of two Mason canning jars and two tops, containers used by bootleggers.

"That's why I called you," said Caffy.

The solemn group watched silently as the CSI team examined the body, bagged his hands, poured tire and foot prints, took photographs, and performed all the tasks that had to be completed before the body could be moved.

Sam said, "Who discovered the body?"

Caffy jerked his thumb over his shoulder and said, "Kids back there were out for a midnight walk on the beach. Came across the body and thought it was a drunk. When they tried to wake him up, they realized they couldn't. Poor kids. Scared the socks off of them."

"Mind if we talk to them?" asked Sam.

"Help yourselves. Don't think they'll be much help except for fixing a time of discovery," Caffy said.

Travis and Sam walked up to the couple. They were huddled together in the lee of the dune, and the girl trembled uncontrollably. She was petite and appeared to be swallowed up by an enormous light blue sweatshirt that had Carolina printed in large white letters across the front. The boy was shirtless, apparently having literally given her the shirt off his back. They were both barefoot.

"How you doing?" asked Travis while simultaneously flashing his badge.

"Not so good," said the boy. "Susan is real cold. Any idea how long we have to stay here?"

"Wouldn't think long. See that big guy in the uniform down there? His name is Sheriff Caffy. As soon as the lab boys finish checking out the scene, we'll go in. He may or may not have questions for you, but we won't forget you. I really don't think it will be much longer," said Travis.

"You okay?" Sam asked the girl directly. "You're shaking like a blender."

She nodded, and with chattering teeth said, "I'm just so cold."

"The night air's cold, but you also had a shock. See what we can do," said Sam. Then he turned toward the beach and shouted, "Hey Dicky, how 'bout getting these kids some hot coffee. They need it. Especially the young lady."

The uniformed officer gave a thumbs up and started up the dune. "Thanks," said the girl. Every time she spoke, she shook harder.

Sam patted the girl's arm and gently tapped the boy's shoulder with his fist. "We won't forget you," he said and winked.

Travis and Sam returned to the scene, and Sam stood beside Nona and watched as the lab boys gathered their gear to move out.

"Well, what you got, doc?" said Caffy.

"Looks like we got a male, white, between the ages of 40 and 50. Appears to have died about three or four hours ago. Nobody I know." He lifted the yellow tape and added, "Come on down."

Caffy, Travis, and Sam approached the body. "How did he die?" asked Caffy.

"Shotgun," said the examiner. "Blew his belly wide open. Crabs got in him."

"Any casings?" asked Sam.

"Nope," said the examiner.

"Won't get any help from ballistics then," added Travis.

"Maybe the shooter's a duck hunter...you know, shotgun and all," said Sam.

"Well, that should really narrow it down," the sheriff said caustically. "How many duck hunters you suppose we got on the islands?"

Caffy bent down to take a closer look at the victim. The victim was lying on his side, so Caffy reached to turn him over for a closer. As he grasped the shoulder, they saw movement...a slow stirring in the abdominal area near the wound. "My God," exclaimed Caffy, "Is he still alive?"

Caffy quickly flipped the body onto his back and as he did he shrieked, "*AGH*" and frantically backed through the sand and away from the corpse.

"What the.?" said Travis as he and Sam cautiously bent over the dead man. Almost imperceptibly the flesh around the gapping black wound moved. At first it moved very slowly, and then more forcefully. Finally a head emerged, and a crab wiggled out of the corpse's abdomen and headed fearlessly towards the surf.

"That's the most disgusting thing I ever saw," said Caffy as he shivered and struggled to stand up.

Travis held out a hand and gave him a tug. "So much for crab cakes," he said.

Sam was still staring at the body. "You know this guy, Caffy?" he asked.

"Well let me try again," said Caffy mustering nerve and looking down at the face of the victim. "Well, I be damned," he said. "If it ain't old Maynard Dwayne Drane."

"You mean this is 'blue eyes' husband?" asked Sam.

"Huh? What are you talking about 'blue eyes'?" asked Caffy with a puzzled look on his face.

Travis said, "Don't pay him any mind Caffy. What he meant is…is this Eve Drane's husband?"

"Sure is," said the sheriff. "I'm surprised, too. He's been on the lunatic fringe for a long time, but he was one resourceful fellow…real hard to pin down. I'd begun to think nothing would kill him."

"The bigger they are the harder they fall," Sam said simply.

Suddenly the men heard a cracking sound behind them. Without turning around, Caffy said. "Don't go messing up the crime scene with those damned peanut shells, Shucks." Then he spun around and added, "Where the hell you been anyway?"

Shucks threw some nuts in his mouth and pocketed the shells. Then he said lamely, "I was checking out places Maynard Dwayne Drane might frequent."

"Well tonight he *frequented* the beach," snapped Caffy.

Travis interrupted in an effort to take the heat off of Shucks. "Think this might be moonshine related?" he asked.

"Or drugs," said Caffy. "How 'bout you two pitching in till we nail this thing down?"

"Sure," said Travis. "Want us to question the witnesses?" Then he added, "That is unless you want Shucks to interview them."

"No, you two do it," Caffy said. "Shucks, you help out here."

Sam and Travis were glad that the sheriff gave Shucks a break, and they headed toward the couple huddled by the dune.

"Told you we wouldn't forget you," said Sam winking at the girl. She smiled weakly.

"Can you tell us what time you found the body?" asked Travis.

The boy said, "Well, we didn't actually clock it, but I think it must have been around one thirty or one forty five."

"Tell us exactly what happened," said Sam.

The boy said, "Well, we'd been at this party up the beach. And a little after one people started leaving. We'd been drinking beer, and so we thought we'd walk for awhile before driving back to our motel." He paused to see what the reaction of the officers would be to his admission that they'd been drinking.

"Good choice," said Travis, "not to drink and drive."

The boy seemed relieved and continued hastily, "We were sorta splashing around at the edge of the water when we saw somebody just laying there. We thought he was drunk, and I was afraid the tide would come in and wash him out so I went up to him and grabbed him by the shoulder and shook him. I said 'hey buddy get up' but he didn't move. Then I realized he was dead."

"So what did you do then?" asked Sam.

The boy turned and looked toward a condominium complex and said, "We ran up to those condos and told the guard at the gate what we'd found. He called the police, and they said we should stay here until they got here. And not to touch anything."

"You did exactly right," Sam said. "We'll check with the guard about the exact time."

"Then you did touch the body?" said Travis.

"Yes, I did," said the boy with a worried look on his face. "But I didn't know he was dead. I thought he was drunk."

"Hey, that's okay," Travis reassured him. "You didn't know."

Travis knelt down to get the names, addresses, and telephone numbers of the young couple and as he did, he heard a crunching sound. He looked under his shoe at a pile of crushed peanut shells. He asked, "Have any other policemen been up here?"

The boy answered, "Only the officer that brought us coffee." Throughout the entire interview the girl shivered and said nothing.

"You know what," Travis said to the shaking girl, "I think we need to have you checked out at the Outer Banks Hospital. You might be suffering from shock."

The girl turned a tear-streaked face to him and nodded. Sam shouted down to the uniformed officer who had brought them coffee, "Hey Dicky. How about running these two over to the Outer Banks Hospital. Think this little lady might need some attention."

After they helped the girl to the squad car, Travis and Sam walked across to the condo gatehouse. The shift had not changed so the guard the couple reported the body to was still on duty. He consulted his records and reported that the couple came to his station at one forty five. When Sam and Travis returned to the beach, the body was being loaded on a stretcher.

"Wrapping it up here," said Caffy. "Tide is moving in fast. Pretty soon there won't be no crime scene. Thanks for helping out tonight," Caffy pointed to the broken jars being bagged by a crime scene officer and said, "Like I said, I smell moonshine all over this one. Just exactly what our friend Maynard

Dwayne Drane was up to, I don't know. The lab boys should have something for us tomorrow. Hate like the dickens to break into your vacation like this, but I'd like for you to be there. Say about one? Sure 'preciate your help."

"Forget it," said Sam.

"Sure, we'll be there," said Travis.

The two frustrated fishermen trudged wearily up the dune. Travis said, "Do you believe that some things just weren't meant to be?"

"You talking about our fishing vacation?" said Sam. "Know what you mean. We might as well have stayed in Seaboard."

"Yeah, well the fishing trip and other things too," said Travis.

"Oh, I see," Sam said wisely. "Yeah, Trav, sadly enough I do believe that some things were never meant to be."

CHAPTER 12

WEDNESDAY MORNING

Travis and Sam would not be defeated. They grabbed a couple of hours sleep, snatched their fishing gear, walked up the dune, and took their place on the beach with the other dogged fishermen. Fortunately, the fish were active this morning, and at noon they presented Reba with a half bucket of blues, spots, and channel bass. As usual she thanked them profusely saying that her freezer was almost full. Travis and Sam thought that she must have one big freezer.

They only had an hour to shower, dress, and get a bite to eat before meeting with Sheriff Caffy so lunch was a couple of hot dogs and a milk shake to go from the Dairy Queen. They walked into Caffy's office smelling like onions and French fries.

"Glad you fellows had lunch," said Caffy. "We'll just work on through."

Travis and Sam recognized all the people assembled in the sheriff's office. There was the medical examiner and his main assistant, Shucks, Dicky, the officer who took the kids to the Outer Banks Hospital, and Nona Godette.

"Why don't you kick us off, Doc?" said Caffy.

The medical examiner handed Sheriff Caffy a document then he flipped open a spiral pad and began, "That's a copy of the official autopsy report. The victim is identified as Maynard Dwayne Drane, five foot ten, one hundred and sixty eight pounds, age 51, Caucasian. The victim sustained massive damage to the abdominal area as the result of a shotgun blast. He bled to death. It appears that the time of death was approximately 10:30 pm. Body discovered at 1:45 am. Time was verified by the guard at the condo and by the 911 recording here at headquarters. Any questions so far?"

"What about the weapon?" asked Shucks.

"Well, I'm gonna get to that in a few minutes," said the doctor. "Let me tell you this first. We found four sets of footprints. The two barefoot prints belonged to the kids who found the body. The other prints belonged to two other people. One set was a size 11 men's shoe. Big Foot wore a cheap boat shoe that you can get at any discount or dime store. The other looks like a flip-flop sandal…same thing, cheap and available in a dozen places around here. Now the flip flop slipped around so much that I couldn't get an accurate size on it. Do know it was lots smaller than the boat shoe. The interesting thing is that either these two were really heavy guys, or they were carrying something. And I say they were carrying the victim because Maynard Dwayne Drane was not killed on the beach."

"Now that is interesting," said the sheriff. "What's your evidence?"

"For one thing," said the Doc, "there was no blood. Like I said, this guy bled to death. There should have been lots of blood. Another thing, we didn't find a gun or any shotgun casings. There was also a short drag mark. At one point the perpetrators got tired and dropped him. So they dragged the body for about five feet to the edge of the water."

"Well, how do you suppose they got him down to the beach in the first place?" asked Nona.

"They drove him down. Sometimes it's hard to get tire prints in the sand, but we got a real good set. It's the same kind of tire used on a Jeep Wrangler. And the kicker is….are you ready? The kicker is that it's the same tire print we lifted in the hit/run accident. You know the one involving the young girl, Elizabeth Early."

"Holy socks," said Sam.

"Are you sure?" said Travis.

"Sure as rain," said the Doc. "Checked them both out this morning. The jeep that hit Elizabeth Early is the same vehicle that hauled Maynard Dwayne Drane's body down to the beach."

"But where's the jeep now?" said Nona.

"Ah, Sheriff, that's what I was doing last night. I was trying to locate the vehicle used in the hit and run. You see…that would have been the same one used in the murder last night," said Shucks hoping to regain favor with his boss.

The sheriff ignored him. Shucks was abashed. "Okay boys…and girl…"

the sheriff added rubbing his hands together, "it looks to me like we got ourselves a companion case. I can think of all kinds of motives for people wanting old Maynard Dwayne Drane dead, but what we've got to do is come up with the motive that applies in this particular situation. Sorry fellows," he said looking at Travis and Sam, "but now your friend Doo-Wop Early is high on that suspect list."

Travis and Sam must have looked concerned. "Don't worry, though," the sheriff continued, "We also got a wife."

"That's suppose to make me feel better?" thought Travis.

"You know sheriff," said Nona, "if we lined up all the people who had a reason to want Maynard Dwayne Drane dead, we'd have a line from here to Hatteras."

"Thank you, Nona," thought Travis.

"Well, go at it any way you want to sheriff," said Doc. "But somebody went to a lot of unnecessary trouble if you ask me."

"What you mean?" said the sheriff.

"What I mean is that is wasn't necessary for anybody to murder Maynard Dwayne Drane, he was already dying." There was a gasp, and Doc continued, "Drane was dying of liver cancer. He was eaten up. Couldn't have lived more than six months. So somebody went to a lot of trouble for nothing."

"Who would want to kill a dying man?" said Shucks

"Maybe whoever killed him didn't know he was dying," said Nona Godette.

"Or maybe the murderer couldn't wait six months," said Sam.

"Yeah, maybe Maynard knew something that he shouldn't have, and they needed to silence him sooner rather than later," added Travis.

"Well, I've said it once and I'll say it again," said Caffy. "This smells like moonshine or drugs to me. Has Mrs. Drane been notified?"

"Not by us," said Doc.

"Well, I suppose that's one of the first things we need to do. Notify her, and get a statement." He looked straight at Travis. "How about you doing that Travis?"

"Okay," Travis said weakly.

"Then we need to find out all we can on Mr. Maynard Dwayne Drane. Find out what the heck he's been into lately," Caffy said slamming his fist into the palm of his hand.

CHAPTER 13

This time Travis drove a little slower as he crossed the Washington Baum Bridge to Nags Head. When he turned off highway 158 onto Ocean Acres he hardly noticed the scrumptious aroma emanating from Pig Pulling Barbecue. He meandered through the subdivision until he reached the stand of yaupons that cloistered Eve Drane's spruce, modest house. He pulled onto the shell driveway and the car made a crunching sound that was unusually loud almost intrusive in this peaceful setting. He turned off the engine and sat silently mustering the grit he needed to ring the doorbell.

Finally Travis mounted the steps to the small stoop. He didn't need to ring the bell because his arrival was announced by loud woofs erupting from the enormous white head framed in the window.

"Hey, Misha," said Travis. "Remember me?"

The Samoyed answered with the big Sammy smile characteristic of the breed. Travis heard movement in the hall, and the door opened unleashing a mass of white fur with big paws that quickly found their way to Travis's shoulders.

"Get down, Misha," said Eve. "I can't seems to break him of the habit of jumping up."

"Oh, that's okay," said Travis.

"Yes, but it's not okay with everyone. Won't you come in?" she said struggling to restrain the dog.

Travis followed her back into the kitchen and she motioned him to a chair at the kitchen table. "I've just made a pitcher of ice tea. Won't you have a glass?" she said moving toward the kitchen counter.

"No," said Travis. "Mrs. Drane, I'm afraid I have some bad news for you." He hated it when he had to say those words.

Eve turned slowly and walked back to the table. She sat down and looked at him solemnly. Travis sat too.

"Mrs. Drane…" he said.

"Please don't call me that. Call me Eve," she said.

"Okay, Eve," he said. "I'm sorry to tell you that last night your husband was found…"

"Found? What do you mean *found*?" she asked.

"Please let me finish," said Travis. "Eve, Maynard is dead. His body was found last night on the beach." He paused to let her process.

Eve dropped her face in her hands. She stayed like that for what seemed an interminable length of time, but when she finally raised her head, her eyes were dry, no tears streaked her cheeks. She had not been crying, she had been hiding behind her hands. Hiding from more pain and disappointment caused by Maynard Dwayne Drane.

"You're surprised I'm not crying," she said. It was a simple statement, not a question. "At the risk of sounding melodramatic, I haven't any tears left. I wept so many years for Maynard and then two years ago I finally accepted that he would never change. The only changes I have any control over are changes that I make in myself."

She stood and walked to the kitchen counter. "I'm having a glass of ice tea," she said. "Do you want one or not?"

"Yes, thanks," said Travis. As Eve busied herself with the tea, Travis' eyes roamed about carefully scrutinizing the room. The floor was clean and freshly polished, no dirty dishes cluttered the sink, magazines were neatly stacked on the coffee table, and the gun rack above the fireplace was empty. Both the shotgun and twenty-two were gone.

Eve sliced lemon wedges, filled two glasses with ice, added tea, and set the drinks on the table. She lifted a glass to her lips then set it down without taking a sip. "Lemon?" she asked pushing the saucer of wedges across the table.

"No thanks," Travis said and took a hefty swallow of the sweet drink. He reached into his pocket and took out a small spiral pad and a pen. "I need to ask you some questions."

"Fine," she said. "Then I'd like to do the same."

"Of course," Travis said. "When did you last see your…Maynard?"

"I've caught glimpses of him driving pass the bait shop and passing on the road by the house, but I haven't seen him to speak to in, oh…three, four weeks."

"I see…," said Travis. "Where were you last night?" He fairly blurted out the question.

"At work," she said. "You know that. You dropped me off." She paused, "I did leave early though since we weren't busy."

"Eve, I've been curious about something. You told me that Maynard bought the car for you, in fact, the custom license plate had your name on it."

"That's right," she said in a faltering voice.

"So why did he take the jeep with your name on it and leave you the clunker?" he asked.

"Actually, the jeep wasn't in my name…neither car was. They were both in his name from the very beginning. At the time he got the jeep, we were in serious financial shape. We couldn't pay the bills much less afford a car. Putting my name on the license plate was his attempt to placate me." She looked directly at Travis, "Maynard never did understand me."

Travis returned to questions regarding the night of the murder.

"How did you get home last night?" Travis asked, remembering that she told him she didn't have a car.

"A neighbor came in to buy bait, and I asked him to give me a ride home," Eve said.

"What time was that?" asked Travis.

"A little before ten," she answered.

Travis asked for the neighbor's name, address and telephone number, and she gave it to him. He wrote it down. Then he turned towards the fireplace. "When I was in here yesterday I noticed that a twenty-two and a shotgun were in the rack over the fireplace. Where are they now?"

Eve was silent for a long time. She stared downward and took several sips of tea. Then she slowly raised her head and said angrily, "Well, surely if you noticed the guns are missing you noticed my television is also gone." She took a deep, audible breath and continued, "When my neighbor drove me home I asked him to drop me off at the corner. I like to walk in the evening when it's cool. When I got home last night, Misha was on the porch, the front door was wide open, and lights were on in the house. At first I was startled, but then I realized that if anyone were inside, Misha would be right there with him."

Travis nodded and asked, "Did you see any vehicles around…like up on the road or in the driveway?"

She hesitated and said, "No. There were no cars around." Then she poured more tea. "I came inside and made a quick inventory. I spotted the empty gun rack right away. I suppose Maynard needed money again and took the guns and TV to pawn."

"Did you report this?" asked Travis.

"No," she said.

"Why not?" he said.

"Because I've reported him so many times before and nothing is ever done about it. I'm just sick and tired of going by the book, reporting his crimes, and getting no help," she asserted.

"I'm sorry you didn't get the help you wanted," he said. Then added, "Eve did you know that Maynard was terminally ill?"

For the first time during the interview, Eve showed true emotion. She looked baffled and shocked. She covered her mouth with her hand barely stifling a gasp, bounded from her chair, rushed to the kitchen counter, and gripped the sides of the sink. She stood there bracing herself rigidly.

Travis was startled by her reaction. "Are you alright, Eve," he said.

"What are you saying?" Eve said.

Travis said, this time more gently, "Eve, Maynard was dying of cancer. Cancer of the liver."

"The liquor...he drank himself to death. Is that what you're telling me?" Eve said.

"Well, I don't know cause," Travis said, "But the autopsy clearly revealed that he had liver cancer and didn't have long to live. And you weren't aware of this?"

She turned and walked unsteadily across the room and sat down again at the kitchen table. "No," she whispered.

They sat quietly for quite a while. Only the rhythm from the kitchen clock on the mantle broke the silence. Finally Travis repeated, "You had no idea that Maynard was sick?"

Eve shook her head.

"Do you want to ask me about Maynard's death?" Travis asked.

Eve shook her head.

"Would you just like for me to tell you what happened?" Travis asked.

Eve nodded. So Travis told Eve how a couple of college kids took a moonlight walk on the beach and found Maynard's body. He told her that Maynard was shot, and that the police had no suspects at this time. He told her that the body was at the morgue and that she could make arrangements whenever she wanted to. He did not tell her that the weapon used in the crime was a shotgun. He did not tell her that Maynard's jeep was the same vehicle involved in the hit and run that struck Short Sugar Early. He did not tell her that Maynard was killed somewhere else and his body dumped on the beach. And he didn't tell her that Maynard's jeep was still missing.

Travis had one last question to ask Eve, the question he dreaded most. "Eve, I have to ask you, do you know if Maynard had any insurance…any life insurance?"

Eve set her head high and fixed a angry eye on Travis. "Yes, officer," she said. "Maynard did have a life insurance policy with the Low-Rate Insurance Group, and I am the beneficiary of it. Is that what you wanted to know?"

Travis turned away from her hostile glare and asked, "Do you know the name of the company they signed him up with?"

"No," she snapped. She turned her face towards the window and looked out onto the small, freshly mowed, green lawn. Her expression was expressionless, and he wasn't certain, but he thought he saw a tear in the corner of her right eye.

Travis left Eve sitting at the kitchen table, a pitcher of sweet ice tea and a saucer of lemon wedges nearby. He remembered that his grandmother used to say that sweet ice tea is a southerner's cocktail. Well, Eve was hitting the stuff hard this afternoon.

Travis drove a few blocks to the address of the neighbor Eve had given him. He pulled into the driveway beside a beat up Oldsmobile Cutlass that had an assortment of unidentifiable auto parts strewn around it on the ground. The bottom half of a man hung out of the front of the car where the engine should be and a barrage of profanity floated above the carcass of the rusty automobile. Travis made it a point to slam the door of his jeep unusually hard. The noise caused the mechanic to start, and he banged his head smartly on the hood of the car. Yet more profanity erupted, and the man jerked a greasy, glaring face toward Travis.

"Who the hell are you?" he demanded.

Travis reached into his pocket, removed his identification, and placed it in his dirty, outstretched palm. The man made no attempt to wipe his hands. "I'm Travis White. ABC officer. Like to ask you a few questions."

"What about?" the neighbor said returning the shield covered with oily fingerprints to Travis. Travis made no attempt to clean the shield and carefully returned it to the loose pocket of his shirt.

"About Maynard Dwayne Drane," said Travis.

The neighbor reached for a rag and began to wipe his hands. "So, what's Maynard into now?" he asked.

"Maynard Drane was found dead on the beach last night," said Travis closely watching the neighbor's reaction to the news.

The neighbor took his time cleaning his hands and then tossed the rag on the ground. "Well, Old Maynard finally caught the bus. Can't say as I'm surprised. The only surprise is that it took so long."

"Why do you say that?" asked Travis.

"Well, if you're doing any kind of investigation of Maynard Dwayne Drane, it shouldn't come as a surprise to you that he'd be dead sooner rather than later. That guy lived on the edge. Anybody 'round here'll tell you that it was just a matter of time. And I bet he died in some bizarre way. How'd he die anyway?"

Travis ignored the question. "What makes you think he died in a *bizarre* way?"

The neighbor looked impatient. "Do your own homework. I done told you that Maynard Drane was a fool. Don't take no rocket scientist to deduct that he would die in some unusual way. Probably violent. Now what you want with me? I got work to do."

"I understand that you saw Eve Drane last night," Travis said.

"Is that a question?" the neighbor said sarcastically. Then he added, "Yes, I *saw* Eve Drane last night. I give her a ride home from the bait shop. You trying to make something out of that?"

"No," said Travis. "Should I?"

"Now you listen hear I'm tired of your chicken shit attitude," said the neighbor. "You got something you want to say just say it, otherwise get the hell out of here and let me get to work."

"Okay," said Travis. "What time did you and Eve Drane leave the bait shop?"

"A little before ten," said the neighbor.

"And what time did you drop her off?" asked Travis

The neighbor's face turned red, he took several deep breaths and said, "About ten minutes later."

"Where did you drop her off?" asked Travis.

"At the corner of her street. She said she liked to walk at night," said the neighbor.

"Did you see anyone else walking?" asked Travis.

"No," said the neighbor.

"See any other vehicles?" asked Travis.

"Yes," said the neighbor. "Saw old lady Grimsley who lives two houses up. She was in her 1987 Cadillac poking on home from her prayer meeting."

"Little late to be coming home from a prayer meeting," commented Travis as he jotted the information down in his notebook.

"Not for old lady Grimsley. She prays at the drop of a hat…long and hard," said the neighbor.

"See any other vehicles?" asked Travis.

"Yep," said the neighbor.

"I'm glad Sam's not here. This is like pulling hen's teeth," thought Travis. Then he took a deep breath and asked. "What kind of car was it?"

"A patrol car," said the neighbor.

"What kind of patrol car was it that you saw?" asked Travis.

"Just the usual ill-kept vehicle that the county keeps. Dare County Sheriff Department, old Ford Crown Victoria, smashed in right fender. They don't maintain those vehicles, and it's taxpayers got to replace them. What they need to do is hire some mechanics that know what they're doing," said the neighbor wiping his hands on his overalls.

Travis wondered if he had a particular mechanic in mind. Then he said, "Do you have any information about Maynard Drane that might be helpful to us in investigating his death?"

"So, he was murdered," said the neighbor nonchalantly. "And don't go asking me 'what makes me think that'. Done told you I'm tired of your chicken shit games. I don't know nothing about Maynard Dwayne Drane's business. Anybody got good sense wouldn't want to know. Me and my wife feel real sorry for Eve, and I don't mind telling you that her life will be a lot better with him gone."

Travis said nothing, but inwardly agreed with the neighbor. He slapped his note pad closed and said, "Thanks for your help. Sorry I interrupted your work on the car."

The neighbor waved off the apology, turned, and retreated under the hood of his car. Suddenly a screen door slammed, and a rotund Amazon of a woman, with sweaty, wet hair, wearing a wrinkled blue cotton dress and dirty white apron stepped onto the porch. She frowned and squinted at Travis while wiping her hands on her apron. Travis had never seen such an intimidating woman.

"Claude," she shouted in a deep surly voice, "can't you tell time? Dinner's on the table." She shot Travis a withering glare that served notice that he was not invited, then she banged the screen door and went inside.

Travis went directly to the home of Mrs. Lila Grimsley. As he pulled in front of the house, he spotted a little girl in a green print dress, matching green flip-flop sandals, and a wide-brim straw hat. She was stretching to reach a low-hanging bird feeder with one hand while grasping a plastic bag of bird seed in the other.

Travis walked over to the child and said, "Here, let me help you."

A thin, soft voice said, "Why thank you. I have ever so much trouble reaching this feeder." Then the tiny person turned and Travis started in amazement. The face that smiled sweetly up at him was not that of a little girl but a shriveled, withered face...like the wrinkled face of an apple doll.

"Mrs. Grimsley? Mrs. Lila Grimsley?" said Travis.

"Why, yes," said the sweet little old lady. "Do I know you?"

"No mam," said Travis, and he identified himself.

"Oh, I've never been visited by an Alcohol Beverage Control agent before," she said. "This is exciting."

"Thank you, mam," Travis said clumsily.

"What can I do for you, officer?" she said.

"I just wanted to ask you about your drive home from prayer meeting Wednesday night," said Travis. "Did you see anyone walking in the neighborhood?"

Mrs. Grimsley placed her finger on her temple and said, "Now let me see......no."

"Did you see any cars driving in the neighborhood?" Travis asked.

"No...no, wait. I did see one car. A police car. Does that count?" asked Mrs. Grimsley.

"Yes mam it does count. Did you notice if it was a city police car or a sheriff's department car?" asked Travis

"Oh, yes," she said. "I recognized immediately that it was a sheriff's department car." Then she added almost at once, "I didn't take my eyes off the road though officer. I never take my eyes off the road. I would never have noticed that car at all if he had not been driving on *my* side of the road. I thought how careless for him to drive like that. Don't you think so, officer?"

"Yes, mam," said Travis. He thanked Mrs. Grimsley for her time and started back to his car. As he walked pass the Cadillac, he noticed two over-stuffed pillows placed strategically under the steering wheel.

Travis waved as he backed out of Lila Grimsley's drive. She waved back and watched him drive the car towards Nags Head. Then she considered aloud to herself, "I wonder why he didn't ask me if I knew the driver of the sheriff's department car."

Travis pulled into the paved parking lot of the Low-Rate Insurance Group just as a young man wearing slick navy blue polyester pants, shiny black tassel loafers, and a short-sleeve blue plaid shirt dropped a key in his pocket and hung a CLOSED sign on the door. Travis grabbed a look at his watch and saw it was only four fifteen. He got out of the car and walked quickly toward the office.

The young man spotted him, immediately flashed a toothy bogus smile, and said, "Good evening, sir. I was closing a little early, but I've always got time for another customer. Come in…won't you come in?"

He snatched the CLOSED sign, unlocked the door, and held it open as Travis walked into a small room filled with cheap office furniture that wreaked of cigarette smoke. He motioned to a straight back chair with a cracked plastic seat cover and said, "Have a seat, sir. Have a seat. My name's George Borne, agent here with the Low-Rate Insurance Group. How can I help you?"

Travis reached carefully for his identification still smeared with greasy fingerprints, flashed it quickly, and said, "I'm Travis White, ABC officer. I'd like to ask you a few questions about one of your customers."

The young man's broad smile was replaced with a look of disappointment. "Which customer are you talking about?"

Travis carefully replaced the identification badge in his loose shirt pocket. "I need some insurance information on Maynard Dwayne Drane."

"Maynard Dwayne Drane? He don't have no insurance with us," said the young man.

"Are you sure?" said Travis. "Are you sure that Maynard Dwayne Drane never bought insurance from your company?"

"Now I didn't say that," said the young insurance agent. "I said he don't have no insurance with us now. Maynard took a policy out…let me see." He twirled around in his swivel chair and switched on a computer. He clicked a few keys and repeated, "Now let me see. Drane, Drane, Drane. Drane, Daniel; Drane, Franklin; Drane, Maynard. Here we are. Drane, Maynard took out insurance about fifteen months ago. Beneficiary was Eve Drane, wife. Made

81

one premium payment and dropped it. No more purchases since then. Hey, wait….he even wanted a refund on that single payment." Then he said in a low voice, "Lots of luck, Buddy."

The young insurance agent turned off the computer, twirled back around to face Travis and said, "Anything else I can help you with, officer?"

Travis was stunned. After taking a few seconds to regroup, he said, "Mr. Borne, do you happen to know if Eve Maynard, his wife, knew that he dropped the policy?"

"I wouldn't have any way to know that," Borne said.

Travis stood up to leave. "Thank you for your time. If you should think of anything else about the Drane policy, give me a call." He handed Borne a card.

They walked out into the parking lot. "Say, Officer White," said the insurance agent. "I'd like to talk to you sometime about you own insurance needs. Health, accident, auto. We got it all and real cheap. That's how we come up with our name…Low-Rate Insurance Group. We have this real sweet term life policy…damned cheap…designed to fit the special requirements of people in high-risk professions. As a matter of fact just last year……"

Travis shook his head and fairly ran for his car.

CHAPTER 14

As he pulled out of the parking space in the Dare County Justice Center parking lot, Sam waved weakly to a despondent-looking Shucks. He clicked the signal and turned left towards highway 345, the Wanchese road. Sam felt badly that Sheriff Caffy wouldn't allow Shucks to accompany him to question Doo-Wop Early. And to add insult to injury, Caffy gave Shucks' vehicle to Sam and assigned Shucks paper work. Caffy was still ticked off because Shucks damaged his car in a high-speed chase involving two drunken high school kids. Then to top it off he showed up late at the beach crime scene.

"That's Shucks for you," thought Sam. "Can't seem to catch a break."

But Sam's reason for wanting Shucks to accompany him on Doo's interview was not so much out of sympathy for Shucks but more because he could use some moral support while questioning his old friend.

Sam drove toward Wanchese, pass the Manteo city limits, and turned right onto a bumpy, potholed road hardly wider than a footpath. It twisted like a corkscrew through dense scrub trees to a clearing by a creek. Facing the creek was a small neat clapboard house set in a patch of thick green neatly mowed grass. The house had a row of tomato plants growing along side the porch that extended the entire length of the house. Near the shoreline of the creek that was fuzzy with algae, a heron waited motionless for his next meal, and in the distance a nutria's cry pierced the air. On the porch a shirtless old man wearing bib overalls nodded in a rocking chair, a wooden cane gripped tightly in his gnarled hand. His white hair and beard made his face appear blacker than it really was. When Sam closed the car door the old man slowly opened his eyes and wiped dribble from his chin.

"Hey, Pop Early," said Sam walking towards the porch.

"Sam," said the old man in a shaky voice. "I bin 'specting you. Come on up cheer."

Sam walked to the porch and sat down on the top step. "How you doing, Pop?"

"Not much good. Not much good atall, Sam. Ain't bin worf nuffin since Short Sugar got hurt. Cain't git it outta my haid dat somebody done dat to our baby. How come, Sam?"

"I don't know, Pop," said Sam. "But I'll tell you one thing. I won't rest till I find out the whole truth behind this thing. Pop, I need to talk to Doo. Is he home?"

"Yeah, he be here. He be sleep all day. Out las night lookin' and talkin' to erbody bout Short Sugar bein' hurt," said Pop. "I'll go git 'em."

Pop rocked forward, used his cane for leverage, groaned, and rose slowly. He flexed his knees several times before taking the few steps to the screen door and disappeared inside.

In a few minutes the door opened, and Doo leaned against the frame. His eyes were swollen and bloodshot. He wore jeans with no belt, and they hung carelessly low around his skinny waist. He was barefoot and didn't wear a shirt. Sam could count his ribs.

"Hey, Doo," said Sam. "You making it alright?"

Doo-Wop walked slowly onto the porch dragging his feet with each step. He walked over to the porch rail, braced his arm against the post, and laid his head in the bend of arm. Suddenly his shoulders began to shake. First slowly, then convulsively. Cries of anguish exploded from the miserable man.

Sam went to him and placed his arm around his shoulder. They stood there silently, somberly for what seemed to be an eternity each man not daring to move not wanting to sever the bond being revived between them.

Finally Sam slipped slowly aside and gave Doo a firm pat on the back. "So. Tell me about Short Sugar. How's she doing?" said Sam.

"Better. She doin' better. Dey tolt me she cin come home inna few days," said Doo.

"Good. Good," said Sam. "Trav said tell you that he'd see you later today. We got caught up in a case, and he's working an angle. Anyway, he said say 'hey'"

"Hey, back," said Doo-Wop. "Sam, I donna know what git inta me a hollaring at ya'll lak dat. Guess I musta bin bout haf crazy. I bin so flustrated. Flustrated 'bout why someone do dis to my baby. Flustrated caus' I dun know who done it. Flustrated 'bout the hospital bills. Jest plain flustrated. Pleeze forgive me."

84

"Doo…nothing to forgive. Being upset when someone hurts your child is a parent's right of passage. We were sorry to see you so strung out, but guy, you had every right to be crazy," said Sam. "Let's not talk about it ever again. Okay?"

"Okay. Tell Trav?" said Doo.

"Sure," said Sam. "Now Doo, I have to tell you about the investigation into the hit and run. Let's sit."

The two men sat down on the steps. Doo-Wop's face turned expectantly to Sam. Sam said, "Doo, we've identified the car that struck Short Sugar."

Doo-Wop's haggard face took on new life. "You say?" he said.

"Yes," said Sam. "Using the tire prints as evidence, we determined the make of the vehicle, a Jeep. Then the Jeep dealer in Nags Head gave us a list of local Wrangler owners. We started checking them out. Then we uncovered evidence that pointed toward one particular vehicle."

"Do dat mean you got de jeep, Sam? De jeep what run down my baby?" Doo said with great excitement.

"In a way…," said Sam.

"What ya mean 'in a way'?" Doo-Wop said a puzzled look on his face. "Ya got de jeep or no?"

"No, Doo," said Sam. Quickly he added, "We don't have the jeep, but we have the owner of the vehicle."

"Well, dat be okay den," said Do- Wop. "I don't care nuffin 'bout no jeep. I jest want dat driver *under* de jail. Whair he be anyhow?"

"Doo, that's the tricky part. You see we have the owner down in the morgue," said Sam watching Doo-Wop's face carefully. "The owner was found dead on the beach last night. Two college kids walking the beach found him."

Doo sat solemnly staring out onto the creek. A powerboat roared pass, tossed a wake that looked like a soft white pillow upon the shoreline, and sent the feeding heron scurrying into the air. "How ya know he be the one dat owns de jeep if'n he be daid?"

"The name of the dead man was on the list of jeep owners living on the island. Jeep Dealer gave it to us," said Sam.

Doo-Wop thought about this for a few minutes and said, "But if'n ya don't got de jeep what belonged to him, how de ya know dat it was his perticuler jeep dat hit Short Sugar?"

Sam said, "There were tire tracks on the beach near the body. Those tracks matched the tire tracks at the crime scene where Short Sugar was hit. Of course, we don't know that the owner was driving the car when it hit Short Sugar. But we do know that the same car that struck Short Sugar was used to take the jeep owner's body to the beach."

"And you ain't got de jeep?" Doo-Wop asked.

"No," said Sam. "Apparently the body was dumped on the beach, and the murderers drove off in the jeep."

"Murderers?" exclaimed Doo-Wop. "Ya sayin' he wuz murdered?"

"Yes," said Sam.

"How ya no he won't killed hit and run lak my baby?" said Doo-Wop.

"Because," said Sam, "he was killed by a shot gun blast to his stomach."

"Oh, sweet Jeezus," moaned Doo-Wop. He dropped his face into his hands and covered his eyes. Finally he raised his head, looked at Sam and asked hoarsely, "Sam, who be dis murdered man dat own de jeep what run over my baby?"

"His name is Maynard Dwayne Drane," Sam said.

"Oh, Jeezus. Sweet Jeezus," repeated Doo-Wop. "Sam dat man ain't nuffin but trash. Jest plain white trash."

Sam simply nodded his head in agreement. They sat silently, and Sam allowed Doo-Wop time to process the information he'd given him. A hot breeze stirred the September air and the leaves on the trees moved slowly allowing slits of lights to penetrate the thick foliage. Doo was a simple man but Sam knew that he was also very wise, especially wise in street smarts.

Doo finally spoke. "So, Sam, ya come all de way out cheer jest to tell me 'bout finding de owner or de jeep or what? Is dare sumpin else ya wants from me?"

"Yes, Doo," said Sam. "Anytime we have a murder we have to check out those who might have a reason to want to harm the victim. Since it is likely that Drane was the driver that hit Short Sugar, there certainly wouldn't be any love lost between the two of you. Understand what I'm saying?"

When Doo-Wop's voice sounded like an automaton, "I understan dat I fret fo my baby til I almost be crazy, and din I gots to defend myself ginst a murder charge."

"Whoa, now partner," said Sam. "That's not what I'm saying. Not what I'm saying at all. We just need to know where you were last night. That's all. Believe me we're asking a lot of people that question. You'd be amazed how many people didn't like Maynard Dwayne Drane." To himself Sam thought *Please let him have an alibi.*

"I wudn't be 'mazed," said Doo-Wop. "Dat boy gots mo enemies dan a hound dog got fleas. Las night I et suppa wid Pop and den I go down to Willy Joe's Place to haf a few beers and talk bout how to get hup for de hospital bills."

"Okay, that's good," said Sam taking out a pad and pen, "what time did you leave the house...after eating supper with Pop?"

"Lemme tink," said Doo-Wop.

Before he could answer a voice from inside the house said, "He lef har 'bout nine o'clock."

"Pop's right," said Doo-Wop. "It wuz 'bout nine o'clock."

"You go straight to Willy Joe's Place?" said Sam.

"Straight dare," said Doo-Wop.

"Stay there all evening?" asked Sam.

"All evenin," said Doo-Wop.

"What time did you get home?" asked Sam.

"Now lemme see," a far-away look crossed Doo-Wop's face.

"'Bout leven o'clock," the voice from inside the house answered.

"Guess Pop's right again," said Doo-Wop. "I cudn't sware to hit beings I wuz so taxed."

"You mean too much to drink?" asked Sam.

"Yes," said the voice from inside.

"Doo, do you recall who else was at Willy Joe's that might have seen you come and go?" asked Sam.

"Well, I dun't lak to be givin out de names of folks a drinkin down at Willy Joe's, but you might ax Willy Joe hisself. Abody wud know he hat to be dare," said Doo-Wop.

"Will do," said Sam. He flipped his note pad shut and stuck it back into his shirt pocket. "One other thing, Doo. Do you own a gun?"

"Ya knows I do, Sam," said Doo-Wop. "I gots that ole twenty-two rifle I uses for squirrel hunting."

"No...a shot gun?" said Sam.

"No shot gun," repeated Doo-Wop.

"Well, guess that about wraps it up here, Doo," said Sam. "I'll be going on down to Willy Joe's Place."

"Not jest yet," said the voice from inside, and Pop Early stepped onto the porch with a plate stacked high with soft-shell crab sandwiches and dill pickles in one hand and a six pack of Pepsi Colas in the other. Doo and Sam broke off a couple of Pepsis, "Want one Pop?" asked Sam.

"No tank ya, Sam," said Pop. "I'll jest tak a drink of sweet water."

The three men sat silently, devoured the crunchy, succulent sandwiches and crisp pickles, and pulled long swallows of Pepsi from cans that dripped icy sweat.

Finally Doo broke the silence. "Duz ya believe me, Sam?" he asked "Will ya take my part."

Without hesitation Sam said, "Yes, I believe you Doo, and I'll take your part."

The wind rustled the leaves and a gray squirrel crept stealthily onto a low-hanging limb and dropped cautiously onto the ground beside a tomato plant. He sat upright on his hind legs, wiggled his nose, looked straight at the spectators, grabbed a red tomato, and scurried back up the tree to safety.

"Lose mo of dem maters dan I eats," said Pop. "But I dun't care. Dey's got to eat too."

Sam and Doo-Wop nodded their heads in agreement and reached for another soft-shell crab sandwich.

Sam followed the Wanchese Highway a couple of miles to where both sides of the road were skirted by woods so thick that sunlight could hardly penetrate the branches and vines that sheltered the swampy ground below. The woods were alive with cicadas. He pulled into a muddy parking area filled with ruts so deep that you could fill them up with water and raise catfish. The lot was strewn with beer cans, liquor bottles, fast food wrappers, a rotting athletic shoe, a couple of beat-up pickup trucks, and several hammered old gas guzzlers.

Sam surveyed the place a few minutes before grabbing his badge and sticking it on the front of his shirt. Sam's badge had gained him uncontested entrance to many anomalous places in his career, and Willy Joe's was the kind of place that ABC officers didn't usually go into alone. Sam knew that Travis would give him hell for going it alone today, but Sam got to know Willy Joe over the years. Besides it wasn't Willy Joe that he needed to watch but rather the low lifes that frequented his establishment.

Willy Joe's place was a juke joint housed in an abandoned Texaco service station. The old gas pumps were still in place with the broken glass that once bore the big red T against a white star, and the only paved area in the whole parking lot was the crumbling concrete in front of the pumps. Last year's Christmas lights still hung along the roofline waiting for next year's holiday.

Sam walked towards the laughter and loud voices coming from inside the joint and creaked open the rusting screen door. The rotting floor squeaked when he stepped inside and the room fell silent. He felt startled, piercing eyes riveted on him as the door slammed behind him. The joint was not air conditioned and the smell of sweat, stale beer, cigarette smoke, and marijuana hung heavy in the air. There were four screenless windows and flies buzzed the room avoiding the sticky fly tape that hung from the ceiling. Curtains that were little more than dirty tatters hung from the windows and occasionally puffed in what little breeze found its way into the room.

Sam easily spotted Willy Joe Loomis seated at the bar. He wore a wide brim Panama hat with an oily red sweatband, a shirt cut from a tropical print, hip hugging pants that hung low and looked two sizes too small, and a gold necklace and watch that matched his large gold front tooth. Sam moved toward him undeterred. From behind Sam heard the scurry of retreating footsteps, the slam of the screen door, and the rapid crunch of running feet in the parking lot. Willy Joe's face was rippled with perspiration as he flashed Sam a contrived smile and said, "Hey, occifer come on in."

A slender young light skin woman with a blue rag wrapped around her head stood behind the bar. She didn't look up but continued to put beer cans in the cooler. "What's up, Willy Joe?" said Sam sidling up to the bar, then turning slowly to scrutinize the customers.

"Tings be on de up and up," said Willy Joe, his smile never leaving his face. "I bin cardin' and cardin'. Ain't no underage beer sales go be hair."

"Good, Willy Joe. That's good," said Sam. "You keep on carding your young customers, but that's not why I'm here today. Need some information."

Willy Joe looked skeptical. "What kinda infomation?"

"Want you to help me clear up something. You know about Short Sugar Early's hit run don't you?" said Sam.

"I knows what I hairs," Willy Joe said cautiously. "Mostly from Doo-Wop Early."

"Right. Well I was just down to Doo's house. We think we got the guy who ran down Short Sugar," said Sam in an effort to put Willy Joe at ease.

Willy Joe looked relieved. "I's glad. Real glad for de Doo-Wop. He's a bin a frettin' and a frettin' 'Bout worried hisself sick," he said.

"Now what I want to ask you is this. Was Doo down here at your place last night?" said Sam.

Willy Joe looked puzzled. He hesitated for quite a while then said reluctantly, "Yeah, he be hair last light."

"Good," said Sam. Willy Joe looked relieved again. "Can you tell me what time he came in and what time he left?"

Willy Joe rolled his eyes upward in deep concentration. "Now lets me see," he said. "He come in hair 'bout...'bout nine. Wudn't ya say, Tess?"

The young woman with the blue rag on her head closed the door to the cooler, patted her cold hands on her face, and said, "Yeah, 'bout nine."

Sam said, "And what about when he left?"

Willy Joe deferred to Tess again, "Whatcha tink, Tess?"

"I'd say round leven or so...maybe a few minits pass," Tess drawled.

Sam must have looked pleased because Willy Joe let out a soft sigh as Sam jotted the times down in his notepad and stuck it in his pocket.

"Okay, Willy Joe," said Sam. "Thanks, and carry on. See you soon." And he walked briskly towards the door.

"See ya'," said Willy Joe. And then in a whisper to Tess he added, "But I hopes it ain't real soon.

CHAPTER 15

Travis and Sam pulled into the parking lot of the Dare County Justice Center simultaneously and just in time to watch Nona Godette back out of her parking space.

"Hey, wait up," said Sam holding his palm up gesturing her to stop.

"What's up, Sam?" Nona asked a wicked grin on her face.

"I'm gonna let that one pass," said Sam with a sheepish grin on his face. "Does the sheriff want to see us this afternoon?"

"Well, if you don't have a watch," she said holding up her wrist and displaying her own, "you can't know that it not afternoon any more. It's six thirty. Sheriff's gone. Wants to see us all in the morning."

"That's good," said Sam. "And where are you off to in such a hurry? Date with *Mr. Compliment Each Other* ?"

"What?" Nona said lifting an eyebrow affecting a puzzled look.

"Never mind," said Sam. "Carry on." He smacked the car door gently.

Nona put the car in drive, moved forward a few feet, and stopped in front of Travis. "Watch him, Trav," she said. "He's gone off...not making sense."

"He seldom does," replied Travis, and he waved her off.

Sam waited outside while Travis ran inside the Center to have the lab run a check on the mechanic's oily fingerprints. Soon Travis joined him, and as they were getting into their car a voice stopped them.

"Hey, you two," called Shucks. "Wait up." They waited.

Sam and Travis still felt badly that the sheriff had not sent Shucks on assignment with either of them, and they worried that he would think they were infringing on his investigation. For what it was worth, Shucks always gave his assignments his best shot.

"What's going on, Shucks," said Travis.

"Nothing," Shucks said. "Least wise nothing here. How'd things go for you two? Find out anything?"

"Yeah, as a matter of fact I did," said Travis.

"Me, too," said Sam.

Shucks looked at them expectantly, and Travis felt a surge of pity. "Tell you what, Shucks," Travis said, "Why don't you go out to eat with us? We'll fill you in."

Shucks was so elated that he began to shift from one foot to the other. "Sure. Great. Where ya'll going?"

"Let's go somewhere different tonight," said Sam reasoning that Nona might show up at Guthrie's with *Mr. Compliments Each Other*. "How about the Oyster Shell on Virginia Dare Trail?"

Shucks couldn't hide his excitement at being invited to join them. "Great," he said starting towards his car. "I'll follow you there."

The Oyster Shell was a combination bar, grill, and dance floor. In spite of the fact that Travis and Sam busted the proprietor a couple of times for selling alcohol to underage customers they felt welcome and actually had a pretty straight relationship with the owner now. The place sported a tropical motif and everything was arranged around a circular bar that was covered in wicker-like material and strung with colorful electric-lighted lanterns. Rattan chairs were pushed under matching tables with lighted candles reflecting off the glass tops. Couples gyrated wildly as an enormous jukebox pulsated green, blue, and red lights and pumped out earsplitting music non-stop.

"This racket is off the Richter. Let's move to the back," shouted Sam above the commotion. They chose a table in a corner as far away from the jukebox as possible.

A cute young thing wearing cut-off faded jeans, a halter made of a tropical print, and a string of artificial flowers around her neck in essence skipped to their table. Then with batting eyelashes and a saucy smile she said, "What can I do for you guys?"

Sam thought about that one for a few minutes then settled on another comment he felt more appropriate. He affected his *I can't believe I've finally met you look*, looked straight at the plastic flowers hanging from the waitress' neck and said, "Wow! Just look at this boys! Have you ever seen such a beautiful lei?"

The waitress fingered the plastic flowers, grinned and said, "They look real don't they?"

"Oh, I'm sure they're real," said Sam.

The waitress giggled. The men ordered a large platter of oysters on the half shell served on a bed of shaved ice and a pitcher of beer for starters. As the cold beer and raw oysters slid down their throats, Travis and Sam lay open the events of the day to Shucks.

Sam related his interview with Doo-Wop and Pop Early. He told how Doo-Wop and Pop contended that the only gun Doo owned was the twenty-two he used to hunt squirrels. Both Pop and Doo readily admitted that Doo hadn't worked the night of the murder, but added that he was at home drunk until nine pm. At nine he went to Willy Joe's Place where the other commiserated with him until around eleven pm. Then he came home, fell into bed, and stayed there until Sam found him this morning. Sam described Doo's remorse for having railed at Travis and him earlier. Sam also emphasized that both Willy Joe and Tess confirmed that Doo was at Willy Joe's Place until around eleven pm. Then Sam leaned back, put his hand behind his head, and waited for Travis to give him hell for going into Willy Joe's Place alone,

And hell it was. "Sam you damned fool. You got a death wish or something? You just can't wait to get your lights punched out can you......" and blah, blah, blah.

Finally, "Trav, my man, you're right. I'm a damned fool. I sure as hell won't do something that stupid again," Sam lied.

Travis knew Sam was lying and that Sam's kind of risks was certainly dangerous to his partner, but being a risk taker was what made him such a good agent. Shucks watched and listened with envy as he witnessed the obvious loyalty the two men felt towards each other. Shucks never felt so alone and inept in his life.

Then it was Travis' turn to report about his day with Ms. Eve Drane. Travis reported that she left work a little before ten, got a ride home with a neighbor who dropped her off at the corner of her street rather than her driveway because she liked to walk at night. He told how she claimed that her house was broken into, the dog left outside, the lights turned on, and a television and two guns stolen. This really got Sam and Shucks' attention. Travis explained that he talked with the neighbor who verified that he indeed drove Eve home from work and dropped her off at the corner. Eve told him that Drane had a life insurance policy naming her as the beneficiary, and she claimed not to know that Drane was dying. Then Travis threw in the clincher…Eve wasn't aware that Drane had dropped the life insurance policy.

"Whoa, there buddy," Sam raised his eyebrows expressing shock. "Looks like there's more to little Miss Blue Eyes than meets the eye. How do you feel about all this, Trav?"

Shucks looked confused. Then a light went on and his baffled expression changed to comprehension. "Travis," he said, "are you besotted with Eve Drane?"

Travis and Sam looked perplexed. Then they burst out laughing. "Besotted?" said Sam. "Besotted? Yeah, Trav are you besotted with Eve?"

The two men bent double with laughter and soon Shucks joined in. Their boisterous guffaws caused heads to turn and faces to stare. As Travis and Shucks continued the whoopla, Sam suddenly fell silent, his eyes glued on the dance floor.

Finally realizing that Sam was quiet, Travis said, "Sam, what's the matter?" Then his eyes followed Sam's to the dance floor. There was Nona Godette undulating wildly, provocatively, sensually, her eyes transfixed on *Mr. Compliments Each Other*.

"Sam, Sam, what's the matter?" Shucks asked.

Travis leaned towards Shucks and whispered, "Sam is *besotted* with Nona Godette."

Sam dropped his fork, threw down his napkin, and pushed his chair back nosily. "Let's get the hell outta here." And he headed for the door.

Shucks snatched up the ticket. "I'll get this boys," he said. "Where we going now?"

Travis and Sam were almost out the door. "To Guthrie's, Shucks. See you there."

CHAPTER 16

They pulled into Guthrie's parking lot. Travis drove while Sam stared sullenly out the window. Travis felt it best not to intrude, so they waited in stony silence outside the restaurant for Shucks. Travis realized that Sam had some things to work out for himself, but he sure wished that Shucks would hurry up and get there.

Shucks finally pulled into the parking lot. "Hey Shucks," said Travis. "Didn't mean to run out and leave you with the tab. How much we owe you?"

"Not a cent. Not one red cent," said Shucks. "This one's on me." Shucks felt exhilarated. He felt included...a part of the crowd. Travis said 'see you there'. That's an invitation! The Three Musketeers, he fantasized. After all now he was privy to personal details about his new buddies...they were *besotted*. Both of them. How many other people knew that?

Travis said, "You don't have to pick up the tab, Shucks."

"No, I want to," Shucks said. "After all what are friends for, huh?"

Travis said, "Thanks." And they went inside.

The usual off-season crowd was inside Guthrie's. They were eating and drinking and laughing, but the noise level was far below the raucous milieu they'd left at the Oyster Shell.

"Hey, fellas. Got you a table right over by the window," Irene greeted them with a wide, sincere grin. "or would you rather go to the bar first?"

"No bar, Irene," said Travis. "Just find us a nice quiet place."

"You got it," she said as she winked, grabbed three menus, and led them to a corner table by the window. "Guess what? Doo's back tonight, and he's his old self again. Says Short Sugar is going to be coming home real soon. You know, he adores that girl, and I can see why. She's a sweet little thing and smmmart."

Sam spoke for the first time. "Glad to hear that, Irene. Thanks for telling us."

"Want I should tell him you're here?" she said.

"That's okay," said Sam. "I spoke with him earlier today."

"I should have known," Irene said and smiled knowingly.

They sat silently and gazed out upon the sound where tiny white caps retreated and then surfaced again like small white feathers floating on the water. A full orange autumnal moon hung low in the dark sky and cast tiny flicks of light like precious gems upon the dark emerald water.

Their thoughts were abruptly interrupted when a high-pitched, nasal voice said, "Hello, I'm Candi. I'll be your server tonight. Can I bring you something to drink?"

The three men looked up to see the bartender who had described Nona and her companion as *compliments each other.*

"Well," said Sam. "What happened to you? Get demoted because they found out you're too young to be behind a bar?"

"No," she said indignantly. "For your information, I was PROmoted. Tips are better for waitresses than bartenders, so Guthrie let me change jobs. Do you want anything to drink or not?"

Travis answered quickly, "Black Radishes all around."

She scribbled down the order furiously, shot them a look to kill, turned on her heels, and walked towards the bar. Suddenly she stopped, returned to the table, and glared down at Sam. "By the way, your girlfriend was by earlier tonight. She sure does look good with Chuckie Ryan. She was hanging on his every word. But why not? What girl wouldn't be interested in the explorations of a tall, dark, handsome scuba diver. I know I would." She tossed her hair as if to say 'one up for me, bud' and started to walk away again. Then she turned again and added, "Just so's you understand what kind of explorations I'm referring to…he explores shipwrecks."

She left the men with their chins practically on the table. "No tip for you, Chickie," snarled Sam. "Still bet she's underage."

"She's not, Sam," said Travis. "We checked Guthrie's employee's out last spring."

"Still, Travis," said Shucks, "She had no right to sass off at Sam like that. That's ill-mannered."

"Ill-mannered? Yeah, she was that," said Travis.

"Ill-mannered?" said Sam. "Where the hell do you come up with these words, Shucks…besotted, ill-mannered?"

"Well, they work, don't they?" said Shucks.

"They sure do," Travis said reassuringly. "She was definitely ill-mannered."

Travis ordered the steamed shell combo. Sam ordered Hatteras clam chowder and a shrimp salad. And Shucks got a hamburger with all the trimmings and French fries. Confident she was now points ahead in her verbal battle with Sam, the waitress took their order without saying a word.

"What the hell kind of name is Chuckie Ryan?" said Sam. No one offered an answer.

"So he's a scuba diver," said Travis. It was a statement, not a question.

"Yeah, scuba diving is a big thing right now," said Shucks. "It's become one of the biggest attractions on the banks. They got diving schools here and everything."

"What'd she mean explore shipwreck?" asked Sam.

Shucks jumped right in. He finally had something to contribute to the conversation. "The shipwrecks off the coast of the North Carolina Outer Banks are what make this such a popular place to scuba dive. Bet you didn't know that over six hundred ships wrecked along the North Carolina coast."

"Six hundred?" said Sam.

"Six hundred resting on the bottom of the ocean for eternity," Shucks said dramatically. Travis and Sam smiled and encourage him to continue. "Actually it's suspected there may be even more than six hundred, but they don't have the documentation to verify them. The earliest wreck dates all the way back to 1585."

Sam and Travis looked surprised. That was all the encouragement Shucks needed. "That's right 1585. A British ship, Tiger, sunk out in the Ocracoke Inlet. The weather out here's always been a real hazard to mariners. So many of these ships wrecked in the fog and storms. Just think about being out on a ship when one those tropical storms come roaring up the coast."

"I can see how the weather could really tear up those earlier vessels," said Sam.

Shucks was delighted. He had Travis and Sam's attention. He slipped his chair closer to the table, leaned forward, and continued eloquently, "Storms are bad, yeah. But wars are too. Confederate and Union battles sent many a gunboat to a watery grave. And the Monitor, she was a Union Ironclad equipped with a rotating turret, still lies out there in those waters. It was swamped in a gale and sunk in 1862. Then World War I German U-boats sank a whole bunch of ships. Then came World War II, and Nazi submarines just littered the coastline with freighters and tankers they sunk. In fact so many ships were sunk that the coastline became known as torpedo junction."

"Oh, I've heard plenty of World War II Outer Banks war stories. You can't grow up in eastern North Carolina and not know about 'torpedo junction'," said Travis. "My dad had this old friend out here who told him that the Outer Bankers would get up early in the morning, go out on the beach, and collect all kinds of debris from sunken ships that the tide brought in...pictures, books, records, pieces of the ship, personal belongings. Sometimes they would find papers and letters written in German. They'd just walk along the beach and pick up this stuff. And the incredible thing about it was that the rest of country seemed to be oblivious to the fact that this was happening right here...just a stone's throw from an American shore."

"Can you imagine how that would play today?" said Sam. "CNN would be on the spot...scene, lights, cameras, live interview...'what did you find this morning Mrs. Jones'?"

Travis picked up the interview, "And 'tell us how you felt when you found that picture'?"

They laughed until they hurt. Shucks never got so much attention in his life, and he reveled in it. He continued with his narration. "Yes, sir. So many ships were sent to a watery grave that the whole North Carolina Coastline is also called the *Graveyard of the Atlantic.*"

"Shucks, you're amazing," said Travis. "How'd you know all this stuff?"

Shucks grinned shyly, "I love it...every since I was a boy, I love it. I read everything I can get my hands on about the Outer Banks. I was born and raised out here you know. If you don't know 'bout you home....well, you ain't educated."

"I think you're right, Shucks," said Travis.

"Me too," said Sam, "but tell me one thing, Shucks. How does Chuckie Ryan get out to those shipwrecks? And what does a scuba diver do once he gets there?"

"Well, Sam," said Shucks, "I can't answer exactly about Chuckie Ryan, but I can tell you that some of these shipwrecks can be reached from the beach right down here at Nags Head."

"You don't say?" said Sam.

"Sure," said Shucks. "There's a couple of wrecks down at milepost eleven off the Bladen Street access. There's a tugboat called the Explorer and a Federal gunship, the Huron. They're maybe only two hundred feet off the beach."

"Really? As many times as I fished that beach, I never knew there were shipwrecks that close," said Sam.

"Yeah, fish like shipwreck. Use them for homes," said Shucks. "There's a couple of others you can reach from the beach down off milepost seven. The Kyzickes, a tanker, and a freighter called the Carl Gerhard. That makes four wrecks that are easily accessible from the beach, and they attract scuba divers."

"Shucks, you're a walking Outer Banks Encyclopedia," said Sam.

Shucks looked embarrassed and said, "Thanks."

"No kidding. I had no idea you knew all this stuff. I'm impressed," Sam said sincerely.

Shucks was never happier. He didn't want the night to end. He knew these compliments were sincere and somehow it made up for the lousy day he'd had shuffling papers back at Dare County Justice Center.

The waitress with an attitude walked up and handed tickets to each man. She looked at Sam and smirked, "No need to wait around for your girlfriend, Sam. Chuckie's group is going out tomorrow morning so he won't stay out late tonight."

"How do you know?" asked Sam.

"I heard them say," she said tauntingly.

"Whatta you mean group?" asked Shucks.

"Chuckie and some friends swim out to wrecks, dive down, and check em out," she said. Then she turned and slithered away.

"Let's get outta here," Sam said for the second time that night and walked towards the cash register.

"Hi, hon. She give you a hard time?" asked Irene reaching for Sam's ticket.

Travis spoke up, "No, Irene, everything's okay. Good shrimp tonight. "

Irene wouldn't be put off. "Sam what do you say? Was she rude?"

"No, everything's okay. Irene, honey, right now you're the only bright bulb in the marquee of my life," Sam said and gave her a wink.

Outside Sam was real quiet, but Travis decided to take a chance and venture into the minefield called Nona. "Sam, why don't you just forget her?" he asked knowing full well that was easier said than done.

Sam shook his head. "I don't know what it is Trav. But Nona's one of those women who can tell you to go to hell in such a way that you look forward to the trip."

Travis shook his head and walked towards the car with Sam. Shucks lagged behind. "See you in the morning, Shucks," Travis said.

"Me, too," said Sam.

Shucks didn't answer, so Travis walked back to him and said, "Shucks, you alright?"

"Yeah, sure. I'm alright. I was just thinking," said Shucks. "Did you know that Maynard Dwayne Drane used to be a scuba diver, and that he spent a lot of time exploring the ship wrecks. In fact, a couple of years ago he was caught trying to sell some artifacts from one of the wrecks. You see those wrecks are like a museum, and it's against the law to plunder them. Anyway, just thought what a coincidence that Chuckie Ryan is a diver, too"

CHAPTER 17

A white Corvette drove onto the parking area of the Bladen Street public beach access. Veils of gray wispy clouds floated idly over a full white moon that was encased in a wide feathery rain ring, and ocean winds blew in cold and steady.

The silhouettes of a man and a woman sitting in the car showed clearly against the moonlight. For some time, the two images sat apart heads and hands moved in conversational gestures. Finally the man got out, walked to the passenger side of the car, opened the door, and extended his hand to the woman who turned in her seat and slipped gracefully out of the Corvette.

The couple walked hand and hand to the gazebo just below the steps that led to the beach. The woman hugged her arms tightly to her body and shivered as the wind whistled up from the ocean whipping her hair wildly about her face. Her companion reached out, drew her to him, and held her tightly. And they stood like this for a long, long time. Then the woman began to struggle…first a push against his chest and then her gestures became more intense, more animated as her arms and fists waved futilely. She'd been caught off guard. Then she suddenly pushed him away, affected a stance, and executed a martial movement that flipped the man and sent him crashing smartly to the floor and on his back. Surprisingly, the man offered no defense. She stood over him, hands on hips, and the motions of her head indicated that now she was in control of the situation. Then she stormed out of the gazebo, crossed the parking lot, and headed towards the go-cart establishment on the other side of Virginia Dare Trail.

The man pushed himself up slowly, brushed the sand off his clothes, shrugged, and turned towards the Corvette. Then something caught his eye.

He looked in the direction of the departing woman. She was nowhere to be seen. Then he squinted and stared out on the ocean just beyond the breakers. A light blinked one, two...one, two...one, two, three...one. Then the sequence was repeated. He hurried to the car, opened the glove box, grabbed a flashlight, and raced to the beach. He looked again in the direction the woman had taken. Satisfied that she was no where in sight, the silhouette pointed his flashlight in the direction of the signal and duplicated the sequence...one, two...one, two...one, two, three...one.

Travis and Sam arrived back at the Sand Trap. This time, Travis was sullen and introspective. Sam waited for him to say something, but patience was not Sam's strong suit. Finally he could take it no longer.

"Okay, Trav," Sam said. "Let's have it. What's eating you? You still thinking about the scuba connection between Ryan and Drane?"

"Well, that certainly gives us something to think about," said Travis. "We need to check that out tomorrow. But...."

"But what else?" said Sam.

Travis sat down on his bed. He stared into space blinking his eyes as if trying to clear his head of some muddled thought. "What?" repeated Sam.

"Sam, when we were telling Shucks about our interviews this afternoon, I left something out. I wanted to run it by you before I told anyone else," said Travis.

"Well, run it by," said Sam impatiently.

"When I interviewed Eve Drane's neighbors this afternoon, two neighbors reported that the night of the murder, they saw a patrol car in the neighborhood," said Travis. "They said it was a Dare County Sheriff's car, and it had a damaged right front fender."

Travis had Sam's attention. "Go on," he prompted.

"This evening when we pulled into the Dare County Justice Center, I noticed that Shucks' patrol car is damaged."

"And?" said Sam.

"It's the right front fender that's smashed," said Travis.

"So, you think it was Shucks patrolling the Drane neighborhood?" asked Sam.

"Yes," said Travis.

"Well, what's so suspicious about that?" asked Sam.

"What is so suspicious is that Shucks never mentioned it. The next day at the briefing, he never said he was in the Drane neighborhood. He just said he was out looking for the perp."

"So?" prompted Sam.

"So, at that point in the investigation, Drane's name hadn't come up as a suspect so why did he chose to check out the Drane neighborhood?"

"I can see where you're coming from, partner," Sam said bluntly, "But it's a real stretch to think that Shucks could be involved in a murder just because he wasn't specific about where he had been cruising."

"I suppose you're right," said Travis. "But for some reason, I didn't want to ask him about it tonight. Just a feeling that I shouldn't. I'll say something to him about it tomorrow."

Travis realized that he no longer had Sam's attention. Sam clicked off the bedside lamp, lay down with his arm behind his head, and stared up at the ceiling lost in Nona Land.

When Shucks left Guthrie's, he felt exhilarated. Working on assignment with Sam and Travis generated a new feeling of competence and confidence in his job that he'd never felt before. But then when they invited him to dinner and shared personal feelings with him, his spirits were elevated to heights he hadn't experienced since joining the Dare County Sheriff's Department. So what should Shucks do with this newly found confidence? Shucks did what he always did when he was too keyed up to go home to his small, quiet room above Mrs. Johnnie Lowe's garage. He flipped the left turn signal of his car, waited for the on-coming traffic to pass, and turned into the parking lot of the Dare County Justice Center.

Without the usual hubbub of daily law enforcement activities, the building was unnaturally quiet...almost macabre. Shucks stopped before several tall metal file cabinets. He check the labels on each drawer...A-B, C-D. He rolled open the second drawer. Davis...,Day,....Drane. He removed the voluminous folder, stuck it under his arm, closed the drawer and headed for his desk. Shucks' heels clicked sharply against the floor as he made his way through a large austere room partitioned by small cubicles each equipped with a metal desk, a PC, a swivel chair, and one four-drawer filing cabinet.

Shucks sat down at his desk, opened the bulky file folder, covered with greasy finger prints and other unidentifiable smudges, and began to sort through the criminal life of Drane. Maynard Dwayne Drane, born 1952, Kitty Hawk, North Carolina, name of father, name of mother, name of wife, no children. It was indicated that Drane had a juvenile record. Juvenile records were kept in another file, so Shucks made a note to pull it later. Next, he examined the cover sheet that indexed each charge the Dare County Sheriff's office made against him. June 3, 1964, petty theft, probation; October 5, 1966 car theft, charges dropped; February 14, 1969, DUI, 30 hours community service; July 6, 1969, assault and battery, charges dropped; November 24, 1972, DUI, repeat, 30 days in county jail; January 3, 1975, sale of untaxed alcohol, dismissed; February 15, 1978, drunk and disorderly, five hundred dollar fine and seven days in jail; January 1, 1979, extortion, charges dropped; January 30, 1981, auto theft grand, charges dropped; December 23, 1981, disturbing the peace, $300 fine; May 12, 1982, possession of moonshine, one year probation; March 16, 1984, petty theft, charges dropped. Shucks wondered at all the dropped charges. And then nothing until 1992 when the offenses began again. Shucks stopped and ran through the dates again. Since he was twelve years old, Maynard D. Drane had consistently run afoul of the law. Why this lapse of eight years in which he appeared to go straight? Shucks drummed his pencil on the desk, bounced his foot up and down nervously, and stared into space. Then he flipped back to that personal data sheet and noted that Maynard and Eve Drane married January 1, 1985.

"He must have tried to play it straight for a while after the wedding," Shucks said aloud.

On a separate sheet, Shucks found a record of domestic disturbance calls made to Nags Head Police. It included arrests and restraining orders against Drane for charges ranging from disturbing the peace to assault and battery.

Shucks began to organize the evidence sheets according to specific incidences. Soon stacks of papers covered his desk, and sheets cascaded to the floor. Shucks was so absorbed in his research that he didn't notice the officer standing at the opening to his cubicle blowing into a Styrofoam cup filled with something hot and steaming.

"Hey, Shucks you looking to break the big one tonight?" the officer taunted.

"Don't bother me, Clelon. I'm busy," Shucks said not looking up from his desk.

The officer grinned, shook his head, blew into his cup again, and sauntered down the hallway, leaving the sound of laughter in his wake. In the distance Shucks could hear the banter, "Hey, Marty. You guys be careful not to disturb old Shucks tonight. He's working on a big one." Laughter erupted and echoed through the cavernous room.

Shucks tried to ignore the ridicule. He thought, "Just wait till we crack ole Maynard Dwayne Drane's murder. Me, and Sam, and Travis. Travis…Think I'll try calling him Trav. That's what Sam calls him sometime. Wonder how Travis would feel about that? I'll try that out tomorrow. 'Hey, Trav. What's up?' Yeah, sounds good. Those creeps down the hall don't know nothing."

The piercing ring of the phone interrupted Shucks thoughts. He snatched the receiver and barked, "Okay, you creeps, cut it out. Some of us got more to do than sit around all night drinking coffee and thinking up monkeyshines to pull on other…"

An earsplitting voice shouted into his phone causing Shucks to jerk the receiver away from his ear. "Nona. Nona, is that you?"

Profanity followed sarcasm and Shucks took on a defensive demeanor. "Now, Nona, you've got no cause to talk to me like that. I ain't done nothing to you."

The harsh voice mellowed, and Shucks listened intently. Finally he interrupted and said, "Well, are you alright, Nona? You sure?"

Shucks listened purposefully. "Sure I'll be right there. Now tell me again exactly where you are?"

Shucks felt euphoric. Could the day get any better? First, dinner with Trav and Sam. Then he was taken into their confidences. Now, the gorgeous, spirited, Nona asked him…yes, HIM, for help. No, it couldn't possibly get any better than this.

"Now, stay where you're at, Nona. Yes, yes, I know exactly where that is. Now you stay put," he repeated, "I'll be there before you know it. And stay calm. Just stay calm," he said excitedly. He slammed down the phone, pushed his chair away from his desk forcefully, and barely avoided being dumped onto the floor.

THURSDAY

Travis slept erratically. Something hiding in his subconscious ate away at his composure and robbed him of sleep. The illuminated digital clock finally clicked up a five. Travis threw back the sheet, pulled on a pair of swimming trunks and a white tee-shirt, found his running shoes, and headed for the door.

He slipped off the chain, released the deadbolt, and slowly, quietly opened the door.

A fine mist like cotton hovered above the parking lot. He climbed out of the mist, up the small dune that was constructed to protect the motel property, and down the slope to the beach. The sun rose out of the east like a spectacular rosy sphere igniting the horizon and turning the ocean a brilliant pink.

Travis decided to run to the pier and back…about three miles. He jogged slowly at first, his shoes digging into the sand causing him to use muscles that he hadn't used in a while. He gradually increased his speed, and by the time he reached the pier his tee shirt stuck to his chest and his hair was matted by perspiration. Then he turned, retraced his steps to the Sand Trap, and gradually began to slow down.

A cold front was moving in and the air became cool and crisp. A storm was headed up from the south, and in the distance, Travis could see rain falling through the early morning sunlight. He raced toward the rain. He began to increase instead or lessen his speed. Closer and closer he came to the rain. Now he was breathing heavily and welcoming cool air into his parched lungs. He breathed deeper and deeper. Then the rain pelted him, first gently then savagely. The cold air, the rain, the released energy…and suddenly it happened. He remembered. Remembered what had been nagging him every since the night Maynard Dwayne Drane was found murdered on the beach.

Travis reached the dune protecting the Sand Trap motel. He took the dune in a few vaults, raced through the parking lot, threw open the door, and yelled breathlessly, "Sam….Sam….wake up. I know what it is. I remember what's wrong with the picture."

Sam bolted out of his bed. He didn't know whether to reach for his gun or slug the person who woke him so abruptly.

"What the hell?" he said.

"Sam, Sam guess what…" Travis said giving himself an opportunity to breath.

"Guess what? Well, I guess I won't have to go the bathroom to take a pee," he said. "What's the matter with you man? You want to get yourself shot?"

Travis flopped on the side of his bed, took slow, deep breaths, and allowed his heart to gear down. Finally he said hoarsely, "Sam, I finally remembered what's been gnawing at me about Shucks. Remember the night of the murder when we were talking to the kids who discovered Drane's body. They'd moved over against the dune, as far away from the body as they could without leaving the area."

"Yeah, they'd been told not to leave," said Sam trying to keep things clear.

"Yes, I know," said Travis, "but while we were questioning them, I remember stepping on something that shouldn't have been there."

"You gonna tell me you stepped in dog shit?" Even under these circumstances Sam couldn't resist.

"Come on, Sam," Travis said irritably. "I remember stepping on something that crunched. When I looked down, there was a pile of peanut shells."

Travis paused to give emphasis to what he'd said. Then he continued, "And when I asked the kids if any other police officer had been up there with them they said only Dicky to bring them coffee."

Travis had Sam's attention now. He thought for a while then said, "So what you're saying is one of four things happened here. One...The kids are lying. Two...The kids were eating unshelled peanuts and dropping the shucks on the ground. Three...Dicky was eating unshelled peanuts and dropping the shucks on the ground. Four...Shucks was eating unshelled peanuts, on the scene BEFORE the kids discovered the body."

As always, Sam was quick. Travis simply said, "You want to figure the odds on each of those scenarios?"

CHAPTER 18

Travis and Sam arrived at the Justice Center before things swung into high gear. They noticed that Shucks' car was in its usual parking place, and Sam wondered aloud if he'd even gone home the night before. The sheriff's parking place was occupied and right beside of his car was Nona Godette's car.

Travis said, "Looks like everyone whose attending the meeting is already here."

Sam looked towards the place reserved for Doc. "Doc's late," he said.

"He's not late. The rest of us are early," said Travis.

They entered the building and the duty officer said, "How you doing Travis?"

"Good, Willard," said Travis.

Willard said, "Sam, Shucks says he needs to see you before the meeting starts. He's down in his office."

"Thanks, Willard," said Sam. "I'll grab a coffee and head on down there."

Travis and Sam stopped at the giant sized aluminum coffee maker, chose the large-size cup, filled it with the thick black brew, and ignored the creamer and sugar. "I'll find Caffy while you go to see Shucks," said Travis.

"Right," said Sam heading towards Shucks' cubicle.

When Sam entered the cubicle, he found Shucks sitting behind a desk the top hidden beneath stacks of paper.

"Whoa, Shucks," said Sam. "Don't strike a match with all that paper laying around or the place will go up in smoke."

"Hey, Sam. Glad you caught me before the meeting. Got something to tell you. Pull that chair up real close and sit down," Shucks said conspiratorially.

Believing that Shucks was off on some hair-brained idea, Sam decided to humor him, so he pulled the chair close to Shucks, put his arm on the desk, and bent in real close. "What's up, Shucks?" he whispered.

"Sam, last night after we left Guthrie's I decided to come back here and check out Maynard Dwayne Drane's jacket. I wasn't here long before I got an urgent call," said Shucks.

Sam continued to play along. "An urgent call to a sheriff's office?" said Sam. "You think that's unusual, Shucks?" he said.

"I think this urgent call was unusual, yes," said Shucks.

Sam grinned, "Well, tell me what was so unusual about it."

"What was unusual was that the call was from Nona, Sam," said Shucks. "Nona was in trouble."

Sam immediately looked grave. "What happened, Shucks?" his voice hoarse.

Shucks told Sam he'd received a phone call from Nona and she was 'mad as a wet hen'. She told him she was not on police business, but was stranded, and needed someone to pick her up. He told Sam that she hadn't shared the particulars of her ordeal, but she had demonstrated her knowledge of dock-side profanity and shared her opinion of low-life males who have only one thing in mind...getting a woman on her back.

"Then she said this strange thing, Sam," said Shucks. "She said 'well, I showed him his back'. That's what she said. 'I showed him his back'," Shucks repeated. "I sure can't swear by it, but I think Chuckie Ryan had something to do with Nona's ordeal."

"And I think you're right, good buddy," said Sam slapping Shucks on the back. Sam stood and began to pace back and forth.

"Good buddy. Sam called me good buddy," thought Shucks. "This just keeps getting better and better."

Then Shucks said, "Sam, you won't tell Nona I told you about this will you? Not that she swore me to secrecy, but I don't want her to think I've been talking about her behind her back. Know what I mean?"

Sam stopped pacing and looked at Shucks. "I know what you mean. And you're right. I don't want her to know that I know, anyway," said Sam. "But I'm sure glad you told me. Thanks."

"That's what friends are for, good buddy," said Shucks. He thought that sounded okay.

"See you at the meeting," said Sam, and he hurried off to find Travis.

Travis was sitting in the sheriff's office reading the Raleigh News and

Observer. He looked up, snapped the paper, and turned to the next page.

"Find the sheriff?" asked Sam.

"He's in the can," said Travis. "What did Shucks want?"

Sam glanced down the hall. Caffy and Nona Godette were walking down the hall balancing cups of hot coffee. Nona was laughing for some unknown reason, and Caffy had a scowl on his face.

"Trav," said Sam. "Don't say anything to Caffy about the peanut shucks at the murder scene just yet."

"Why not?" Travis asked in a surprised voice.

"Tell you later. Just hold off," Sam faced the door, smiled, and said, "Good morning, Sheriff Caffy. Morning Officer Godette."

"Morning yourself, Sam...Travis. Where's the hell's the rest of the crew? Doc, his man...what's his name, and Shucks. Where the hell is Shucks?" said Caffy.

"I'm here, Sheriff," said Shuck scurrying into the sheriff's office. "Just going through..."

"Well, least wise you're here," interrupted the sheriff. "Now if the Doc's spirit will ever move him, maybe we can get this show on the road."

"Here, sheriff," said Doc, his assistant in tow. Doc ambled slowly into the office obviously not intimidated by the sheriff's brusqueness. He took his time carefully positioning his chair so he wouldn't have to move his head so much to look at each person. He continued slowly, "You know, sheriff, keep going off over little things like this, and one of these days, you're gonna stub your toe and have a heart attack."

"Yeah, yeah, yeah," growled the sheriff. He fingered a file folder on his desk, opened it and said, "Okay, Sam, why don't you kick us off. So...how was your day?"

"Think it was better than yours," said Sam.

"That don't take much," said Caffy. "Carry on."

So Sam pulled out his small spiral notebook, flipped a few pages and began. He reported his questioning of Doo-Wop. He told them that Doo had not worked the night of the murder. He'd been at home drunk. He'd slept most of the day, then left home at 9 pm, and went to Willy Joe's Place where he continued drinking. He stayed at Willy Joe's Place till around eleven, then returned home drunk, and fell asleep until the next morning when Sam arrived at his place to interview him. The time he left for Willie Joe's and arrived back home were verified by Pop, Willie Joe, and Tess, the bartender. Sam also reported that Doo owned one gun...a twenty two rifle used for squirrel hunting. The gun was still in the house. Finally, Sam told them that Doo-Wop had reported to work last night, and appeared to be calmer, and more in control of himself.

"Huh," said the sheriff. "You check out the gun."

"No need for that, sheriff," Doc interjected. "Not if you're thinking of the murder weapon. There's no doubt about it, Drane died from a shotgun blast not from a twenty-two."

"Right," said Caffy. "What do you think, Sam?"

"I think he's straight," Sam said simply. "He had motive, sure. Drane, or at least Drane's jeep, was involved in hit/run of Short Sugar. But Doo was drunk, at home, and at Willy Joe's at the time Drane got his. And there's no shot gun connecting Doo to the crime. No, I think he's clear."

"Well, don't go writing anybody off just yet," said Caffy. "Let's keep an open mind on this one. Okay, Travis, you're on. How did the grieving widow take the news?"

Travis said, "Not too bad actually…"

"Well, I'd be suspicious if she was too grieved," scoffed Caffy. "He put her through hell and back. But, of course, that's why we've got to run a close one on her. So let's have it."

Travis began. He told them again that she had not wept for Maynard Drane. He reported that she left work a little before ten. The time was verified by a co-worker. Eve then caught a ride home with a neighbor, walked from the corner to her home, and found that her house had been burglarized. A shotgun, a twenty two, and a TV were missing. She didn't report the break-in because she claimed to have gotten no help in the past. Caffy grunted. Travis reported interviews with two of Eve's neighbors who confirmed the times she'd given him. Travis told how Eve knew that Drane had life insurance, and that she was his beneficiary. She did not, however, know that the policy lapsed or that Drane was dying of cancer.

"Alright Doc," said Caffy when Travis indicated he was through reporting. "Now you got your shotgun. You look around, Travis?"

"No, I didn't have a warrant. Besides, I went there to notify," said Travis.

"Notify and question," the sheriff elaborated.

"Yeah, notify and question," repeated Travis.

"Well, looks like we've got something here," said the sheriff. "Not quite sure what it is, but let's keep digging. Sam, I'm not ready to cut Doo loose completely yet. For one thing, that Willy Joe is a swamp rat. Now I know Pop Early, and he's alright, but he's his pop, so let's keep on him."

Then Caffy turned to Travis. "There's a lot to check with Ms. Drane, Travis. Far as I'm personally concerned, she's one fine lady. Never heard anyone say anything bad about her. But that scoundrel, Maynard Dwayne Drane, was a mean man. He put her through years of hell. And she's right. We didn't do much. The public's always shocked at how little we can do before the criminal acts. But as far as this case is concerned, that's another kettle of fish. She certainly had reason and motive to act against him. I want to know more about those missing guns."

They sat silently for a while. Finally Doc moved to the front of his chair and said, "Well, Sheriff, it's all interesting, but nothing I've heard here this morning changes my findings. My report stands as is. Sheriff, if you need any other lab work done, let me know. But right now, I got a date with an old man just waiting to have his funeral. By the way, Travis, those fingerprints of Eve Drane's neighbor checked out okay."

"Thanks, Doc," said Caffy. "Let's ponder the situation, and come in here at three and talk about where to go now. So since there's nothing else to discuss we'll just..."

"Sheriff, sheriff," said Shucks, his voice cracking. The sheriff turned towards him wearily. "I been checking into the victim here. Looking into Maynard Dwayne Drane, his criminal record and all. And I ran across something you might want checked out."

"Okay, well go on, Shucks. Get to it," said Caffy testily.

Shucks continued this time with more confidence. "Last night Sam, Trav, and I discussed the fact that Drane was a scuba diver."

Sam glanced at Nona. Her eyes registered surprise, and her jaw dropped slightly.

"Yes, sir," said Shucks gaining even more confidence when he realized that the sheriff looked interested in this new information. "Well, I learned that Drane wasn't just somebody out for a Sunday afternoon dive. Drane was an expert diver. In fact he was certified to teach scuba diving and worked for short periods of time at several diving schools. His last job was over here at the White Water Scuba Diving School in Nags Head. He took tourists who were qualified divers out to explore the shipwrecks. Now I don't know why he couldn't keep a job, or why he worked at so many places, but I do know that at the time Drane was murdered, he was taking tourists out to explore the wrecks."

Sheriff Caffy stared. He was speechless. Finally he said, "Well, I be damned, Officer. You may just have stumbled onto something. How'd you come up with this?"

"Just phone calls and such," Shucks said. Then trying to sound professional he added, "I try to keep some sources for cases like this."

Caffy continued to stare. Then he repeated, "Well, I be damned." After a few minutes he roused himself, looked at Sam and Travis and said, "You three discovered this scuba connection last night?"

Sam wanted to give Shucks as much credit as possible. "Shucks is the one who told us about it. And you know the devil's in the detail, and Shucks is the one who dug up the details…with his sources and all."

"Okay," Caffy said rubbing his hands together. "How 'bout you three getting on this scuba slant. I don't know how that could tie into moonshine or drugs, but let's check it out."

"You'd be surprised," said Travis. "A drug agent friend of mine told me that one time some dope smugglers floated a bunch of coke in on the tide. It was wrapped in plastic and taped on an inner tube."

The men stood to leave. Then Nona said, "Sheriff, I'd like to tag along with them. I'm real interested in this scuba diving angle."

"Up to these three. Far as I'm concerned, it's okay," said the Sheriff.

"Okay by me," said Travis. "Shucks?"

"Sure," said Shucks. He had arrived. Trav even asked for his opinion.

Sam grinned and moved in close to Nona. He said, "I'd love to work more closely with Nona. In fact, the closer the better."

Travis, Shucks, and Nona rolled their eyes and walked out of the room.

CHAPTER 19

Travis, Shucks, Nona, and Sam drove to the Dairy Queen where they washed down hot dogs, nachos, and French fries with large diet cokes.

"So," said Travis, "what are we looking for at the White Water Scuba Diving School?"

Sam stuffed a handful of French fries in his mouth, began to chew, and without swallowing mumbled, "Well....I'd say we look for anybody who had a connection with Maynard Drane. Now that could be his employer or a friend."

"I don't know, Sam," said Shucks. "Drane seemed to be pretty much of a loner. Not many friends. Think most folks were scared to have anything to do with him."

"Hey, that's okay," said Sam. "Talking with his enemies might be more informative than talking with his friends."

"Know your friends well, but know your enemies better," Nona said whimsically.

"Huh?" said Sam.

"Oh, nothing," said Nona. "Just something daddy used to tell me."

"Now that's insightful," Sam said staring at Nona judiciously.

"Okay," said Travis. "Stay focused."

They left the Dairy Queen parking lot, followed highway 158 to the next traffic light, then turned right to Virginia Dare Trail. The corner building was constructed of concrete blocks painted blue, and outside a large white sign with blue letters read White Water Scuba Diving School. There was only one car in the parking lot, a 2001 white Jaguar. They exited the patrol car and looked through the large front window. A tall, tan, muscular man with slightly graying brown hair scrutinized them over wire framed half-glasses. They walked to the entrance and opened the door. A bell attached to the door frame shook, and before it stopped jingling, a voice said, "Good Morning, officers. Interested in some scuba diving lessons?"

The voice was one of authority…strong, loud, quick, and confident. The four officers didn't answer immediately but peered painstakingly around the sparsely furnished room. Metal desks outfitted with PCs, modems, scanners, telephones, and wire baskets spilling over with sheets of paper and colorful brochures stood at each end of the room. A long, centrally located worktable held a variety of brochures, applications, discount coupons, and at one end a fax machine. The walls were plastered with sea charts and maps of the Outer Banks. A sign that read Diving Equipment was posted over the entrance to a large room where tanks, snorkels, wet suits, flippers, and all sorts of diving equipment were displayed for sale.

"I'm Travis White, ABC officer, and this is my partner, Sam Barnett. This here is Officers Nona Godette and Shucks Twine."

The man looked puzzled and said, "ABC? What's that?"

Sam said, "Alcohol Beverage Control, sir."

The man smiled and said, "Well then you've got the wrong place. I don't sell liquor…or any kind of alcohol…here."

"That's not why we're here," said Sam. "Sorry, we didn't get your name."

"I'm Jay Reynolds, instructor and owner of this place," he said. "Well, come on in. If you're not here for lessons, how can I possibly help you?"

Shucks spoke up. "Mr. Reynolds, we're making inquiries about one of your employees, Maynard Dwayne Drane. What can you tell us about him?" Sam and Travis were surprised to hear Shucks speak so self confidently.

Mr. Jay Reynolds on the other hand seemed to lose his confidence. He stammered, "Maynard Dwayne Drane? He's not one of my employees. I fired him outright a month ago."

"Wasn't his work competent?" asked Nona.

"Absolutely," said Reynolds. "As a matter of fact, he's the best diving instructor I ever had. And he got along real well with the customers…especially the women."

"Then why did you fire him?" asked Sam.

"A couple of reasons. One is because he's a loose cannon. He took too many risks, and when you run an outfit like this you need prudent people working for you. One bad accident is all it would take to put a diving school like mine out of business. So, I let him go."

"You said a *couple* of reasons," said Shucks, not missing a beat. "What's the other reason?"

Now Reynolds really appeared apprehensive. "The other reason I fired him was because he was selling moonshine. I guess that's why you're here, huh?" he said looking at Travis and Sam.

"Tell us about the moonshine," said Travis.

"Well, as I said, at first I thought I'd found a real winner. Then this summer I started getting some kids in for lessons. I noticed they hung around the parking lot with Maynard after they finished their lessons. I didn't think anything of it at first, then one day I saw him pass a paper bag to one of the kids, and the kid handed him money. The first thing I thought of was drugs, and I confronted Drane about it right away."

"What did he say?" asked Sam.

"Well, he passed it off with a joke when I asked him about selling drugs to the kids. He said 'Jay, I swear to you on a stack of bibles, I ain't never sold no drugs in my whole life'," Jay Reynolds paused and shook his head.

"What then?" asked Nona.

"He played off this conversation for several days. Guess he was trying to make his claim more believable by joking about it. He went around saying things like. 'Ole Jay thinks I'm a drug dealer don't you Jay? Think I look like a druggy?' and he's affect this twisted stance and put on a stupid facial expression, and we'd all laugh and that would be the end of it for awhile. Then one day, Maynard showed up drunk. At first I couldn't believe it, but you could smell it all the way across the room. Fired him on the spot. Gerald here took his class and that was the last time I saw Maynard Dwayne Drane."

"How did you find out it was bootleg whiskey Drane sold to the kids?" asked Travis.

"Simple," said Jay Reynolds. "Gerald asked the kids. They admitted it and laughed about it like there's nothing wrong with buying moonshine. They bought it by the jar…you know a canning jar. By the way, officers, why in the world would anybody buy that stuff? You wouldn't know what in the world went into it."

"The kids probably bought it because they're under age and can't buy alcohol legally," said Sam.

"You're not going to take the names of my customers are you? That would be bad for business. Besides the kids are out-of-staters, and I already fired Drane," said Jay Reynolds.

"No, we won't take those names. The buy would be here-say. The kids told Gerald and Gerald told you. No hard evidence. Besides, we can't arrest Maynard Dwayne Drane now anyway," said Sam.

"Why not?" asked Jay Reynolds.

"We can't arrest Maynard Dwayne Drane because Drane is dead," said Sam. The four officers watched closely as Jay Reynolds face registered genuine shock.

After a few minutes of silence, Nona asked, "Mr. Reynolds, did Drane have one place in particular that he liked to dive? A place he used regularly?"

Reynolds recovered, but when he spoke his voice sounded gravelly, dry. "Sure. Maynard liked to dive out from the Bladen Street Public Beach Access. There's a couple of wrecks out there real close to the beach and easy to reach. Took his students there all the time."

Nona flinched.

"Thanks for your help, Mr. Reynolds," said Travis, and he extended his hand. Jay Reynolds shook his hand vigorously and then extended a hand to each of the others in turn. As he'd shook the last hand he said, "By the way, how did Maynard die?"

"Maynard Dwayne Drane was murdered, Mr. Reynolds," Shucks said dramatically.

Jay Reynolds's hand covered his mouth and stifled a gasp.

The patrol car pulled into the parking lot at the Bladen Street Public Beach Access. Nona shivered as she stepped onto the same pavement she'd stormed across the night before, leaving Chuckie Ryan to brush the sand from his clothes and rub his wounded pride.

"What a jerk," she thought. But she was really angry at herself. What a fool she'd been. Showing off with the new guy on the beach. Parading Chuckie around in front of Sam and Travis like some kind of trophy. Making an absolute ass of herself.

They walked across the pavement towards the steps leading to the beach. Travis spotted the historical plaques posted in the gazebo.

"Hey, Sam, let's take a look at this before we go down to the beach," Travis said and walked up the steps of the gazebo. Sam followed him.

Nona continued walking towards the beach. "I've read all that before. I'm going on down to the beach," she said.

Shucks said, "Me, too. I'm going with Nona."

Sam and Travis began to read the information posted by the National Parks Service about the two shipwrecks just beyond the breakers at this point. "In the early morning of November 24, 1877, the Huron a U.S. man-of-war steamer displacing 541 tons, ran aground just north of Jockeys Ridge. Of the 103 people on board, 98 perished making it one of the worst shipwrecks on the Atlantic Coast. The tragedy of the wreck was compounded by two factors. The first was the close proximity of the wreck to the shore. The Huron lays only 250 yards from the beach in 25 feet of water raising the question why the crew didn't simply swim to shore. The second bit of tragic irony was that there was a nearby life-saving station. But it was deserted because the active service season had not begun. Much of the Huron wreck is still intact today making it a favorite wreck for scuba divers to explore, and at times parts of the ship's hull can be seen from the beach. Buoys mark the eternal resting place of the ship.

"Not far from the Huron, another ship wrecked just 150 yards offshore. It was a tugboat, the Explorer. It sunk in December 1919 in only about 20 feet of water. This wreck is seldom visited by divers, because most of it is covered with sand."

"Fascinating," said Travis. "These are the wrecks that Shucks told us about."

"Yeah, you know that guy continues to surprise me," said Sam.

"By the way, Sam, you didn't tell me why I should hold off on telling Caffy about the peanut shucks on the beach and Shucks patrolling Drane's neighborhood the night of the murder," said Travis.

"Later, Trav" said Sam. "I'm not sure I know myself."

Travis looked puzzled. "Come on, let's go down to the beach," said Sam.

While Sam and Travis read the historical information posted at the gazebo, Shucks joined Nona at the beach, and they stood looking out on the ocean. The ocean took on a rosy hue as twilight settled. Seagulls circled above them hoping for an evening handout, and a little three-toed bird on long skinny legs chased in and out of the surf searching for food the retreating waves left behind.

"Shucks, this is where I popped Chuckie Ryan last night...well, not down here on the beach but up at the gazebo."

"Nona, now you got to tell Sam and Travis about that," said Shucks, not telling her that he'd already snitched to Sam.

"How can I do that? I feel like such a fool," said Nona. "You see, I practically forced Chuckie to bring me here."

"You what?" said Shucks.

"I practically forced him to bring me here," she repeated and then continued hesitantly, "I went to Guthrie's expecting to spend the evening with Chuckie. As I walked in, I saw him at the bar talking to a stranger. I crept up quietly intending to surprise him."

"Well did you? Surprise him that is," prompted Shucks.

"Yes and no, I suppose," said Nona. "As I reached the bar, I heard Chuckie say something like 'Don't worry, I'll be down at the Bladen Street Beach Access on time'. Thinking that they were planning a beach party, I stepped up and said, 'Sounds like a party going on. Thanks I'd love to come'."

"What did Chuckie say?" asked Shucks.

"What could he say? He looked shocked, of course, then he recovered, put his arm around my shoulder and said, 'By all means. It wouldn't be a party without Nona.' The guy he was talking to just faded."

"But Nona, if Chuckie were up to something illegal, why would he invite you to be there when it went down?"

"What I think is that he never intended that I would stay. He made sure I'd be gone by then," she said.

"How could he be sure?" asked Shucks.

"By behaving like the most loathsome, disgusting, low-life of a slime ball I've ever come in contact with. He knew I wouldn't tolerate his disgusting moves. He knew I'd bolt out of there. He just didn't think I'd look back at the beach," her face was flushed and hot.

Shucks didn't like seeing Nona like this. He glanced in the direction of the gazebo and saw Travis and Sam coming down the steps.

"Nona, you got to tell them," Shucks repeated.

"Shucks, there's something else I didn't tell you," Nona said.

"Well, hurry up," urged Shucks. "Go on."

"As I was crossing the parking lot I looked back at Chuckie. He got up, brushed himself off, and then something down at the beach caught his eye. He stood there looking out into the surf, and then I saw what he was staring at. A light flashed right out there," Nona said pointing to the buoys.

"A light?" said Shucks. "What kind of light?"

"Oh, I don't know. Probably a flashlight or something like that," she said. "Anyway the flashes were in a certain sequence, like a code."

"How do you know it wasn't some fool kids diving at night?" asked Shucks.

"I don't think so," said Nona. "You see, Chuckie ran back to his car, got a flashlight, went back to the beach, and returned the signal. Then you drove up and I split."

"Now it still could have been some fool diving at night, but you've got to tell Travis and Sam anyway. You can't let your embarrassment interfere with an investigation. When you're part of a team, Nona, you can't keep secrets from your partners," Shucks repeated the line that Sam and Travis used on him at the hospital.

At this point, Travis and Sam walked up. "Just take a look at those buoys. They look close enough to wade out to," Travis said pointing to two buoys that looked like white Clorox bottles bobbing just off shore.

"I see what's meant by the irony of the tragedy now. It's incredible that so many people could die so close to shore," said Sam.

The four officers stood silently, almost reverently, looking out at the buoys that marked the watery graves of the 98 seamen.

Finally Shucks broke the silence. "Sam and Trav," he said. "Nona's got something to tell you."

CHAPTER 20

They drove back to the Dare County Justice Center in silence. Nona was embarrassed at her disclosure that Chuckie Ryan was a bona fide creep and probably a criminal. Shucks was relieved that he hadn't made any blunders while interviewing the owner of the White Water Scuba Diving School and felt genuinely pleased he'd played a part in setting the record straight between Nona and the Seaboard boys. Travis mulled over the connection between Maynard Dwayne Drane, the White Water Scuba Diving School, Chuckie Ryan, moonshine, and the signal from the beach. And Sam's mind darted back and forth between Nona and Drane, Nona and Shucks, Nona and moonshine, Nona and Chuckie Ryan, Nona and signals on the beach, and Nona and Nona and Nona.

They pulled into the parking lot at Dare County Justice Center. As they headed towards the building, Travis said, "Nona, don't worry about Chuckie Ryan. You're not the first person to get broadsided in an investigation. The important thing is we recovered."

"Trav's right, Nona," said Sam. "Without your connection to Ryan, we'd never know about the beach signal thing. Granted we don't know where that'll go, if anywhere, but we sure need to check it out," said Sam.

"Sam's right, Nona," added Shucks. "And if you think there's something peculiar about those signals, then I do, too. I trust your judgment."

"Thanks, guys," said Nona. "I admit that I feel naive. You'd think a law enforcement officer would do a better job of recognizing such a scoundrel."

As they entered the building, a derisive voice said, "Well, lookee here. Here come de posse."

"Shut up, Clelon," said Shucks. Then to the others he muttered, "That

121

guy'll never grow up." Clelon grinned, and he and two other men walked out the front door.

Sam and Travis laughed and headed to the sheriff's office.

Caffy was shuffling through stacks of papers so thick that it was impossible to see the top of his desk. He stopped what he was doing, looked up, and said, "Well, the prodigals have returned. Learn anything down at the diving school?"

They sat. "Sure," said Sam. "We learned a lot. Ended up with more questions than answers though."

Travis gave Caffy the rundown on their trip to the school. He explained that Drane was an expert diver, that he instructed at White Water Scuba Diving School, and that he was fired for selling moonshine to kids. He reported that no one at the school had seen him since he was fired, that flashlight signals were spotted from Drane's favorite diving spot on the beach, and that Chuckie Ryan returned those signals. He did not mention that Nona was the one who witnessed the signals.

"Who saw the flashlight signal?" asked the sheriff.

The men waited for Nona to answer this one. "I did Sheriff," said Nona. "I was with Chuck Ryan at the beach, and as I walked away, I saw the light signals. He signaled back."

"He know you saw him?" Caffy asked.

"No, I'm pretty sure he doesn't," said Nona.

"We might be able to use that," he said. Nona breathed a sigh of relief when the sheriff didn't press further about why she was at the beach with Chuckie and why she left without him.

"Well, I haven't been sitting on my hands back here," said the sheriff rubbing his rough hands together.

"Don't keep us in suspense, sheriff," said Shucks. "What's up?"

The sheriff was surprised, yet pleased, that Shucks was becoming more outspoken. "Well, I'll tell you, Officer" Cafffy said. "Those stolen guns down at Eve Drane's house kept gnawing at me. Couldn't get pass the fact that one of the supposedly stolen guns was a shotgun, and the murder weapon was a shotgun. Never mind the fact that that little old gal has plenty of reasons to want to see Maynard Dwayne Drane dead."

"So, what happened?" asked Travis anxiously.

"What happened is that I got a search warrant and sent some men out there to search the place. When they come back here, I want to know for sure one way or the other if that shotgun's in her house." The sheriff seemed pleased with himself.

122

No one spoke. The sheriff looked disappointed. "Well," said Nona, "if there's nothing else right now, I have a ton of paper work to do." She stood and left the room.

"Me, too," said Travis. "Not that I have paper work, but I think Sam and I should call in a report ." And he quickly followed Nona.

The sheriff looked baffled. "What'd I do?" he asked. "Suddenly everybody's in a hurry to get outta my office. I got B.O. or something?"

Sam laughed nervously, "Naw, Sheriff, it's just that this is unfolding awfully fast. Guess it's hard to keep up."

"Huh," said the sheriff. Sam and Shucks stood and started to walk out. "Wait a minute, you two. What was Nona doing with Chuckie Ryan down at the beach at night?"

Sam and Shucks turned, their mouths open.

"And why did she leave the beach by herself?" he added.

"Why don't you ask her about this, sheriff?" asked Shucks.

"'Cause I'm asking you," said Caffy. Sam and Shucks walked back to their chairs and sat down.

"Well it's like this…." Sam began.

Travis tore across the Washington Baum Bridge. The air smelled of salt and fish and rain. A light drizzle peppered his windshield and a fine multicolored mist emanated from the hot asphalt. He stopped for a traffic light on highway 158 and waited as fishermen with long, disappointed faces deserted their beach posts and drove home in SUV's carrying empty coolers and idle fishing rods that wiggled uselessly in their spikes. He turned onto Acres View, and meandered back into the subdivision until he reached Eve Drane's driveway. He pulled in and stopped in front of the simple, peaceful bungalow.

The activity taking place inside, however, was anything but peaceful. A patrol car with Dare County Sheriff's Department on the side was parked on the grass in deep ruts on the lawn. A Nags Head Police Department car was beside it. The front door to the house was wide open. Eve Drane sat on the front steps in the drizzle, her wet hair pasted tightly against her head, her face pale and slack. Misha's soaked furry white head lay despondently on her lap his brown eyes looking up at her sad and confused. He raised his head as Travis pulled up in the driveway. The tips of his white fur were sprinkled with droplets of rain that looked like tiny crystals of sleet. He recognized Travis, immediately beamed the famous Sammy smile, and bounded toward his friend.

Travis leapt from of his jeep, patted Misha, and rushed to the porch. "Eve," he said, "are you okay?"

Eve raised her tear-streaked face, shook her head, and nodded in the direction of the open door. From inside Travis heard banging and thrashing about. He took the steps in one stride and rushed into the house. There was complete chaos inside. Cushions from chairs and sofas were scattered on the floor, drawers were open and contents spilled out, closet doors were open and clothes were strewn carelessly about the room, cabinets were open and pots and pans lay on the counter tops. Even a large bag of dry dog food was emptied in a pile on the kitchen floor.

"Clelon," yelled Travis. "What the hell do you think you're doing?"

Clelon turned a surprised face to Travis, but he quickly recovered and said, "What the hell do you think I'm doing, Travis? I'm conducting a search of these premises. Object of interest being one shotgun alleged to have been stolen. And I repeat….alleged."

"And you think you're gonna find a shotgun in the kitchen drawers?" Travis said. "Is this mess necessary?"

"But out, Travis," said Clelon. "This ain't none of your business. Sheriff sent me out here, and I'm merely doing my job. So you just back off."

Travis walked across the room and stared down at a pile of lacey undergarments that lay exposed in a heap on the floor. "And this?" he asked, a tinge of disgust in his voice.

Clelon smirked and said. "That drawer might be big enough to hide a shotgun."

Travis shook his head and said, "Or not."

Clelon's neck was red and blue veins protruded from his neck. "What's it to you, Travis? You ain't got no cause to come in here criticizing my procedures. What the hell difference does it make to you how I do the job?"

A rustling sound caused the men to turn in the direction of the doorway. They turned to see Eve. One hand on the doorframe steadied her and the other grasped Misha's collar that was almost hidden by his thick white coat. Rain dripped from his fur creating puddles on the muddy wooden floor. Suddenly the dog began to shake. First slowly, then vigorously, flinging water on the walls, the furniture, the mess on the floor, and onto the clean, freshly pressed uniforms of the officers.

"Damn! Get that mutt outta here," Clelon barked. "Before I shoot him."

Travis stepped in front of Misha. "The dog stays, Clelon. It's his territory."

Clelon and the other officers used handkerchiefs and their shirtsleeves to dry their face and arms. "Well, we're through anyway. Let's get outta here men."

Then Clelon turned to Travis and said, "Just cause we didn't find the shotgun tonight don't mean she don't know where it is. Can't live with a toad like Drane for over ten years and not get warts." Then he looked at Eve and said, "See you later, Missy."

Travis started across the room, fury exuded from his face. One of the Nags Head Policeman reached out and grabbed his arm. "Let it go, Travis," he said. "It ain't worth it, buddy."

Travis stopped, looked at Clelon, breathed heavily and said, "Clelon, you stepped over the line here today. You were the officer in charge, and you stepped over the line. Don't think I won't report this."

Clelon grinned wickedly, looked at Eve and let his eyes wander slowly up and down her body. "Well, Travis, old buddy, maybe you been stepping over the line a little bit yourself."

Travis started to lunge, but the policeman held his arm tightly. "He ain't worth it, Travis. I tell you he ain't worth it."

Clelon turned and sauntered out of the room.

Eve and Travis stood motionless and listened as car engines started. One car spun its wheel on the grass, and they could hear mud and sand being tossed up as the ruts on the lawn dug deeper into the earth. Then they heard the sound of pebbles striking the sides and bottom of the car as it raced down the driveway and burned rubber on the street.

Eve remained motionless at the door. Her hair was soaking wet and rivulets of rain streamed down her forehead and onto her shoulders. Her shirt stuck to her body as transparent as a thin wet tissue and her jeans were so wet that they looked black instead of blue. She began to shake, first slightly, then uncontrollably.

Travis moved to her quickly and gently led her inside, kicking the door closed with his foot as if trying to shut out the maliciousness that occurred there. He led her to a chair in the kitchen and had her sit down. She did not speak. "Stay here," Travis said.

In the bathroom he found that the clothes in the hamper were dumped in the middle of the floor, but fresh towels still hung on the rack. He snatched two big ones and hurried back to the kitchen. He didn't say anything as he gently dried her hair, her face, her shoulders, and finally her legs and feet. He draped the second towel around her, and said, "I'll heat some water."

He found the teapot amongst the pots and pans on the floor, filled it with water and began to search for tea amidst the clutter of packaged foods and canned goods on the kitchen counter. Then as he waited for the water to boil, he began to place things back in cupboards.

"I don't know where you keep things, Eve," Travis rambled on, "but clearing the floor and counter tops may help a little."

The teapot whistled and Travis put a tea bag in an oversized OBX mug and filled it with boiling water. "Here," he said and placed the steaming cup on the table. "I'm going to help you clean up this mess tonight."

Eve's eyes looked weary and frightened. "No," she whispered. "I can't. I'm just too flattened to do anything."

They heard a crunching sound and turned to see Misha eating the dry dog food that was strewn on the floor. "Poor guy," said Travis. "He doesn't know what the hell is going on," said Travis.

Eve smiled. Then she began to shake again spilling tea in her lap and on the floor and table. She began to cry. "Eve, I don't want to complicate things for you anymore than they already are. Clelon won't be coming back tonight, so maybe it'll be best if I just leave."

Her eyes were wide and frightened. "No. No, please don't leave me here tonight. I can't take anymore. I just can't take anymore," she sobbed.

Travis reached down and drew her up. He held her close and stroke her damp hair. "Shhh…" he said. "Okay. Okay. I'll hang around. But you've got to get out of those wet clothes. You go change, and I'll start a fire in the fireplace."

She walked out of the room like an obedient child. Travis discovered that a fire had already been laid in the fireplace with old newspaper, kindling, and several seasoned logs. He opened the damper, struck a match on the stone hearth, and touched the match to the dry paper. An eager flame leapt up and ignited the kindling and logs. The fire felt warm and comforting. Travis picked up cushions and a throw and placed them on the sofa. Suddenly he felt exhausted. He stared into the fire and began to do a rerun on the events of the day.

Travis heard the sound of water running and realized that Eve was taking a shower. He leaned back and let his head rest on the back of the sofa. He was tired and hungry and angry. What possessed Caffy to send a dumb slug like

Clelon to search the house of a woman who was living alone, who'd been abused by her husband for ten years, and had just identified the jerk's body. Clelon liked to control situations, and it didn't really matter to him if the object of his control was browbeaten, worn out, and all alone. In fact, this seemed to make Clelon come on stronger. The son-of- a.......

Suddenly the sound of water stopped and the house fell eerily still. Travis raised his head and stared into the fireplace. The logs snapped and cinders exploded and danced onto the stone hearth. Blue and orange flames reached upward towards the chimney where air and life and energy emanated. Then he heard the rustling sound of movement and looked towards the bedroom door. Eve was standing there like a statue in a wax museum, her expression dismal, hopeless. She wore slide-on bedroom slippers and a long blue bathrobe made of some soft snug material. Her hair was damp and neatly combed and her cheeks were flushed and hot from the steaming shower.

Travis stood and moved quickly toward her. He could smell her wet hair and the aroma of the citrus-scented shampoo she'd used. He took her hand in one hand and her elbow in the other and supported her as she walked to the sofa. Shadows from the fire danced on her face. Her blue eyes were red and swollen, and her neck was flushed and speckled with tiny red blemishes from the hot spray. Her lips were dry and cracked, and she had applied something oily to them and to a red area under her nose.

"Let me get you something hot to drink," said Travis.

"No, I don't want any more tea," she said.

"Would you like something stronger?" he asked. Then he remembered Drane's drinking problem and quickly added, "that is if you have something stronger here."

"Yes, I would, and I do. Some brandy. It was in the cabinet above the sink. I have no idea where it is now. " She spoke helplessly.

The brandy was not above the sink, but Travis found in setting in the sink under a pile of dish clothes and paper napkins. It was hopeless to look for brandy snifters, so he grabbed a couple of juice glasses and poured generous amounts of brandy into two of them. He stepped over Misha who was sprawled across the kitchen floor and walked back to the sofa. He handed a glass to Eve.

"Misha doesn't seem to be any worse for wear," said Travis. "He's out like a light."

Eve looked sadly at the sleeping dog. "He didn't know what to think of the policemen's harshness. Especially the man who appeared to be in charge.

Everybody loves Misha, and he's always been treated gently. Even Maynard liked him," she said, and then added, "but what's not to like about Misha.?"

Eve took the brandy, sipped it slowly and said, "Thanks. I'm not much of a drinker, but tonight was enough to make a Baptist preacher reach for the bottle."

"Let's not talk about that tonight, Eve. We can talk about it later," said Travis. "You'll just get all riled up and won't be able to sleep, and you're exhausted."

She took another sip of brandy, then stared at the glass, and said, "I'm not used to this, you know. But I think I'll sleep."

Travis set his glass on the table, moved forward on his seat, and said,

"Well, I guess you'd better call it a night. I got something to take care of, so I best be on my way. You gonna be okay?"

Eve suddenly bolted upright, spilled brandy on her robe, and cried in a panicky voice, "No, please don't go. Don't go. I can't stand to be alone just now." And she began to sob. Deep spastic moans rolled up from her throat, and she curled forward hiding her face in her hands.

Travis was taken aback. He wrapped her in his arms and rocked her back and forth like you would a frightened child. "Sh. Sh," he whispered and smoothed the damp hair away from her face. "I'm not going anywhere. Not yet anyway."

Travis slipped back into the seat, pulled her close to him, and cradled her head in the curve of his shoulder. She soon stopped sobbing and became incredibly still. Then she was asleep with her mouth slightly open and her hand tucked under her cheek. Occasionally her hand or leg jerked slightly, and soft cries or moans escaped from the dark stash of memories created by the events of this awful night.

Travis sat motionless, and stared wide-eyed and unblinking into the licking flames. Flames. Flames. He recalled flames...other flames. Flames that inflicted the greatest pain he'd ever endured, pain that ripped the very life and purpose out of his life. Flames that brutally introduced him to mortality and took the light of his soul and snuffed it out like a cold breath upon the flame of a candle.

All night he sat staring transfixed by the fire, and when the gray light of dawn pierced through slits of the partially-closed curtains, Travis slowly eased Eve from his shoulder, laid her on the sofa, and covered her with a throw that he found on the floor. He stood and found that his back and legs ached. He rubbed his stiff shoulder where Eve's head laid so many hours. He stoked the fire, uncovered burning embers, and added logs. Soon the logs ignited and flames leapt high. He reached toward the warmth and rubbed his hands together vigorously.

Travis turned and looked down at Eve sleeping peacefully...so delicate, so trusting, so vulnerable. Then suddenly his thoughts flashed to Ginny and to a happier, less taxing time. The emotion he felt was so strong, so real and passionate, so in the present, that Ginny might have been standing beside him. He felt that her spirit was trapped in a wrinkle of time...a specter drawing him back into a more contented, less troubled past. Sadly, Travis turned and walked quietly out of the house.

CHAPTER 21

FRIDAY

Sam cursed the alarm clock, rolled over, and looked at Travis's empty bed. "Well, well," said Sam. "Looks like old Trav got lucky."

He rolled out of bed, showered, dressed and headed out the door. His lungs stung when he inhaled the cold, salty air, and he zipped his jacket high around his neck. He quickly wiped condensation from his windshield, jumped into the Cherokee, fastened his safety belt and headed towards Don and Ollie's Place. Business was light at Don and Ollie's this morning, so Sam whipped into a space right in front of the steps and took the three risers in one jump. He sauntered into the restaurant, leaned against the checkout counter, and fixed a look on Ollie intended to melt the heart of the coldest woman. Ollie was counting back change to a customer and without missing a beat flashed Sam a grin and winked.

"Have a good day, sir," said Ollie dismissively to the departing customer. Then she grabbed a napkin wrapped around some flatware and stepped from behind the counter.

"Come on, handsome, give you the best seat in the house," she said.

Sam followed Ollie through the dining area eyeing her full, firm posterior. "You know I'll go anywhere you wanta take me, Sweetchops," said Sam flashing his famous toothy grin.

"Sam, that you trying to hit on my wife again?" a voice bawled from the kitchen.

"Sure is Don," said Sam, "and one of these days she's gonna take me up on it. Then who'll bake your biscuits?"

Ollie threw her head back and laughed. Then she slapped Sam on the shoulder and said, "Get outta here, Sam. One day some gal's gonna take you up on your offer, and it'll scare the socks off of you. Coffee?"

"Yeah." Sam said.

Ollie poured thick hot liquid into a large white mug. Sam reached for a sugar packet, tore it open, and shook the contents into the cup. He lifted the cup to his nose and breathed deeply. "Ah, smells good. You know just how I like it Ollie. Hot and sweet."

Ollie guffawed. "Just get outta here." And slapped him on the shoulder again.

Soon Don, wearing a food-stained apron, came out of the kitchen. He walked to Sam's table and set a plate of fried eggs, country ham, grits, and biscuits with white gravy on the table. Then he turned a chair around and straddled it. "So, where's the better half of the Seaboard boys?"

Sam looked real sage, raised an eyebrow, and slowly, meticulously spread butter on his hot homemade biscuits. "Oh, I reckon he's still out and about," Sam said mischievously.

Don leaned forward and opened his eyes in mock surprise. "You don't say? You mean old Travis' been out a tom-catting all night?" Then he turned toward the cash register and said in a stout voice, "Hey Ollie, guess what? Trav got laid last night."

"What you say? Well, shut my mouth," said Ollie. She threw down the wet cloth she'd been using to wipe tables, stomped across the room, and stood looking down expectantly at Sam.

Sam said, "Now did I say that? Did I say that Trav got laid? No, I didn't. I just said that he'd been out all night. Probably working some crime scene, or gathering evidence, or arresting some crook that's a threat to this peaceful, seaside community."

"Yeah, yeah, we know," said Ollie. "Who is she, Sam?"

Almost in slow motion Sam broke a piece of biscuit, used it to soak up the egg yolk on his plate, popped it in his mouth, and chewed slowly. After sufficient time had passed to peak his audience's curiosity, he said, "Well, now remember I didn't say *lay* but Trav was last seen hauling buggy down in the direction of Eve Drane's house."

"Sam, shut your mouth," bellowed Ollie slapping him on the shoulder again and chuckling unashamedly. "That just does my old heart good. She's one sweet girl, Sam. He couldn't do better if I picked her for him myself. And after all she's been through. She deserves to have a man that'll take care of her. Poor little thing."

"Listen to that drivel, Sam," said Don shaking his head. "A man has one night out with a woman, and Ollie's got him hog-tied and ready to butcher."

Sam shook his head, but Ollie would have none of it. "Now you two listen up," she said. "Trav's not been out of the barn in a long time, and he's gonna feel awkward so don't you two go to making him feel embarrassed. You hear me, Sam?"

Sam grabbed his shoulder and shied away from another possible slap. "Now would I do that, Ollie?" asked Sam standing up and tossing some bills on the table. "Besides, I didn't say *lay*."

Sam pulled into the Dare County Justice Center just as Travis was getting out of his car. Travis slammed the car door so hard that the vehicle shook. His face was pale and frozen in rage. He stomped across the parking lot and headed towards the building.

"Hey Trav, wait up," yelled Sam. Travis continued to walk. Sam ran towards him, caught his arm, and spun him around. "Trav, come on. Put it in cruise, man. Who took your last piece of gum?"

Travis stopped, shaking with anger. "That damned Clelon Purvis. I'd like to mash his potatoes. I've never known such a low-down agitator in my life…"

"Whoa, whoa there, buddy. Clelon Purvis? What in the world have you got to do with Clelon Purvis? I thought you went out to Eve Drane's place last night," Sam said.

"I did go to Eve Drane's house last night and that's where I ran into Clelon Purvis," said Travis. "He and a couple of other guys were trashing her place. And I mean trashing. There wasn't any need for that, Sam, except it made old Clelon feel like he had some kind of power over a helpless female."

"What?" said Sam. "I knew Caffy got a search warrant, but I never thought about Clelon being put in charge of a search."

"Well, he was. And he's gonna pay," Travis said starting for the building again. Sam grabbed him again and steered him towards the car. "Okay, Trav, let's go over here, sit in the car, and you tell me everything that happened. Then we'll go see Caffy, and if we don't get no satisfaction, I'll help you punch out Clelon's lights."

Travis let himself be guided towards the Cherokee, his angry subsided slowly. When Sam was there, things got clearer and problems lessened.

Travis knew they wouldn't actually 'punch out Clelon's lights', but he knew that they'd find some way to exact justice if Caffy didn't reign Clelon in. They talked for a long time. Mostly Sam talked...cracking jokes about Clelon and what they could do to him. Finally, Travis was laughing. The tensions from the confrontation with Clelon, his sleepless night, and his reminiscences of Ginny slowly diminished.

The two men walked up the steps and into the building. Inside they spotted two familiar faces leaning against the wall outside Sheriff Caffy's office. One man wore a green polyester jacket with ATF in bright yellow letters on the back and a green baseball cap with the John Deere logo stamped on it. His jeans were clean but faded, and his athletic shoes had seen better days. The other man was tall and slim, almost skinny. His face was skeletal. His eyes recessed. He wore an old naval aviator's cap and a leather bomber jacket with a faux fur collar. And even though it was not that cold, the jacket was zipped up to his chin. The heels of his cowboy boots were so run over that he almost walked on the side of the shoes. This made the limp of his right leg even more noticeable.

The two men spotted Sam and Travis at the same time. Green jacket said, "Hey lookee here. The Seaboard boys. Just who we're looking for."

"Hey, Tom, Stretch," said Travis. "What's up?" Tom Mayes was an Alcohol, Tobacco and Firearms agent out of Washington, DC, and Travis and Sam worked with him on jobs that involved moonshine and unlicensed whiskey smuggled from their territory across state lines.

"Called Raleigh, and they told us you were on vacation out here. Now I find that you're up to your elbows in some murder case. How did that happen?" asked Tom.

"Just lucky, I guess," said Sam. "You out here on business or pleasure?"

"Business, unfortunately," said Tom. "Know you're working with the sheriff on a murder case, but I need your help, too, if we can work something out. I'm waiting to talk to Caffy now. See if he'll cut you loose for a few hours."

"Well, we've got business with the Sheriff, too," said Travis. "Let's go on in." And Travis started towards Caffy's closed office door.

"Ah, Travis, I wouldn't do that if I wuz you," Stretch drawled in an authentic Eastern North Carolina dialect. "Caffy's got some guy in there with him, and he's really shaking his peanuts. Don't know what the man did but the sheriff's real peeved."

Raised, angry voices penetrated the door and echoed down the hall bouncing off the walls and tiled floors. Suddenly the door swung open, and Clelon Purvis stomped out slamming the door behind him. His face was red, and veins protruded from his forehead. Sam even thought he saw a pulse pounding through the thick crimson skin on his neck. Clelon stared wide-eyed and opened mouth at the four men. He paused, looked at Travis, started to say something, thought better about it, turned, and stormed off.

"Hey, Trav," said Sam, "think the sheriff might have already taken care of your little problem?"

"Not my problem," said Travis, "Eve Drane's problem. I sure hope he handled it. I'd hate to think someone like Clelon might be laying for her. There's all sorts of ways he could make her life hell…you know speed traps, license checks, stuff like that."

"Well, whatever happens to Clelon, it'll carry more weight coming from Caffy," said Sam.

Tom said, "Let's go on in and see what the sheriff thinks about you two going out with us."

Stretch knocked on the door. An angry, deafening voice thundered, "What the hell is it now? Can't even eat my breakfast." Then there was a pause and Caffy added impatiently, "Well, come on in. Come on in. What cha waiting for, your birthday?"

The men shook their heads, grinned and opened the door. Sheriff Caffy was leaning over his desk with a jumbo mug of coffee in one hand and a powdered sugar doughnut in the other. The front of his shirt was sprinkled with sugar, and his desk was covered with white residue. He sunk his teeth into the doughnut and tore away half of it sending another flurry of sugar and crumbs onto his desk. He set the doughnut on a paper napkin, wet his fingers with his tongue, touched them to the white powder on his desk, and then licked each finger clean. He lifted his coffee cup and sipped loudly. Then he frowned and said, "Cold. What the hell does it take to get a hot cup of coffee around here? Doris," he yelled.

A middle-aged woman wearing a tan polyester pants suit, brown comfort shoes, and bifocals chained around her neck walked slowly into the room and gave the sheriff a tired look.

"How about getting me a cup of *hot* coffee?" said the sheriff.

"Be glad to sheriff, beings I've got nothing else to do this morning," she said unsmilingly and slowly left the room.

"Independent that one," said the sheriff. "Yeah, sometimes she's too independent, but I don't know what I'd do without her. She understands me. Know what I mean?"

134

All four men nodded knowingly. Then the sheriff said, "First off, Travis, I know about Clelon's actions last night so no need to start in about it."

Travis started to say something, but Caffy raised a palm and continued, "Never occurred to me that Clelon would go off half cocked like that. Didn't occur to me he'd be so rough on a lady who'd been through so much grief, a lady we might need to help us at some point in this investigation. Now I'm afraid she'll get lawyered up and refuse to talk to us at all. I know Clelon don't always run on all four cylinders, but he's all I had last night and that's that. I take full responsible for the decision, and Clelon now has full responsible of cleaning the lock-up down in the jail."

Caffy paused. Doris walked in and handed the sheriff a steaming cup of something hot. "Now that I've fed you, do you think I can get back to my work?" she said. Then she turned to the four men and said disdainfully, "What about you gentlemen? Coffee? Tea? Milk?" They stepped back and shook their heads vigorously, "No mam," they said in unison.

The sheriff laughed, shook his head, and winked. "She looks after me." Then he returned to the events of the previous night. "Now Travis, even before I talked with Clelon this morning, I learned that you walked in on that unfortunate situation at Eve Drane's house last night and you found it vexing…"

"Vexing? That's putting it mildly. How did you find out about it anyway?" asked Travis.

"Let's just say there's an open line of communication between the Nags Head Police Department and the Dare County Sheriff's Department. Now, I'm not gonna warn you about becoming personally involved, and I'm not gonna caution you not to take matters of discipline into your own hands, because I know you to be an intelligent, professional agent. Besides, you don't work for me, you're working with me…and I appreciate all your help," Caffy said.

Travis nodded. "I should have known you'd handle it, Sheriff. And I admit it got personal."

"Well, now that all this has been sufficiently thrashed out," said Caffy, "to what do I owe the pleasure of a visit from the illustrious ATF?" Caffy stood, wiped his hands on his pants, and extended a hand to Tom and Stretch. "Pull up a chair…all of you."

The men sat down. Tom said, "Sheriff, we got wind that large quantities of moonshine are being moved up the southeast coast, through eastern North Carolina, and on up north. Scuttlebutt has it that eighteen-wheelers travel up

I-95, stop at designated spots along the way, pick up moonshine, and by the time they reach their destinations, Washington, Philly, Baltimore, New York, they've got a full load."

The sheriff interrupted, "Tom I never will understand why folks up north buy the stuff. Hell, they've got more bars up there than you can shake a stick at."

"I won't argue with you there, sheriff," said Tom, "but there's big market for moonshine in back-street bars and juke joints. Hey, it's tax-free liquor. And there's always the street people. You know winos, runaways...anybody looking for a cheap way to get drunk fast. And some of that stuff can get you there fast."

"These bars you speak of, do you just walk in and order moonshine?" asked Caffy.

"No, sir," said Tom. "Usually the people who run the joints pour moonshine into empty liquor bottles that still have labels on them and sell it as the real stuff."

"And the customers can't tell the difference?" asked Caffy.

"Sheriff, the customers in these places fried their taste buds years ago. They couldn't tell the difference between Jack Daniels and liquid Drano. You see, our concern is not just the sale of untaxed booze, this stuff can kill if the bootlegger doesn't know what he's doing."

"So I've heard. Travis and Sam here told me that they use all kinds of ingredients to add a little kick to their brew....anti-freeze, Drano, wood alcohol. What I don't understand is why this stuff don't kill em all," said Caffy. "So where do we come in?"

"Well," Tom continued, "a few days ago, we had a truck inspection on I-95 just below the Virginia state line. We were operating with a small staff, and eventually the trucks really stacked up. Then we realized that the line wasn't moving at all. We walked back to investigate and found an abandoned eighteen-wheeler. Apparently when the driver realized we were inspecting, he just hopped out, went down to the interstate, and hitched a ride to Lord only knows where. Anyway, when we checked out the truck, that was stolen by the way, we discovered that it was packed from top to bottom, front to back with moonshine. And it was heading north."

"Well, I'll say. If that ain't the damnedest! But what's this got to do with us?" Caffy repeated.

"The truck obviously made a long haul up the East Coast picking up moonshine at different points, but we recognized one brew we'd seen many times before. And we know it's from out here," said Tom. "So we started pulling in every snitch, every bum, and every drunk we could think of to interrogate. And one name kept coming up over, and over. Maynard Dwayne Drane."

"Maynard Dwayne Drane?" A chorus went up in unison.

Sheriff Caffy leaned across his desk. "Son, I'd do anything I could to help you in this situation, but I'm afraid you're a little bit late."

"What do you mean?" asked Tom.

"Maynard Dwayne Drane is dead," Caffy said simply. "It's his death we're investigating."

"Damn. The ultimate escape, huh?" Tom looked defeated. He thought for a second and then added. "What about the others?"

"What others?" asked Sam.

"Surely if you've got a set-up as big as Drane's you don't work it alone. He must have had somebody working with him," said Tom.

"Hate to disappoint you again," said Caffy. "But Drane was a loner. Always was, up to the very end. Didn't trust nobody enough to have a partner."

Tom sighed. "Well, so much for the bootlegger. That only leaves one thing left to do."

"Find the still," said Travis.

"Right. Find it and bust it. Can't have some hiker running across it and deciding to go into business for himself," said Tom turning to Travis and Sam. "This is your territory, and if anybody can find it, you can. We can do an aerial search. Best method for an initial search of these swamps. Stretch here can take us up. You just tell him where to go, and he can take us so low that you can reach out the window and touch the treetops. He's got his Cessna gassed up and out of the hanger right now."

"I don't know," said Travis, "Our orders are to work with the locals here until the bootlegger's murder is solved."

"When I talked with Raleigh," said Tom, "They said they're okay with it if the sheriff is."

"Sheriff?" said Travis.

"How long?" asked the sheriff.

"Just today I hope," said Tom.

"Okay by me then," said Sheriff Caffy. "I got a couple of officers working the case, too. They'll hold things down till you guys get back in. Besides, finding that still might give us some leads in the murder investigation."

The men stood up and the sheriff shook hands with Tom and Stretch again. "Always good to see you boys," he said. Then he turned to Travis and said, "You think Ms. Drane will talk to us after that fiasco last night?"

"I don't know," said Travis. The sheriff held his eye. Travis added, "I'll talk to her."

"Good," he said. "And Stretch don't be a doing any of those barn-storming stunts with the Seaboard boys on your plane. I need them."

Stretch just grinned, and as the men walked into the hall they heard the sheriff yell, "Doris, don't we have no *hot* coffee around here?"

CHAPTER 22

Nona Godette stood in the corridor of the Dare County Justice Center her hands wrapped around a big mug of hot tea. She watched intently as Sam and Travis got into an unmarked car with two men she didn't recognize.

Nona heard a snap behind her and a voice interrupted her scrutiny. "Hey Nona," said Shucks. "What you staring at so hard?"

She recognized the scent of Old Spice after-shave lotion and without turning she said, "Hey Shucks." Shucks cracked another peanut and tossed the shells in a nearby planter.

Nona eyes were riveted on the car as it drove out of the parking lot and disappeared behind a stand of pine trees. "Did you see them?"

"Yeah," Shucks answered simply.

"Do you know who those two men are with Travis and Sam?" she asked.

"Yeah," he said and dug into his pocket for another peanut.

"Well, are you gonna tell me who they are or not?" she asked irritably.

"Gosh Nona, you didn't ask me who they are. You asked if I saw them," Shucks said defensibly.

Nona set her coffee mug on the window ledge, leaned in close to Shucks, and said slowly, "Shucks, do you know those men Travis and Sam left with?"

"You don't have to get in my face, Nona. The men are Tom Mayes and Stretch Pugh," said Shucks.

"Hummm. I wonder what business they have with the Seaboard boys." Nona mused aloud.

Shucks squeezed two nuts, picked out the meat, and tossed them in his mouth. "Well, you didn't ask nothing about their business," Shucks crunched as he spoke. Nona turned and shot him an infuriated look that made Shucks step back and bump against a large potted rubber plant. He quickly added, "Tom, he's with the ATF out of Washington DC, and Stretch is a pilot. I don't know any more."

Nona spun around and glared in the direction of the vanished car as if summoning it to return. "What are Travis and Sam doing with ATF?" she demanded.

"I told you I don't know nothing else," Shucks said quickly and reached into his pocket for more peanuts.

"I thought the four of us were suppose to work this case together. Remember how you lectured me about teamwork? You said something like 'if you're on a team you can't keep secrets from your partners'. Now those jerks have gone off on their own. I'll not be a token member of this team," she said anger rising in her voice. She glared at Shucks and said, "Do you understand that?"

"Hey, don't tell me, Nona," Shucks said calmly in an effort to placate her. "Tell somebody who can do something about it."

She said, "Maybe I will. Just maybe I will." And she marched in the direction of Sheriff Caffy's office.

Nona rushed through the sheriff's open door, collided with Doris, and watched helplessly as a flurry of papers and folders floated to the floor.

"Nona!" screamed Doris.

"Doris, I'm so sorry. Here let me help you," Nona dropped to her knees and began to gather up the papers. "Can I help you sort these?"

"No, no you've done quite enough, thank you," Doris said heatedly snatching the papers and folders haphazardly. Then she turned and stomped out of the office.

Thinking it would not be wise to get mixed up in the fray, the sheriff sat silently at his desk and watched. When Doris was gone Nona took a deep breath, stood, straightened her slacks, and turned toward the business at hand....the sheriff.

"Can I do something for you, Nona?" the sheriff asked tiredly. His morning seemed to be getting worse and worse.

"I hope you can," said Nona defiantly. "I certainly hope you can. Sheriff, I had been under the impression that the Seaboard boys, Shucks and I were to work the Drane case together."

"Well, as a matter of fact, Nona," said Caffy, "I was under that impression, too. Of course, who am I to say? I'm just the sheriff."

Nona ignored the barb and continued, "Well, I wish someone would tell

me how the four of us can work as a team, if two members of the team go off
on their own and don't let the other two members know what they're up to."

Sheriff Caffy shook his head as if trying to clear his thoughts. "That would
be interesting to know, Officer," said the sheriff. "Did you have any
particular *team members* in mind…you know who are going off on their
own?"

"Yes," said Nona. "The Seaboard boys. They're off right now with an
ATF agent. Shucks and I have no idea what's going on. And I'd like to say one
thing, please…"

"Just one?" the sheriff said wearily.

Nona ignored the interruption and continued, "When I was told to work
this case, I thought I had a real assignment. Now it looks like I'm just a token
member of the team. I don't like that, Sheriff. I don't want to be a token
woman law enforcement officer."

Now the sheriff's face took on a grave look. "Are you through, Officer?"
And he waited for her to answer.

"Yes," she said.

"First off, you are assigned to this case. And yours is not a token
assignment. I expect you and Shucks to work with these ABC agents until we
find out who killed Maynard Dwayne Drane…"

"But what about the ATF?" she interjected.

"Don't interrupt me, Officer," the sheriff said softly, but firmly. "Now if
you had walked in here like somebody with good sense and asked, instead of
storming in and running poor Doris down, I would have told you that Travis
and Sam are assisting ATF Agent Tom Mayes in an aerial search. They'll just
be gone a few hours. ATF is not involved in our murder investigation. ATF
don't *care* who killed Maynard Dwayne Drane. They got their own
headaches. They just want to find his still and bust it up, and the Seaboard
boys know the best places to look for it."

"Oh," Nona said weakly. "Thanks." And she turned toward the door.

"Just wait a minute," said Caffy. She turned and looked at him, her face
and neck flushed. "You gotta learn to bank your fire till you really need it.
Now Nona, you're a good officer, but I'm telling you to get that chip off your
shoulder. I don't assign people to any case as a token. I assign the best people
I can think of for that particular case. But I'll tell you one thing, if you expect
me to explain my decisions to you every time you get your dander up, you'll
find yourself sitting behind a desk most of the time. Is that clear Officer?"

"Yes, sir," she said meekly and scurried out of the room.

Sheriff Caffy cocked his elbow on the desk and rested his forehead in hand. "Doris," he shouted, "Doris, get me a couple of Tylenols...extra strength."

The car sped towards the airstrip located on the outskirts of Manteo. "Where you think we oughta check first?" said Tom.

Sam said, "I agree with Caffy about Drane working alone. From what I gather, that guy was paranoid. I don't think he'd trust his own mother to work his still."

"And if that is the case," added Travis, "He'd need to keep an eye on his business. So I think he'd keep it close to home."

"Makes sense to me," said Tom. "And it would have to be secluded and not easily accessible."

"So where to gentlemen?" said Stretch.

"I'm thinking right here at Nags Head and Roanoke Island area," said Sam. "Let's do Nags Head and slightly north of there. Lots of scrub forests down there."

"Sounds like a plan," said Stretch as he turned by a sign that read Dare County Regional Airport.

The facility was not built to accommodate large planes just two, three, or four passenger planes and small commuters. The paved airstrip was short, narrow, and interspersed with cracks. Small patches of coarse green grass had taken root in the sandy soil underneath the runway and pushed its way through the fissures. Somehow it managed to survive the battering of plane tires that rolled over it. There was a metal hanger and a small office building. An old Cessna 172 was tied down in an adjoining lot, and Stretch pulled the car onto the field beside it.

He got out of the car and said, "Be out in a minute." Then Stretch hobbled towards a hanger as quickly as his bum leg would take him.

Stretch joined the navy and became a pilot when he was only eighteen years old. Even though he was young, had only a high school education, and was so skinny that it appeared he could be easily sucked into a jet engine, he showed extraordinary knowledge of planes and exceptional skill in flying them. Over the years, Stretch created an impressive reputation for flying. At the age of thirty eight, after serving twenty years, Stretch retired from the military and transferred his skill of flying navy planes to flying crop dusters over the fields of eastern North Carolina.

As the farmers of the area strived to eek out a living from the land, they planted every plot of earth that government allotments would allow. They planted crops in fields surrounded by woods; fields within a hundred feet of farm houses, country stores, and schools; and fields underneath high-voltage power lines. Stretch never refused a job. But it was the power lines that finally brought him down. He was dusting a triangular-shaped field with power wires stretching across the northern point. Just beyond the field was a thick stand of tall long-leaf pines. He remembers pointing the nose of his Cessna downward intending to dust low across the widest point of the field first and top the power lines. Then he'd pull up quickly and avoid the pine trees. The power lines were the last maneuver he remembered until he woke up in the hospital with his leg in traction and hurting like hell. He'd gone in too low. The power lines snagged the plane, and crashed it into the pine trees. He later learned, however, that slamming into the trees probably saved him because the pines tore the wires lose from the little crop duster and allowed the rescue people to reach Stretch and pull him out.

That was the end of Stretch's crop-dusting career. He decided to go into another business by himself. Now he owned his own plane and operated his own less hazardous business, and he liked it that way. He advertised No Flying Job is Too Small. He flew sightseers above the shimmering sands of the Outer Banks coastline. He was hired to fly his plane low over the beaches trailing advertisement banners written in bold black letters. He made emergency flights to places that larger planes couldn't get into, and he picked up quite a few surveillance jobs for law enforcement.

Sam, Travis, and Tom watched the Cessna 172 taxi onto the little runway. The three men ran across the field and pulled themselves aboard. Travis took the seat beside Stretch, and Sam and Tom slid into the back. As Stretch revved-up the engine, he tossed a wad of bubble gum into his mouth and handed a big bag to Travis.

"Here, pass this around," he shouted, "Keeps your ears clear."

"Thanks," said Travis as he unwrapped a piece of Super Bubble and handed the bag back to Sam.

The plane gathered speed as it shook and bumped its way down the narrow runway. Then the nose lifted, and the passengers watched as buildings, cars, and woods drifted farther and farther downward. Stretch banked in a northeasterly direction and headed out over the Roanoke Sound towards the Nags Head Woods.

Gems of sunlight bounced off the water, and water fowl fishing for their next meal squawked and complained at the noisy interruption. As the plane reached the other bank, the men looked down upon lush, steep wooded dunes that make up a part of the 1,400-acre maritime forest. The Nags Head Woods are termed maritime because it grows under the influence of the ocean. In other places where there are high winds, salty spray, lack of fresh water, and poor soil, land would be desolate. But on the Outer Banks, a ridge of dunes shelter the woods and provide a growing place for hearty beech, hickory, oak, and, of course, pine for which the Tar Heel state is well known.

True to Tom's word, Stretch took the plane low over the trees. Sam and Travis looked out upon round treetops that looked like plump green satin pillows that had been casually tossed there. They flew slowly, meticulously back and forth over the forest. They scanned five miles of public hiking trails that snaked past ponds and swamps that teemed with plant and animal life. They were looking for any sign of a footpath that led away from the main trails and into the thick forest that could so easily provide a hiding place for an unscrupulous undertaking. They stared down at the faces of hikers and watched them mouth obscenities at the low-flying plane they feared might disturb the protected songbirds. Using binoculars, they scrutinized steep ridges and bridges that crossed the lovely ponds and salt marshes. Finally they flew up and down the shore of the Roanoke Sound while below kayakers enjoyed a day on the sparkling water.

"So what do you think?" Stretch shouted above the roar of the plane's engine. "You wanta take another look at anything here?"

"Far as I'm concerned, we've seen it all," Sam shouted back.

"Right," Travis agreed. "This would be a hard place to hide a still what with the rangers and hikers. Although, I've seen stills in more conspicuous places than this."

"Like where?" asked Stretch.

"Like in out-houses, barns, smokehouses, and basements," replied Travis.

"Whoa!" shouted Stretch. "So where to?"

"Let's fly on over to the Alligator River National Wildlife Refuge," Sam yelled from the back.

"You got it," said Stretch, and he banked the plane west and headed toward the Croatan Sound.

Although in Dare County, the Alligator River National Wildlife Refuge is not on Roanoke Island but lays across the sound on mainland Dare and Hyde Counties. Soon they crossed the Croatan and were flying above a vast expanse of swamplands that make up the Refuge. The men realized that a search of this preserve would take much longer and be far more tedious than the Nags Head Woods search. The refuge encompasses 150,000 acres of lush, swampy wetlands that provides a perfect habitat for a variety of wildlife such as wood ducks, alligators, black bears, red wolves, deer, a variety of fish, and an assortment of small amphibians. It's a perfect place for a bootlegger to set up shop. In the center of the refuge is 46,000 acres of swampy land that's owned by the Air Force and used for a practice bombing range. The scene below appeared dark, inhospitable, almost impenetrable.

The plane swung low and they watched a big heron work the beach of the Alligator River for his dinner. Not far from there, an alligator appeared to be resting on the warm sand. Suddenly it reared its head and slid unbelievably fast back into the safety of the murky water. Then Sam nudged Travis on the shoulder and pointed to a startled young deer that had been feeding dangerously close by.

"We interrupted the 'gator's dinner," he shouted. Travis nodded.

"Now if I were gonna hide a still," shouted Tom, "this would be the place I'd chose."

Stretch used the same search strategy he'd employed in the Nags Head Woods search. But from the air, the hiking and wildlife trails did not appear to be as clearly defined as the ones they'd inspected earlier. Travis pored over a map of the Refuge and pointed out spots that warranted close examination. They dissected the map and then flew low over first one small section of the wilderness then another. Close attention was paid to observation platforms, especially if they appeared to be abandoned. They even checked out the docks that were used for canoe tours. They analyzed forest shadows, animal paths that disappeared into the swamp, and tricks of light that played off Spanish moss that clung to sinister-looking cypress trees.

"This is hopeless," shouted Stretch. "There's a million places a bootlegger could hide a still down there. How do you ever find one in these swamps?"

"Hey this is a great place for a still," said Travis.

"To answer your question about how to find the damned things…well, it just takes talent," Sam shouted back.

"And patience," added Travis.

Travis doggedly continued to pan the acres of wetlands below with high powered binoculars. Suddenly he fixed the binoculars on an object below. Travis shouted, "Whoa, hold it right there."

"This ain't no helicopter, Travis," shouted Stretch. "We'll have to circle back." And he turned the plane and headed back to the area they'd just flown over.

The binoculars never left Travis's eyes, and he twisted in his seat to maintain the optical target.

"What you got, Trav?" shouted Sam.

"Metal," replied Travis.

"Metal?" Stretch seemed confused.

"Yeah," said Tom. "Metal where metal shouldn't be…right in the middle of a swamp."

"Take her as low as you can, Stretch," instructed Travis. "See that area that looks like a salt marsh…over there to the right."

"See it," Stretch acknowledged.

"Okay, now see there's a dark patch that looks like a little ridge…no, no, take her back to the right. Yeah," Travis exclaimed excitedly. "Just focus on that dark spot and take us in as close as you can."

"Got it," Stretch confirmed. He banked the little plane again and circled back for another fly-over.

"Think we've found ourselves a still, boys," Travis shouted excitedly and passed the binoculars back to Sam. He immediately began to mark the map indicating the approximate location.

"Damn tooting," shouted Sam as he studied sunlight bouncing off some metal object below.

Using his own binocular, Tom gave the object the once over and exclaimed, "Hey you've got an eagle eye, Travis. It's a still, alright."

"Circle back again, Stretch. I want to get a fix on it," said Travis.

Stretch circled the spot again, and Travis got a position fix using a GPS receiver.

"Okay, Stretch," shouted Travis beginning to fold his map, "that's a confirmation. Take her home."

Soon they were over the Croatan Sound and headed for Manteo Regional Airport. Stretch shouted, "Hey, that was fun, and it didn't take as long as I thought it would."

Suddenly a tremendous roar shook the cabin walls of the small Cessna 172. The plane began to vibrate violently and rock back and forth. It dropped about twenty feet like a roller coaster out of control, and the waters of the Croatan rose swiftly upward, upward towards the little plane. The sound was earsplitting, the shaking terrifying. The windshield shuddered and threatened to crack wide open.

Stretch was caught completely by surprise but almost immediately began struggling to bring the aircraft under control and steer it up from the murky waters that already served as final resting place for several small aircrafts. Finally the plane leveled out, and Stretch began to pull it up to the standard altitude for flights approaching Dare County Regional Airport. The noise was subsiding and although the plane was no longer shaking, the men were.

"What the hell?" shouted Tom.

"I thought this was the time," said Sam throwing his head back against the headrest. "I really thought this was it."

"Stretch, what happened?" screamed Travis.

Stretch was pale and shaking. His fingers were glued to the controls. Without speaking he stared wide-eyed and speechlessly through the windshield as an F-16 jet rocketed ahead of them, tipped its wings, and disappeared.

Finally Stretch spoke, his voice shaking, "Must have wandered into a No-Fly area. Just some fly-boys from Langley out spotting imaginary targets. You know…war games."

"Well next time I hope they ask if we want to play," Sam said contemptuously.

CHAPTER 23

Nona sat at her desk immersed in a sea of paperwork. Her confrontation with Sheriff Caffy left her frazzled and she found it hard to focus on tasks she found mundane and time consuming. She reached for a half-empty cup, missed, and sent cold coffee spilling onto a pile of neatly stacked papers. She grabbed a box of tissues and began to sop up the rapidly spreading puddle of brown liquid when the phone rang.

She jerked up the receiver, "Yeah?" she barked.

"Nona, this is Doris," a tired voice said.

"Oh, Doris," Nona said contritely, "Sorry, I just had a little mishap here."

"Another one?" Doris said coldly. "Well when you recover, the Sheriff wants to see you and Shucks. ASAP."

Sparing no tissues, Nona quickly mopped up the spilled coffee, tucked her shirt into her slacks, and ran out to find Shucks. He was leaning casually against a wall talking to another officer, shucking peanuts, and dropping the shells into a planter. A sizeable pile of shells suggested that he'd been standing there a long time.

Without even slowing down, Nona said, "Let's go Shucks."

"For heaven's sake, Nona," he said. "Where to?"

"Caffy wants to see us right away," she called over her shoulder.

Shucks pocketed the unshelled peanuts and quickly fell in behind Nona. "What about, Nona?" he said nervously.

"I don't know, Shucks," she said. "If I knew we wouldn't have to go to his office would we?"

"Well no....," Shucks didn't get to complete his sentence because he slammed into Nona who had stopped abruptly to take a deep breath before walking into the Sheriff's office.

"You wanted to see us, Sheriff?" Nona asked nonchalantly.

Caffy looked up and answered Nona as if the row earlier that morning had never taken place. "Got a report of a vehicle in the water on the sound side just over the Oregon Inlet bridge. It was spotted by a birdwatcher from an observation platform. The guy called the park ranger and the ranger verifies. There's a tow truck down there down, but they've got orders to hold off till you arrive, so get on it."

"Yes, sir," said Shucks, as he and Nona turned and hurried out of the office.

Shucks pulled out of the parking lot of the Dare County Justice Center and with lights flashing and sirens wailing, he drove across the Roanoke Sound Bridge and straight to Highway 12. The patrol car sped pass Bodie Island Lighthouse, and they were soon on the bridge that climbed and snaked across the shallow Oregon Inlet.

Nona glanced down at men in waders casting their lines hopefully into the waters of the sound. She watched charters move cautiously through the channel toward blue water carrying optimistic fishermen ready to take on the challenge of marlin, bluefin tuna, or even a sailfish. For a moment, Nona's mind clicked back to simpler times. She thought nostalgically of the hours she'd spent with her dad on his charter and how he'd taught her the ways of the fisherman. Suddenly the car bumped onto the highway on the south side of the bridge, and Nona was back in the present, with Shucks, and speeding to a scene.

"Slow down, Shucks, we'll pass it," said Nona. The words were no sooner spoken than they saw the flashing lights of a tow truck, and Shucks exited right into a small parking area next to a waterfowl observation platform.

"What we got here?" Nona addressed the park ranger.

"Looks like a vehicle down in about six feet of water. Too murky to tell anything about it right now. Guy over there spotted it before the tide came in," the ranger jerked his thumb in the direction of a man and woman. They both wore hiking boots, long jeans, and long-sleeve shirts for protection against biting insects. Expensive binoculars hung around their necks, and the woman was snapping a digital camera into a carrying case.

Shucks addressed the couple, "Need you to stick around for awhile. I'll have to get a statement." The couple nodded.

"I went ahead and called the tow truck," the ranger said stating the obvious.

Nona turned to the tow truck operator. "Can you get to her while the tide's in?"

"No problem," the tow truck driver answered.

"Okay, let's take her out," she said.

The driver nodded, kicked off his boots, grabbed a chain and hook, and waded in clothes and all. When the water was about chest high, he stooped down, allowing water to lap at his chin. His hands generated little ripples of muddy, salty brine as he explored the submerged vehicle searching for the right spot to attach the hook.

"Ah!" he finally said. And he secured the chain and slowly waded ashore.

Without taking time to put on his boots, the tow truck driver jumped into his truck and started the engine. The submerged vehicle had sunk deeply into the mud, and it resisted the truck's effort to free it. After several tries, the rear end of a vehicle slowly emerged from the brackish water. It was completely covered with silt and muck and the color was barely distinguishable.

When the vehicle cleared, Nona and Shucks waited for water to stop pouring out of crevices, and then they stepped forward for a closer look. Wearing gloves, Shucks opened the front door on the driver's side. Nona did the same on the passenger's side. More water and small sea life that had already taken up residence in the vehicle spilled out. Shucks wiped his hand across the hood.

"We got a black Wrangler here," he shouted. Nona did not respond. Shucks walked to the rear where Nona stared at the back of the jeep. Shucks looked at where Nona gawked. She had cleared the muck from the license plate on the back of the jeep, and the number that appeared was EVI-112.

Although Doo-Wop and Irene arrived early at the hospital in Elizabeth City, they found Short Sugar already dressed and sitting in a chair by the window. Since Irene didn't report to work at Guthrie's until eleven, she insisted on driving Doo-Wop to pick up Short Sugar who was being released from the hospital that day.

"How you feeling, honey?" asked Irene as she walked quickly across the room and took Short Sugar's hand. Irene was shocked to see the bruises and the wires that held Short Sugar's jaw together.

"Actually, I feel pretty good," said Short Sugar. "I'll feel much better when I get home though."

"And Gran-Pop and ole Doo-Daddy gonna feel better having you dare," Doo said, a smile spreading across his face.

"Alright young lady," a commanding voice said from the door, and a nurse in white slacks, white shoes, and a stethoscope dangling around her neck pushed a wheel chair into the room. "You've been sprung. Today's your big day."

The nurse would not allow Doo-Wop to help Short Sugar move to the wheelchair. "Hands off," she commanded. "She's my responsibility until she's in your car," she said with authority and grasped Short Sugar's arm.

Irene had put pillows and blankets in the back seat of her Corolla and when Short Sugar was buckled in securely and comfortably they began the drive back to Manteo. Irene drove unnecessarily cautious as if a treasured porcelain doll were resting on her back seat. Short Sugar awoke early that morning, so once she was comfortably situated the vibrations of the car quickly lulled her to sleep. Irene glanced in the rear-view mirror at the sleeping girl the multicolored beads attached to her braids laying motionless on the white pillow.

"How could anybody leave such a helpless little angel lying beside the road?" Irene thought.

Then Irene glanced at Doo. The wide toothy grin he'd flashed at the hospital was gone, and tears rolled down his cheek. "You okay Doo?" asked Irene.

"I be alright," he said. "I jest hopes my baby be."

Irene pulled out a tissue and handed it to him.

"Tank you," he said. "Some of dese tears be fo sadness dat my baby bin hurt. Some of dese tears be fo joy dat she be cumin home."

When they finally arrived at Doo-Wop's house, Irene breathed a sigh of relief, unbuckled her seat belt, turned to Short Sugar, and shook her knee gently. "Wake up, you're home, honey," she said, "and I see somebody whose been waiting for you all morning."

Short Sugar opened her eyes, looked towards the porch, and smiled. Gran-Pop Early was sitting in his rocker wearing bib overalls with no shirt and work shoes with no socks. He rocked forward in his chair and used his cane as leverage to stand. Then he said, "'Bout time. You'll be wanting your lunch, I s'pose. Come on in cheer fo I feeds it to de dogs."

Short Sugar laughed weakly, "Grand-Pop, we don't have any dogs."

Grand-Pop studied his granddaughter with keen eyes that had witnessed happiness, births, sickness, sadness, loneliness, and death. He stared into his grand-daughter's eyes and saw the determination of youth, and although he grieved for her pain he applauded her grit. The drive and the walk from the car to the house was the most activity Short Sugar had experienced since being hospitalized, and she gladly accepted help from Doo and Irene. They each held an elbow and supported her up the steps and inside where a delicious aroma permeated the whole house.

"My something sure does smell good, Pop Early," said Irene. "Now I know who taught Doo how to cook."

"Jest sum chickin and dumplins," said Pop. Then he addressed Short Sugar's chewing problem. "And don't you go to complainin' none, Short Sugar. 'Cause I'm agonna mush dem dumplins up so's they'll be soft as smashed taters."

With that the homecoming was interrupted by the sharp ring of the telephone.

"Now who dat be a callin' here at dinner time?" Pop Early said irritably.

Doo-Wop reached for the phone and said, "Dis be the Doo-Wopper." Then there was a long pause. "Ya dun't say?" Doo-Wop's face took on an odd expression. Then he mumbled something that sounded like "thanks" and hung up.

"Well, who be dat, Doo, cause you to be a lookin lak dat," asked Pop Early.

"Dat wuz de poolice," said Do-Wop.

"De poolice?" repeated Pop. "What fo dey be callin' you, Doo?

"Dey callin me to tell me dat dey done found de car what hit Short Sugar," said Doo.

Pop Early walked over to Doo-Wop and looked him straight in the eye. "Doo, tweren't jest a car dat hit Short Sugar. It wuz dat white trash Maynard Dwayne Drane. And don't you fergit it."

CHAPTER 24

Stretch waited patiently beside the ATF van while the three men talked on cell phones. Travis reported their findings to the Raleigh office. Sam filled in Sheriff Caffy. And Tom called Washington. Each described the sighting they suspected was Maynard Dwayne Drane's still, and they recommended going in to confirm and destroy it. Soon they joined Stretch at the van.

"Okay with Raleigh to take it out," said Travis.

"Same with ATF," said Tom.

"Caffy's gonna send over a couple of uniforms to go in with us. They'll meet us at the end of Buffalo City Road off US 64," said Sam.

"Shucks and Nona?" asked Travis.

"Nope," said Sam. "Seems like Nona and Shucks have their hands full right now."

"What's happened?" Travis asked anxiously his mind immediately switching to Eve.

"They've found Drane's jeep," said Sam. "It was in the sound just south of Oregon Inlet Bridge."

"Got anything from it yet?" asked Travis.

"Not yet. It's been towed to the shop. I wonder what they can tell after it's been in the water so long," said Sam. "Well, let's head out."

"Okay if I tag along?" asked Stretch. "I'd like to see how this plays out."

"The more hands, the better," said Travis.

Tom drove left out of the airport onto highway 64. Soon they were crossing the bridge over Croatan Sound and headed for the mainland. They passed the sign that read Alligator River National Wildlife Refuge and soon turned onto a road marked Buffalo City Road. They drove to the end of a dirt road and parked.

"We'll wait here for Caffy's men to show. Where the heck is Buffalo City anyway?" Tom said peering into the dense forest. "I don't see anything but swamp."

"This is the *site* of Buffalo City," explained Travis. "Buffalo City was a town built by three logging men from Buffalo, New York back in 1870. That's how come the name Buffalo. They came down here and discovered a wealth of trees. So they bought 168,000 acres of swampland and built themselves a logging town. It was a fairly big city, too. It had a couple of hotels, a school, a general store, lots of moonshine taverns, and the population got to be as much as 3,000 people."

"And they lived in this swamp?" asked Stretch.

"Those people were survivors and very ingenious," said Travis. "They built wooden railroads through the peat bogs and used the waters of the river and sound to transport the lumber. It was a thriving place."

"What ever happened to it?" asked Tom.

"Trees ran out, and the lumber company went belly up," said Sam.

"What about those 3,000 people?" asked Stretch.

"As I said, they were very ingenious. The lumber played out at the height of prohibition making the town perfect for bootlegging. It was isolated, had the water and railroad transportation, so all they needed was a product."

"Moonshine?" said Tom.

"Why not?" said Sam. "Many a southern gentlemen had their own still. I read somewhere that even George Washington made a fortune selling moonshine."

Travis said, "I understand that Buffalo City became real famous during the prohibition. They ran moonshine from Philadelphia to Atlanta, Georgia with little or no interference from the Feds until after prohibition ended."

"What happened after prohibition ended?" asked Stretch.

"Government regulations. The government regulators came in and closed them down," said Sam.

"The people tried to stay on here," said Travis, "but it didn't work. They tried farming. But as fast as they cleared the land, the swamp would repossess it. They finally just gave up and pulled out. There's still some remains of the town...rotting buildings and such."

"Ironic that Drane would choose this place to hide his still," said Tom.

"Why not? It's a tried and true spot for moonshiners," said Sam.

The men heard the clamor of a car on the dirt road, and turned to see a Dare County Sheriff's car. It pulled up beside them. Travis grabbed the aerial map he'd marked, and climbed out of the van. He recognized the two uniformed officers, shook hands with them, spread the map on the hood of their car, and began to go over the details of the search.

They entered the swamp by a hiking trail and walked about a mile into the wild beautiful wetlands. They walked along a steam that cut back and disappeared into the woods. A grouse was startled by their presence and rose from its nest at the stream's edge, and a deer drinking from the same stream reared its startled head and darted into the woods. They crossed an arm of the swamp and examined ravine after ravine in an effort to locate the dark area shown on the map that marked where they would leave the trail and go into the woods.

"This is not as simple as it looked from the air," said Stretch. "Every steep bank looks like it could be the dark area we're looking for."

"It's a challenge," said Sam. "Takes years of practice. And fortunately, we've had years of practice."

"Wait," said Travis referring to the GPS and pointing to a thick bed of ferns growing at the edge of the trail. "If I'm reading this right, we go in here."

The men veered off the hiking trail and made their way into the swamp. The woods were dark, lonely, and full of shadows. Giant trees and humble bushes were so thick that at times they couldn't see fifteen feet in front of them. A curtain created by strands of moss and tangled vines almost shut out the sunlight, and they had the feeling that they were intruding on some primeval sacred place.

The forest vibrated with sound…the hum of cicada; the twitter of nesting birds; the bleep of nutrias; the chatter of squirrels; the cry of water fowl. On the ground there was a thick carpet of leaves and underbrush, and slimy creeping things moved in the rotting vegetation. Wild grape, nettles, and blackberry thorns tore at their clothes, and the deer flies plagued them. They splashed through murky swamp water and dry stream beds. The musty smell of the swamp filled their nostrils. The men realized how easy it would be to become mesmerized by the awesome surroundings, but reminded themselves it was necessary to remain vigilant for snakes and alligators.

They reached a ravine with a tree lying across it. The log appeared to be rotten and unsubstantial.

"Shall we try it or take another tack?" asked Travis.

"I say give it a try," said Sam. "Old Drane may have planned for a rotting log to put us off his trail."

Although there wasn't much of a drop from the log to the ravine below, the men crossed cautiously one at a time.

Sam's notion paid off. About twenty feet beyond the log crossing, they saw it. Maynard Dwayne Drane's still. It was tucked away under a steep bank, and a clear stream trickled quietly in front of it.

"Do I know my bootleggers or what?" Sam shouted exuberantly.

The men moved in to take a closer look, and Travis immediately began taking photographs. The still was situated above a pit filled with ashes. The contraption was made of galvanized steel. One end of a car radiator was attached to the still, and the other end was attached to a huge container that stood ready to collect the liquid that passed through the radiator. The container was empty, but a sour smell emanated from the still. Tom investigated and discovered that it contained slop, the corn meal mixture that is left over from the previous cooking. Apparently Dwayne Drane planned to used the slop again.

"Say, this is some set-up," Stretch said breathing hard to catch his breath. "I never saw one of these before."

"This is nothing, Stretch," said Tom. "This is a real cheap one."

"That's old Dwayne," said one of the uniformed officers. "He was nothing if not cheap."

"Why do you say it's cheap?" asked Stretch.

Sam explained, "When you find a quality set-up, the still is made of stainless steel, and a copper tube is used to collect the vapors. Here you got a galvanized steel still that's been soldered together, and that car radiator there was used in place of copper tubing to condense the vapors. Drane probably threw this whole set-up together for three, four hundred dollars."

"Cheap stills like this are hazardous. Good source of lead poisoning," said Tom.

Travis finished shooting photos, and went over to investigate the contents of four tightly closed large metal drums. Animal footprints covered the containers and the ground around them. Scratch marks were etched into the metal, and one barrel lay on its side.

"Sam hand me that crowbar," he said.

Sam brought the tool to Travis, and they pried off the lids. Inside the barrels, they found cornmeal, sugar, yeast, and some unidentifiable powder.

"Well, we found Drane's moonshine ingredients," said Travis.

"Yeah, but what the heck is this?" asked Sam. He licked his finger, touched it to the powder, and sniffed it.

"No telling. Must be Maynard's special ingredient," laughed Tom.

"Maybe its Drano," said Stretch.

Stretch laughed. "Don't laugh," said Tom. "Bootleggers have been known to use Drano for that extra kick."

"Lead poisoning, Drano," said Stretch. "Why the world would anybody buy this stuff?"

Sam and Travis tapped the lids back on the barrels tightly, and rolled them aside.

"How do you suppose he got the moonshine out of here?" asked one of the officers. "He couldn't tote moonshine out the way we came in."

"I suspect if we follow that stream," said Travis, "we'll come out somewhere in the river."

"Okay boys, let's tear her down," said Sam as he wielded a pick axe against the still spilling the slop onto the ground.

The other men followed suit, and soon a pile of shattered, twisted metal was strewn where Maynard Dwayne Drane's handiwork once stood.

Sam said, "Let's get out of here before it gets dark. I want to try to exit by following this stream. I think this was how Drane got his moonshine out. What do you want to bet that it leads to the river?"

"No takers here," said one of the officers. "Floating the stuff down this stream has got to be the only way."

The water was knee high, so they walked along the banks of the stream through marsh grass and thick green ferns. Slanting shadows cut through leafy branches and cast eerie shadows along the stream bank. Bushes rustled in the breeze, and they could hear the sound of animals scurrying off in the woods close by. Then the stream widened, and they were suddenly standing on the banks of the Alligator River.

"There she is," said Tom. "Drane's transportation route."

Flattened marsh grass and broken cattails evidenced that the river bank had been utilized, and a trail of compressed mud and sand at the water's edge indicated that a boat had been banked there.

"Now where the heck do we go from here?" asked Stretch.

"Try walking over that way," said Travis pointing west. Stretch turned and looked in the direction Travis indicated, and there only a couple of hundred yards down the riverbank was a parking lot for the Alligator River National Wildlife Refuge. Then looking out upon the river Stretch saw three fishermen bobbing about in a Carolina Skiff.

"What was he thinking?" said Stretch. "This is a heavily traveled area. He could have been spotted."

"I'm sure that Old Maynard worked at night," said Sam. "Besides, how does that old saying go…if you really want to hide something, put it in a conspicuous place?"

The sun was setting as the men drove across the bridge to Roanoke Island. A crimson glow splashed the clouds that floated just above the western horizon, and a gray mist of departing sunlight hovered over the Croatan Sound. The air was warm and a gentle breeze blew off the water.

They dropped Stretch off at the airport, and headed to the Dare County Justice Center. The parking lot was almost empty, but they recognized the few cars still there. The spot marked *RESERVED FOR SHERIFF* was occupied, and they spotted Shucks' and Nona's cars. The men were caked with mud, covered with scratches, and briars had torn at their clothes. They entered the nearly-deserted building and walked straight to the sheriff's office. There they found Caffy, Nona, and Shucks kicked back with coffee in their hands.

"What took you so long?" said Sheriff Caffy.

"Long?" said Sam "We weren't gone long. This was a walk in the park compared to some hunts I've been on. Why did you miss me?" He looked at Nona and winked. Nona rolled her eyes and turned a shoulder to him.

Caffy laughed and said, "Get yourselves a cup and take a load off. Want to hear about your day."

"I could use something stronger than coffee," said Tom. "But I guess this'll have to do."

Tom, Sam, and Travis took turns reporting. They told about using the aerial map and GPS to locate the site, described the cheap still they'd smashed, and told how Drane moved the moonshine out of the swamp by water.

"Sounds like a good day's work," said Caffy. "I'll get with the park rangers and see about getting that debris cleaned up. Wouldn't want somebody else going in there and recycling what's left."

"Not much left to recycle," said Travis. "but there is a lot of debris. The barrels containing ingredients ought to be taken out and discarded before they rust and the contents spill out. We don't want the wildlife to get in it. No telling what's in that one barrel."

"Hey, let's hear about the jeep you found," said Sam.

Shucks told them about the discovery, the identification, and that the vehicle was in the shop to be checked for evidence. Sam noticed that Nona allowed Shucks to do all the reporting.

"So what have you got at this point?" asked Travis.

"Only that it's Drane's vehicle, and it's clear that he hit something. With Elizabeth Early's description and the damage to the front of the vehicle it's pretty conclusive that it's the vehicle that struck her," said the sheriff. "Was he driving the jeep? I don't know. But we're headed towards a strong case."

"And we still don't know how the vehicle got in the sound," added Shucks.

"Right," said the sheriff. "But don't worry. We'll tear the jeep down to the frame looking for evidence if we have to." Caffy stood up, raised his arms and stretched. "Well, can't do anything else now, so let's call it a night." They followed the sheriff out of the building and watched him drive out of the parking lot.

"So where do you guys plan to eat tonight?" asked Tom.

They decided to meet at Guthrie's for dinner. As Nona backed her car out of the parking space, Sam lifted his palm signaling her to stop.

"You'll be there won't you?" he asked with unprecedented awkwardness.

Nona lifted an eyebrow and smiled. "Why Sam, I wouldn't miss it for anything."

While Sam showered, Travis took advantage of the privacy to call Eve. He waited anxiously as the phone rang three, four, five, six times. He was just about to hang up when a breathless voice said, "Hello."

"Eve, this is Travis. Travis White. You doing okay?"

"Oh Travis, yes, I'm fine," she said. Then there was an awkward pause. Neither knew what to say next. Finally Eve said, "Thank you for staying last night, Travis. I was…was not myself I'm afraid."

"Well, that's understandable," said Travis. "Eve, I was wondering if…well, if you're not busy…I was wondering if I could maybe stop by tonight. If that's okay?"

Eve gave a little laugh. "I'd love that Travis, but I have to work."

"Oh," said Travis, disappointment apparent in his voice. "I'm sorry…I should have…I'm sorry."

Eve interrupted, "But I sure could use a ride home after work. If it's not too late for you to pick me up."

Travis jumped at the chance. With great excitement he said, "No, no it's not too late. I'd be glad to drive you home. See you then." And he started to hang up.

"Travis, Travis," Eve cried, "Don't you want to know what time I get off work?"

Travis felt his face flush. "Uh yes," he said. I was just going to ask you...what time do you get off work."

Eve laughed. "Eleven o'clock."

"Eleven o'clock. Yes, eleven. I'll pick you up at eleven," Travis stammered.

"Goodbye, Travis," said Eve.

"Bye Eve," and he clicked the off button and dropped the phone like a hot coal. "WHEW!" he said.

Travis heard a snicker from behind him and turned to see Sam standing at the bathroom door clutching a towel around his waist.

"Well, well," Sam said with a wicked grin. "Looks like my old buddy, Trav, will be conducting further investigation tonight."

CHAPTER 25

Travis and Sam arrived at Guthrie's and spotted Tom and Stretch sitting at a round wooden table for six by a window. A half-empty beer pitcher suggested that they had already begun to unwind The usual tranquil view beyond the window was cloaked in darkness, and only an occasional light from a fisherman's boat could be seen bobbing up and down in the sound. Travis and Sam walked directly to the dining room and joined them.

"Looks like you two have several up on us," said Travis eyeing the pitcher and their empty glasses.

"Pull up a chair and take a load off," said Tom. "Let's see about catching you up." He motioned to Irene who was working the cash register and playing hostess in the off-season.

She nodded, said 'good night' to a departing customer, and walked back to their table.

"Well, if it ain't the Seaboard boys again. You snuck right by me. Ya'll alright tonight?" Irene said.

"Irene, honey," said Sam with bogus sincerity in his eyes, "Now that you're here, how could anything not be right? The only thing that could make life better is for you to bring us a couple more glasses and another pitcher of beer. By the way, is Doo-Wop working tonight?"

"He sure is," said Irene. "And things are running lots smoother in the kitchen with the old Doo-Wop in charge. Thanks to the Seaboard boys here." She placed a hand on Travis' shoulder and smiled broadly. "You want a menu, hon?"

Travis patted Irene's hand and said, "We will later. Have to wait for Shucks and Nona. They haven't been in have they?"

"Not yet honey," she said. "But it's early. And you know Nona. She's got to put on a lot a war paint before making her grand entrance. Guess you'll just have to wait a while."

"And it'll be worth the wait," Sam said dreamily. He quickly realized how immature that sounded. He looked embarrassed, and his face turned red.

"Hey, Sam," said Stretch. "you ain't blushing are you?"

Tom said, "I got something I've been wanting to asked you guys ever since I met you."

"What's that Tom?" asked Travis.

"Now how long have you two lived in Seaboard?" Tom said.

"All our lives. You're talking about half a century there," said Travis. "Why do you ask?"

"Well, how long does a guy have to live in Seaboard before they stop calling him *boy?*" Tom asked.

Sam threw his head back, laughed, and said, "That's just part of the 'good ole boy notion'. In Seaboard you're called boy as long as there's a living man in town older than you."

Tom laughed. "Thanks for clearing that up for me, Sam."

"Any time, Tom, any time," said Sam.

At that moment, the door opened, and Shucks walked in. Recognizing the laughter from the dining room, he walked straight back to the table.

"Hey, fellas," Shucks said pulling up a chair. "What's so funny?"

Travis told Shucks how Sam let down his guard and revealed his obsession with Nona. "That's no surprise to me," said Shucks. "I've known for a long time that Sam was taken with Nona. My surprise is that he's embarrassed about it."

"Where you been, Shucks," asked Sam in an effort to take the heat off of himself. "Thought you'd get here before us."

"Oh, I've been over to see my Aunt Lila. She lives by herself, and I thought she might want to hear about my day," said Shucks.

Travis said, "I didn't know you had an aunt, Shucks."

"Sure," Shucks said. "Actually she helped raise me. Every night I go by or call, and she asks how my day was. Usually I don't have anything to tell her...not anything real exciting anyway. But today was pretty darned exciting, so I wanted to tell her about it in person. That made me run a little late."

Tom said, "That's good, Shucks. Real good that you have family nearby...or I guess nearby. Where does your aunt live anyway?"

"She lives over close to Nags Head Woods. Just off Ocean Acres. Not too far from Pig Pulling Barbecue. She just loves that barbecue, too. Matter of fact I picked some up for her tonight...."

Travis interrupted, "Shucks, does your aunt live close to Eve Drane?"

"Not too far. Why?" said Shucks.

"Does she drive a car?" asked Travis.

"Yes, Travis, she does," Shucks sounded concerned.

"What's this all about, Travis?" asked Sam.

"Yeah, Travis," said Shucks, "I know she's old to be driving but she's real careful. She never takes her eyes off the road. Why she could drive right pass you in that big old Cadillac of hers and never see you. She pays strict attention to the road."

"Shucks, is your aunt's last name Grimsley?" asked Travis

"Travis, you're starting to worry me," said Shucks. "Yes, she's Lila Grimsley. Now why are you asking?"

Travis relaxed. "Sorry, I didn't mean to worry you, Shucks. It's just that I've met Lila Grimsley, and I didn't know that she was your aunt. She's a real nice lady, Shucks."

Shucks relaxed and grinned. "That she is. As I said, I try to check on her every night. She lives alone. How did you meet Aunt Lila, Travis."

"I talked with Eve Drane's neighbors after the murder. Lila Grimsley was one of the neighbors I interviewed. She said she saw a sheriff's car. Could have been your car she saw that night," said Travis.

"It was. Wednesday night is her prayer meeting night. I just like to drive by and make sure everything looks okay when she goes out at night," said Shucks. He hesitated and added. "Ah, Travis, I never mentioned this to Sheriff Caffy. You know about checking on my Aunt Lila the night of the murder. I was afraid to tell him I was doing something personal while on duty. You won't mention it, will you?"

"Of course not," said Travis. Inwardly Travis breathed a sigh of relief. This answered the question of why Shucks was cruising around in Maynard Dwayne Drane's neighborhood the night of the murder. Now if he only knew how peanut shells got on the beach where they shouldn't have been.

The conversation turned to the events of the day. Shucks was especially exuberant. He drew from a bottle of Corolla and related again how Maynard Dwayne Drane's jeep was found submerged in the sound, how they'd had it towed, and speculated about evidence that the shop would uncover. Then he asked dozens of questions about the discovery of the still...its exact location, description, how they'd smashed it, and how Drane transported the moonshine out of the swamp. He repeated over and over how he wished he's been with them at the Alligator River National Wildlife Refuge *bust*, as he called it.

"Hey fellas," said Shucks, "Answer this question for me if you can."

"IF we can?" said Sam. "You ask it...we'll answer it."

"Well, I always wondered why they call bootleg whiskey moonshine."

"Now Shucks, if we're gonna have a quiz session, you'll have to come up with tougher questions than that," boasted Sam. "It's called moonshine because night is the most undetectable time to work a still. Also at night there's not as much chance that someone will catch a whiff of the stench."

Shucks reiterated how he would 'give anything' to go on a *bust*, and assured them that he'd be available to assist them at the 'drop of a hat'.

When Shucks stopped to take a breath, Sam laughed and said, "Hey Shucks, you're really wired tonight."

They were all getting a kick out of Shucks' enthusiasm. The successes he'd experienced the pass couple of days boosted his confidence and created an entirely new Shucks.

Suddenly the door opened, the room fell silent, and in floated Nona in all her splendor. Her blonde hair was braided into one long plait and interlaced with iridescent green ribbon. She wore a simple green, ankle-length dress made of a thin gauzy material. The skirt was full and the way it clung to her body left no question but that there was little underneath. The bodice scooped low like a big green crescent moon barely eclipsing the creamy white mounds of her breasts. A soft red leather belt was tied around her waist, and she wore no jewelry save earrings of multi-colored stones that bounced and swung as she pranced into the room. The joie de vivre of her entrance seemed to energize the diners, and silence quickly turned to lighthearted chatter.

Nona walked straight to their table and said, "Hello, boys." She placed a hand on her hip and looked down at the men commandingly. When she spoke again, her voice was husky, "Hope I didn't keep you waiting."

"Well, you sure..." Shucks began.

"Not at all," interrupted Tom as he stood and pulled out a chair. "We were just...ah...we were...what were we doing?"

They all laughed. Nona sat down.

"Nona, when you change out of your uniform, a magnificent metamorphosis takes place," said Tom.

Sam smirked. "I wish I'd said that," he said.

"Yeah, Tom beat your time, Sam," Travis jibed.

Shucks continued the banter, "Well, I don't think Sam could ever wax that eloquently."

They gawked at Shucks.

Then Travis said, "*WAX ELOGUENTLY, WAX ELOQUENTLY*! Shucks, where do you get this stuff? The other night it was besotted...."

"Besotted? Did you say besotted?" asked Stretch.

"What's besotted," asked Tom.

"You know...besotted this, besotted that," Sam picked it up quickly fearing that besotted would be explained in terms of his being obsessed with Nona. "Explain this waxing eloquently, Shucks."

As Shucks expounded on his explanation of *waxing eloquently*, he did not mind that the others were laughing. He knew that tonight they were laughing with him not at him.

Finally Sam slapped Shucks on the back and said, "Shucks, my man, you're amazing. Ain't he amazing?"

Suddenly Sam realized that the other people at the table were not looking at him. They were staring intently in the direction of the bar. He turned and saw Chuckie Ryan standing at the bar with two strangers. Sam did not recognize Chuckie's drinking buddies, except that they presented the same imposing figure as Chuckie...very tall, very dark, very athletic, and very handsome. The table fell silent, and they all looked at Nona. At first she appeared to be surprised, and then her face took on a cool, poised look of self confidence. She pushed her chair away from the table, stood up, and began to walk slowly, purposely towards the bar. Sam started to stand up, but Shucks put a hand on his arm.

"Don't do it, Sam," Shucks said. "Nona's got a tongue as sharp as a shark's tooth, and she can take care of herself. She'll resent your interference." Sam sat back down.

As Chuckie lifted his glass he saw Nona approaching. He smiled broadly, but the smile disappeared quickly when Nona reached the bar and faced him doggedly. The spectators back at the table could not hear what was being said, but the demeanor and body language of the two indicated that Nona had a lot to say, and Chuckie offered little rebuttal. Chuckie's two companions stood wide eyed and open mouthed at the spectacle taking place before them. Soon all eyes at the bar were upon Nona and Chuckie. Then Chuckie set down his glass, threw a bill onto the bar, and retreated through the door with his companions right behind. The bartender walked over to Nona, said something, and started to pick up the glass. Nona waved his hand away from the glass. She said something to the bartender, and he left and returned with a paper bag used for carry-outs. Using a cocktail napkin, she placed the glass in the bag, walked back to the table, and carefully set the bagged glass down.

Nona collapsed into the chair. "Whew!" she said.

"Looks like you really rattled old Chuckie's chain," said Sam.

"You alright, Nona?" asked Shucks.

Nona sat up straight, regained her composure, and said, "I'm alright. The bigger they are, the harder they fall."

"What's with the glass?" asked Travis.

"Something just doesn't feel right about old Chuckie, Duckie," said Nona. "I want to run a finger print check, see what we come up with."

Sam leaned forward and said, "I think that's a good idea. I keep thinking of Chuckie and Drane's interest in diving. I don't think Chuckie was after buying moonshine, but diving allowed the men's paths to cross, and now Drane's dead. It's just makes sense to look at that connection."

"Good. I'll send in for a fingerprint check first thing in the morning," said Nona, a look of satisfaction on her face. "Now let's order. I'm hungry."

Tom motioned to Irene, and she walked immediately to the table. "Bet you've worked up an appetite, honey," said Irene as she passed out menus. "I was glad to see you put that guy in his place. He just seemed to think too highly of himself…if you know what I mean."

They all agreed with Irene's opinion of Chuckie and ordered lavishly. The discovery of Drane's jeep, smashing the still, meeting with Sheriff Caffy, and Nona's confrontation with Chuckie Ryan left them all ravenous. They ate heartily and with little conversation.

"The perfect end to a great day," said Shucks as he tossed his napkin on the table and pushed his chair back.

They all muttered in agreement and began to discuss splitting up the bill. Travis looked at his watch nervously.

"Say Sam, let me give you this. Take care of my part will you?" He handed Sam a bill, stood up and announced, "Uh, I have another commitment."

Sam grinned broadly. "Sure, Trav, I'll be glad to take care of your part so you can take care of your other *commitment.*"

"Travis, you need any help?" asked Shucks. "If you do, I don't have any place else to go."

Travis was already out the door. Sam said, "Shucks, Trav doesn't need any help with what he's going to do. Believe me."

"Well, if you say so," said Shucks. "Just trying to be helpful…."

They walked to the parking lot together. Stretch said, "Shucks, you could help me if you don't mind."

"Sure," said Shucks.

"Drop me off at my place in Manteo. It's out of the way for Tom since he's staying over at Nags Head," said Stretch.

"Sure Stretch, sure. See ya'll tomorrow," he said over his shoulder and led the way to his car.

Tom climbed into his rental car, threw up a hand, pulled out of the parking lot, and headed towards Nags Head.

"Well, alone at last," said Sam turning to Nona.

Nona did not say anything. Sam was surprised at the feeling of ineptness that suddenly swept over him. After all, this was what he'd waited for every since he met Nona Godette...to be alone with her, to have a chance to overwhelm her with his charisma, to chance to demonstrate his moves. What was happening? He felt like a star-struck kid trying to get up the nerve to ask a girl out on a first date.

After what seemed like an eternity of silence, humiliation set in, and Sam said simply, "See you tomorrow, Nona." And turned and walked towards his truck.

"For someone who talks big, you sure do give up easy," Nona said from behind him.

Sam turned, and she walked towards him. "I'd like you to do something for me."

The old Sam suddenly resurfaced, grinned, and said slyly, "I'm always at your service, Nona."

"Well, that was a quick recovery," Nona said.

Sam laughed, and then in a more serious tone said, "What do you want me to do?"

"I want you to go with me to the beach. Down to the Bladen Street access. I want to go to the beach at night and take a careful look at the spot that Chuckie Ryan signaled from. We might notice something we missed the other morning."

"Nona, I can't think of anyone I'd rather spend an evening on the beach with than you," the old Sam replied. He opened the door to his jeep, bowed lowly, and held out his hand to Nona. She climbed in making no effort to cover her knees as her green skirt slid up on the plastic seat covers.

CHAPTER 26

Doo-Wop returned to work at Guthrie's leaving Grand-Pop Early to take care of Short Sugar. Grand-Pop Early took seriously the responsibility of caring for his granddaughter. His feelings for Elizabeth rose above the feelings of love, devotion, and commitment typical of proud grandparents. Tonight he was not just taking care of his lovely, intelligent granddaughter. He was safeguarding hope, opportunity, and accomplishment for his future progeny...descendants that will have transcended the bonds of slavery, poverty, and ignorance and in doing so would validate the significance to his own wretched life.

Grand-Pop Early had already checked on Short Sugar a dozen times, but once more he opened her bedroom door and crept into the room. He looked toward the single bed by the window. The moon was up, and stars blanketed the cobalt blue sky. The silhouette of tree branches waved gently in the breeze. The curtains were slightly parted, and a slice of moonlight shone brightly on the girl's face.

With alarm, Grand-Pop Early moved swiftly across the room to her bed. His fearful eyes reflected a primitive belief that had survived centuries...an African belief that evil is invited in when moonlight shines on a sleeping person's face. Grand-Pop Early quickly reached across the bed and closed the curtains tightly shutting out the glow.

When Travis arrived at the bait shop, he was troubled to see the place dark. He pulled into the parking lot, jumped out of his car, and took all three steps in one leap. He reached for the door handle and shook it. Locked.

Then from the dark corner of the porch a voice said, "Travis, I'm here."

He turned to see Eve sitting on the plank bench with a young man Travis recognized as a clerk in the shop.

Travis crossed the porch and took her hands pulling her up. "Hey, it gave me a scare when I saw the place dark and all locked up." He squeezed her hand.

"I'm sorry," she said. "We weren't busy, so we just closed early. Hours are pretty erratic in the off-season. Travis, I'd like you to meet David. David works at the shop, and he kept me company till you got here."

Travis shook hands with the young man. "Thanks, David," he said. Turning to Eve he added. "I feel so foolish. I was just sitting down at Guthrie's shooting the breeze with some of the guys. I could have been here earlier."

"Not to worry," smiled Eve. "David is very good company." The young man smiled shyly.

Travis slapped David on the back and said, "Thanks, again pal."

They were silent as they drove towards Eve house. Eve smiled and looked out the side window. Travis glanced at her surreptitiously. Finally he reached over and clicked on the radio.

"You like music?" he asked.

"Yes," she said pleasantly.

"What kind do you like?" he asked as he nervously turned the selector knob passing several stations.

"Oh, I usually listen to the beach music station," she said.

"Me, too," he said as he moved quickly to that station and increased the volume. "How's that?"

"That's good," she said.

When they couldn't think of anything else to say, they drove in silence and allowed the music to fill the void. The windows were open, and the breeze felt cool and invigorating. Although the night was still, there was the smell of rain in the air, a warning of an approaching storm. They only passed a few cars, and when they turned onto Ocean Acres they noticed that Pig Pulling Barbecue was dark, the parking lot empty.

"Not much night life here this time of year," Eve said.

"Suits me fine," said Travis. "Night life on the beach means work for me."

The car crunched onto the shell drive of Eve's house. Almost simultaneously, a deep, loud woof was heard. When Travis looked in the direction of the barking he saw an enormous white head with peaked ears and a smiling face. The animal was excited and threatened to come through the window if they didn't move faster.

"I think Misha sits there the entire time I'm at work," said Eve.

"He's just watching the street like any good watch dog," said Travis opening the car door for Eve.

Eve unlocked the front door and a hundred pounds of white, wooly dog bounded from one to the other registering his complaints at having been left alone so long. Travis rumpled the dog's thick coat and scratched behind his ear. Eve was gentle and reassuring and spoke to him as if he were a child., "Misha, I told you I'd be home at eleven. I always try to keep my word. Good dog. Now outside. It's been a long time between visits with Mother Nature."

The dog let go with one more round of woofs as if to get in the last word, turned, and headed for the woods. Eve closed the door and walked towards the back of the house. Travis looked around him. He was amazed. When he left that morning, the house was a disaster. Mud tracked onto the floors, even the contents of the refrigerator strewn about. Now, the house looked as it had the first time Travis saw it…neat, orderly, clean.

"Eve, how did you do it? How did you clean up the mess so quickly. Did someone help you?" Travis said.

Eve laughed. "No, I cleaned it myself."

"You should have waited. I wanted to pitch in tonight," said Travis.

Eve placed her purse on the kitchen counter, removed her sweater, and looked at Travis appreciatively. She said, "Thank you Travis for wanting to help. Thank you for taking my part in that ordeal last night. But this was something I had to do myself." She moved to the refrigerator and took out a pitcher of sweet tea.

"Tea?"

"Yes," Travis said. "But I really don't understand why you wanted to clean up after Clelon Purvis yourself."

Eve filled the glasses with ice and set them on the kitchen table. They sat down, and she continued, "I suppose you could say that cleaning up last night's mess was symbolic. I was in a sense cleaning up Maynard's mess for the last time. Every time I put something in a trash bag or scrubbed up muddy footprints, I told myself that I'm doing this myself, and I'll never have to do it again." She paused and took a sip of tea. Then she said simply, "It was really therapeutic."

Travis smiled. "Eve Drane, you're one remarkable lady."

"And that's another thing," she said. "I'm taking back my maiden name. I will no longer go by Eve Drane, I'll be Eve Dunbar."

Travis reached across the table and took her hand. He said, "Hello Eve Dunbar. Glad to meet you. I'm Travis White."

They laughed and leaned towards each other, their lips so very close. Then suddenly there was a furious scratching at the front door, followed by a demanding 'yap'. They were both jolted to attention. Eve laughed, "That's Misha."

"We'll have to do something about his timing," said Travis.

"He's so afraid he'll miss something." Eve laughed and walked towards the door.

"And he almost did," muttered Travis.

Eve went to the door, let Misha in, and returned to the table. She moved her chair closer to Travis, took his hand, smiled, and said, "You know how I spent my day, now tell me what you were up to."

Travis told Eve about the search of the swamp, the discovery of Maynard's still, and how they destroyed it. He was afraid that the story of finding the still would ruin the moment, but much to his relief, it did the opposite.

"Well, Travis, it looks like we both took care of Maynard today. Now we have a clean slate," she said wearily.

"Eve," said Travis his voice taking on a more serious edge, "I want to talk to you about something. First of all let me tell you that Sheriff Caffy was appalled by what happened here last night. He certainly never intended that one of his officers do something like that."

"I know," said Eve. "Sheriff Caffy called me this morning."

"Good," said Travis. "Also, the Sheriff wanted me to ask you if you'd be willing to come down and talk to him about Maynard. You know, we still haven't solved his murder."

"You don't think I'm a suspect do you?" she asked.

"Absolutely not," he said.

"Then I'll do it," she said. "I have been thinking about doing a little investigating of my own."

"Eve, don't do it," Travis said with alarm. "Don't go off on your own digging up stuff about Maynard and his *business acquaintances.* If you think Maynard was bad, he's nothing compared to some guys that get mixed up in bootlegging. They'd make life with Maynard seem like a day at Disney World. Eve, promise me you won't do anything by yourself." Travis's eyes were fearful, imploring.

Eve sighed and said, "Okay. I'll leave the investigating up to you and the Sheriff."

"Promise?" he wanted further assurance.

She smiled. "Promise." How comforting it was to have someone show concern for her, she thought.

Eve fed Misha while Travis built a fire. It wasn't cold but the fire created a peaceful, romantic ambience. Eve turned on the radio already tuned to the beach music station, lighted several candles, and placed them strategically about the room. Shadows flickered in the dark corners and the smell of burning wood filled the room. They sat in comfortable silence and watched as orange and blue flames licked at the wood that popped and crackled and then fell into glowing embers beneath the grate.

The hectic day began to catch up with them, and exhaustion set in. Travis' arm rested protectively around Eve, and she laid her head on his shoulder. He gazed down at her lovely face with a nest of freckles sprinkled across her pixie nose. Her feet were tucked under her and a woolen throw covered her lap. Eve lay very still, and Travis's eyelids grew heavy. He stifled a yawn.

"Eve, it's getting late," he said. "I've got to get back to the Sand Trap. I know...."

Eve stirred. "Don't go, Travis. Please don't go."

She arose slowly, took Travis's hands, and tugged gently. They stood and embrace. Then without another word, they moved towards the bedroom. Misha, who had been sleeping in a far corner of the room, raised his head, watched the couple go into the bedroom, yawned, and went back to sleep.

Sam drove to the Dare County Justice Center so Nona could secure the glass with Chuckie Ryan's fingerprints on it. As he waited outside, he considered the interesting situation in which he found himself. How long had he played cat and mouse games with Nona Godette? How many nights had he lay awake thinking of unique ploys to get her attention? How much time had he spent thinking up come-backs to her quips? How often had he blown a chance to be with her because of some jibe he couldn't resist throwing her way? Now he was alone with her and all her exciting eccentricities. Alone with the untouchable Nona Godette.

"And how will I screw it up this time?" he asked himself. Sam felt like a character out of some capricious romantic comedy.

He heard the door to the Center slam and looked up to see Nona bouncing down the steps. "Okay," she said as she opened the car door. "The glass is locked up safe and sound. Let's do it." Sam decided to let that one pass.

They drove in silence across the bridge and into Nags Head. There were few lights on in the houses along the way, and many vacation cottages were already boarded up. Some deserted streets looked like the set from a science fiction movie. They arrived at the Bladen Street Access and pulled into the parking lot.

Sam said, "Exactly where did Chuckie park?"

Nona thought for a few moments and then said, "Over there. Two spaces over from the gazebo."

Sam pulled into the same spot. They got out of the car. Sam looked toward the go-cart establishment shop the street. "Show me where you were when you saw Chuckie return the signal."

They walked towards the parking lot entrance, and Nona stopped. "I was right here," she said. "I saw Chuckie return to his car, get what I would later realize was a flashlight, return to the platform, and give that signal."

Sam stood where Nona had stood. He looked at the car and then towards the platform.

"Okay," he said and walked towards the steps.

They climbed the steps to the platform overlooking the beach. "Now tell me exactly where Chuckie stood when he signaled," said Sam.

Nona walked forward on the platform, turned towards the beach, and chose a spot. "Here," she said. "He stood here."

Sam moved to where Nona was standing and looked out over the ocean. Although clouds were creeping up from the horizon, the silver moon was full and high illuminating the beach. Mist and froth from the ocean rolled across the sand, and in the distance they saw the white plastic markers bobbing up and down. The white caps that floated above the wrecks looked like beckoning hands beseeching onlookers to join the occupants of the sunken ships.

Sam walked to the edge of the platform and used a night vision scope to study the ocean just beyond the breakers. The surf was beginning to build, and there was a heavy ominous stillness that precedes a storm. He descended the steps and walked for some time along the beach in the shadows of the dunes. Then from the southern horizon, lightening flashed giving a clearer view of the shoreline, and an angry sweep of wind blew in from the ocean. Sam quickly retraced his path, but soon rain fell in torrents. Although impeded by the sand he jogged in the direction of the steps. Rain pelted his face, his shoes quickly became waterlogged, and his clothes drenched. He finally reached the steps breathless and soaked. He assumed that Nona took refuge in the car, and was surprised when he looked up at the platform. She was standing in the same spot he'd left her. Her face shone with rain and her dripping hair was glued to her head. Her wet dress clung to her long legs and white breast. Concern etched on her face.

"Sam, quick," she shouted. "It's dangerous to be on the beach when it's lightening."

Sam mounted the steps quickly, and they raced for the protection of the car.

"Nona," he said searching the car for something to use as a towel. "You should have come back to the car. You're soaked." Then he looked at her. Her head was thrown back upon the headrest. She was breathing heavily, and her breasts heaved with each breath. Sam watched this erotic motion and waited for her breathing to become less labored. Finally she sat quietly.

Sam said, "Nona, what ever made you take up with the likes of Chuckie Ryan?"

She turned her face towards him and said softly, "Stupid! I got tired of waiting for you...Mr. All Talk and No Action."

Sam couldn't believe what he'd heard. "What? What did you say?"

"Come here, you," she said as she pulled his face towards hers.

Back at the Sand Trap they raced to Sam's apartment. They struggled to open the screen door that had slammed stuck by the wind. Once inside, they stripped off the wet clothes that clung stubbornly to their bodies, and let them drop in piles on the floor. They dove for the bed and buried themselves beneath a mound of blankets, sheets, and spreads.

Outside the wind blew strong and whistled around the corner of the building. The windows rattled, fierce thunder shook the walls, and enormous drops of rain walloped the windows. A glow from distant lightening penetrated the thin curtains and illuminated the hungry couple that seemed to draw energy and stamina from the fierce storm outside.

Finally they lay together exhausted, a tangle of slippery, wet arms and legs. They clutched each other desperately afraid to sleep. Afraid of dropping into that chasm of loneliness that they'd finally climbed out of.

CHAPTER 27

SATURDAY

A giant white canine paw nudged Travis into wakefulness. He opened his eyes and stared directly into brown almond shaped eyes set in that enormous white head with peaked ears. A dangling pink tongue protruded from the side of the dog's mouth, and Travis laughed at the animal's ridiculous smile.

"Hey, Misha," Travis said sleepily. "You're certainly not who I wanted to wake up with."

As Travis got out of bed, an uncertain feeling swept over him. He had not been with another woman since Ginny's death. He didn't feel guilty, but he did feel apprehensive. After so many years of loneliness he found someone to fill the emptiness, and he was suddenly afraid of losing her. He dressed hurriedly and walked to the kitchen.

The rain had stopped, and the wind that blew in through the open window was little more than a breeze. The radio was still set to the beach music station, and Otis Redding suggested that you *Try a Little Tenderness.* The smell of fresh coffee, sausage, and hot biscuits filled the room, and the table was set for two. Eve gave Travis a timid smile, looked away awkwardly, and continued to busy herself at the stove. This was what Travis feared. She had regrets. Regrets that last night was merely the result of loneliness, need, lust. He felt a surge of panic. He'd found her, and now he could lose her.

Travis crossed the room, gently grasped Eve's shoulders, and turned her to face him. He looked deeply into her eyes, and said, "Eve, don't be sorry. Please don't. We can take this as slow or as fast as you want to. But please tell me that you don't think last night was a mistake."

She looked at him warmly, reached up, and took his hands. "Travis," she whispered. "I'm so relieved. I couldn't sleep last night because I was afraid I'd wake up and you would be gone. After so many years with Maynard, it will take me a long time to completely trust anyone. Please be patient. Please try to understand."

"Hey, I'm the most patient, understanding guy you'll find. You'll see," Travis pulled her close and looked down into the bluest eyes he'd ever seen.

When Sam awoke, he realized the rain had stopped. Light filtered through the thin curtains, and he heard the squawk of gulls gliding above the beach in search of tasty morsels that the storm washed ashore. When he turned over, he was startled to find the other side of the bed empty. He sat up abruptly and looked at the clock. Eight o'clock. He also noticed that his car keys were gone. Pulling a bed sheet around his waist, he went to the window, threw open the curtains, and stared at the empty parking space where he'd parked his car the night before. Two men carrying fishing rods and tackle boxes walked pass the window, gawked at Sam, and roared with laughter. Nonchalantly Sam dropped the sheet, bowed deeply, and shouted, "Have a good day, gentlemen."

As Sam showered, he relived his night with Nona. And what a night it was! His only regret was that they wasted so many years with rivalry and wars of words. When he walked back into the bedroom, he was jolted into reality. Travis was sitting on the bed tossing an iridescent green ribbon back and forth in his hands.

"So, what's up, Sam?" he said with a sly grin on his face.

Sam smiled broadly. "Same as you, I'd suspect," he said.

They both laughed nervously. "Where's your car?" asked Travis.

"Think I've been carjacked," Sam said. "Gotta be sure to report it when I get to the Sheriff's office."

Travis drove them to the Buttermilk Biscuit Shop on the by-pass. They ate three country ham biscuits and large coffees and discussed what to do next. First, fax reports and pictures to Raleigh regarding the discovery and destruction of Drane's still. Then, meet with Sheriff Caffy, Nona, and Shucks to decide on the next step in the murder investigation of Maynard Dwayne Drane.

"Eve is willing to come in and talk about Drane. Don't know how much help she'll be though. The picture I'm getting of Drane is that he was big on secrets. Anyway, she even offered to assist in the investigation," Travis said with s smile.

"Hope you nipped that idea in the bud," said Sam. "If she thought Drane was bad...."

Travis interrupted, "Not to worry. I nixed that right away. But I was impressed that she'd entertain the idea. That gal is something else. Yes, she is."

"Don't go dreamy on me now, Trav. We got people to see and places to go. So let's have at it," Sam said as he stood and tossed his napkin and cup in the trash.

When they pulled into the parking lot of the Dare County Justice Center, they spotted Sam's Cherokee.

Travis pointed and said, "Now that we've located your stolen car, I'll turn the keys to this vehicle in to Sheriff Caffy."

"Yeah, I gotta investigate this theft thing first," said Sam as he swung from the car.

Once inside Sam made a beeline for the desk of Officer Nona Godette. There she was scrubbed and fresh in her starched, pressed uniform and looking every bit as tantalizing as she'd looked the night before when rain and wind lashed her clothes and pasted them against her wet body. 'She sure cleaned up nice,' thought Sam.

Sam cleared his throat and said solemnly, "Officer, can you tell how to go about reporting a stolen car?"

Nona looked up, cocked an eyebrow, and said, "Maybe I can help you."

"I just bet you can," Sam said.

"Can you tell me the circumstances under which your car was stolen?" said Nona.

"Well," said Sam, "I was temporarily...ah...distracted."

"I see," Nona said and leaned across the desk. "Care to elaborate on what kind of distraction."

"It's like this," said Sam bending to meet her. "There was..."

Sam did not have a chance to finish. Nona's phone rang.

"Damn," said Nona and reached for the receiver. Godette here," she said.

A tired voice said, "Nona, this is Doris. Sheriff Caffy wants to see you...*again*"

"What about?" Nona asked anxiously.

"Nona, if I knew *what about* I could tell you and you wouldn't have to bother him," she said.

"Does he want to see Shucks, too" Nona asked hopefully.

"No, just you. Better hurry up, Nona, he's real cantankerous," said Doris

"Cantankerous?" Nona repeated nervously, "I'll be right there." And she hung up.

"Who's cantankerous?" asked Sam who heard Nona's part of the conversation.

Nona stood up and began moving towards the hall. "Sheriff Caffy. He's already on my case. This could be bad, Sam. Real bad."

Nona hurried to Sheriff Caffy's office. She stopped at the door, took a deep breath, and knocked.

"Come," boomed Caffy.

Nona entered all smiles. "You wanted to see me Sheriff?" she said.

"Close the door," he ordered.

Sheriff Caffy looked up from his desk and motioned for Nona to enter and sit down. Then he slowly lay down his pen, leaned forward, and said very softly, "Officer, do you lay awake nights trying to think of ways to vex me? Must I look forward to starting every morning with some crisis that you've manufactured? Is this a test? Are you trying to see how far you can push before I shackle you to a desk?"

"Sheriff, I don't understand," said Nona. "What's going on?"

"What's going on, Officer," said Caffy, "is that we are once more being visited by the law enforcement elite. I use that term in jest, because I don't think the Feds are any better at law enforcement than the locals. Especially down here..."

"The Feds?" Nona said in surprise.

"Yes, Officer, the Feds," said Caffy, "And don't interrupt me. If you are surprised, just imagine how surprised I was when I got a call from Washington this morning saying that an FBI agent and two INS agents will be paying us a visit this afternoon at one o'clock. Now when I asked what their visit was in regard to, guess what they said."

Nona looked scared. "I have no idea."

"I was told that their visit is in regard to fingerprints submitted for identification by one of my officers. Now I didn't really have to ask because I felt pretty damned sure that I knew *which* officer, but to be on the safe side anyhow I asked 'which officer'. And guess who they said."

Nona said weakly, "Me."

"Yes, Nona, you," the sheriff said. "Now before I make an even bigger ass of myself, looking like some hick sheriff that don't know what the hell's going on in his own department," It was at this point that he shouted, "I WANT YOU TO TELL ME WHAT THE HELL'S GOING ON."

Suddenly the hubbub from the outer offices ceased. The silence was startling and for a moment Nona sat speechless. Sheriff Caffy's eyes were fixed mercilessly upon her.

"I know now what they are talking about, Sheriff," she said hesitantly. "What I did wasn't a breech of procedure. You see, I got these fingerprints of a possible suspect, and had them faxed to Raleigh for identification. I don't know anything about how the FBI or the INS got involved in this."

"Who was this suspect?" asked the Sheriff.

"It was Chuckie Ryan," said Nona.

The Sheriff leaned back in his chair and tapped his pen on the desk. Finally he said, "How did you get the prints?"

Nona told Sheriff Caffy about having dinner at Guthrie's, confronting Chuckie Ryan, how she lifted his prints, and then had them faxed to Raleigh for identification.

"Did you secure the evidence?" asked the Sheriff.

"Yes, sir. I brought the bagged glass here and locked it up until this morning when they were sent to Raleigh," said Nona.

"So tell me just who was at this little dinner party last night," said the Sheriff.

"The Seaboard boys, Shucks, Tom Mayes, and Stretch," said Nona. She was beginning to relax feeling that the possibilities of her being canned were diminishing.

"Where's Mayes now?" asked the Sheriff.

"I believe he's already gone back to DC. But the other guys are in the building," said Nona.

"Better get them in here. We need to brainstorm this thing before the Feds descend upon us," said the Sheriff.

Nona hurried out of the office as Sheriff Caffy shouted, "Doris, get me two extra strength Tylenol and a cup of coffee. And this time make it hot."

News that Nona was in trouble with Sheriff Caffy again spread through the building like wildfire. Heads turned away as she hurried through the halls looking for Sam and the others. She found Shucks, Travis, and Sam huddled together talking in whispers. As she approached, they bombarded her with questions.

"He wants to see us all right away," she said, made a hundred and eighty degree turn, and began walking back toward Sheriff Caffy's office.

As they rushed through the halls, Nona briefly filled them in on the reason why the Sheriff had raked her over the coals. When they reached Caffy's door, Doris was walking out of his office. She looked harried and shot Nona a look that would kill. The four stepped aside quickly and allowed her to pass.

The Sheriff was throwing tablets into his mouth and washing them down with hot coffee. He motioned them into the room and said, "Close the damned door." Shucks closed it.

The Sheriff said, "I suppose Nona told you that we are to receive a visit from the Feds this afternoon. What I need to know is how did Washington get involved in this? And why do they want to talk to us? You see, even though I've had lots of practice dealing with surprises…thanks to Officer Godette, here…I still like to know what the hell to expect when I go into a meeting with people at the federal level. So, give."

They had never seen the Sheriff so distraught. After a few moments of silence Travis said, "I think I can shed some light on how the Feds got involved. When prints go to Raleigh, they're flagged if the suspect is wanted for questioning by the FBI or other federal agencies. So what I'm thinking is that when Ryan's prints went through Raleigh, they were found to be flagged, and were sent on to Washington to whatever agency wanted to question them."

The Sheriff leaned back in his chair and tapped his pen on the desk. Finally he said, "So what does it tell us when the FBI and INS are the interested agencies?" he asked.

"FBI could be any of a countless number of federal charges," said Sam. "As for Immigration and Naturalization Services, that usually speaks to illegal entry into the country."

"Just what do we know about this Chuckie Ryan?" the Sheriff said looking at Nona.

Nona said, "Not that much. He came to the Outer Banks this summer. And we already told you, he likes to dive and explore sunken ships. And that's how he appears to spend most of his time."

"Employed?" the Sheriff asked.

"Not that I know of," Nona said.

"Where's he from?" the Sheriff said.

"I don't know," said Nona.

"What DO you know about this guy, Officer?" the Sheriff said.

Nona was beginning to feel foolish. She said weakly, "Not much, Sheriff. I only saw him socially…you know danced with him at public places like Guthrie's, things like that."

Sam intervened, "Sheriff, there was no reason to gather information on Chuckie Ryan until after we made this connection between him and Maynard Dwayne Drane."

"The diving connection, you mean?" asked the Sheriff.

"Yes. We intended to discuss that connection some more at briefing today," said Sam. "When we talked to the owner of the diving school, we discovered that both Drane and Ryan dived regularly near the Huron and Explorer wrecks down off the Bladen Street access. That's where Nona saw Ryan flash what appeared to be signals from the beach."

Sam hesitated, looked at Nona and then continued, "Last night after Officer Godette secured the glass with Ryan's fingerprints on it, she and I went down to the beach and checked out the signal area at night. We decided to recommend a more in depth investigation of Ryan's involvement in the murder of Drane. Thing is, you got that Washington call before we could update you."

"Hmmm." The Sheriff thought about this for a few minutes. "Where's this Ryan been staying?" he asked looking at Nona again.

"I don't know," she said. "As I said, I always saw him in public places."

Shucks, who had not spoken during the entire meeting, leaned forward and said meekly, "Ah, Sheriff, I know where Chuckie Ryan lives. Over at the Long Leaf Pines Apartments. He showed up around March 15 and has been there every since. A two bedroom place is rented in his name only. He paid six month's rent in advance. And he paid in cash." Shucks sat back and looked around at his astonished listeners.

After a few minutes Sheriff Caffy said, "Shucks, how'd you get all that?"

Shucks replied humbly, "Well, when Chuckie Ryan's name kept coming up, I thought it best to keep an eye on him. First off, we needed to know where he lives. So I got his address from the diving supply shop, went by, and talked to the Long Leaf Pines Apartment manager."

"When?" asked Nona.

"This morning," Shucks said.

After a few minutes, the Sheriff said, "Okay, the Feds will be here at one o'clock. See if you can find out anything else about Ryan, and for crap's sake don't scare him off. See you at one."

The four stood and walked towards the door. The Sheriff stopped them by saying, "By the way, Shucks, that was quick thinking. You, too, Nona."

As the office emptied, Doris stepped into Caffy's office. "You too, Nona?" she feigned shock.

"Yeah, I'm surprised, too," said Sheriff. "And you know what else...that Shucks has really come around. I used to think he was dumb as a stump, but he's turned into a regular Columbo."

CHAPTER 28

Travis hung up the phone and sat looking at the tablet on the desk.

"Okay," said Sam. "Let's have it. What did you get from Raleigh?"

"They're going to fax us this morning, but she read me what they have anyway," said Travis. He studied his sketchy notes for a few minutes and then said, "Let's see if I can read my own handwriting. Okay. Charles (Chuckie) Alonzo Ryan, alias: Carlos Ramirez, C.J. Ryman, Fredrick Sears. Born November 18, 1957, New York City. Distinguishing marks: tattoo of a scorpion on his left shoulder blade. Known Previous Employment: dock worker, ship yards, tugboat captain, diving instructor. Wanted For: Passing bad checks, forgery. Considered to be extremely dangerous.

Travis passed the note pad to Sam. "Bad checks, forgery? Why do you suppose the INS would be interested in someone wanted for passing bad checks and forgery?"

"Guess it would depend on what he used the money for and what he forged. This is out of our league," said Travis.

"Yeah, I know what you mean. Give me a good ole boy bootlegger any day. That's our game," said Sam.

Shucks and Nona cruised pass the Long Leaf Pines Apartments in an unmarked car and saw no sign of Chuckie Ryan's vehicle so they pulled into the parking lot and walked to the office. The manager was talking on the phone and motioned them in. They looked around the Spartan office. A metal file cabinet, a computer, desk, and two straight chairs comprised the entire furnishings of the room. There were no curtains, only metal blinds, and the windows were streaked from the salt water air.

The manager made no effort to rush his phone conversation, and Nona and Shucks began to worry that Chuckie would return and find them there. They stood by the window anxiously watching the street.

"If you're looking for Chuckie Ryan, you missed him," the manager said hanging up the phone.

Shucks and Nona spun around in alarm. "You mean he's checked out?" asked Shucks. "Thought you were going to call me if he tried to check out."

"Don't get yourself in an uproar," said the manager. "He ain't checked out. He's just gone away for a few hours."

"How do you know he'll come back?" Nona said envisioning Sheriff Caffy's reaction to the news that he was gone. After all, one of the last things he'd said was 'don't scare him off'.

"'Cause he said so. He's all time doing this," said the manager in a matter of fact manner.

"Doing what?" said Shucks.

"Why taking his visitors home or wherever he takes them," he said. "When he has company, they stay for a day or so, then Ryan comes in here and asks me to keep an eye on things while he drives his friends back. Sometimes he's gone a few hours, sometimes overnight."

"You said he took his friends back. Back where?" asked Nona.

"I don't ask," the manager said impatiently. "I leave tenants alone as long as they don't disturb anybody and pay their rent on time. And Ryan's rent is paid through this month. I figure what they do is their business. I ain't running no dormitory for kids here…this is an apartment building. And I rent only to adults."

The two officers frowned. Finally the manager said, "What?"

"I suppose I'm still afraid he won't come back," said Nona.

"You don't have nothing to worry about," said the manager. "Ain't nobody going to go off and leave all that equipment up there."

"Equipment? What kind of equipment?" said Shucks.

"All sorts of video and stereo equipment and a real state of the art computer, printer, fax…you name it, and he's got it. No, ain't nobody going to leave all that behind."

Nona's interest was peaked. "Computer?" she said.

"Sure," said the manager. "You want to see it? I got extra keys right here."

"No," Shucks answered quickly. "We can't go in there without a warrant."

"Well," said the manager, "Go get one. Then I'll let you in."

"You've really been helpful," said Nona, "And I'd sure like to get my hands on that computer, but we don't have cause to get a warrant."

Shucks took a card out of his pocket. "I want you to give us a call when Chuckie Ryan gets back in. I don't care how late it is, we need to know. We don't want him to take off."

A look of concern crossed the manager's face. "What am I suppose to do?"

"Nothing," said Nona. "You don't do anything. Just call us at one of those numbers. We'll do what has to be done."

Now the manager's voice was anxious, "This is serious isn't it? Is he dangerous?"

"We don't know, sir," said Nona. "All we can say is that we want to question him."

Shucks and Nona drove straight to the Justice Center, found Travis and Sam, and repeated the conversation with the manager of the Long Leaf Pines Apartments. In turn, Travis handed them copies of the fax that had just arrived from Raleigh.

Nona looked startled. "Dangerous? Hey, I was alone with him. What *have* we got here?"

"And how does this tie in with the murder of Maynard Dwayne Drane?" said Shucks. "Drane couldn't get away with passing bad checks around here. Nobody around here would even take a check from him. And he wasn't smart enough to be a forger. Shoot...I'd be surprised if he could write. Do you suppose there's no connection between Drane's death and Chuckie's night signals on the beach?"

"No," said Nona. "There *is* a connection. I just feel it."

"So now we're going to add woman's intuition to the mix," said Sam.

Nona shot him a withering look. "Careful Barnett," said Nona. "You don't want to go there again."

"No mam. Sorry. Bad habit I'm trying to break," Sam answered repentantly. "What was I thinking?" he thought.

"I sure would like to get into Chuckie's computer," Travis said returning to the business at hand.

"Maybe we can get some help from the Feds on that," said Shucks.

"I doubt it," said Sam. "They're coming down here in regard to their own case, not ours. Anything they uncover will go to that end."

"You know what I keep asking myself...does this have anything at all to do with bootlegging?" said Nona

"Somebody sure wanted us to think it did. Don't forget the smashed Mason jars at the scene of the crime," said Sam.

"Right," Shucks mused and nodded his head. Then he looked toward the glass front of the building. "Lookeeee there," he said and pointed to a large black car with tinted windows pulling into the visitor's parking space.

"Here come de Feds," Sam said mockingly.

Three grim looking men swung out of the car and stormed the steps of the building. They wore dark suits, white shirts, and ties.

"All they need for the part is a fedora and dark glasses," Nona said derisively.

They entered the building and stood motionless looking around the lobby. Then they marched to the desk of the duty officer, spoke briefly to her, and headed in the direction of Sheriff Caffy's office.

It wasn't long before Doris raced down the halls looking anxious and annoyed. "Where have you been?" she demanded. "They're here and the Sheriff wants you in his office right now."

Doris wheeled around and started back toward Caffy's office. She stopped several times and motioned the four officers to hurry.

When they walked into the Sheriff's office the four federal agents made no effort to stand until they saw Nona. Then they stood reluctantly, nodded, and directed their attention back to Sheriff Caffy.

Caffy addressed Travis, Sam, Shucks, and Nona "These are the three federal agents up from Washington DC to talk to us. This here is Jesus Martinez, and over there is Franklin Farmer. They are from the Immigration and Naturalization Service. Over here is George Thomas Williams of the Federal Bureau of Investigation." Without speaking the four agents nodded in acknowledge of their introductions.

Caffy paused and then continued, "Now these are the four officers who are working on a murder case and stumbled across a possible connection between our victim and Chuckie Ryan," said the Sheriff. "These two gentlemen are North Carolina Alcohol Beverage Control officers, Sam Barnett and Travis White." The federal agents didn't look impressed. The Sheriff continued, "These two here are Dare County law enforcement officers, Shucks Twine and Nona Godette. It was Officer Godette that linked our murder victim to your fugitive. So…what do you want to talk about?" the Sheriff said tossing the ball to the agents.

Speaking with a Latino accent Martinez said, "Perhaps we can start by your telling us about your murder case." He looked from one officer to the other.

Finally Travis spoke up. He told the agents about Maynard Dwayne Drane's murder on the beach and of the discovery of jars often used in the sale of bootleg whiskey. He explained that according to the lab, Drane had not been killed on the beach.

Shucks reported that Drane's jeep was used in a hit and run crime. The vehicle was eventually discovered in the sound and was being checked for evidence as they spoke.

Then Sam explained how the investigation of Drane's activities, led them to Chuckie Ryan. He described Drane and Chuckie Ryan's interest in diving. They both explored sunken ships, especially the Huron and the Explorer. And they both used the Bladen Street Access.

Farmer said, "And you became suspicious of Ryan just because he and Drane dive from the access?"

"Well, it's not that simple," said Shucks. "Go ahead, Nona, tell them."

Nona slipped to the edge of her chair. She was aware that the agents' eyes were riveted on her, and she couldn't understand the reason for the intensity. She told them how she'd spent the evening with Chuckie Ryan, and after dancing they went to the beach. She recounted how she left the beach first and looked back to see lights flashing beyond the breakers. She related how she hid and watched as Chuckie returned the signals.

"Miss Godette…" Farmer began.

"Officer Godette," corrected Nona.

"Well, then *Officer* Godette," continued Farmer. "How did you first meet Charles Ryan?"

"I met him at Guthrie's" said Nona.

"Guthrie's? What is this Guthrie's?" asked Martinez.

"It's a restaurant and bar. They have a juke box and people go there to eat and dance," said Nona.

"And after you met Ryan in this bar, how far did your relationship progress?" asked Farmer.

Nona squirmed, and Sam looked angry. Then Nona composed herself, looked Farmer straight in the eye, and said resolutely, "There is no *relationship*. He is an acquaintance. I'd run into Chuckie at Guthrie's, and we'd have a couple of drinks and dance."

Martinez fired next, "Really? Then why would you go to the beach at night with someone you met in a bar, who was a mere acquaintance?"

Nona was dumbfounded.

Then the FBI agent spoke for the first time, "Do you think that Chuckie Ryan took you to the beach to have sex with him?"

"What?" cried Nona.

"Do you think that Chuckie Ryan took you to the beach to have sex with him?" FBI Agent Williams repeated.

Sam's face turned beet red, and he started forward in his chair. Travis placed a restraining hand on his arm.

"Okay, that's enough." It was Sheriff Caffy. "Officer Godette don't say another word. Now let's talk about what's going on here." He placed his arms on the desk and thrust his angry face in the direction of the Feds. "Now you guys call me up from Washington, DC and say you want to talk about a federal fugitive. I say come on down, be glad to help. I get my team together, and we come in here with cooperation on our minds and what happens? You don't tell us didly squat, and you treat my officer like she's a suspect instead of a Dare County law enforcement officer."

Caffy rocked back in his chair and let his tirade soak in. Finally he continued, "Now I don't want you to think that this is the first time we've worked with federal agencies. Matter of fact, someone from ATF was down here just this week. We want to cooperate, and we want to communicate. But the operative word is communicate not interrogate. So, we're gonna take a twenty minute break. Then we'll come back and see if the climate don't change in here."

Sheriff Caffy stood dismissively, and his office emptied rapidly. Nona was the first out the door with Sam and Travis close behind.

"Doris," shouted the Sheriff.

Doris's appearance was instantaneous. "What do you need, Sheriff? Coffee? Tylenol?"

"No," said the Sheriff. "Take care of Nona."

"What? Me take care of Nona?" Doris said incredulously.

"Yes, you. I don't see any other woman in here," the Sheriff said.

Doris left his office in a trot and headed straight for the only sanctuary in the building off limits to men...the women's restroom. There she found Sam and Travis standing sentry by the door. Doris gave them a heated look, pushed the door open, and went inside.

Several minutes passed before Doris walked out. She stopped, faced Sam with her hands on her hips, and demanded, "What did you do to her?"

"Me?" Sam said in a stunned voice. "I didn't do anything. It was the Feds. They came down here like gang-buster swinging their weight around..."

Doris interrupted, waggled a finger at him, and said, "I don't like this, Sam. I don't like this one bit."

Then she spun around and stormed back to Caffy's office.

"What'd I do?" said Sam. "I didn't..."

Travis said, "Come on let's wait in the lobby. We shouldn't be hanging around the women's toilet. We'll get arrested as perverts."

They returned to the lobby and joined Shucks who was watching the three federal agents walk back and forth in front of the building. Martinez was a chain smoker and lighted at least one cigarette from a butt, Farmer appeared agitated, while Williams, the FBI agent, was doing all the talking.

"Now doesn't that inspire confidence in America's finest?" The men turned to find Nona standing behind them. Travis had expected to see tear-streaked cheeks and red swollen eyes, but instead her look was dour.

"Hey, you okay?" Sam asked.

"Sure," Nona said. "Busted a mirror."

"What?" said Shucks.

"Floor-length mirror in the women's room. I kicked it. Cracked like thin ice," she said simply. They all laughed.

"Good," said Sam.

Travis eyeballed the federal agents and said roguishly, "I think we oughta go on down to Caffy's office. Already be there when they walk in. Let's see how the fed's like it when they have to walk through our gauntlet."

CHAPTER 29

When the federal agents returned to the Sheriff's office, they halted abruptly at the door and gaped at the four officers sitting stone-faced and waiting silently to reconvene. Their hesitation was short-lived, however, and they quickly picked their way through the maze of straight chairs to their assigned seats.

Sheriff Caffy, who had a gift for the dramatic, let the silence rest on the gathering for a while. Finally, he spoke to the federal agents, "Now we have been very forth coming in sharing information with you fellows. I'm thinking that now it's time for you to reciprocate. If Chuckie Ryan is as dangerous as this fax says he is, as Sheriff of Dare County North Carolina I have a right to know what I'm dealing with," he waved the fax he'd received before them. "So what have you got?" Then he sat back, laced his fingers across his chest, and waited.

Seconds passed, and then INS agent Farmer said, "I'm not sure how much..."

"If you have received a fax on Chuckie Ryan's record, then it should not come as a surprise that he is a dangerous person," FBI agent Williams interrupted loudly. Then he lowered his voice and continued, "As you know, Charles Alonzo Ryan was born in New York city. His mother's name was Mary Katherine Ryan an Iris-Catholic immigrant who worked the bars and the streets of New York. His father was Asner Mohammed of Middle Eastern origin. Country unknown. They were never married. Mary Kate raised her son alone and tried hard to teach him to resent his Middle Eastern heritage. In fact, that is why she gave him the middle name Alonzo. For years she claimed his father was Mexican. Her subterfuge backfired, however, and Chuckie became a teenager, rebelled, left home, and embraced his Middle Eastern legacy. With me so far?"

Sheriff Caffy waited for any questions then said, "Your report is simple enough, but what's this screw-up from New York City doing in Dare County?"

"Good question," said Williams. "That was what I asked when I found out he'd turned up on the Outer Banks of North Carolina. But it's like a puzzle. When you keep placing pieces, it starts to make sense. Ryan always spent a lot of time around the docks in New York. He worked odd jobs at the harbor, and when he left New York, he naturally gravitated to the waterfronts. Over the years, he worked ports and marinas from Maine to Florida. He worked on barges, tugs, and sailboats. He became an expert diver and a licensed instructor."

Williams's audience was getting restless. Finally Travis said, "If you know that he was an expert diver, then you must know of his interest in sunken vessels. And we've got plenty of those along the Outer Banks. They don't call these waters the Graveyard of the Atlantic for nothing, you know. This area was bound to attract him eventually."

Williams said, "I think Ryan was attracted to more than the sunken vessels along the North Carolina Coastline. But let me continue. Ryan didn't make enough money as a dock worker and seaman to satisfy the standard of life he desired. So he stumbled upon a way to supplement his income."

Now his audience's interest heightened, and Sam said, "And just what did he do to supplement his income?"

Williams said, "You have to realize the Charles Alonzo Ryan is not a stupid man. Unfortunately for us, he is very intelligent. Chuckie discovered a skill that became very profitable to him."

"Don't tell me making moonshine," said Travis.

"Oh no, that certainly wouldn't suit his life style," said Williams. "Chuckie discovered that he was very talented at forgery...particularly reproducing people's signature. So for a few years he made a lucrative income by stealing blank checks, filling them in, and forging signatures."

"Well, I can tell you right now," said Sheriff Caffy, "we haven't had any reports of that sort of crime out here."

"I'm just giving you this background so you'll understand just what we think Ryan's been up to this summer," said Williams. He paused for effect.

"Ryan's business of forging checks did so well that he expanded it," Williams continued.

"And that's where the Immigration and Naturalization Service came into play," said Farmer.

"So Mr. Know-It-All, Big Shot FBI Agent is gonna let someone else talk," thought Nona.

"Ryan started forging ID for people who entered the country illegally," Farmer said. "As Agent Williams said, Ryan was shrewd. First he'd find out the year of the illegal's birth. Then he went to a cemetery in a small town, found the tombstone of a child who was born that same year, go to the courthouse, and get an official birth certificate."

"Can you do that?" asked Shucks.

"Sure," said Farmer. "This procedure has been used for years. After securing a birth certificate, other identification is simple to procure. And what Ryan couldn't procure, he made. He sold social security cards, driver's licenses, library cards, voter registration cards, and all kinds of membership cards. His scheme was brilliant. He used the right kind of paper and plastic coatings. Brilliant. Absolutely brilliant." Farmer actually appeared to admire Chuckie Ryan's talent.

Then Sheriff Caffy said, "We don't run into that caliber of crook down here, but I still think we would have picked up on this kind of activity if it was going on here."

"I agree," said Martinez. "I don't suppose there would be much of a market for Chuckie's talent among the locals. But here's how I think the Outer Banks comes in. Ryan took his talent to yet another level. In addition to supplying false ID for illegals, he began to assist them in entering the country."

"Now you've got my attention," said Caffy.

"Yes," said Martinez. "I'm sure you've all seem boat loads of illegals coming into Florida from the Caribbean area. Well, there's thousands of miles of seashore on the Atlantic Coastline. Florida receives a lot of attention because the entry attempts are so visible, but it is by no means the only coastal area used to enter the country illegally."

"I think I see where you're going here," said Shucks.

"Right," said Martinez. "What better place to enter than the Outer Banks. It's remote, sparsely populated, and very little surveillance. Picture this…a boat that doesn't draw a lot of water, like a sailboat or a fishing boat, brings the illegal as close to shore as possible. Then they put a dinghy over the side, and a person from the ship rows the illegal to a designated spot even closer to shore. He drops his passenger off, and he swims in. There's someone on the beach to meet him and provide him with all the identification he needs. Home free…as they say."

"And the buoys over the Huron and the Explorer could serve as markers…you know, the designated spot," said Shucks who was really getting into it. To him, this was the stuff that law enforcement was made of. The others still looked doubtful.

Farmer picked up on their skepticism, "It's not so incredible if you look at it from the point of view of the illegal. When he drops off the dinghy, he can see a marker showing him exactly where to swim, and it's a short distance in shallow water. Then when he reaches, the beach, he meets someone who supplies him with a place to stay, clothes, American money, and false ID. And there's probably transportation to a nearby city where he can get lost in the crowd."

"The manager said that Chuckie was driving his guest 'back'," said Nona.

"Nona, are you….," Sam began. But he was interrupted by Doris standing at the door.

"Sorry to interrupt," Doris said. "But there's a man on the phone who says he's the manager at the Long Leaf Pines Apartments. He's real excited and says it's urgent that he speak to Shucks right away."

Shucks looked at the Sheriff. Caffy said, "Go get it." Then he turned to the federal agents and explained, "That's where Chuckie Ryan lives."

They waited anxiously. Shucks finally returned excited and uneasy. "He's back. Chuckie Ryan just pulled up in the parking lot at the Long Leaf Pines. And he's alone."

"Well folks," said Sheriff Caffy. "I think this calls for a little strategizing…Doris, coffee all around."

CHAPTER 30

A mud splattered white sedan with West Virginia license plates pulled into the parking lot at the Bladen Street Access. Three casually dressed, middle aged male tourists got out and stretched. One man wore jeans with a wrinkled plaid shirt, and an expensive pair of binoculars was strapped around his neck. The second man was dressed in shorts and a tee-shirt that was inscribed with the slogan, JOIN THE NAVY, SEE THE WORLD. The Third man had on a baseball cap, jeans, and a shiny pink windbreaker over a black tee-shirt. He carried a digital camera.

The tourists walked to the gazebo and conversed as they read the account of the sunken ships and studied the maps. Eventually they walked up the steps to the platform overlooking the beach. They pointed to the buoys, spoke animatedly, and took turns looking through the binoculars. Then they slowly walked down the steps and onto the beach. Surfers were riding huge waves created by the incoming tide, and two bikini-clad female divers swam from the wreckage site of the sunken ships and plodded ashore.

Pink Shiny Windbreaker was busy clicking pictures. After taking shots of the wreckage site, wildlife, and the surfers, he approached the shapely divers and spoke with them. At first they giggled and shook their heads, but finally they struck seductive poses and allowed him to take several pictures. Then they ran sniggering towards the steps.

Two of the tourists sat down on the sand, observed the surfers, and took turns using the binoculars, while Plaid Shirt walked along the beach. When he returned, his companions stood, stretched, and followed him back up the steps to the parking lot.

The three stomped their feet and brushed sand from their clothing. Then they climbed into the sedan, and slowly exited the parking lot. The car turned left on Virginia Dare Trail driving toward the by-pass intersection. There it turned left, crossed the Washington Baum Bridge over the Roanoke Sound, and entered into the parking lot of the Dare County Justice Center.

The sedan parked beside a large black vehicle with tinted windows and the three tourists got out. Pink Windbreaker quickly removed the West Virginia license plates and replaced it with a North Carolina one. Plaid Shirt popped the trunk of the black car and placed the binoculars and digital camera inside. Then the three men mounted the steps to the Center, sauntered pass the officer on duty and Doris, and entered Sheriff Caffy's office.

Sheriff Caffy had spent the afternoon hashing over the new information with the four team members. He looked up and said, "So, how was your trip to the beach?"

Farmer, wearing a shiny pink windbreaker, said, "Fascinating! Absolutely fascinating! Those buoys are within spitting distance of land. How come so many seamen lost their lives? It's quite a story and a mystery. I've never seen anything like it. I can certainly understand the attraction to that site. Makes me wish I were a diver. That's a captivating place."

"Yes, it's a captivating place, and the perfect place to land illegals," said FBI agent Williams returning the focus to their purpose for being here. "Let me remind you that this whole thing of people entering the country illegally took on greater importance with nine eleven. And if what we suspect is actually happening, then this is a well constructed plan. It requires coordination among lots of people. Arresting Ryan could lead us to a network of criminals."

"I knew it," Shucks exclaimed, "Outer Banks has always been intriguing…going all the way back to 1587 with the disappearance of the first English Colony right here on Roanoke Island."

Sheriff Caffy cut his eyes at Shucks, ignored his exuberance, and said, "So, where to go from here. This is still supposition. We sure don't have enough to pull Ryan in."

"You're forgetting the computer and records in his apartment," said Nona.

"But we don't even have enough for a search warrant," Sam reminded her.

They sat silently for a few minutes, and then FBI agent Williams said, "If he is bringing illegals in the way we suspect, we'll have to catch him in the act. Then that would certainly give us cause for a warrant to search his computer and files."

"That's easier said than done," said Travis. "We could wait around here for weeks before he brings somebody else in."

"The manager said his rent is paid through the end of the month," said Shucks. "I'm thinking he'll move before then."

"If he gets away, it could take weeks, months, before we find him again," warned Martinez.

"Excuse me, Sheriff," Doris, who had circles under her eyes and a tired look on her face, stood at the door. "That manager down at the Long Leaf Pines wants to speak to Shucks again."

Shucks walked briskly from the room, picked up the receiver on Doris' desk and said, "Officer Twine here."

"Hey, Officer, thought you might want to know that Chuckie Ryan might be leaving real soon," the manager said in a quiet, conspiratorial voice.

"Leaving? How do you know?" Shucks asked excitedly.

"This morning he told me he's expecting more friends to come in. His MO is friends arrive, stay a few days, he takes them home…or somewhere," the manager whispered. He was really getting into the part.

"Okay," said Shucks. "Don't say or do anything that will make him suspicious. We don't want to scare him off. Let me know if anything else comes up."

"Check," said the manager.

"And thanks," Shucks added. He hung up. "I just hate that phony TV cop talk," he said to himself.

Shucks rushed back into the Sheriff's office. "We aren't going to have to wait weeks or months," he said excitedly. "Seems like old Chuckie is on the move."

"What?" said Williams with alarm.

"What I mean is…." And Shucks related his conversation with the apartment manager.

"Sounds like something could go down tonight," said Travis.

"Doesn't give us a whole lot of time to organize," said Sam.

"To be on the safe side, we'll go with the assumption that tonight's the night," said Caffy. Then he shouted, "Doris, step in here."

Doris immediately appeared at the door wearing her jacket and carrying a purse.

"Oh, you going home?" Caffy looked surprised. He seemed shocked to learn that Doris was ever beyond summoning distance.

"Yes, Sheriff, I was. It's after six," she said impatiently.

"Well," Cafffy said with resignation, "If you have to. But before you go, how about ordering up a stack of Reuben sandwiches and making a fresh pot of coffee?"

A hostile look flashed across Doris's face as she jerked off her jacket.

"And Doris," Caffy added offhandedly, "You know those fried pies I like? Order about a dozen of them."

CHAPTER 31

"Hello."

"Eve, this is Travis White," Travis said.

"Yes, I know," smiled her voice.

"Eve, I wanted to let you know that I have to work tonight," he said. "I didn't want you to think that after last night, I just took off."

"Thank you, Travis," said Eve. "I'm afraid that's exactly what I would have thought."

Memories from last night floated through his mind. He could see her blue eyes. He could feel her warmth and smell her scent. Suddenly Travis needed her so much that he ached.

"Eve I want to be with you so badly," his voice was hoarse. "I don't now how long this is going to take. I may get through late tonight, or it may be tomorrow. Can I come over as soon as I'm free…no matter when it is?"

"Yes," she whispered. "Do come over…no matter when it is."

The Bladen Street Access parking lot was empty, and the beach that stretched in front of the sunken ships was deserted. Surfers and divers had surrendered to nightfall, and after dinner beach walkers had gone home to their television sets.

Sam and Travis hid their car under the carport of a pink stucco beach house with a "For Rent" sign in the yard. Now in hooded windbreakers they huddled silently in the lee of a dune seeking shelter from the cold ocean air. The sea was calm and resembled a vast, watery plain. The sand on the briny beach took on a silverish hue as clouds flirted with the moon.

A slight rustling caused them to stare intently in its direction, but they soon relaxed remembering how wind and mist play tricks on the beach at night. Then they heard it again. It was the crackle of dry sea oats under foot. They countered with alarm as their hands reached for their side arms, and they watched as out of the mist two crouching figures crept slowly towards them. Then they relaxed as they recognized the intruders.

"What's going on?" Travis whispered to Nona and Shucks in a hushed voice.

"Everybody's dug in and waiting for the action," said Shucks. "It would be a real disappointment if they didn't show up tonight."

"You two staying warm?" Nona said looking at Sam.

"As warm as can be expected under the circumstances," said Sam.

"Want to trade?" asked Nona.

"Trade?" said Travis.

"Yeah, you take Shucks, and I'll take Sam," she said mischievously.

"Now I don't know if that's a good idea, Nona." said Shucks. "I know how you are."

"And how is that, Shucks?" said Nona playfully.

"Oh, come on, Nona, this is serious," said Shucks impatiently.

Travis said, "Shucks is right. This is serious. So I want to pair up with a serious partner. How about it Shucks?"

"You want to pair up with me, Trav?" asked Shucks. He was delighted. He'd get to work with an ABC officers that he called Trav.

"Sure I mean it," said Travis. "Where's your station?"

"Come on," said Shucks. "I'll show you." And he scurried off into the haze with Travis behind him.

Nona turned to Sam. "Shucks is all keyed up about his first stakeout."

"Aren't you?" asked Sam.

"Aren't I what?" said Nona.

"Excited," said Sam.

"Yeah, but not about the stakeout," she teased.

They sat in silence, their eyes glued on the beach. They checked out every sound that blended with the crash of the sea. They sat beneath the steely stars and used night scopes to search the gray mist. Ribbons of moonlight reflected intermittently off the sparkling sand, and then disappeared when the moon ducked behind a cloud. Hours crawled by like years. Their muscles cramped, their clothes were coated with sand, and mosquitoes had developed a taste for their insect repellent.

Then the sleeping ocean awoke. They heard the thunderous cadence of the waves as swell upon swell crashed salty foam upon the beach.

"There's something arousing about the sound of crashing waves on the beach," Nona said.

"Now don't start something you can't finish," warned Sam.

"Just checking to see if you're awake," said Nona.

Sam laughed and focused the night scope on the sea. He panned back and forth several time, then stopped abruptly, passed the scope to Nona and said excitedly, "Over there...out pass the buoy on the far right."

Beyond the breakers there was a shimmer of white...a sailboat gleamed in the moonlight. It looked to be about forty feet long. Its jib was rolled up, sails tied to the mast, and anchors were being dropped from the bow and the stern of the boat.

"Say, ain't she a beauty," Nona said. "But I don't think they're anchored there for the night. Not if they know anything about the tides and currents around here."

"I don't think they intend to stay long," said Sam. "Keep watching."

Nona said, "Sailboat's an unusual craft to use for smuggling illegals."

"That's what makes it such a good choice," said Sam.

They saw no activity aboard, and for at least half an hour the sailboat rocked gently with the ocean swells.

"Do you think the others have seen her?" asked Nona.

"You can be sure of it," said Sam.

"What do we do now?" asked Nona.

"Wait," Sam said. "Just keep the sailboat, steps, and beach under surveillance."

Minutes seemed like hours. Sam amazed Nona. The restless Sam she knew remained composed, methodical, and patient. He was completely unruffled by the measured pace of the assignment. Nona, on the other hand, was edgy. She hoped her irritation was because this was her first stakeout. "Otherwise," she thought, "I'm in big trouble."

Suddenly Sam whispered excitedly, "Look...at the platform."

Nona watched as a light pierced through the opaque curtain of mist. The signal...one, two,...one, two,...one, two, three,...one. The sequence was repeated several times with no response.

"Maybe he's signaling the wrong boat," said Nona.

"No, wait," said Sam. "Just give them time."

After what seemed to be an eternity, Nona saw the light sequence returned from the boat.

On the other side of the steps, Travis and Shucks peered through a cluster of sea oats and watched the light show.

"It's going down the way we hoped," Shucks whispered excitedly.

"Just hold on," Travis cautioned him. "None of us move till they hit the beach."

Travis no sooner gave the warning than Shucks handed him the night scope and pointed in the direction of the sailboat. Travis watched as figures appeared and scurried about the deck. Soon a dinghy with an outboard motor was lowered from the stern davits, and three shadowy figures climbed down a ladder and boarded the craft. Then they pushed away from the sailboat, started the outboard, and headed towards the buoys. Unknown to them, anxious eyes watched through night scopes as their tiny boat bobbed up and down in the frothy chop.

"What if they capsize?" Shucks asked apprehensively.

"If worse comes to worse, remember, we've alerted the Elizabeth City Coast Guard. They're as eager to put a stop to this kind of activity as we are," said Travis.

The dinghy's progress was slow. For every two feet the small craft covered, it lost a foot. Finally it reached the breakers that seized and tossed it unmercifully.

Travis said, "Just a little farther to the buoys and the passengers could take to the water and ride in on the waves."

However, much to their surprise, when the craft reached the buoys, the boat continued in to shore.

"Trav," Shucks exclaimed, "They're gonna beach her. Why do you suppose they'd do a thing like that?"

"I don't know," said Travis. "Maybe one of his passengers can't swim."

They were so intent on watching the saga unfold, that they almost missed the sound of muffled footsteps in the sand behind them. Travis nudged Shucks, raised his finger to his lips, and ducked. Chuckie Ryan jogged pass them and toward the water's edge. Suddenly, the dinghy made land, three men climbed out, and they began to drag the vessel onto the beach.

"Well, what do you think, Shucks? Time to go in?" asked Travis. But Shucks didn't have time to answer, Sam and Nona were already up and racing down the dunes. Travis and Shucks joined suit. Suddenly the beach was filled with law enforcement officers shouting, "FBI...Police...INS...you're under arrest...get your hands up..."

A helicopter came out of nowhere and trained a spotlight on the sailboat.

Then there was a mighty roar of an engine and a boat suddenly appeared from the direction of the pier, pulled in beside the sailboat, and a voice yelled through an amplifier, "Coast Guard, Coast Guard. Coming aboard."

Chuckie looked stunned. The dinghy operator raised his hands, but the two passengers dropped to their knees and clasped their hands behind their heads. Handcuffs clicked and officers began to read the prisoners their rights.

"Okay, Chuckie," said Sam, "It's over. You have the right…"

But Sam didn't get to finish reading Chuckie his rights. Nona covered Chuckie as Sam secured his weapon and stepped forward to handcuff Chuckie. Chuckie's startled eyes fell on Nona, and his face grew gray with rage. He shrieked a curse, assumed a martial arts stance, and kicked Sam in the groin. Sam folded. As he went down, Chuckie wrenched his gun from him and went for Nona. Nona was caught off guard. Chuckie struck her on the forehead, her knees buckled, and her firearm dropped to the ground. He caught her by the throat with one hand and with the other hand held Sam's firearm to her head.

"Bitch!" he shrieked. "You set me up. I'm gonna…"

But Chuckie didn't have time to make good his threat. Suddenly Travis was there, and his hand crashed down on Chuckie's wrist. Travis wrenched the gun from his hand, released the clip from its magazine, and ejected the round from the chamber. Then he angrily hurled the gun to Shucks.

Travis quickly clicked on the cuffs, and Farmer escorted Chuckie away. Then Travis dropped to his knees beside of Sam, "You okay, buddy?" said Travis.

"I'm okay," said Sam, "but I'm not too sure about my future children."

"You're future children? You're not mature enough to have kids," Travis said.

Then Sam saw Nona, and he crawled towards her, "Nona," he cried.

But Shucks was already there. "Nona, Nona, you alright? Wake up," he said gently slapping her face.

Nona slowly opened her eyes, focused on Shucks and said groggily, "If you slap me one more time, Shucks, I swear you'll never strike another woman."

Shucks grinned, looked at Sam and Travis, and announced, "She'll be okay. Nona's got pluck."

"PLUCK?" they said in unison. "Where in the hell do you get these words?"

CHAPTER 32

As soon as Nona and Sam opened the door to the Dare County Justice Center they heard loud voices reverberating down the empty hall from the direction of Sheriff Caffy's office.

Sam walked over to the officer on duty and said, "What the hell's going on?"

The officer shook his head and jerked a thumb in the direction of the row, "Turf war," he said.

"Uh, oh," said Sam, and he and Nona headed down the hall to defend their ranks.

As they reached the Sheriff's office door, Caffy yelled, "I don't give a happy damn what you have pending against him, we've got a murder right here in my jurisdiction, and until we determine his involvement, he stays put."

"You don't know if he's involved in the murder at all," FBI agent Williams countered.

"And don't forget the hit run," Travis added.

"Right...murder AND hit run," said the Sheriff.

Williams gave Travis a smug look and said, "North Carolina is certainly generous with its government agents. Has anything that's happened today led you to think that Chuckie Ryan's involved in illegal sale of alcohol?"

"In my opinion, it's highly unlikely that Ryan was involved in bootlegging," Travis admitted. "But I said *highly* unlikely. Problem is someone went to a lot of trouble to make us think the murder was alcohol related by planting smashed jars at the scene."

"And as long as it was set up to look like bootlegging, we got to check it out," a voice added.

Sheriff Caffy looked up to see Sam at the door. Then he turned a worried eye on Nona and said, "Nona, what the hell are you doing here? I told you to go to the hospital."

"I went...don't worry...I went. Doctor said I just have a goose egg on my head. No concussion, just a nasty bump," Nona said impatiently. Nona did not like to be fussed over.

"Well, it's your headache," Caffy said, trying to sound unconcerned, "just don't let it interfere in this investigation."

At that point, INS agent Farmer walked in and announced, "I called Washington, and they're sending a truck to pack evidence from Ryan's apartment...that is if we ever get a search warrant."

Caffy erupted, "Now that's another thing. I'm not gonna have any evidence taken out of this county, until we're sure it's not connected to Drane's murder. When things go to Washington, they have a way of disappearing. No sir, my crime scene people are going in there, and they get to pass on anything that leaves Dare County."

"Sheriff Caffy," it was Jesus Martinez of INS whose Latino accent was thicker than ever, "do you realize that you are interfering in a federal investigation of illegal people coming into our country at such perilous times."

"Agent Martinez, YOU don't seem to understand," Caffy said. "I wouldn't interfere with your case for anything in this world. But I expect the same consideration from you. Your case won't turn on whether or not Ryan killed Drane. You already told us that you have him dead to rights for providing false ID and assistance to illegals. And after tonight, thanks to the help of MY team, you got him for assisting illegal entry. Your case seems pretty damned airtight to me. But our case is not. In fact, I don't even know if we have a case against him. But if we do, I'm betting that we'll find corroborating evidence in that apartment. And I want it."

"Okay, okay," said FBI agent Williams lifting his hands in a jester of surrender. "We'll go slow, let your crime scene people in, and nobody takes anything without the other party's knowledge."

"Other party?" Farmer said sarcastically. "What is this anyway..."

"It's what I say," Williams said angrily. Then he turned back to Caffy with a haughty look on his face. "Are your crime scene people competent?"

Caffy looked disgusted. Then he said, "Well, they can read, if that's what you mean."

Fearing that the situation would deteriorate again, Sam said, "Where's Ryan and his buddies now?

Caffy said, "On ice. We've got them isolated from each other. Give them a chance to sweat till we get around to questioning them."

"Sheriff, do you think that's the best thing to...." Williams began.

"Yes Mr. FBI Agent I think that is the best thing to do. If Shucks ever gets back here with that damned warrant, maybe we can go on over to Ryan's apartment and find something to use as leverage when we start prying the truth out of them."

As if on cue, they heard a clamor in the hallway. The Sheriff said, "Sounds like Shucks is back."

Shucks scampered in breathlessly, sprinted across the room, and handed a document to the Sheriff. "Judge says tell you that three o'clock in the morning is no time to be conducting business, Sheriff. He hopes that next time you'll wait at least till daylight," Shucks said with a grin.

Caffy said, "Well, I'll be sure to pass the word throughout our criminal community to please commit their crimes between nine and five." Caffy jerked the document from his hand, stood up, and added tiredly. "Okay Shucks, get the crime scene people up, we're ready to go in."

SUNDAY

Travis and Sam leaned on the hood of the Cherokee and waited patiently for the crime scene people to finish with Chuckie Ryan's apartment. They had seen the Dare County scene people work crime scenes many times and were accustomed to the slow, meticulous way they did things. Agent Williams, however, paced nervously outside the yellow crime scene tape. He wasn't sure whether the slow pace was the result of thoroughness, indecision, or incompetence.

The drapes closed inside the apartment, and the lights flicked off. Then a shaft of bluish light like a flashlight beam filtered through the thin curtains and panned around the room. When the beam disappeared, they could hear the sound of furniture being moved.

Time crept by endlessly. Finally a fiery red ball bounced from the eastern horizon and ignited the sea turning it a rosy red. No matter how many times Sam and Travis witnessed the sun rise over the ocean, it was still magnificent. But today, regardless of the awe inspiring scene, fatigue set in. Sam and Travis wearily watched a triangular fin followed by a black satin back leap from the water as a playful dolphin chased white caps through the surf. Someone brought coffee, compliments of the Long Leaf Pines Apartment manager who was excited by the activity taking place in the building. Soon residents appeared on their way to work. Their questions were disregarded, and they were urged to move quickly to their cars.

Seven o'clock, eight o'clock. FBI Agent Williams and INS Agents Martinez and Farmer were ready to storm the fort when the door opened and a scene person emerged and motioned them inside. Travis and Sam entered quickly with police, county law enforcement, and the Feds into the sanctum of Chuckie Ryan's apartment. Surprisingly, once inside everyone seem to work in concert.

The Feds went straight to the files and computer. Government technicians from Washington arrived and soon the computer was up and running. File drawers were opened and contents examined. But Sheriff Caffy, the Seaboard boys, Shucks, and Nona stared fixedly at the opposite side of the room. A large armoire was pulled out exposing several dark stains with smaller spots around it on the carpet. The area was still damp. There were also dark spatters on the wall.

"Well, well, well," said the Sheriff. "What have we got here?"

The gloved officer said, "When we used the luminal, we found what look like blood stains on the carpet in front of the armoire. Indentations on the carpet over there," and he pointed to the other side of the room, "indicate that the armoire hadn't always set here. So we moved the armoire out and found this." He points to the dark stains on the carpet.

"So what's this gonna tell us," said Caffy.

"A lot I hope," said the scene man. "For one thing somebody moved that armoire in an effort to cover blood stain evidence. Also, we'll check the blood for a match with Drane's."

"And evidence from the carpet and wall hasn't been compromised by the clean-up attempts?" said Sam.

"These guys did a haphazard cleaning job. They didn't begin to get rid of all blood traces," said the scene man.

Caffy rubbed his hands together. "Boys, looks like we hit the mother load!"

"Ah, there's one thing you need to know sheriff," said the scene man almost apologetically, "We didn't find any evidence of a shotgun being fired in here."

Sheriff Caffy's face took on a look of concern. "You sure 'bout that?"

"Yep, positive," said the scene man as he began to collect his equipment. "If that shotgun had been fired in here there would be tissue, lots more blood, plus damage to the room."

"Well ain't that a happy dam?" said Caffy. "And I was all ready to pack this up and go home."

"Find anything that might tie Ryan in with bootlegging?" asked Travis.

"Sorry," said the scene man. "Not yet. If we do, you guys will be the first to know."

Sheriff Caffy appeared invigorated, "Okay, let's go put the squeeze on these bozos."

"Hold on Sheriff," said Travis. "We don't want to move too fast."

"That's right, Sheriff. It takes some time to get DNA results," cautioned the scene man.

"I know that. You know that," said Caffy with a twinkle in his eye. "But the suspects don't. And I want to connect Drane's murder to Ryan before the Feds haul him off to Washington." He tossed his head in the direction of the federal agents who were absorbed in the computer and files.

CHAPTER 33

MONDAY

When Doo-Wop arrived for work at Guthrie's the activity down at the Long Leaf Pines Apartments was all the buzz. As he walked into the kitchen, he was bombarded with questions. Did he know Chuckie Ryan was arrested? Was Chuckie involved in Short Sugar's hit run? Had he talked with the Seaboard boys? And on and on.

It never occurred to Doo-Wop that anyone other than Maynard Dwayne Drane ran down Short Sugar. If there were a connection between Ryan and Drane, then Ryan could also be responsible for running down Short Sugar. Doo-Wop untied his apron, laid it on the counter, and walked out of the kitchen to find Irene. She was setting up the cash register for the day.

"Hey, Doo," she said. "Hear about the goings-on down at the Long Leaf Pines?"

"Yeah," said Doo-Wop. "Dat wha I want ta ax you 'bout. If'n it be alright fo' me ta leave. I needs ta fine de Seaboard boys."

Irene looked concerned. "Sure. Someone can cover for you in the kitchen. But Doo, are you okay? How about I go with you?"

"No tanks, I be okay. I jes have sumping to ax them 'bout," said Doo-Wop, and he left quickly.

Eve called the bait shop and got the night off. There was no problem with taking the time because business had turned slack. Fishermen were leaving the Outer Banks now, returning home with yet another fishing venture to boast of.

Eve spent the morning cooking. She made a lemon cake and put a roast and vegetables in the crock pot. She cleaned the house and even brushed Misha who would gladly have gone without the attention. She turned the radio to the beach music station, and danced around the room with a broom. Candles, freshly cut flowers, and a lovely pink cloth graced the table set for two. A bottle of red wine and two long-stemmed glasses set on the kitchen counter. And now she waited.

Eve thought of the many nights she had waited for Maynard to come home. She thought of the times he either didn't show up at all or was so drunk that the night turned ugly. She remembered the anger, the fear, the humiliation, and the tears. Then she shook her head fiercely to rid her brain of the disgusting memories. That was past…this was now. She knew that Travis would come, because he cared enough to call. And she'd wait for him no matter how late. How could she be so lucky to meet Travis at the lowest point in her life. Travis. She stretched out on the sofa and let her mind drift back to last night. She had been afraid that she'd never feel that safe and loved again.

Eve bent down and hugged Misha's thick, wooly neck. The dog smiled and licked her cheek. She laughed and said, "Don't worry Misha. Travis will come home."

The questioning of Chuckie Ryan and the other prisoners was long and tedious. The men doing the questioning were bushed. The prisoners were exhausted too, but by taking turns with the interrogation the interrogators had the upper edge.

The Coast Guard confiscated the sailboat and took its occupants into custody. They were being held and questioned at the Coast Guard Station in Elizabeth City.

The young man who motored the two illegals ashore in the dinghy was terrified and pled ignorance. He signed on the boat only two weeks ago. He followed the orders of the sailboat captain. He had not met the two men he brought ashore until he was hired. No, he didn't know they were entering illegally. When asked if he wanted a lawyer, he replied, "Do I need one?"

The two dinghy passengers did not speak English, or Spanish, or any languages spoken by the questioners. Or so they claimed. Consequently, interrogation of them proved unproductive. This was of little consequence to the Dare County investigators, however, since the illegals were not in the country when Maynard Dwayne Drane was murdered nor when Short Sugar Early was hit. Therefore, Sheriff Caffy turned them over to the trusty hands of the Feds.

Chuckie Ryan received their greatest effort. Federal agents fired questions after question at Chuckie citing the federal offenses of assisting illegal entry into the country and providing false IDs for them. Dare county officers hit him with questions concerning the murder of Maynard Dwayne Drane, and Travis and Sam shot questions at him about the illegal sale of bootleg whiskey. And they didn't let up. At first, Chuckie refused a lawyer saying he didn't trust "these back-water shysters". And so it went hour after hour for the whole day.

Around six o'clock the Sheriff came out of the interrogation room. He was worn out. His eyes were blood shot, he needed a shave, and his uniform was crumpled. He smelled of sweat and body oil. He stood with Travis and Sam, and said tiredly, "I think he's about to crack."

"He's got to be beat," said Sam. "I know damned well I am."

The Sheriff's eyes fell on a huddled figure sitting on a bench in the lobby. "What's he doing here?" he said nodding towards Doo-Wop.

Sam said, "He heard about Ryan's arrest and wants to know if he had anything to do with the hit and run. We told him we didn't know yet."

"So what's he going to do if Ryan was involved in the hit and run?" the Sheriff asked dubiously.

"He's harmless," Travis said reassuringly. "I think he's just looking for closure."

"Closure? Huh," said the Sheriff. "I could use a little closure from this whole damned case."

The door to the interrogation room flew open and Shucks rushed out. "Sheriff, better get in here. Old Chuckie Ryan's cracking like an egg."

Chuckie was talking, but he wasn't saying exactly what the officers wanted to hear. He seemingly forgot his earlier disparaging remarks about local attorneys. He requested and received a lawyer. So when the officers entered the interrogation room this time, Chuckie was seated with his counsel calmly sipping water from a plastic bottle.

Chuckie affected the persona of perfect innocence as he related his account of the events leading up to the death of Maynard Dwayne Drane. He spoke slowly, deliberately almost as if he'd rehearsed the statement. The scenario he described took place in Chuckie Ryan's apartment. Chuckie Ryan returned home after meeting some "friends" who hitched passage on a boat headed north from the Caribbean. No, he didn't know that his "friends" were entering illegally. No, he wasn't suspicious when they were dropped off-shore and motored to the beach by dinghy. He guessed they were just 'trying to save on travel expenses'. The members of his audience glanced at each other as if to say 'how dumb does he think we are'. But once Chuckie was on a roll, they didn't interrupt him.

Chuckie related how he and his friends returned to his apartment. He showed them their room and turned the television on to watch the evening news. There was a loud knock on his door…like a pounding fist. He was surprised that someone would come by that late. When he opened the door, Maynard Dwayne Drane stood there, a shotgun pointed downward by his side. Drane motioned Chuckie back into the room, and said something to the effect that he saw Chuckie bring the stuff ashore. Chuckie answered that he didn't know what Drane was talking about. Then Drane shoved him against the wall, pointed the shotgun at him, claimed he'd seen the deal go down, and gave him ten seconds to come up with the stuff. Stuff? What stuff? It was at this point that it occurred to "naïve" Chuckie that Drane thought drugs were smuggled in on the dinghy.

Chuckie continued feigning innocence. He claimed he tried to reason with Drane, but Drane was like a maniac. Then his two friends heard the commotion, entered the room, thought a robbery was taking place, and charged Drane. Fearful because Drane was armed, one of Chuckie's friends grabbed a knife from the kitchen knife rack and swung at Drane slicing him across the abdominal area. Drane doubled over. The shot gun went limp, but he didn't drop it. Drane then stumbled backwards out of the apartment. No shots were ever fired in the apartment. Chuckie and his friends used only their strength and the kitchen knife to defend themselves.

"It was a definite case of self defense, pure and simple," Ryan declared candidly.

When asked why he had not called the police, Chuckie maintained that he was frightened, and his friends didn't want to get involved with the cops. They acted out of desperation. The tried to clean up the blood in the apartment, but were unsuccessful so they moved the armoire over the spots.

Travis and Sam listened intently to Chuckie's story. Nothing they learned seemed to implicate Chuckie in the sale of illegal alcohol. However, they still had no explanation for why the broken Mason jars were planted at the scene. Was Drane's murder the work of rival bootleggers? Was it just a ruse to throw the police off some more sinister crime? Was it some kind of personal vendetta?

The FBI and INS agents were also less than satisfied with the explanation they got concerning Chuckie Ryan's involvement in illegal entries and false ID. He denied any knowledge or involvement in these crimes, and demonstrated strong indignation at such "accusations". He attempted to play the Feds and local law enforcement officers against each other by appearing to cooperate with the locals while stonewalling the Feds. His strategy was to convey the attitude, "See…I'm cooperating with the locals, why would I lie to the Feds?"

Chuckie finally signed a less than satisfactory statement for Sheriff Caffy, and Caffy and the Seaboard boys walked down the hall toward the Sheriff's office. Once inside Sheriff Caffy sat behind his desk, rocked back in his chair, and tapped his finger tips together.

"Well, if this ain't a fine kettle of fish," he said. "When we walked in that apartment and saw those blood stains, I thought we'd wrapped it up tight. We got to talk about this."

Sheriff Caffy rolled forward across his desk and shouted, "Doris, come a runnin'."

Doris *slowly* appeared at the door not one bit amused by the Sheriff's joke.

"You rang?" she said tiredly.

"Doris, get Shucks, Nona, and the Doc up here on the double. I don't want to go home tonight without some kind of an assessment of what we got here," said Sheriff Caffy.

Doris withdrew as slowly as she'd appeared. A measured pace was her only protest against his offhanded manner.

"Chuckie Ryan figured he'd rather take his chances down here in Dare County than Washington, DC. He'll claim self defense. He knows that folks here abouts consider Maynard Dwayne Drane to be one step below a slug. So he figures public opinion will work in his favor," Sheriff Caffy said. Then holding up Chuckie Ryan's signed statement he added "I can buy the story about Drane being stabbed in the apartment, but I just don't think the fight ended with that injury."

Nona and Shucks scurried into the Sheriff's office. Doc was close behind but moving at a much slower speed.

Sheriff Caffy went over Chuckie Ryan's entire statement again. Then he said, "Like I was telling Travis and Sam, I don't think the fight ended with Drane getting stabbed in that apartment. I think they took it some place else and finished the job. So what do you think?" He looked from one face to the other.

"Does this mean that if we don't find the location of the crime that Chuckie will walk," asked Shucks crestfallen.

"No, Shucks it don't mean that," said the Sheriff. "What I mean is that now we know pretty much what Ryan's defense will be, and it's our job to plug up any holes in it. What do you think, Doc?"

"Well, I don't think I can add much to what you already have, Sheriff," said Doc. "As my man down at the scene told you, if there had been a shotgun blast in that apartment, we would have found tissue, shotgun pellets, and probably some damage to the wall or furniture. We didn't find any of that…just some blood. Now mind you I'm not saying that your suspect didn't murder Chuckie Ryan, I'm just saying if he did murder him it wasn't done in that apartment."

"Did you find the knife in the apartment?" Sam asked.

"Yes, we did," said Doc. "It had been washed but again, they did a lousy job and blood showed up when we tested it. Drane was cut."

"Then why didn't you find a knife wound when you did the autopsy?" asked Nona.

"There was tremendous damage to the abdominal area from the close range shotgun blast and the crabs got to him so any indication of a cut was obliterated," Doc answered.

Travis remained silent. The Sheriff said, "How come you ain't put your two cents worth in Travis?"

"I don't know. His story leaves so many loose ends I'd like to see tied up. Why the Mason jars by the body? What about the missing shotgun," said Travis.

"Well the shotgun could be at the bottom of a river or sound," Caffy said. "Let's just continue tying up the ends. In the meantime, we'll document the investigation and turn it over to the prosecutor. There is one thing though, I ain't about to cut Chuckie Ryan loose to anyone…not even the Feds. Shucks, when the Feds get through questioning Mr. Ryan, book him for murder."

"Yes sir, Sheriff," said Shucks.

"We've all had a full day and a long night. Let's break out of here and go home for a good night's sleep. Tomorrow we'll start wrapping things up."

When Caffy left his office Travis said, "Sam, I'm heading over to Eve's. Told her I'd be by when things settled here. Can you take care of Doo?"

"Sure, no problem. Got a little under-cover work to do tonight?" Sam teased.

"Cut it out, Sam," Travis said edgily. "Eve's…Eve's special…"

"Hey, I know she is, or you wouldn't be *besotted* with her," Sam said clipping Travis lightly on the shoulder with his fist.

Travis looked indignantly at Sam and rushed out the door.

Sam joined Doo who had not left his post on the hard bench all day. "Hey, Buddy, how you holding up?" asked Sam.

"I be holing up bitter when I knows if'n Chuckie Ryan had any ting to do wid my Baby's painful condition," said Doo-Wop.

"Well, I think I can put your mind to rest there," said Sam. "We just got a statement from Ryan. From what we learned, I think we can safely say he was not involved in the hit run of Short Sugar. Drane was most certainly the driver."

"Praise be," exclaimed Doo clasping his hands together and lifting his eyes heavenward. "Sam, I jest don't tink I could take any mo of dis. I needs to put hit to res."

Sam placed his hand on the weary man's shoulder. "I know. I know."

"What he say dat lits you know dat he won't in on de hit run?" asked Doo-Wop.

"According to Ryan's statement, Drane was injured in the early morning hours in Chuckie Ryan's apartment. So you see Short Sugar was hit *before* Drane was killed and *long before* he went to Ryan's apartment."

"So you's sayin dat Drane hit my Baby befo' he went to Chuckie Ryan's aparment," Doo-Wop wanted to make sure he understood.

"Right. That's what Chuckie Ryan's statement indicates and the evidence supports," repeated Sam. "Now I have an additional theory of my own about Drane's involvement in Short Sugar's hit run," said Sam. "Mind you, this is not evidence…just my take."

"Go head," prompted Doo-Wop.

"Drane was driving from the direction of the Alligator River National Wildlife Refuge, so I think he'd been working his still that day. More likely than not he was delivering moonshine to customers. He was driving fast, hit

Short Sugar, and kept going because he had illegal alcohol in his possession and didn't want to be stopped by the law," said Sam. "Of course, like I said, this is supposition on my part."

"Make sense ta me," Doo said nodding his head.

Then Sam said, "Come on. Let me give you a ride home."

"No tanks," said Doo-Wop. "I bes go back ta work. Dis be da busy time."

"Good," said Sam. "I'll drive you. I'm on my way there now to hook up with Nona and Shucks."

When Sam walked into Guthrie's, he found Shucks already seated at the bar. He was being hit with a barrage of questions about the arrest of Chuckie Ryan and the two *mysterious* strangers. Always the consummate cop, Shucks would not reveal any information that might 'compromise their case' against Ryan, but he basked in the glory of the attention he was getting.

"Hey, here's one of my partners now," Shucks said hoping everyone caught the 'partner' thing. "What took you so long, Sam?"

"Just tying up loose ends, partner," grinned Sam.

"It can't get any better than this," Shucks thought to himself again.

Sam too was hit with a deluge of questions, but he begged off and directed the questions to the only representative of Dare County law enforcement present…Shucks Twine. Shucks beamed. Then suddenly the place became quiet, heads turned toward the entrance, and in sashayed Nona in all her splendor. Tonight she wore a simple yet seductive black thing. A single string of pearls dangled from her neck and bounced playfully on her bosoms. The back of the dress was cut down to her waist exposing her smooth, white back, and her shiny black sandals clicked loudly on the tile floor as they headed towards the bar.

She looked straight at Sam, raised an eyebrow, and said in an enticing voice, "What's a girl got to do to get a beer around here?"

"Just show up, honey," said Sam. "Just show up.

Irene came to tell them that she had a table for three by the window. As they followed her through the restaurant, Sam complained about having to look at the nutrias, to which Nona snapped, "What a wimp. Sit with your back to the window."

Then Sam came back with, "I'll show you wimp." And smacked Nona on the rear.

The conversation revolved around the murder of Maynard Dwayne Drane and the arrest of Chuckie Ryan. Shucks said, "You know, I won't ever feel the same way about that spot on the beach where they found Maynard Drane's body."

"What do you mean 'feel the same' about that spot on the beach?" asked Sam.

"Well, you see, that used to be one of my favorite places to seek reverie," said Shucks.

"*Reverie?* " said Sam. "Oh, come off it with the words, Shucks. What the hell do you mean?"

"What I mean is that I used to go to that very spot when I had troubles on my mind," said Shucks. "You know, like problems at work and such. I'd just go there, sit on the dunes, watch the ocean, and work through whatever's troubling me."

"You go there a lot?" asked Sam.

"I guess a lot," Shucks looked puzzled.

"And eat peanuts," said Sam.

"Yeah," Shucks said. "And eat peanuts…"

"And drop the shells in the sand," said Sam.

"Well sometimes I pocket them, but what difference does it make if I drop them on the sand? They're biodegradable," Shucks said defensively.

"Shucks, my friend, you are absolutely right. They are biodegradable. You just go right ahead and drop those shells, good buddy. Go right ahead," Sam said excitedly and thought, "Just wait'll Trav finds out how peanut shells got on the dunes at the murder site."

A waitress appeared, and Sam recognized little Miss Compliments Each Other. She gave Sam a flippant look, turned to Nona and with a pitiful expression said sadly, "I heard about your boy friend. You must feel awful. I'm so sorry."

Sam said, "Don't be. Nona decided to dump him…they didn't really 'compliment each other' after all."

"What?" asked Nona.

"Oh, never mind. Just an inside joke," said Sam winking at the waitress. "Now let's order. Food! I'm so hungry my stomach's shaking hands with my backbone."

CHAPTER 34

Travis drove the unmarked vehicle he borrowed from Dare County Justice Center and headed towards Nags Head. He no sooner crossed the Washington Baum Bridge than he was zapped by fatigue. He had neither eaten nor slept for hours, and he was grimy and disheveled. He lowered the car window and breathed the clean salty air allowing it to penetrate and soothe his throbbing muscles. As he began to relax, he fought sleep. He roused himself when he almost missed the turn onto Ocean Acres. He drove pass Pig Pulling Barbecue, and his stomach protested loudly as the aroma of hickory smoke and North Carolina barbecue filtered through the air. Suddenly, hunger transcended fatigue.

He arrived at Eve's house, and had no sooner turned off the engine when the front door flew open. A massive heap of white wool piled out of the house, braced his gigantic, front paws against the door of the car, and smiled at his weary new friend. Eve was close behind admonishing Misha as she always did, and he ignored her as he always did. The sight of the two of them rushing across the yard gave Travis just the boost he needed. He opened the door, and she fell into his arms. And for a long time they just stood there holding each other desperately, fearful that this fragile bond would vanish.

Eve pushed him away slowly and said, "You'll be wanting your supper now."

Travis sighed, "I don't think I've ever been so hungry in my life." And they wrapped their arms around each other's waist and headed for the house with a big, white, wiggling dog tagging happily behind them.

"Why don't you wash up while I get the food on the table," Eve suggested.

When Travis looked in the bathroom mirror, he gasped at the gaunt face that stared back at him. He was shocked that fatigue and loss of sleep could take its toll so quickly. He had heavy stubble, and dark rings circled his sunken, bloodshot eyes. He used the tiny razor Eve gave him, washed his face, and dampened and combed his hair. "Purely superficial, but it'll have to do," he muttered. Scrumptious smells from the kitchen drew him out to satisfy a more pressing need.

Three servings of pot roast and two glasses of wine later, Travis sat across the candlelit table, ate lemon cake, and related the events of the last forty eight hours.

Eve said, "Tell me about your day." She hesitated. "You can't understand how strange it feels to be able to ask that."

"What do you mean?" asked Travis.

Eve ran her finger round and round the rim of her wine glass. Then she looked up and said, "I was never able to ask Maynard to 'tell me about his day'. His days were filled with secrets. Secrets he shared with no one. And when I learned about the bootlegging, I didn't want to ask. I really didn't want to know about his day."

Eve smiled and looked at Travis. "But you are different. I can ask you, Travis. So tell me about your day."

Travis told Eve about the stakeout at the beach, the arrest of Chuckie Ryan, and the statement he gave about Maynard Dwayne Drane's late night visit to his apartment.

"He swears he didn't kill Drane. That Drane was only injured in a knife fight in the apartment and then ran away," said Travis. He did not divulge the fact that blood evidence tended to support the claim that Dwayne was not shot in Ryan's apartment.

Eve sipped her wine and asked softly, "What do you think, Travis?"

"I think Chuckie Ryan killed Maynard Dwayne Drane. I don't know where yet, but I'll tell you one thing…we'll find out," said Travis.

Eve stood and began to remove the dishes from the table. Travis rose to help. Eve took a plate from him and said, "No, please let me do this. Let me do this for you…for us. Tell me, what do you think will happen to Chuckie Ryan?"

"IF we've got enough evidence, and IF he is charged with first degree murder, and IF he's found guilty, he could be executed or get life in prison," said Travis."

Eve dropped a fork in the sink. The clatter seemed to unnerve her, and she jumped.

"Eve, are you alright?" Travis asked as he moved quickly to her side.

Eve was looking down into the sink as if searching for the source of the racket. She quickly straightened and said, "Yes, I'm fine, Travis. I suppose everything that happened this week is finally catching up with me."

Travis took Eve in his arms. "Oh, Eve. That was damned insensitive of me. Coming here tonight and discussing Maynard's death and the investigation as if it had no connection to you at all. You must be thinking, what kind of man is he anyhow."

Eve pushed away from Travis, looked him straight in the eye, and said, "Travis White I was thinking no such thing. I know what kind of man you are. I'm just still reeling from all that has…"

Eve didn't finish her sentence. Travis drew her to him. Eve threw her arms around his waist and clutched him fiercely, desperately. He held her until her arms relaxed. Then he pushed her back and kissed her with a hunger he'd suppressed too long.

When they finally parted, Eve said, "I'm glad it's over. Over for both of us. Maynard spoiled so many nights for me. I'm not going to let him spoil this one. "Now you take this wine and sit by the fire. I'll join you in just a minute."

Travis went willingly. As the wine and the warmth of the fire took effect, he began to relax, and soon he dropped into a much needed sleep. When Eve came in she smiled down at him, carefully took the wine glass from his hand, and covered him with a throw. Then she kissed his cheek, nestled close beside him, and laid her head on his shoulder. Travis stirred slightly. Then he slipped his arm around her, and drew her to him.

Outside the wind whispered softly, and the cry of a night bird pierced the darkness. Flames from the fire in the fireplace created little patterns that danced on the ceiling. A log burned through and fell from the grate sending embers and sparks of fire onto the hearth. The lingering smell of pot roast, scented candles, and smoke from the fire drifted through the house.

Travis floated in and out of sleep. He suddenly became aware of a heavy weight on his right foot and his leg began to tingle. He tried to move his foot and couldn't. He sat up and looked down to see Misha sleeping peacefully, his huge head resting on his foot. As Travis slipped his foot free Eve stirred. She turned, looked up at him, and smiled. He bent and kissed her lovingly then desperately, longingly. Eve slowly backed away and stood. She led Travis toward the bedroom. Misha sensing that the party was moving to the other room trotted along behind them. When they got to the bedroom door, Travis gently pushed him back, "No, partner, you're not invited." Travis closed the door. Misha lay down outside the room, chin on his paws, and without a trace of his Sammy smile.

Eve and Travis made love hungrily, desperately as if there would be no other time. Gone were the feelings of betrayal that Travis feared would condemn him to a life of loneliness and grief. Eve aroused a protective instinct in Travis. He hadn't had this feeling for years, and it felt fulfilling. When their passion was spent, Eve slept with her arm on Travis's chest and her leg wrapped around his. Her damp head lay on his shoulder and her hair smelled of gardenias. A cool breeze rustled the curtains and the sound of cicadas and tree frogs could be heard in the distant woods and swamps. Travis fell quickly into a deep peaceful sleep where none of the tribulations of his job could intrude.

Travis was not sure why he awakened so abruptly. Perhaps it was years of sleeping with one ear always tuned to the unexpected. But tonight he awoke with a start. His hand searched the other side of the bed. It was cold and empty. A glint of moonlight filtered through the curtains, and he turned to see that the clock read 3:30 am. He swung out of bed, pulled on his pants, and started towards the closed door. He opened it slowly, and noticed that Misha was not at his post. He stepped down the short hall and into the den. He saw her there at the kitchen table, Misha at her feet. A beam of moonlight illuminated her face. And when he came closer her realized that her cheeks were wet. Wet with tears.

Travis walked quickly across the room and knelt beside her. He took her chin between his fingers and turned her face toward him. He kissed her salty cheeks and said, "Eve, honey, what's the matter? Oh, Eve did we move too fast? I want to take care of you, not complicate your life. Eve, please tell me what's wrong. Give me a chance to make it right."

New tears rolled down her face. She closed her eyes in an effort to stop the flow. Travis reached for a napkin and began to dab at her cheeks. "Eve? Please, what's wrong?"

She opened her eyes now and looked at Travis sorrowfully. "Travis," she said, "I killed Maynard."

CHAPTER 35

TUESDAY

It was barely daylight when Sam and Nona pulled into the parking lot of the Dare County Justice Center. The space marked Reserved for Dare County Sheriff was already occupied. Before they could step out of their car, Shucks' car sped into the parking lot and screeched to a halt beside of them. Shucks jumped out and immediately began to blather.

"What's going on, Sam? Do you know what's going on? Nona? I never heard the Sheriff sound so grim." As he spoke, Shucks' eyes panned the parking lot. "Where's Travis? You seen Travis? Oh lord, I sure hope nothings happened to Travis. Sam…"

But Sam and Nona were already scurrying toward the building. They took two steps at a time, and Sam called over his shoulder, "We don't know no more than you do, Shucks."

The three of them burst into the reception area and Nona started to speak. The officer on duty shook his head and jabbed a thumb towards Sheriff Caffy's office. They rushed in that direction.

The three breathless officers burst into Caffy's office and stopped short. Sheriff Caffy sat behind his desk concern etched on his face. He leaned forward with his elbows propped on his desk. He repeatedly snapped the point of a ball point pen in and out. A tape recorder set idly by.

Seated across from him in a straight-back chair was Eve Drane. She looked so small and frightened like a snared rabbit. She wore no make-up. Her hair was disheveled, and her blue eyes were rimmed red. She wore a white blouse and a blue print skirt with a sweater draped about her shoulders.

She was looking down at her hands that clutched a damp tattered tissue.

Sitting beside of Eve was a slender young man dressed in a tan sport jacket, dark brown pants, a crisp yellow shirt, and a striped tie. He held a legal pad and pen efficiently on his lap. Beside his chair was a briefcase that looked so new as to question if there might be a price tag still inside. Sam recognized him as Samuel Jourdan a young man who recently passed his bar exam in North Carolina and set up practice in Manteo.

Seated next to the wall was Travis. He leaned forward with his elbows on his knees, his eyes riveted on Eve. He looked a mess. He was wearing the same clothes he'd worn the night before. His hair was not combed, and he needed to shave. Sam thought that the last time he'd seen his friend look so distraught was at Virginia's funeral. His instinct was to rush over and console his friend, reassure him. But console, reassure him for what?

"Well, hail, hail, the gang's all here," Sheriff Caffy said. "Nona (Nona started fearful that this early morning meeting was the result of something she'd done.) Nona, it appears to me that you've got some competition."

"C-C-Competition? I don't follow…" Nona said.

"What I mean," Sheriff Caffy interrupted, "is that you are no longer the only one creating headaches for me. Seems like our friend Travis aims to pull my chain some too."

Shucks, Nona, and Sam all began to talk at the same time.

Sheriff Caffy raised his hands in a jester of silence. "I believe you three have met Mrs. Eve Drane also none as Mrs. Maynard Dwayne Drane. This here is her lawyer, Samuel Jourdan. It appears that Mrs. Drane has something to report to us that could not wait till regular office hours. So I saw no reason for you three to get a full night's sleep and miss this latest development. Of course, Travis over here don't sleep anyhow so he's more or less responsible for the timing of this meeting."

Shucks, Sam, and Nona looked from Eve to Travis to the Sheriff too dumbfounded to speak.

The Sheriff looked at Samuel Jourdan and said, "Counselor, I understand you've spent some time conferring with your client already, and seeings I don't know what the hell this is all about, I'm just going to read Mrs. Drane her rights. Do you think that is appropriate?"

"Yes, I most certainly do," said the lawyer.

Sheriff Caffy reached over and clicked on the tape recorder and read Eve her rights. He began the interview. "Mrs. Drane, I'd like for the record to show that you contacted me by telephone this morning at five thirty am. Is that correct?"

"Yes, that is correct," said Eve.

"And you asked if you could come in here immediately for a conference. Is that correct?" asked the Sheriff

"Yes," said Eve.

"And you also told me that you would be accompanied by your lawyer, Samuel Jourdan and Travis White, North Carolina Alcohol Beverage Control Agent. Is that correct?"

"Yes," said Eve.

"Is your lawyer here with you now?" asked the Sheriff.

"Yes, he is," said Eve.

"Let the record show that present at the interview is Samuel Jourdan, lawyer for Eve Drane, Travis White and Sam Barnett North Carolina Alcohol Beverage Control Agents, Nona Godette and Norman Twine Dare County law enforcement officers. I'm Sheriff Grady Caffy."

Sheriff Caffy paused and searched the face of each one present. Satisfied that everyone understood why they were assembled, he rubbed his hands together and continued, "Now Mrs. Drane since you were the one who called for this meeting, I'll just sit back and ask you to tell us in as much detail as you can exactly why we're here."

Eve looked up into the eyes of Sheriff Caffy. She wet her lips. "I wanted to tell you…." She whispered.

"Excuse me Mrs. Drane, could you speak a little louder please," Sheriff Caffy said. He pointed to the tape recorder and pushed it closer to her.

Eve cleared her throat. This time her voice cracked and she spoke too loud. "I wanted to tell you that I killed Maynard."

The room fell silent. Sheriff Caffy gaped at Eve. Shucks and Nona's jaws dropped. Sam's eyes went immediately to Travis. Travis dropped his face into his hands and slowly shook his head. Sam wanted to go to him to reassure him, but reassure him how. He couldn't move. He felt as if he were glued to the spot.

Sheriff Caffy reached over and clicked off the recorder. "Are you okay with this counselor?"

"This is what my client wants," said Jourdan.

Sheriff Caffy clicked on the recorder again. "Alright Mrs. Drane, tell us what happened."

CHAPTER 36

Eve spoke in monotone and her report was succinct. Her eyes seldom left the twisted tissue in her hand as she told her story.

Eve learned of Maynard's latest brush with the law, the hit run crime, on Monday when Travis came to her home to ask about Maynard's Jeep. When Travis finished interviewing Eve, he drove her to work. What Eve did not realize at the time was that Maynard hid in a nearby stand of scrub pines and watched them drive off. Maynard, concerned that Eve was being driven to the Justice Center for further interrogation, followed them into town. He watched as Eve went into the bait shop to report for work, and Travis drove off. Satisfied that Eve would work at the bait shop until closing, Maynard drove back to the house. He searched in all the usual places for hidden cash, and when he found none he snatched the guns and television set and took them out to the Jeep. In the process, Misha went outside. Travis drove off leaving the dog in the yard. Misha was not accustomed to being unrestrained while Eve was at work. He ambled onto the porch, lay down with his chin on his paws, and waited for Eve to come home.

The bait shop closed a little before ten. Eve's neighbor, who was in to buy bait, offered to drive her home. When her neighbor drove her home she asked him to drop her off at the corner explaining that she liked to walk in the evening while it was cool. When she got home Misha was on the porch and the lights on inside. Eve went inside and found the guns and TV gone. Eve knew exactly what had happened. Maynard had needed money and when he found none, he took the guns and television to pawn.

Eve began some household chores…threw a load of clothes in the washer, put away the dishes, and folded some clothes. It was then that she realized that

Misha was still outside. She went to the front door and called him. He was no where to be seen. Finally after calling several times, she heard him bark from the woods just beyond the house. Fearful that he was hurt, she rushed into the woods and straight into Maynard Dwayne Drain. He had used a line from the scuba equipment he kept piled in his Jeep to tie Misha to a young, slender pine tree. Fearful that Maynard had harmed the dog, Eve dropped to her knees beside her beloved companion to check him out. She spoke soothingly to Misha as she checked him for any signs of injury. Relieved that she found no wounds, she turned her attention to Maynard.

She looked up at him and shouted, "You know he doesn't like to be tied up." It was then that she saw the blood. His shirt was ripped and a red stain spread across his chest.

"Maynard, what have you done now?" she said in a hoarse voice.

"What do you mean *what have I done*," he said. "Just one time couldn't you say what have they done to you? No. No. It's always *MY* fault. What have *I* done?"

"Maynard, I'm not going to listen to any more of this. I know you're in trouble again, and I'm not getting involved," Eve said and she turned to untie Misha. As she turned still kneeling, Maynard lifted his foot and pushed her over.

"Yes, you will listen to me, Missy. And yes you will help me," he said. "I saw you with that policeman. Yeah. That's right I know everything you do. If you think you'll get any help from them you are wrong. You know why? Huh? You know why they won't help you? It's because every man…even a policeman…knows better than to get involved in another man's domestic affairs."

"We have no domestic affairs, Maynard," said Eve as she raised herself on her elbow and glared up at Maynard. "And I'm not going to help you period."

Maynard grinned. "Well, if I don't have the kind of wife that's gonna stick by me and help me out when I need it, then I don't need a wife at all."

Maynard slowly raised his shotgun. "So Missy, you want to be separated? You want to be divorced? Well, you're gonna get your wish…permanently. First, I'm gonna take out this worthless cur, and then I'll make myself a single man."

Maynard pointed the shotgun at Misha. Eve crawled forward and grabbed the barrel of the gun, pulled herself up, and wrestled with Mayard until the barrel was pointed to the ground. They struggled for the shotgun Eve realized that Maynard's strength was ebbing. Probably from loss of blood. She finally managed to wrest the gun from his grasp, and Maynard fell backwards. He groaned as he hit the ground. He looked at Eve with fury in his face.

"You are going to die, bitch. You and your mangy mutt," he growled. And he struggled to stand.

Eve pointed the shotgun at Maynard. "Don't do it Maynard," she said. "Don't make me shoot you."

"You? Shoot me? Ha! Why you haven't got the guts," he said and lunged toward Eve.

Eve fired one shot. A look of surprise filled Maynard's face. He looked down at the front of his shirt where the blood stain grew larger and larger. He looked incredulously at Eve and simply said, "You shot me." He fell forward on his face.

Eve dropped the gun. There was no need to check Maynard's vital signs. The rapidly spreading pool of blood confirmed that the very life was running out of him. Eve quickly untied Misha, and they ran to the house. Eve checked Misha again to make sure he was not injured. He seemed okay. Only his pride was hurt after being restrained. Eve waited anxiously fearful that someone heard the shot and would telephone or come over to see if she were okay. Thirty minutes passed without any phone calls or inquiries, she breathed a sigh of relief reasoning that either no one heard the shot or no one identified the noise as a gun shot.

Now her thoughts turned to Maynard. Call the police? She remembered what Maynard said about men not wanting to get involved in other men's domestic affairs. She thought about the times she'd called the police and they were either unwilling or unable to help her. Eve concluded that this was again a situation she must handle herself. But how?

Perhaps she could hide or bury Maynard's body. There were certainly enough places on the Outer Banks to hide a body so it would never be found. But could she handle it…physically handle it. Maynard was not a small man. She doubted that she could even lift him into the Jeep. Her thoughts were abruptly interrupted by the ring of the telephone. She moved anxiously to the phone and slowly lifted the receiver.

"Hello," Eve said apprehensively.

"Eve, this is David," the young familiar voice of the bait shop clerk said.

"What? Oh, David," said Eve.

David hesitated. "Did I call at a bad time?"

"No, no David. I, I was ah just getting ready for bed," Eve said.

"Well, okay. I just wanted to know if you'd like me to pick you up in the morning since we're both scheduled to go in early," asked David.

"Oh, David, tomorrow? Pick me up? Ah…," Eve stammered.

"Eve is there something wrong?" asked David

"Wrong?" Eve repeated.

"There is something wrong Eve," David said. "Are you alone?"

"Yes," whispered Eve.

"Are you hurt?" asked David.

"No," Eve said and then she began to cry. "David, I don't know what to do."

"Okay, Eve, sit tight. I'm coming over," David said confidently then added pleadingly, "if that is okay."

"Oh, yes, David. It is okay," Eve whispered, "And David, please come very quietly."

"Alright then," David said.

David must have called from a nearby public phone because he arrived quickly. He cut his lights as he drove into Eve's driveway. He crept to the porch and tapped lightly on the door. Inside, Eve jumped not expecting David to get there so fast.

Without turning on the porch light she opened the door and hurried David inside.

"What's going on, Eve? Is Maynard around?" David asked nervously. His eyes searched the room.

"David, Maynard is around, but he can't do any harm…not any more," Eve said.

"Eve, what do you mean?" the young man asked his confidence ebbing.

Eve dissolved into tears. David didn't know what to do. He shifted from one foot to the other repeating her name, "Eve, Eve, Eve…"

Eve finally gained control. "Oh, David I killed Maynard," she said.

"You what?" asked David.

"I shot him…" and Eve told the young man exactly what happened when she came home and found the wounded Maynard Dwayne Drane hiding in the woods beside her house. She explained her reluctance to call the police. Then she described her dilemma at not being physically able to move Maynard's body.

David paced back and forth wide-eyed as Eve told her story. When she finished, she stood and looked at him as if to say 'what now'. They were silent for a while and then David said, "Show me the body."

Eve led him out the front door. Fearful of turning on the porch light, they waited allowing their eyes to adjust to the darkness. Then Eve walked cautiously across the yard and into the woods. It wasn't until they were well into the woods that Eve turned a small flashlight on the body.

"He's dead alright," said David. "He's got to be dead. Look at all that blood."

"I know, David, I know he's dead," said Eve, "but what am I going to do with him?"

David looked over his shoulder at Maynard Drane's Jeep then down at the body.

"Okay, here's what we can do," he said finally, "I'll back the Jeep up to the very edge of the woods, and we'll drag the body to it. Then we'll put him in the passenger side and get him out of here."

"Yes, yes," Eve coaxed, "and then what?"

"Well, we'll dump him somewhere way away from here," said David.

"Yes, it will just look like a bootleg buy gone bad," said Eve getting into the game.

"Right," said David. "But it'll take two of us to put the body in the jeep and two to take it out."

"Okay, you drive Maynard's Jeep and I'll drive your car," said Eve. "Or we could do it the other way around. You drive your car and I'll drive the Jeep…except he…he'll be in the Jeep."

David interrupted, "No, no, that's okay. I'll drive the Jeep." He reached down and lifted Maynard's arms.

"We'd best decide where we're taking him before we leave here," said Eve.

David dropped Maynard's arms and they hit the ground with a thump. "Yeah, right we need to decide where we're going to dump him."

They stood in silence for a moment then Eve said, "How about the beach? Fishermen will go out early and find him there."

"Do you want that? Do you want them to find him, Eve," asked David in surprise.

"Yes, David I do. I can't just dump him in the swamp or something. I killed him. The least I can do is bury him," Eve said.

"Well, okay if that's what you want," David said reluctantly. "I'd want to lose him forever, but that's just me. The beach it is."

Fearful of drawing attention, David put the Jeep in neutral, and he and Eve pushed it to the edge of the woods. Then they dragged Maynard's body to the passenger side and lifted it into the seat. He raced back into the woods, retrieved the shotgun, and tossed it into the back of the Jeep. Then he studied Maynard in the passenger seat.

"He just looks like a drunk," said David.

But Eve wasn't looking at Maynard. "Oh, David, look at the blood on the ground."

"We'll worry about that tomorrow. Just kick some leaves over it for now," said David and he began kicking pine needles and leaves over the blood.

Eve wasn't moving. "Come on, Eve," David said impatiently. "We'll do a better job tomorrow. Right now just cover it with leaves."

"But David, look at the blood on the Jeep seat," Eve said.

David finished kicking leaves and walked back to the Jeep. "Well, as much as I hate to say this, Eve, we're gonna have to ditch this Jeep."

"And me without a car," Eve murmured.

David jumped behind the wheel of the Jeep and started the motor. "Just follow me Eve." And he tossed her the keys to his car.

David drove to a road that ran in front of a condominium complex. The beach below was heavily fished by the residents of the condominiums. He stopped before driving the Jeep down the dune to the water, and Eve pulled up behind him. She parked David's car on the side of the road and crawled into the back of the Jeep amidst scuba equipment and some of Eve's old canning jars that Maynard used to bottle his bootleg whiskey. Then David drove the Jeep close to the water's edge taking care not to get so close that he'd get stuck in the sand. Eve and David lifted Maynard's body out of the Jeep and dragged it closer the waves. Eve's flip flops kept slipping and this made it difficult for her to balance her end of the body. They finally dropped the body and dragged it the last few feet. They placed Maynard's body close to the surf, dropped it, and made their way back to the Jeep.

As they were climbing in the Jeep Eve spotted the Mason jars in the back of the Jeep.

She grabbed a couple, tossed them back towards the body, and said, "Now the police will surely think it was a bootleg sale gone bad. Let's go."

David drove the Jeep up the dune and onto the road again. He stopped beside his car. "Eve, we got to get rid of this Jeep," he said. "No kidding. It's no good to you with blood stains on it."

"I know," Eve said. "Any ideas?"

"I think so," he said, "just follow me."

David drove the Jeep out to Highway 12. He drove pass Bodie Lighthouse and over the Oregon Inlet Bridge. Just beyond the bridge, David pulled into a small parking area. He motioned Eve to park in front of a waterfowl observation platform. He then turned and backed the Jeep to the water, put it in neutral, and hopped out.

"I don't know, Eve," David said, "I'm afraid the Jeep is gonna get stuck in the mud."

David walked around examining the situation. "I think the best thing to do is pull up, put it in reverse, gun the engine, and let it hit the water. When it hits the water, I'll roll out."

"Oh, David," said Eve, "That sounds dangerous. Let's just try to push it in."

"No, no," said David, "Gunning it is best. We can't take a chance of getting stuck in the mud. Now I'll just wipe our prints off and we'll be ready to roll."

David tore off a part of his shirttail and began to wipe places on the Jeep that they might have touched. Then covering a part of the steering wheel with the fabric, he jumped into the Jeep, turned the key, and gunned the engine. The Jeep launched backwards. As it hit the water, David bailed out. The Jeep disappeared quickly in the briny water.

David ran from the water, grabbed Eve's hand, and headed for his car. "We're outta here," he said.

When they crossed the Oregon Inlet Bridge David turned right onto a dirt road that twisted through marsh grass to a favorite spot for inlet fishing. He grabbed the shotgun that lay in the back of the Jeep, opened the car door, and raced to the water. He tossed the weapon forcefully. It spun out over the inlet and splashed down beside a yellow channel marker.

David killed the car lights as he turned onto Eve's street and slowly pulled into her driveway. He parked the car close to edge of the woods. Clouds floated continuously across the sky allowing an occasion peek at the bright, full moon.

"What about the blood in the woods," Eve whispered.

"We gotta take care of that as soon as possible," David said. Adrenalin diminished, he was beginning to shiver.

"David," Eve put her hand on David's arm. She realized he was in distress. "Do you want to come in?"

"No, no. We've gotta take care of that blood," he said shakily. He was breathing hard. "Suppose someone comes out here in the morning to ask more questions, and they decide to look around outside. No, we got to take care of that blood."

"How should we do that?" asked Eve.

"I don't know," said David. He reached for the car door handle. "Let's take a look now."

"Now? But David…" Eve was too late. He had opened the car door and was headed across the lawn towards the woods. Eve grabbed the flashlight, jumped from the car, and raced after him.

David was standing in the woods looking down at the ground. "Where was it exactly? The leaves are disturbed here and weeds trampled but…" He kicked the leaves about. Eve shined the flashlight on the spot.

"Hey look. A lot of the blood soaked into the ground. I don't think it looks like as much as before. What do you think?" David exclaimed excitedly.

Eve looked carefully. "I think you're right, David. It doesn't look as bad," she said carefully. "But you can still see some. We've got to do something."

Eve and David stood in the woods and discussed how best to conceal the blood evidence at the crime scene. The moon occasionally bounced from behind a cloud and shined through the tree branches just enough to create a menacing atmosphere. The two conspirators were faced with the reality that there were only a few hours of darkness left in which to complete the job.

Using a garden hose from Eve's yard, they saturated the blood soaked ground with water. Then they brought armfuls of leaves from various spots in the woods. When they moved leaves they were careful to scatter nearby leaves in such a way as not to leave a trail of bare spots. Then they used the leaves they'd gathered to cover the watered-soaked area. After the spot was concealed by leaves, they backed out of the woods. As they went they plumped up foliage so as not to leave a path from the lawn to the location where Maynard's body fell.

The first light of day was chasing the moon from the sky. They had worked all night.

"Come inside, David," said Eve.

"No, I gotta go, Eve," said David.

Eve looked at David's rumpled, dirty clothes and nodded. "You can't go like that, David," she said.

David looked down. "Geez," he said, "I guess I can't."

"Come inside. I'll find you something to wear," Eve said and walked towards the house. David followed.

The hands of the kitchen clock pointed to five o'clock, and Misha let it be known that it was his turn to go outside.

"Will he go over there?" David said nodding toward the spot they'd just left.

"I don't think so," said Eve. "He's a creature of habit and that is not his bathroom territory. But I'll keep an eye on him. Meantime here are some clothes." She tossed him a pair of jeans and a short-sleeve tee shirt.

David caught the pants and shirt and held them at arms length. "Are these his?" asked David staring at the clothes.

Eve shrugged. "That's all I have, David. Besides they are clean and pressed. Why don't you shower and change. Then I'll do the same." She moved to the window to check on Misha. The dog saw her look out and raced back towards the house.

When David came out of the bathroom, he saw a pot of coffee and two mugs on the kitchen counter.

"Have some coffee, David. I'll clean up and then we better get to work," said Eve as she started towards the bathroom.

When Eve reached the bathroom she stopped and leaned against the door frame. Then she turned and said, "David, for years I have been so alone. I didn't think I had a friend in the world. Maynard convinced me of that. I felt so isolated and afraid. I had no one to turn to for help. Now I have a job, and I have a friend. Thank you, David, for being my friend."

"Uh, you're welcome," David blushed. Eve disappeared into the bathroom.

When Eve finished her statement, she sat silently still staring at the tissue in her hand which was now in shreds.

Travis still leaned forward with his elbows on his knees, his eyes riveted on Eve. Shucks' face took on a perplexed expression as if he feared someone was playing a prank. Sam looked at Travis with concern in his eyes. Nona's mouth was open, and she shook her head in disbelief. Samuel Jourdan tapped his pencil on the yellow legal pad he held on his knee. You could hear a pin drop.

Sheriff exhaled loudly, rocked back in his chair, and said, "Mrs. Drane, I need to ask you the full name of this young friend who helped you out."

Eve looked up at the Sheriff. Tears welled up in her eyes. "Sheriff, please don't blame him. This was all my fault. David just stumbled into the situation innocently. He's only sixteen years old. He's virtually alone. I couldn't bare it if I were the cause of his getting in trouble. ."

"Mrs. Drane," Sheriff Caffy interrupted sternly, "I want you to give me the name of the young man who helped you move Maynard Dwayne Drane's body and helped you sink his Jeep. And I want it now."

"Sheriff Caffy." Samuel Jourdan began, but Eve touched his arm to silence him.

"His name is David Luther. He is, as I said, a clerk at the bait shop," said Eve. "But please Sheriff, he's just a boy. He was just trying to help a friend in trouble. He's not a criminal."

"Huh," scoffed the Sheriff, "we'll see. In the meantime Counselor, I have to talk to my team about these latest developments your client landed on me. So, why don't you two go on down to a conference room and give us a little time to chew on this."

Caffy reached over and clicked off the tape recorder.

"Sheriff, if you don't mind…" began Jourdan.

"Counselor, I do mind," Sheriff Caffy said. "I've been up all night, ain't had no coffee, and you and your client come in here and drop a bombshell on me. Now, I'm gonna have my coffee, and I'm gonna have a conference with my team whether you like it or not. We'll make you comfortable and try to be more considerate of you and your client than she was of us."

Sheriff Caffy reached over and punched the intercom button. "Doris, you here yet?"

An irritable voice replied, "Where else would I be?"

"Well, come on in here then," Caffy said and released the button.

Doris entered immediately and stood at attention in the open doorway. "Nona, you take Mr. Jourdan and Mrs. Drane down to Conference Room A. Ah, see if there is ah, anything Mrs. Drane needs. Shucks, you go down and tell Doc to come a runnin. Doris, we're gonna need coffee and lots of it. See if you can't get a pot hooked up down in the conference room for Mr. Jourdan and his client too and some of those cake doughnuts with little sprinklely things on them."

As Doris turned to leave Sheriff Caffy added, "Oh, and Doris, make sure the coffee's hot." Doris shot him a look to kill and stomped out. Caffy added, "Nona, you and Shucks get back in here as soon as you can."

Everyone scurried to follow Sheriff Caffy's orders except Travis and Sam. Sam moved to Travis and said, "How you holding up, buddy?"

CHAPTER 37

When they assembled Sheriff Caffy looked around at the solemn faces of his team. Doris entered pushing a cart that held a coffee maker and a large platter of cake doughnuts with little 'sprinkley things' on them. One look at the assemblage told her this was a serious situation.

Sheriff Caffy stood and walked over to the cart. "Come on and get yourselves some coffee and a doughnut. These doughnuts make a mess, but I can't get on with my day without one." Everyone did as instructed and then returned to their seats.

Sheriff Caffy blew into his cup and took a couple of loud sips. Then he opened wide and bit into his doughnut sending tiny sprinkles onto his desk. "See what I mean? They're a mess but worth the trouble. I tell you what, let's just listen to Eve Drane's statement again while we eat breakfast."

He reached over and clicked on the tape player. They listened without interruptions to the tape. When it was finished Sheriff Caffy reached over and clicked it off.

A few more minutes of silence passed. Then Sheriff Caffy said, "Travis, since you dropped this bomb on us, why don't you start off. How and when did you find out that Eve Drane killed her husband?"

Travis said, "Last night. Well, it was really morning."

Sheriff Caffy raised an eyebrow. "Go on."

"Last night I had dinner with Eve. At her house. During the evening she asked me about the arrest of Chuckie Ryan. I told her about it...generally. Don't worry I didn't divulge evidence or anything. She asked what would happen to him if he were found guilty. I told her that he could get life or the death penalty. At first it didn't seem to bother her that much, but later I suppose she felt guilty about the possibility of someone paying for a crime she'd committed. So she broke down and told me that she murdered Chuckie Ryan."

Travis stopped and panned the room looking for allies. He continued, "Don't you see. She felt guilty. She didn't want someone else to pay for something she did."

Travis paused again. Everyone still appeared dumbfounded. "It was Eve who wanted to come in. She wanted me to call Sheriff Caffy immediately and tell him that Chuckie didn't kill Maynard…she did. She didn't want the wrong person to be sent to jail or executed."

"I can believe that," Nona said finally. "I *can* see her living with the knowledge that she killed a slim ball like Maynard Drane, but I *can't* see her living with the knowledge that someone else was doing her time." Travis looked at her appreciatively.

Encouraged Travis continued, "She didn't even want a lawyer to accompany her. I insisted that she call him. He came over, and she told him what she'd told me. I thought having the lawyer here would save us time."

"Well, thank you for that, Travis," Sheriff Caffy said sarcastically. "There's just one thing I want to ask you, Travis," and he looked Travis straight in the eye, "did you spend the night with Mrs. Drane last night?"

"Yes," said Travis defiantly.

"Okay then," the Sheriff said with finality.

The room fell silent. Pondering what to do next, Sheriff Caffy did the only sensible thing he could think of. He stood up, walked to the coffee cart, and reached for another doughnut. Then ever the consummate host, he passed the platter around to the others. When everyone shook their heads in a pass, he said, "Suit yourselves." Then he placed the platter on the cart and returned to his chair behind the desk.

"Doc," said Caffy, "You heard what these two squirrels did to the crime scene. Running around with a garden hose and kicking leaves all over the place for Christ sake. Think you can salvage any evidence there?"

Doc smiled, "Sure Sheriff. What these two did certainly didn't *destroy* the scene. Considering the amount of blood, squirting a garden hose on the spot is not going to remove all traces of blood from the ground, leaves, and other debris there."

"You sure about that?" asked Caffy.

"Sure I'm sure," said Doc. "Also, a shotgun blast at close range as she described is bound to have left tissue evidence. That was one big hole in him."

The Sheriff looked around at the other members of the team who still sat in a state of shock. "Come on folks, wake up. You can't tell me that after all we just heard you don't have no questions."

Sam said, "Doc, what about the part of the statement where Eve claimed that Drane showed up with a cut on his abdominal area. You find anything to substantiate that?"

"Well," said Doc, "we already covered that with the Chuckie Ryan discussion. If Drane was cut, the knife wound was obliterated by the shotgun blast and crabs. So nothing she said changes my opinion there."

"But she described a lot of blood on his shirt when he showed up at her house," said Shucks.

"It doesn't take a horrendous injury to make a wound bleed a lot," said the Doc. "I don't doubt that he was bleeding when he got to Eve Drane's house, but I can confidently say that it was the shotgun blast that killed Maynard Drane."

"What about Purvis's search of Eve's house," said Nona. Anger flashed across Travis's face as he thought of Clelon Purvis ransacking Eve's house.

Nona continued, "Why didn't he find evidence of the shooting?"

Sam said, "He wasn't conducting that kind of a search. He was focused on finding a shotgun on the premises."

"You're right, he wasn't conducting that kind of search...he was more interested in rummaging through personal effects," Travis said angrily.

"Now that's water under the bridge," said Sheriff Caffy sternly. "Don't want to get side tracked. We got a man down in jail that we are charging with murder....by the way, Shucks, have you charged him yet?"

"No sir," said Shucks, "When I left here last night, the Feds were still working him. I'd planned to charge him this morning."

"Good," said Caffy, "we got enough to hold him for the time being what with assault on Drane and the charges the Feds have. He ain't going nowhere till we get this straightened out. So hold off on the murder charge for the time being."

The Sheriff rubbed his red eyes and brushed the crumbs off the front of his shirt. Then he eyed Travis. "Travis, do you think Eve Drane is telling the truth about shooting Maynard?"

"Yes, Sheriff, I do," Travis said simply.

"Okay, let's talk about how Eve Drane's story agrees with police findings. First of all, she knew exactly where the body was found on the beach," the Sheriff said.

"Also, she knew about the Mason jars. She even admitted to tossing them," added Sam.

"Sheriff," said Shucks, "I been thinking about those Mason jars. Shouldn't we check for her fingerprints on them?"

"Won't make no difference, Shucks," Caffy said. "They were her canning jars. Stand to reason her prints are probably on them."

"She knew where the Jeep was dumped," said Shucks.

"She also collaborates Chuckie's claim that he didn't shoot Maynard that he was cut in his apartment," said Nona.

The Sheriff rubbed his hands together. "Okay then," he said, "let's check it out. Shucks, get yourself a crew and see if you can find that shotgun. Don't forget she mentioned a channel marker. Good luck. You're in charge."

Shucks had just been handed the sword. He'd made the grade. He was the man. "Yes sir," Shucks said boldly, and he shot up and scurried out of the room to follow orders.

"Doc, we got another crime scene for your guys down at Eve Drane's place. See what you can salvage. Garden hose, kicking leaves," the Sheriff scoffed.

"Don't worry, Sheriff," said Doc, "if it's there, we'll find something." Doc ambled out of the office.

"Nona, got a two-fer for you," said Caffy. "First we're gonna have to hold Eve Drane till we get to the bottom of this. You being our only female officer, I want you to make sure she's taken care of. After she's safe and sound behind bars, go down there and pick up David Luther for questioning. Remember, he's a juvenile."

"Yes sir," Nona said and headed in the direction of the conference room.

The Sheriff leaned back in his chair, stretched wide, and yawned. "Guess this leaves me with the unpleasant task of bringing our Federal friends up to date. I'm still not ready to send Chuckie packing till I can get a handle on Eve Drane's story. Also I got to contact the DA and bring him up to date."

"What do you want me to do?" asked Sam.

"Sam, I can't think of any reason to use the services of ABC any longer beings this was domestic not alcohol related" said Caffy.

"Guess that goes for me, too," said Travis.

"Travis, you'd be off the case under any circumstances. Hell, you're personally involved with a suspect. On the one hand I'm disappointed that you'd get romantically involved with a suspect in a murder case. But on the other hand, I admire you for putting the law above your personal feelings and bringing her in."

"I didn't *bring* her in. I accompanied her," said Travis.

"Well, whatever," said the Sheriff. "Anyhow your actions may ultimately allow us to solve this case, and I'm grateful for that."

Sam stood. "I suppose there's no reason for us to hang around. What say, Trav?" he said.

Travis did not move. "Sheriff, I understand that you don't want nor need us to work the case anymore, but can I ask you a question off the record?" Travis's eyes pled with Sheriff Caffy.

Without hesitation Sheriff Caffy said, "Shoot."

"What do you think will happen to them?" Travis asked plainly.

The Sheriff leaned back in his chair and tapped his fingers together. "Travis," he said, "I won't pretend to be a prosecutor. All I can do is give you my best guess. As far as Eve Drane is concerned," he held up a thick folder, "we got arrest records for Maynard for bootlegging, assault, theft, bad checks, breaking and entering. We got a folder full of domestic complaints. We got a restraining order. We got domestic assault. Now I'm not saying just because a person has a record it's okay to shoot them with a shotgun, but I will say that Eve Drane has plenty to back up her charge of self defense." The Sheriff dropped the folder on his desk.

"Now what she don't have is a legal justification for all she did." The Sheriff clicked the charges off on his fingers, "one, interfering with the investigation of a crime; two, destroying evidence; and three, lying to a law enforcement official." It was on number three that Sheriff Caffy pointed a finger at Travis. "Same goes for the boy. He is an accessory after the fact."

"I remember David," said Travis. "I met him one night when I picked up Eve at the bait shop. He is just a kid."

Caffy frowned. Travis looked beaten. Sam remained standing. The Sheriff continued, "I don't know how the DA will handle this, Travis. Maynard Dwayne Drane was a menace to the community," Caffy tapped the thick folder. "DA would be hard pressed to find a jury hereabouts to come down on an abused wife defending herself...especially if she defended herself against the likes of Drane. But now this thing of moving the body, I do not know."

Travis stood, "Thanks Sheriff. When can I see her?"

"I'll let you know," Sheriff Caffy said. "Where will you be?"

Travis told him, and he and Sam walked solemnly out of the building. When they reached the car, Sam said, "Want to stop by Guthrie's and get a beer?"

"No thanks," said Travis.

"What do you want to do then?" asked his friend.

"I want to go fishing," said Travis.

"Good idea," said Sam as he plopped behind the wheel.

CHAPTER 38

SOME DAYS LATER

Travis waited nervously for Eve to be escorted to the visitor's room. The room was silent except for the hands of the wall clock that ticked away each second. With each tick, he thought of how he was alone again. The door handle clicked and he jumped. He stood as Eve walked slowly into the room. She looks so pale and small in the starched blue uniform. Her hair was combed back severely from her face making her blue eyes look more prominent and frightened. She sat down and looked down at her hands folded on the table.

Travis reached for her hands and she jerked them away and put them in her lap under the table. "We can't touch each other," she whispered.

Travis was taken aback. He'd never thought that he couldn't touch her, hold her, and console her. He forced a smile and said, "That's okay. There'll be plenty of time for that later on."

"Oh Travis," she said her eyes brimming with tears. "Will there be a later on?"

"Of course there will," Travis said reassuringly. "But Eve you don't have to stay here. You could be out on bond in an hour. You mustn't punish yourself like this."

Eve wrung her hands and looked somber. Travis continued, "Is that what you're trying to do? Punish yourself?"

Tears ran down Eve's cheeks, and Travis knew he'd said too much. Eve's life was finally her own. She was able to make decisions for herself, and this is what she wanted to do…or needed to do.

"How's Misha?" Eve asked, fresh tears welling up in her eyes.

"Nona says he fine. He misses you, of course, but he is definitely a lady's man. He sticks to Nona like glue."

"I really appreciate her taking care of him. He's big but he's still so helpless," she said.

"Well, not as helpless as you think," Travis smiled.

"Travis, you don't have to do this. Don't feel like you have to stick by me just because..." she didn't finish but looked down at her hands again.

Travis smiled. "Is that what you're thinking? You're thinking I'll *stick* by you just because we spent the night together."

"It's not just that, Travis," she said. "Just think of your job. You're in law enforcement. How well does it set for you to have a girl friend who is arrested for killing her husband? How well does it set for you to have a girl friend in jail? Oh no, Travis, I care for you too much to ruin your life like that."

Travis smiled again, "Eve, I don't know how it will set for me to have a girl friend who has gone through what you're going through, but I'm not planning to stick up for a girl friend, I'm planning to stick up for my wife."

Tears rushed down Eve's cheeks. She reached across the table and grabbed Travis's hands. "Oh, Travis..."

"Eve," the guard said, "hands under the table....please." And she smiled.

EPILOGUE

It was a perfect Indian summer evening, the breeze gentle, the air filled with the smell of burning leaves. Trees caught the glow of a crimson sunset that stretched across the cobalt blue sky. Their leaves looked like wedges of fire ignited by a blaze swept down from heaven.

Inside the small, historic Seaboard Methodist Church long tapered white candles threw shadows against the white walls, and the sweet scent of lilies and gardenias mingled with the musty smell of ferns. The soft glow of departing daylight filtered through the stained glass windows, and heavenly figures smiled down upon the couple kneeling at the alter. Guests smiled happily as they strained to hear the vows Eve and Travis whispered.

Then with a resounding cord from the organ, the couple stood and kissed briefly. And as melodious chimes echoed from the steeple, Travis and Eve turned and began their first walk together as husband and wife. They walked slowly down the red carpet pausing to smile broadly at those in attendance. Eve looked like a woodland nymph wearing a simple, white, floor-length cotton gown and a crown of fresh baby's breath on her head. Travis was handsome in his dark suit and crisp white shirt, and it occurred to Eve that this was the first time she'd seen him wear a coat and tie.

As they reached the churchyard, the ebbing sunlight pierced the yellow leaves and scattered golden beams upon the grass. Shadows of branches dappled the sidewalk with intricate patterns. The couple did not hurry away. They mingled with guests and thanked them for coming to share their happiness.

Travis talked with his neighbors, mostly answering questions about Eve. Eve knew that as the community newcomer with a past, she would be the topic of conversation for months to come. But Eve was comforted by small town customs. Tradition allowed that it was permissible for those within the community to discuss, even gossip, about each other. After all, this was just showing interest in one's neighbor. However, should outside threats arise, citizens were capable of joining ranks, circling the wagons, and coming to the fiercest defense of their own.

Sam did not stray far from Shucks and Nona. Nona was drawing almost as much attention as the newly weds. Not wanting to upstage the bride, Nona dressed in a fashion she termed "drab"…a simple black dress However, it was impossible to conceal Nona's obvious qualities. More and more the men slipped awestruck glances her way, and soon Nona began to behave like Nona…enticing, fascinating, flirtatious.

Eve overheard a conversation between two elderly ladies who looked like fine porcelain dolls and smelled of lavender and moth balls. "I'm so glad Travis found someone like Eve. He's such a nice boy," one lady commented.

"I know," her companion whispered, "And she seems to be a nice girl, too."

Eve smiled remembering how Travis explained Seaboard's 'good ole boy notion'. "As long as there is a living man in town older than you, you're called boy." Eve thought, maybe there's a 'good ole girl notion', too.

Eve watched admiringly as Travis greeted people. He was so at ease, his face glowed with happiness and contentment. Suddenly tears filled Eve's eyes, her life of pain and humiliation gone forever. She and Travis were together. This was their time.

Printed in the United States
65263LVS00004B/82-105